The Twenty-Year Itch

LINDA KELSEY

The Twenty-Year Itch

HODDER &
STOUGHTON

First published in Great Britain in 2010 by Hodder & Stoughton
An Hachette UK company

1

A CIP catalogue record for this title is available from the British Library

Hardback ISBN 978 0 340 96332 6
Trade Paperback ISBN 978 0 340 96333 3

Typeset in Plantin Light by Hewer Text UK Ltd, Edinburgh
Printed and bound by Clays Ltd, St Ives plc;

Hodder & Stoughton policy is to use papers that are natural,
renewable and recyclable products and made from wood grown in
sustainable forests. The logging and manufacturing processes are expected
to conform to the environmental regulations of the country of origin.

Hodder & Stoughton Ltd
338 Euston Road
London NW1 3BH

www.hodder.co.uk

In loving memory of Samuel Cohen (1915–2008)

With special thanks to Yehudi Gordon, Melissa
Calvin, Gordana Prelevic and Camilla Rodger.
Any factual errors are mine, not theirs.

Chapter One

'He's packing. *All by himself!* I can hardly believe what a grown-up boy he is. Making an absolute hash of it, of course, but you have to let go, don't you? Let them learn by their own mistakes.'

I'm on the phone to Gemma, my sister. She knows me too well. 'Julie, you sound slightly hysterical,' she says. 'Perhaps I should pop over.'

'Me? Hysterical? Not at all. Look, I've been through this gap-year business twice before. First with Tess, then with Katy. I'm used to it.' I'm holding the cordless phone to my right ear. The middle finger of my left hand is doing its customary twiddle. Twiddling a lock of blonde-highlighted hair in a continual circling motion just above my left ear. I'll regret it. I always do. Yesterday I went to the hairdresser. At eight in the morning, before work. An act of pure defiance, I'd thought at the time, observing myself dispassionately in the mirror, being blow-dried to unaccustomed sleekness. You see what we can do, my smooth, shiny, confident hair seemed to say back to me, we can survive this.

Together we can survive this.

'You look different,' he'd said to me in the evening, but of course he couldn't identify what exactly was different about me. Men never can. And I wasn't about to enlighten him. 'Nice,' he'd said, as I left the room.

'Too late for nice now,' I say to Gemma, voicing my thoughts.

'Sorry, Julie, but I seem to have lost your flow . . .'

'Yes, well, I suppose I am a little distracted. You see I went to the hairdresser.'

'And . . .'

'And nothing. I just thought you'd like to know.'

'Have you been drinking? You sound a bit barmy,' says Gemma. 'Not that I'd blame you for being drunk or barmy given the circumstances.'

'What do you take me for, Gemma?' I reply, keen for this conversation to meander, to wander with neither aim nor direction, for as long as possible. 'It's ten o'clock in the morning. You know I never start on the gin before eleven a.m. on a Saturday. I tell you, last time I popped into the bedroom – on the pretext of needing to empty the wastepaper basket – he was scratching his head. Either he's got lice or he's completely flummoxed. A bit of me just wants to take over like I always do. He's never had a clue when it comes to packing.'

'Don't even think about it, Julie. Just self-medicate – surely there's something in your medical arsenal that will calm you down – and read the newspapers.'

'But I could offer. It will mean he'll be finished in half the time, and he may even get to the airport on time and not miss his flight.'

'JULIE!'

'What?'

'This is not your call. It's out of your hands. Why are you hanging around, torturing yourself like this? Leave the house or something. I'll meet you for a coffee if you like.'

'What do you mean torturing myself? I'm having fun. It's a genuine spectator sport, watching him make a complete prat of himself. Anyway I can't go out, he might need me.'

'You're crying, aren't you? I can tell.'

'Rubbish . . . Well, maybe just a bit.' I give the hair-twiddling a rest and touch the corner of one eye with the back of my wrist. Definitely moist. 'I mean you're entitled to, aren't you? It's what you do when they leave the nest. Especially the last of the bunch. But they come back, don't they? They don't leave you for ever.'

'It's not the same, Julie. We're not talking about Tess and Katy. We're not talking about the girls. We're talking about Walt, Walter. You remember who Walt is, don't you? Walt is your husband.'

I pull a tissue from the sleeve of my sweater and blow my nose vigorously.

'Of course I know it's Walt. I mean you don't go to the hairdresser because your son is going back-packing. But if your husband is buggering off for a Gap Year, well, going to the hairdresser makes some kind of sense. A statement of sorts.'

Dammit, I can feel the tears welling up. I was determined not to do this. Gemma was always the cry-baby of the family, but I'm supposed to be made of sterner stuff. Our mother had always said there'd been a mix-up in the birth-order, that from the moment I could talk – and boss and manage and organise – I had usurped Gemma's older-sister role. Gemma didn't seem to be bothered by it, she was so dreamy and sweet natured that she could go along with my plans while keeping a space free in her head to create the stories that helped her shine in English lessons at school, and eventually led to her becoming a writer. Gemma cried easily, but that's because she was so sensitive to other people's pain. She never cried because she felt sorry for herself.

'I wish I was there so I could give you a hug,' says Gemma.

'Oh Gemma, I honestly think it would be easier if he had another woman. Or had gone gay on me.' The truth is that however much I go over it in my mind, I'm still mystified as to why Walt's doing what he's doing. This leaving me for the Scarlet Macaws of the Brazilian rain forest, before heading for a flock of Australian sheep and moving on to some Indian yogi in a loincloth who spends all day standing on his head does *my* head in. And all this uncertainty about what's going to happen when he comes back. *If* he comes back. 'I don't get it, Gemma, I really don't.'

'Neither do I, but you're going to be all right you know.'

'I don't know about that. But I suppose I'm luckier than most. I do have the girls and my work and all my friends, and of course you and Antony.' My fingers travel automatically back to the tangled knot of hair behind my left ear. So much for the twenty-four quid plus tip I spent at the hairdresser yesterday. I'm sure the scarecrow look was not what my stylist had in mind.

'Zis will show ze barztard,' he had said, admiring his handiwork and spraying a swirling mist of lacquer somewhere in the region of my head.

'Well, maybe not me *and* Antony,' says Gemma.

'What? Sorry, I don't understand . . .' My thoughts are darting around like fireflies searching for a mate on a summer's night.

'Well, you've been a bit wrapped up. Don't get me wrong. Understandably wrapped up. I didn't want to mention it.'

'Mention what?'

'That I'm thinking of seeing a lawyer.'

'Antony is a lawyer.'

'A divorce lawyer, Julie. A *divorce* lawyer. I couldn't ask Antony to handle our own divorce. In any case, he only does corporate.'

'That's not funny, Gemma. I mean this whole thing with me and Walt isn't exactly a joke.'

'I know it's not a joke, Julie, and believe me, I'm not kidding either.'

'But . . . but Gemma. You can't. You absolutely one hundred per cent definitely can't. I simply won't allow it.'

'Why can't I?'

'You just can't. It's impossible. Ridiculous. I won't be able to cope.'

'*You* won't be able to cope?'

'Jesus, Gemma, I had no idea. Well, of course I did have an idea, but not that it was this serious. Just because you had a holiday fling three years ago and are killing yourself with guilt and remorse, that's no reason to leave. You love Antony . . . Even *I* love Antony. Well, except when he's being a pompous prick or expecting the boys to be performing seals, but his heart's in the right place.'

'Well then, you can marry him. With my blessing. Keep it in the family, that would be really cosy. And I can assure you that my holiday fling has absolutely nothing to do with it. I knew you wouldn't understand. I should have kept my big mouth shut. At least until the dust of Walt's departure . . .' Gemma halts mid-sentence, as if suddenly aware that whatever she says is going to sound crass.

'It's just such a shock, Gemma, and your timing isn't exactly . . .'

Another phone rings, playing the opening bars of 'Goodness Gracious Me' . . . *Oh doctor I'm in trouble . . . Well, goodness gracious me* . . . The ring tone was Walt's doing, not mine. Being too technically incompetent to set up my own I asked Walt to choose something for me – something subtle but distinctive, and not too intrusive. This is what he came up with. I laughed a lot when I first heard it. Now every time it rings I want to hurl it at the wall. Or is it really Walt I want to hurl? When he's gone I'll change it, and I won't ask anyone to help me this time. I'll do it on my own. ON MY OWN. Three little words I hate even more than my ring tone.

'It's the mobile, I'd better take it, it might be Tess to tell me about the ultrasound.'

'Of course take it. We'll talk later.'

'Gosh, Gemma, we could do double dates.'

'I can't imagine anything more horrible.'

'Me neither.' And then despite everything I begin to laugh. And then Gemma's laughing, too. I can picture her putting down the receiver with a big grin lighting up her toothy mouth, a mouth which she customarily covers with her hand, just like Japanese women do when they giggle. Gemma has never liked her big, white teeth. Teeth too big for her sweet little face, so she covers her mouth from habit, even when no one else is there to see.

As I grab the mobile from the kitchen table I'm still chortling. 'Hi, darling,' I manage to splutter. 'Tell me the good news.'

It's not Tess on the other end though, it's Aggie.

Aggie is one of those women who never introduces herself. She doesn't even do that annoying thing of saying 'Hello, it's me,' leaving you to wonder who the hell me is. She just launches right in.

'Glad you're having such a good time. What's the joke? Fucking Armageddon here,' she says.

'I was expecting Tess,' I say. 'I'd better be quick. What's up?'

Aggie is a drama queen. Armageddon could be running out of Touche Eclat, or a stray chin hair.

'He knows everything. Last night. He extracted a full confession.'

'*Everything*?' I know exactly to what Aggie is referring. Everything means the catalogue of affairs that Aggie has been conducting throughout her twenty-year marriage to Charles. The paramour revolving door, as our gang likes to call it. The *liaisons dangereuses* that have kept her marriage all tickety-boo, as she has always insisted. Or rather the affairs that kept her marriage tickety-boo so long as Charles didn't know about them.

'I'm such a fool. I played too close to home. My first mistake in all these years. He's chucking me out. I may have to come and stay for a while. Just until he agrees to take me back. He has to take me back, he has to . . .'

'You know Walt is leaving later today,' I say, deliberately changing the subject. I really can't deal with Aggie's histrionics right now. Not after Gemma's bombshell, which I take far more seriously. I've always believed that Charles is fully aware of Ag's antics, and has simply chosen to ignore them for a quiet life. If my theory is right, and he has been complicit all along, surely it won't take long before he shrugs it off and continues as before. I decide to say none of this for now. What I want is Aggie off the phone as soon as possible in case Tess is trying to get through.

'Of course I know,' says Aggie. 'That's why I thought I might move in. Keep you company for a bit. Oh, I'm sorry, are you all right? Am I being terribly tactless? You sounded so cheery when you picked up the phone.'

Sometimes you put up with your friends despite their complete unsuitability for the job.

I'm suddenly aware of a particular patch of skin, just above my armpit, around the join where my arm meets my chest. It's been flaring up lately, intermittently itching and burning. And there's a matching dry, red patch on the other side. *Pruritis* to give it its proper name. I can't help it – you can take the girl out of medical school, but you can't take medical school out of the girl.

My skin is trying to tell me something. Of course! It's not just a stress symptom, it's a physical manifestation of what's happening to my marriage, and indeed the marriages all around me. It's the twenty-year itch. And it appears to be catching.

'You still there?' asks Aggie.

'Sorry, yes. Just that I was thinking that all this stuff that's going on, it's like a virus. It's like MRSA, only it's not just in the hospitals, and it's not bacterial, it's out here, in the general population.'

'You've lost me, Dr Broadhurst. You know I don't do this medical stuff.'

'Miss Broadhurst to you. I'm a surgeon, remember. And there's nothing medical about it, Aggie. I was just musing on my itchy skin and then I got to thinking about all the people I know whose relationships are falling apart. And it made me think that the seven-year itch has been replaced in the twenty-first century by the twenty-year itch. Itchy armpit as marriage metaphor.'

'But I've been itchy for at least fifteen of the last twenty years. The difference is I don't want my marriage to end.'

'Where did we go wrong, Ags?'

'Search me, Julie my friend.'

The sound of a man dragging a suitcase across the floor in the room above brings me back to the present.

'We'll have a war council later. Once Walt is out of the house.'

'Around seven thirty?'

'Seven thirty will be fine. And I'll get Gemma and Valentina to come, too. At least Valentina has a head on her shoulders. Despite what she's been through.'

'And a happy marriage.'

'Well yes, but at this rate even her marriage could be over by tonight. No, that would be the worst. I shouldn't have said that, even as a joke.'

'Hang on in there, Julie.'

'You, too, Ags. Bye.'

A beep sounds out from my mobile. It's a text from Tess, and it has an image attached to it. I press the bar to access the picture and a grainy, barely discernible image of a 12-week-old foetus appears on the screen.

'My baby!' says the accompanying text. 'All is well. Beautiful/ handsome genius cooking nicely. And if you think you can tell the sex, I don't want to know.'

'Walt!' I screech, racing out of the room to the bottom of the staircase. 'Walt, come here. Quickly. It's Tess. The ultrasound is fine. The baby's fine!'

A moment later Walt's head and torso lean over the banister. A long-distance blur of an outline so familiar that I don't need my glasses to help me fill in the features. The thick head of curly hair, made up of coiled springs in gun-metal grey streaked with black, reaching to below his collar and giving him a professorial air. The full, slightly feminine mouth. The still visible scar, tracing a jagged path along his nose, the result of a football boot spike slicing through it when he was a boy and a stitch-up job by someone who hadn't learned to sew. And, most important, the stubble, which by mid-afternoon, despite daily shaving, would be clearly visible. For so many years, just by thinking about it, I could conjure up the sensation of his stubble lightly grazing my lips as I kissed his cheek or chin. It would send a tremor right through me. But that was then.

'You see, grandma-to-be, I told you everything would be all right.' I can hear the smile in Walt's voice, and his acknowledgment of just how much this baby means to him as well as to Tess. I'd really rather Walt was horrible to me all the time. At least then I'd have something to fight back against. When he's being kind, which is often, I feel utterly helpless.

I click on the text again. A new baby I can understand. I can absolutely see the point of that. A new life? For me? At fifty-three? Whatever for?

Chapter Two

When I walk into the bedroom I find Walt crouching next to his enormous back pack, shuffling stuff around. He turns and looks up at me over his shoulder with that look. It's a look that takes me right back to the start, a look that seems to be asking a question, but isn't quite sure how to phrase it, or whether he dares to ask it at all. That very first time, in the café around the corner from the hospital, he just looked at me, and then at Tess, who was wriggling around on the chair next to me, then back at me again. There was something quizzical about his expression. I guessed he was thinking, where's the father? Later I found out I was right. He'd been attracted to me right away but assumed I was out of bounds. In the end it was me who started the conversation. He was too attractive to let slip. If I hadn't said anything he would have continued to glance surreptitiously when he thought I was looking the other way, trying – and failing – to pluck up courage to make the opening gambit.

Far from sapping my confidence at the time, being a single mum to Tess gave me a certain boldness. Wrapped me in a warm security blanket. There was a real one for Tess, an imaginary one for me, cocooning me from the moment I knew I was pregnant. Together Tess and I were quite a team.

Tess had started lobbing little bits of lemon drizzle cake in Walt's general direction, which gave me the perfect excuse. 'Stop that *now*, Tess,' I admonished my three-year-old daughter. 'Sorry,' I said, turning my attention to Walt. 'She's just learned the art of throwing, but not what not to throw.'

'She's adorable,' Walt had beamed back, and had immediately started to engage Tess with a nonsense rhyme about crumbs and thumbs and big fat tums and sticky-out bums that I assumed he'd made up on the spot. There was something about its clunky spontaneity that made me warm to Walt right away, and Tess liked it because it was just a little bit rude, and a bit like the words to a song. 'Crum, bum, tum, thum,' she laughed on that day, all day, and for the week that followed.

Something catches in my throat, like a pearl of pomegranate, and I have to turn away from Walt and leave the room.

I don't know where to put myself. I go back downstairs, try to be busy, in the study at the computer, checking emails, googling, putting paper into neat piles, and moving them round on my desk, but I can't concentrate. It's as though a feather duster is tickling at my insides, making it impossible to sit still.

I get up and wander into the hallway, stopping at the floor-to-ceiling bookcase to pull books randomly from the shelves. I find myself aimlessly flicking, halting occasionally to stare at a page. The letters and words, impossible to read without my glasses, bleed into one another, devoid of shape or meaning.

So I go upstairs again, deliberately sprightly and springy on the oak boards, so as not to let my feet betray my heart. I decide to go into Katy's room and ... well, just look around I suppose. If Katy, the daughter Walt and I made together twenty years ago, was a standard sort of girl, there'd be a job for me to do. Tidying up and sorting the debris she'd have left behind before going back to university, where she is reading geography, for the start of the second term of her first year. But Katy isn't your average young woman, at least as far as domestic standards are concerned. Katy's room has the kind of hygiene record that every hospital ward should be aiming for.

I don't suppose it would go down very well but I'm seriously thinking of suggesting a tour of Katy's bedroom to the head of cleaning staff at the hospital where I work. Spotless, clutterless, pristine perfection. Like a room-set for a magazine. Books on the shelves stacked in different sections according to theme and subject and within each section books arranged in descending order of height. CDs stored alphabetically by artist in drawers on rollers under the bed. Three cushions propped up on her bed cover, neatly overlapping and pointing up towards the ceiling, each at exactly the same angle. Desk drawers lined with scented paper; pens, pencils, erasers, postcards, stamps, writing paper, each stored in their own place. A box folder for personal letters, another for correspondence from her university, one for her old school reports. And inside the cupboards, too . . . I know what I'll find but I can't resist opening them, if only to marvel at how different a mother and daughter can be. All her summer T-shirts colour-coded in neat piles on the open shelves, spare bras stored in plastic bags, sandals and light shoes packed away in boxes at the foot of her cupboard, with Polaroids of each pair stuck to the outside of the boxes for easy identification.

Dear, difficult, vulnerable Katy who tries to compensate for her chaotic hormonal state with everyday order and control. The tidier Katy is, the more jittery it makes me feel. She's clearly borderline obsessive, but I would hesitate to diagnose OCD. I keep telling myself it's a phase, something she'll grow out of when she starts to feel more comfortable with herself. Am I the first mother in the world to wish her offspring's bedroom were more of a mess?

Every few seconds I look at my watch, fretting about the time, about when Walt needs to check in at the airport, but I'm determined not to say anything. I don't even intend to go back into our bedroom, not with him still there, but I'm drawn in as if pulled by powerful magnets. Now it's my own cupboard I find myself heading towards. The huge armoire that sits to the right of the fireplace.

One of the sweetest memories of my life with Walt is of those early days – or rather nights – after Katy was born, when Walt would light the gas fire and I would sit close to it in an armchair inherited from my grandmother, and give Katy her 2 a.m. feed in the warm glow of firelight. Sometimes Walt would go back to sleep. Other times he would prop himself up on pillows, one hand behind his head, and watch from the bed, a sleepy smile on his face, as Katy sucked at my breast. I felt that as a family we had been vacuum packed. Nothing from the outside could permeate, long-lasting freshness guaranteed.

I open the armoire, remove a sweater from the shelf. I shake it out, examine it, try to decide whether or not to put it on, even though I was dressed for the day hours ago, and have no real intention of changing. It's just something to do, to keep me close to Walt without giving him the impression that I'm hovering. And so, with a couple of deft movements and a raised-knee manoeuvre, I refold the jumper from a standing position and replace it exactly where it was before.

I note that folding a sweater while remaining upright and with no surface to rest it on is something I do really well. It has a kind of clarity to it. A satisfying simplicity. I could get a job in Gap. There's one just round the corner from the hospital. A job that wouldn't use up quite so much of me. Leave something over for . . .

I'm aware of the silence, but I don't know how to fill it. Walt's head is deep inside his own wardrobe, the wardrobe that stands to the left of the fireplace opposite the bed. I can see my reflection in the open mirrored door of his cupboard, as well as in the mirror of my own armoire. Too many mirrors.

I scrutinise myself. For clues. Clues in my appearance as to why Walt might be leaving. I can't deny that there is more of me than there used to be, especially round the middle. The jawline has gone a little fuzzy. And my eyes look somehow smaller, less alert, probably as a result of my eyelids not holding up as well as they used to. But I wouldn't say I've let myself go. I do care about how I look, but I don't obsess about it. When too many pounds pile on I cut out wheat for a couple of weeks, or announce a no-alcohol fortnight, and I shrink back again. Well, not right back, perhaps, but almost. And although I am gym-phobic, I do walk the half hour each way to work and take the stairs rather than the lift up to the fifth floor of the hospital. Could I make more of an effort to firm my flesh, do I need a Gok Wan to come and sort my wardrobe? Yes and yes, but that's not what this is about.

I find myself shrugging at the sight of my middle-aged self and the laughable little knot of hair above my ear. I wonder if Walt metaphorically shrugs when he looks at me. Is he resigned to the way I look? Or indifferent? Or repulsed? It's so long since he touched me that maybe it's gone beyond indifference to repulsion.

I try to redirect the voice in my head. The cupboards, Julie, you were thinking about the cupboards. Even though I have far more clothes than Walt, we each have an armoire to ourselves. This is an equal opportunities household, always has been. His cupboard is full, too, but only because everything is spread out with room to breathe. He and Katy, so very alike. Not that Walt has ever been less than loving towards Tess, who didn't belong to him, not biologically at least. Katy thinks her father has taken leave of his senses. She told him, to his face, that he was being 'totally pathetic'. And she never criticises him. Tess, the psychologist, takes a more balanced view. 'You can't escape yourself when you go away, you know. You'll be with you all the time.'

It's so damn neat inside Walt's cupboard that I sometimes get the urge to barge in there when he's out, or when he's snoring in the middle of the night and disturbing my sleep, and shake things up a little. Put one of his polo shirts in with one of his dress shirts, twin a brown sock and a grey sock, encourage a pair of his trousers to slide off the hanger and onto the floor. There's stuff all over the floor in my cupboard. Unless you want to haul whatever there's no hanging or shelf space for downstairs to the basement, on top of your shoes would seem the next best location as far as I'm concerned. On the outside these cupboards look pretty much the same. On the inside it's Sloane Street designer store versus Cricklewood car boot sale. It's one of the things about Walt that drives me mad. So how come Katy being like this, only far more exaggeratedly than Walt, doesn't drive me mad the same way? How come I'm so much more forgiving of Katy than I am of Walt for almost exactly the same thing? Marriage, that's the difference, I suppose.

The two armoires were bought at auction when we first moved in together. Not exactly a matched pair. Mine – or at least the one I decided had my name on it – was more in the rococo style, with a sensually curved top featuring a shell with flowers and leaves, and small curvy legs. His, I was told at the time, was Henri II style. It was squared off at the top, though decorative, too. Just a tad more masculine. We stripped them down ourselves, then hand-painted them in white, distressing them as was the fashion. It took a whole weekend, what with stopping for sex and sandwiches and sniping affectionately over who was making the faster progress.

Our marriage has been a bit like those armoires. I can feel a slow smile spreading across my face at my own cleverness, before I rein it in, abruptly. I'm not sure that smiling – given the current circumstances – is appropriate. But those cupboards *are* us. I'm surprised that I've never thought of them this way before – and the smile creeps back, despite my best efforts. Look at them, sitting companionably close to one another, separated only by the fireplace, just not so close that you can't tell them apart. Equal in all respects, and yet different. Compatible and yet at the same time completely independent entities. Not a matched pair, but a good match. At least on the outside, as far as appearances are concerned.

Inside, hidden to the outside world, and perhaps even to themselves, there have been different things going on over the years. In his cupboard, the neatness has intensified. In my cupboard, the mess has been mounting. Open those cupboards at the same time, and you'd think no wonder this is where it's ended up. And yet, despite the chaos on my side, it's me who has been relatively calm all these years. He's the one who's been festering away beneath the pristine surface, storing up petty grudges for later. 'Here's one I prepared earlier,' I can almost hear him saying, as he lobs yet another grudge, like a hand grenade, something I'd said years back that had deeply wounded him, and of which I had no memory whatsoever. I wonder if it's a good thing, a positive character trait, that I am able to let things go, to shrug off petty slights and quarrels. Or does it demonstrate a lack of sensitivity? I would like to think the former. I fear Walt would say it was the latter.

I'm tempted to speak my observations aloud. Not the bit about grudges, of course, but comparing our marriage to the cupboards. It's the kind of analogy he'd love. There was a time when Walt would look at me intently as I spoke, and his head would nod, almost imperceptibly – no one but me would ever have noticed it – as if I held the key to the universe in every utterance, however mundane. He so adored me then. Walt must have heard me come in. But this time he's pretending he hasn't noticed. Why doesn't he at least acknowledge me? Oh, what the hell! What difference does any of it make?

As I leave the room yet again, I glance at the marital bed that I have shared with Walt for twenty-three years. What I'd really like to do is crawl into it, pull the duvet over my head, and hide there until this nightmare is over. Until he comes in, too, pulls back the covers and tells me it was all a joke. But the bed is barred to me. I can't get in. It's covered with kit, his kit for the great journey that lies ahead.

The kit is something else I can't come to terms with. There's the iPod, the BlackBerry, the portable SatNav. It's what modern adventurers do. You can't set about finding yourself, the meaning of life, until you've sorted the kit. Start with the kit, then head for the ashram, or the monkey sanctuary or the Amazon rain forest, to commune with nature, never more than five seconds' contact away from your mates back home. There's no Wash n' Go for the male, mid-life adventurer.

Then there's all the stuff I told him he'd need. Well, I'm a doctor after all, and even if I could kill him for going off like this, I don't actually want him to die. So there are the water-sterilising tablets and the Dioralyte and the just-in-case antibiotics for his stomach, and the malaria pills. I even wrote him a list of all the inoculations he'd need, which he could easily have found out about himself from the travel health clinic. As a medical journalist Walt would in any case know all this stuff. It's something I find hard to accept, the idea that Walt probably knows as much about medicine as I do. More maybe. He got right through med school before dropping out, and has read up on vast quantities of research as a journalist over the years. Me? I've specialised, so I know masses about my subject, but not much else. Walt thinks I patronise him and he could be right.

I'm remembering Walt's diatribe against the material madness of London life, his urgent desire to get away to something simpler, more spiritual. 'It's over for me,' he said, months before he told me he was leaving.

'What's over?' I had asked, distractedly, thinking about a pregnant patient whose baby had just been diagnosed with a heart condition that would necessitate surgery within days of it being born.

'This place, this city,' he had said. But that was only part of what Walt meant. I wasn't listening properly. Or rather I chose not to hear.

'Well, you could go to the country,' I said. As a journalist Walt didn't need to live in the centre of London. 'We could increase the mortgage and invest in a cottage and you could spend part of the time there. Or we could sell up and buy a flat in town and a place in the country.'

It was not what I wanted to do but it was a compromise I was willing to consider. In my heart, I hoped this would be a passing fancy, an idea that would burn itself out. But I realise now that it was never *the* country that he wanted, but another country, a country where I wasn't.

Walt, pronounced Wolt, as in Disney. But these days when I think of my husband, I think of Wart, not Walt. On angry days, thinking of him as Wart helps. It helps to convince me, even if it only works for minutes, sometimes seconds, at a time, that I need to excise him from my life. Get the Bazuka Extra Strength Gel, apply judiciously, and let the salycilic acid work its magic. Walt, or rather Wart, will disappear! Zapped from my existence, freeing me to . . . To what? That's the problem. That's the huge, soaring, looming, ginormous problem. Freeing me to what? To be alone. To be lonely. To have sex with strangers. Please God, not that. To pursue my own goals? But I've been pursuing my own goals anyway all these years.

What is this nonsense about a Gap Year? *A Marriage Sabbatical!* The man has gone quite mad. Or I have, letting him get away with it.

The front doorbell rings.

'Damn it,' says Walt, finally acknowledging me. 'It must be my mini-cab. I'm not finished.'

'I'll tell him to wait. How long do you need?'

'Tell him ten minutes. I'll be ready in ten.'

'I'm not sure I can handle the goodbyes,' I say. On impulse I add, 'I'm going to go down the road and get myself a cappuccino. I won't be back until you've gone.' And before he has the chance to reply, I say, 'Bye, Walt. See you in a year. Maybe.'

'Ju—'

Too late. I'm disappearing down the corridor. I run down the stairs and past the hall table, grabbing keys and purse. Stooping on the mat to pick up my boots and the Puffa jacket I'd flung there the night before, I grab at the front door latch. On the porch I collide with an impatient mini-cab driver.

'If he's not down in ten minutes,' I tell him as I struggle, hopping, into one boot at a time, 'you'd better ring again. He's hopeless at time-keeping.'

The driver seems amused by my ungainly hopping and raises an eyebrow conspiratorially, as if agreeing with my statement about hopeless men, but I'm in no mood to be matey. I've got my boots on and I'm gone, breaking into a jog, racing off down the street at the same time as trying to get my arms into the sleeves of my coat. I never jog. By the time I reach the first junction I am already breathless. But I keep on running. At the end of the road I turn a sharp left and within seconds I'm outside the little Polish-owned coffee bar that only opened a week ago, replacing the Romanian-run one that opened and closed the week before that. I shoulder my way in, heart racing, breath coming in short gasps.

'Cappuccino please,' I wheeze, slumping into a chair by the window. It takes me a minute or two to recover my breath. At the table opposite is a mother and child, a little girl of about two sitting in a high chair stuffing a cream bun into her mouth. This has to be the moment, the moment when Walt walks in. This is when we meet for the first time and play the whole thing over from the very beginning.

I raise my cup of cappuccino, and rubbing the condensation away from the window with my other hand, look out through the glass. It's as though I'm watching out for someone, waiting for someone to arrive. But who? I don't realise how much my hand is shaking until coffee spills over and scalds the back of it. The cup rattles against the saucer as I set it down again. I wipe my hand, stinging now from the hot coffee, with a paper napkin, and blow on it, then hug my arms around myself and look once more out of the window. By the time I've stopped staring out into the grey, cold, mid-January day, my coffee is cold and bitter and undrinkable. He's not coming, of course not, how stupid of me. He'll be well and truly on the way to the airport by now. I look out for what I am determined will be the last time and as I do so a silver saloon car drives past with a male passenger in the back. It's him, I'm sure of it. Oh my God, it is, it's him.

I look at my watch, take £1.70 from my purse and place it on the table, then dive back into my purse again for another 20p, for the tip. Act normal, I command myself. I get out a little notebook from my bag and start to write a list. My pen hovers above the pad. The girls are coming round this evening, there's no white wine left and barely a thing in the house to eat. *Hummus, olives, goats cheese, salami.* I can write shopping lists in my sleep. *Grissini sticks, French bread, grapes.* I know exactly what's in the fridge, how many spare Toilet Ducks there are in the cupboard and whether I'm about to run out of stock cubes and matches. I don't even need to check.

Clementines, wine, juice, hot-smoked salmon and mackerel fillets, salad, a packet of almonds with raisins. This is how it is when you've been a wife and mother for as long as I have. It's what I love about domestic life, the certainty of food that can always be replenished, a crisp, new roll on the toilet-roll holder, a fresh, beeswax candle on the dining table. The knowledge that someone else – a child, a husband – will be there, too. Not physically there all the time, that's not necessary at all for peace of mind, but imprinted there, even in their absence.

Act normal, I repeat silently, and everything will be all right. And somehow it is. I leave the café, walk to the supermarket, nod at shoppers I recognise and cashiers who have served me hundreds of times on twice-weekly shopping expeditions over a twenty-year span.

I feel foolish for not having brought the car when I have six carrier bags full of food to carry. So much stuff, much of which will go to waste. But never has a full fridge felt quite so necessary.

Getting home is a struggle, I have to stop every couple of minutes to rearrange the bags as the plastic handles slice painful furrows into my fingers. The ten-minute walk seems to go on for ever.

Dumping the bags on the porch in relief, I rummage in my handbag for the keys. As I open the door I am reluctant to enter. No, it's more than reluctance, it's a rush of pure fear. Is it possible to be mugged by your memories? To be assaulted by an empty house?

I pick up the bags and go in, tentatively, banging the door shut with my bottom. Heading towards the kitchen at the end of the corridor, still dressed in my Puffa, I go about my mundane business. The kettle is switched on, provisions placed inside the fridge and the store-cupboard and the vegetable basket, and empty plastic bags shoved into a drawer. Eco-bags, I think randomly, I really must start buying reusable carriers. I put a tea bag into a mug, add water and milk and stir.

'My husband is going on a Gap Year,' I say aloud, testing the sound of the words as I sit down at the kitchen table. How will I say it when I tell people? Jauntily? Ironically? Bitterly? Contemptuously? As I sip my tea I feel acutely aware of my smallness. I can feel myself shrinking, almost to the point of disappearing altogether. And then, still feeling very small, and with tears beginning to course down my face, I get up and start to potter, bringing out cutlery and plates and platters for the salami, and wine and water glasses and paper napkins. Ten minutes must have passed before I realise that I have forgotten to remove my coat.

Chapter Three

That weekend of Katy going up to university for the first time in early October had started with everyone being tetchy. Walt and I had bickered over whether there'd be room for me in the car in addition to him in the driving seat, Katy and all her paraphernalia: clothes, books, towels, bed linen, pots, pans and a giant supermarket shop, amounting to enough provisions for at least a fortnight.

'It's you or the bean bag,' Walt said.

'How about me *and* the bean bag?' I'd countered. 'That bean bag and I have been through a lot together, and we're not going to be parted now. I'll even sit on it if necessary.' I was keeping it light, though I wasn't feeling light at all about Katy going away. For all the difficulties between us I love Katy with a fierceness that's quite different from the mellow, easy-going love I feel for Tess. The more we clash, the more I feel her vulnerability, and want to protect her. She drives me mad, but she never drives me away. The prospect of her going off to university had me ricocheting emotionally from relief at being able to put some distance between us, to guilt about feeling relieved and anxiety about how she'd cope in an unfamiliar environment. It's not that Katy doesn't make friends, but she doesn't make them easily. There are two girls with whom she has a special bond, but she doesn't do the gang thing, avoids pub gatherings and parties in favour of going to the cinema with one of her mates if they're available. Otherwise she stays in. The fact is Katy doesn't like herself very much and I think she assumes other people won't much like her either. Especially boys.

The way it seems to work – or rather not work – between us is like this. I sense Katy's anxiety and become anxious on her behalf. She picks up on my anxiety, which only compounds her own, and then we row, about the most trivial of things. Like bean bags.

Katy and her two best friends, Mel and Annie, all going up to university in different parts of the country at the same time, had been going on about bean bags for months, and they all eventually agreed that having one was *de rigueur*, the must-have accessory that would give their halls or rented rooms a bit of personality. Four times I'd taken Katy out on the great bean-bag hunt, and each time we came home *sans* bean bag. In Ikea, after losing one another for 20 minutes, she accused me of disappearing on purpose because I was 'pissed off' at her inability to make up her mind. I agreed I was pretty fed up with her dithering, but denied I'd lost her on purpose and she burst into tears and said she hated geography and didn't want to go to university anyway. So I took her to the café for a hot chocolate with pink and white marshmallows floating on the top and a slab of cake, where we made up, and then I felt bad for compounding her weight problem by filling her with calories. If Katy was too fat, it could only be one person's fault. Mine.

I'd been shopping in John Lewis one day the following week when I'd come across what I thought might be the perfect bean bag, but of course I dared not buy it without consulting Katy whose taste I was never quite in tune with and who was likely to think it the naffest, most toe-curling bean bag she'd ever set eyes upon. The way I am with Katy, always fearful of getting it wrong, losing my temper one second, apologising the next, is in total contrast to me in my professional life, when I am never less than cool, capable, competent and in control. In a hospital emergency I never falter. When Katy wobbles, I become a quivering wreck. I do try not to let it show, but I don't always succeed.

Knowing she was mooching around at home towards the end of the summer holidays, I rang Katy and got her to look up the bean bag on the store's website. 'I don't know, Mum, I'm just not sure,' Katy had said.

Here we go again, I thought. I adopted my most patient, reassuring tone, the one I use for terrified patients. 'I have this feeling you're going to love it. Although it's not real suede it's got this really soft suede feel to it, unlike all those other horrible, scratchy ones we've seen. The cover is removable and washable, and it's . . . it's . . . well I'd say it was a prince among bean bags.'

'But isn't beige a bit boring?'

I repeated the mantra. Treat her like a terrified patient, not an exasperating daughter. 'Well it won't clash with anything, and personally I think it's extremely chic. I saw one just like it in *Elle Deco* magazine in the waiting room last week.' I was sitting on the bean bag as I spoke, shifting this way and that to assess its comfort rating and rather enjoying resting my feet in the middle of the furniture department. I'd invented the bit about seeing it in a magazine because I thought it might help Katy to make up her mind, although it could just as easily backfire on the basis of *Elle Deco* not being the sort of magazine you'd want to see something you owned recommended in. What I wanted to say was, *It's only a damn bean bag, why the hell don't you just say yes or forget it.* Even though there are valid reasons for it I don't think it's healthy that I tread so carefully around Katy, and one of these days I'm going to break the habit and just be me. Only not just yet.

'OK, Mum, go for it, as long as they'll take it back if it really sucks.'

'As far as medical science is aware,' I replied, 'bean bags do not have a sucking reflex.'

I detected the slightest hint of a snigger coming down the line, and ended the call with a deep sigh. Surely those multiple small cysts on Katy's ovaries can't be entirely responsible for her inability to make up her mind about anything. Of course, I know that Katy's dodgy hormones aren't the whole story, because she's not this way with her dad. The difference between me and Walt is that I'm always trying to get it right with Katy, and failing, he just says whatever comes into his mind and Katy is generally cool with it.

'No way am I going without the bean bag,' said Katy.

'And no way I'm not coming with you to see the campus and help settle you in.'

'Well then, why don't you drive, Julie, and I'll stay behind,' Walt pitched in, playing the martyr card.

'Oh no, Dad, I really want you to come,' said Katy. I noted she hadn't said the same about wanting me around. 'I'll tell you what,' she continued, 'I'm going to take some of the food back into the house. You do know I'm going to have to share a fridge with at least ten people in my corridor, and this is so over the top it's embarrassing.' At least ten Tesco carrier bags were lined up on the driveway next to the open boot, ready to be stuffed into corners between the suitcases.

'But Katy . . .' I started.

'I'm just not having it,' she yelled at me, and immediately started riffling through the bags one by one, depositing various tins and packets onto the tarmac, defiantly determined to carry them back inside the house. 'I'm moving into a hall of residence on campus, for heaven's sake.' Katy shot me a Hannibal Lecter of icy glares. 'It's not exactly a million miles from civilisation, and I know for a fact there's a supermarket on site.'

'She's right,' said Walt. 'And this way we'll be able to squash the bean bag into the boot between the suitcases.'

'I was only trying to be helpful,' I said, disliking the peevish and put-upon tone that had crept into my voice. 'I do remember what it's like trying to settle yourself into uni, getting to know people, sorting out your work schedule, finding your way around, without having to worry about what you're going to eat. It's no different from what we did for Tess.'

'Well I'm not Tess, unfortunately for you . . .'

'For God's sake, Katy . . .'

She stormed back into the house with her arms full of rejected provisions. I shoved the bean bag into the boot and got into the back of the car. I'd decided, even before war had broken out, that I wasn't going to leave Katy on her own in the back, alone with her thoughts. She was as nervous as a child in the dentist's chair for the first time, which I could tell by the way that she'd started munching at the little skin tags at the side of her nails. She never bit the actual nails when she was anxious, only the tiny bits of skin at the side, sometimes leaving her fingers red and raw around the cuticles.

For my part I preferred sitting in the back of the car. I felt more relaxed and less inclined to ask Walt to slow down or find my foot reaching for the imaginary brake pedal whenever Walt was doing his boy-racer thing. It drove Walt nuts when my foot reached out like that, but it had become automatic and I couldn't break the habit. Better for everyone if I sat in the back and kept my mouth shut.

In fact no one spoke much on the journey. Walt was concentrating on the road, Katy on her fingernails and me on how well or not Katy would cope and hoping she'd find a boyfriend, someone kind who would make her feel good about herself. I wasn't sure geography was a great choice for Katy, as I didn't think it would help her find a career, but at least I didn't have any fears for her on the academic front. It was in a social setting that Katy was awkward, giving the impression of standoffishness when shyness was the real problem.

It was some time after Katy hit puberty that her hormonal problems began. Her periods were normal at the beginning, then started to become irregular from about the age of sixteen, but for a full year she didn't say a word to me about it. It was only when I realised that I hadn't stocked up on Katy's tampons for ages that I was finally alerted.

'Everything all right with your periods, Katy?' I asked one morning over breakfast.

'Well no, actually,' Katy had replied, not looking up from her cornflakes.

'When was your last one?'

'About three months ago.'

'Three months! That's way too long. And the one before that?'

'I dunno. Six weeks, two months, I really don't remember.'

'And before that?'

'Bloody periods, bloody hell. You're doing my head in.'

'You should have told me.'

'But you always make such a fuss. So I've a missed a period or two, so what? I'm not pregnant, am I?'

'I should hope not.' I felt my stomach spasm.

'Of course not, Mum. I'm still a virgin? But you know that. I've never even had a boyfriend.'

'You're only just seventeen. It's not a crime to be a virgin, you know.'

'Yes I do know that, Mum, thanks very much. If I wanted your advice I'd have asked for it. Why are we even talking about this stuff?'

I had found it hard not to lose my temper. 'But your periods shouldn't be so irregular, it's an indication that something's not working properly.'

Katy had simply shrugged.

'Do you have any other symptoms, sweetheart, anything you're not telling me?'

At which point Katy had burst into tears and run out of the room.

I looked at my watch. It was 8.15 and I had a clinic at the hospital beginning at 9.00. If I dealt with Katy now the clinic would start late and finish late and then I'd be late for lunch with one of my colleagues to talk over the research project, which in turn would make me late for the weekly departmental meeting . . .

I raced out of the room and up the stairs and knocked on Katy's firmly closed door. I knocked twice before trying to turn the door handle. The door was locked. 'Let me in, sweetheart,' I cajoled.

'I'm late for school. Why don't you just leave me alone to get ready. Please, Mum, go away.'

'OK, Katy, love, we'll talk tonight. But we do need to get to the bottom of this for your own sake.'

Silence.

I turned reluctantly away from my daughter's door and compartmentalised my concern into a passage of my brain marked LATER. Julie LATER Broadhurst, I thought. Later is practically my middle name.

Over supper that night, a home-delivered takeaway Chinese because despite starting on time I had still overrun my day by two hours and was feeling utterly exhausted, Katy didn't say a word. She knew she was going to get a grilling the minute the aluminium cartons had been gathered and binned.

I was watching her mopping up sauce from the prawns with her middle finger, sucking on it greedily and returning it to the carton to scrape it even cleaner. 'Do you have to do that?' I asked. 'It's extremely bad manners, you know. And one day you'll do it in public without even realising and embarrass yourself dreadfully.'

Katy pulled a face and returned to her finger work, sucking on it noisily to make sure Walt and I knew exactly how she felt about me interfering with her table manners.

'We really do have to talk, Katy.'

'I've got a stomach ache,' said Katy. 'Actually I feel a bit sick.'

'Not surprising, the way you've been stuffing your face.'

'Thanks, Mum.'

'Thanks for what?'

'For being so sympathetic. I mean I might have salmonella poisoning or a burst appendix for all you know.'

'Well then you're lucky there's a doctor in the house, aren't you?' Instead of my temper flaring out of control I suddenly found myself wanting to put my arms around my awkward, grumpy daughter who was so uncomfortable in her own skin. I wanted to hold her tight and soak up her anxieties and absorb them into my own flesh. If only Katy could shed a stone in weight I thought she'd probably shed her spots as well and then she'd feel so much better about herself. But weight was one of those issues that I carefully skated around. My clinics are full of anorexic girls who've stopped having periods and whose bones are beginning to look like Aero bars. I didn't want Katy to become size and diet obsessed.

'I've got a bit of work to do,' said Walt. This was the pre-arranged ploy that would enable me to get Katy on her own.

'OK then,' I'd said, noting with satisfaction that Walt had not only cleared away the debris but also wiped down the kitchen table and the sink. There couldn't be many men around who were as good-naturedly domesticated as Walter.

As he left the room, I turned my attention back to Katy.

'Tell me what's going on, sweetheart.'

'I hate myself, that's what's going on.'

'Come on, Katy, that can't be true, you've so much going for you . . .'

'Oh yeah? Like what? Like the fact that I'm fat and I'm spotty and I don't get periods and my hair's falling out and I'm turning into a man.' Katy was beginning to cry and alarm bells were ringing in my head.

'Hair falling out? Turning into a man? What's all this about?'

'Look at my hair. Look at it!' Katy was close to hysterical. 'Why do you think I've got this stupid side parting? Why do you think I tie my hair back to keep it in place so you can't see how thin it's got?' Katy's hair was dark like her father's, but fine and straight like mine.

'It's normal to shed between seventy-five and a hundred hairs a day. It sounds a lot, I know, but it's perfectly normal.'

'I don't care about your stupid statistics. I don't care what's normal. I'm going to be bald in a minute.'

'Katy, sweet, it can't be that bad or I'd have noticed.'

'You don't notice anything, do you? You're always too busy working or arguing with Dad.'

'That's not . . .' I stopped myself. It was important to stick to the agenda.

'Let me have a closer look, Katy. Let your hair loose and let me take a look.'

'Don't touch me!' Katy shrieked.

'OK. OK. We'll take it slowly. So what's this turning into a man business all about? Not having periods doesn't mean you're turning into a man. It's not possible to turn into a man.'

'Well maybe not a man then, maybe a gorilla.' Katy was utterly out of control, beginning to hyperventilate.

If Katy had been a GP referral and this exchange had been taking place in my consulting room I would have suspected right away what was going on. So caught up had I been in Katy's emotional outburst that I had quite failed to see the obvious. I breathed a slow sigh of relief, stood up from my chair and moved round to the other side of the table so I could sit next to rather than opposite my distraught daughter.

'Let's try and take this calmly, shall we, Katy?' I said, grasping her two hands between mine. 'I think I have quite a good idea what this is all about. And turning into a man or even a gorilla is definitely not your problem.'

Katy continued to snuffle and tremble as I began to gently probe.

'This gorilla business. Does it involve hair in places that as a girl you think you shouldn't be having any hair?'

Katy's head, which had been firmly pointing in the direction of her lap, shot up.

'Like hair around your nipples for example,' I said, trying to give no hint of my own emotional turmoil.

Katy started sobbing again. 'What am I going to do? It's horrible. It's the only thing I ever think about.'

'For a start you're going to show me, and then we'll decide what to do next. Now that it's a problem shared, I think you'll pretty soon feel a whole lot better. Having a mum as a doctor is no bad thing, you know.'

Katy's sobs were growing still louder.

'What it sounds like to me – and we'll have to start with some blood tests to be sure – is a case of PCOS, or polycystic ovarian syndrome. It would explain everything from your periods to your hair. The good news is that it can be treated. You'd never guess how common it is. You may hate statistics but it's estimated that between five and twenty-six out of every hundred women in the UK has PCOS.'

'Do you mean I'll be all right then?' Katy looked at me with her big, pleading eyes as tears ran down her face. 'I mean . . . I mean . . .' Katy was spluttering and I waited to give her time to compose herself. 'I mean I knew I couldn't really be turning into a man, I knew that was ridiculous, but I kept thinking I'd just get hairier and hairier and go bald on top and then I'd have to kill myself.'

'My poor Katy. I'm not surprised you've been worried sick. And I am so very sorry not to have picked up on this before. I'm not such an ogre that you can't talk to me, am I?'

'Sorry, Mum. I know I'm always having a go at you but you have a go at me, too.'

'Yeah, I guess we're just the have-a-go girls, you and me.' I opened my arms for a hug and for once Katy allowed herself to be held. 'Maybe we could have a deal. I'll have a go less, and you'll talk to me more.'

Katy pulled back. 'Mum, are you and Dad all right?'

I felt myself recoiling from the question, but knew that Katy deserved an honest answer. 'I think so, Katy, it's just that we wind each other up over all the sensational stories he has to write for the paper, and I'm not sure there's a solution. He feels trapped by it but he doesn't want to leave because the pay is so good.'

'You're not going to get divorced or anything, are you?'

'Not that I know of,' I said, trying to read the expression on Katy's face. She looked bewildered, as though life itself were too huge a concept for her to grasp.

'Nearly everyone's parents are divorced these days.'

'Well divorce isn't on the cards, so there's one less thing for you to worry about. Would a bar of chocolate help?' I could have kicked myself. A bar of chocolate was exactly what Katy shouldn't have. It wouldn't help her spots, and it wouldn't help her weight, and if Katy turned out to be insulin-resistant as well, which was the case with many PCOS sufferers, it would be extra-important to slim down. But at this moment I simply wanted Katy to feel safe.

'Thanks, Mum, but you know what? I think I'll have an apple.'

After that, whenever things between the two of us reached fever pitch – and they often did – I would remind myself of the apple moment and know there was a way back to it.

Once we had reached the motorway Katy plugged herself into her iPod, and I stared out the window watching trees and road markers whizzing by. I had loved my own university days, forged friendships that still held strong today, despite nearly all of these friends living elsewhere, and many of them on different continents. But I had been so much more self-assured than Katy, and that had made it easy for me. Keep off her case, but keep the lines of communication open. I repeated this to myself over and over. With Tess, if she were annoyed with you, it would always be for a reason you could understand. But with Katy it sometimes seemed you could press the wrong button merely by breathing in her presence.

In the end, after a difficult start, the day had gone well, better than expected. That is to say the first half of the day ended on a high note. The vast, American-style, purpose-built campus had far more green spaces than I had expected. There were lakes with ducks and swans, and picnic areas and every type of tree just beginning to turn to the russets and golds that heralded autumn. The sun was shining and students were milling in groups. A golden place, I thought, and how remarkably young everyone looks. And then I reminded myself that of course that's what they were. For a fraction of a second I had forgotten it was Katy who was starting university and had thought it was the beginning of my own freshers' week, almost thirty-five years earlier. A wave of nostalgia, so strong it made me feel momentarily light headed, swept over me.

'I can feel the atmosphere already, Katy. You're going to love it, love it, love it,' I shouted from the back seat, like an over-excited child.

'That's so typical, Mum,' groaned Katy, pulling out her iPod ear-piece. 'I mean how can you tell? It's all just talk, to make me feel good about being here. What's the rush anyway? I mean we haven't even arrived yet and you're already telling me it's going to be one long fabulous party and a total love-fest with everyone I meet.'

Here we go again, I thought. It's the first time I've opened my mouth the whole journey and I've already said the wrong thing. 'Perhaps I should have stayed home like your father suggested,' I said coldly.

Walt grimaced into the mirror, in the hope that I'd notice, which I did.

'Your mum's right, Katy,' he said, 'it does have a good vibe. Even your insensitive old dad who never notices anything can feel it.' A small victory, Walt agreeing with me rather than taking Katy's side.

'I guess so,' said Katy, softening a little. And then, 'Sorry, Mum. Fact is I'm so nervous I want to throw up, and I know you're only trying to make me feel better, but I can't be so instant and spontaneous to react as you.'

I released my seat-belt so I could lean forward and wrap my arms around Katy from behind, planting a kiss on the side of her face.

'I know, Katy, sweet, it must be very scary. At least everyone else is in the same boat as you'll soon discover.'

After a few wrong turns and stopping to ask several times for directions, we had finally arrived at Katy's hall of residence, a low, two-storey red-brick building, set amongst half a dozen others exactly the same. Once Katy had been name-checked and given the key to her room in the signposted reception area in one of the buildings, the three of us began to unload the cargo from the car. As Katy was turning the key in the lock of her ground-floor room, a big, smiley girl with shiny black hair and shiny dark skin came bouncing up to her.

'Hi,' she said, putting out a hand to shake Katy's, which was unshakeable because Katy was practically hidden from view by the giant bean bag, 'my name's Rani and I've got the room next to yours. That bean bag is cool, you lucky thing, mine's a nasty shiny red plastic thing that my mum bought me without permission.' I grinned to myself, vindicated at last. 'Do you like curry by any chance?' asked Rani.

'Mmm,' grunted Katy, popping her head around her bean bag to smile at her new neighbour.

'Well I don't cook,' she said, 'but you can share a family-sized Bird's Eye frozen with me tonight if you like. And we can explore the campus together unless you have better plans.'

I breathed a sigh of relief. Katy might find it hard at first, but if everyone was as friendly and open as Rani she was going to be OK. No sooner had Walt and I finished helping her to unpack than Katy said, 'Thanks, Dad, thanks, Mum. I'm quite settled now, and it's probably a good idea if I make the effort with my new neighbours. Is that all right with you?' I noted the slight tremor in her voice, could tell she was being brave.

'Of course it's all right with us,' I said, looking at Walt, who nodded in agreement.

'I'm going to take your mother out for a pub lunch,' said Walt, hugging Katy close. I could see a tear forming in the corner of one of Walt's eyes.

Chapter Four

'I have to go.'

I was about to break into the crust of my individual steak-and-kidney pie.

'Then go.' I looked up and noted that Walt was pale. 'You've gone a bit green. Is your stomach playing up? I saw the signs for the toilets to the right of the door as we came into the pub.'

'For God's sake, Julie, I don't need to go to the toilet. And if I did I wouldn't have to ask your permission. That's part of the problem. You treat me like a child.'

'Part of what problem? You're not making sense.'

'I don't make sense to myself any more, so it's not surprising I don't make sense to you.'

'Sorry, Walt, I'm not getting it. You said you had to go. I thought you meant to the toilet. What do you mean by I have to go?'

'I mean I have to go. AWAY. I can't go on like this.'

Walt was talking in riddles. 'Like what?'

'Like with all of this. With my job, with my life, with myself, with you.'

Over the years I've observed the way different patients respond to the breaking of bad news. Because I have a special interest in fertility I am often in the position of offering hope, but sometimes with these things there is no hope of my patient having a baby by means natural or artificial and I have to tell it like it is. There are patients who burst into tears. There are patients who, ridiculous as it seems, try to comfort me: 'Oh it's all right, doctor, you're not to worry, I'll be fine.' And there are those who shut down completely, who show not a trace of emotion, but become exaggeratedly detached and rational. The floodgates will open later. Maybe when they leave the room. Or maybe not for weeks or months to come. All this went through my mind as Walt started to tell me that our life together was unravelling, as though having presented myself with three possible modes of response I was actually free to choose what my response might be.

My fork was still hovering above the pie.

'I wonder if they could re-heat this and give it to someone else. It seems such a waste.'

'Julie, are you listening to me?'

'If food so much as touches my lips, I'll throw up, of that I am certain. Excuse me,' I called, waving at somebody walking by our table who might just possibly have been a waiter. 'I feel a little unwell. Would you mind taking this back?'

'I don't work here,' said a young man with a spiny porcupine haircut and a slimline stripy shirt worn outside his jeans. 'But if you're really not hungry, I'll take it off your hands. My wife over there, the pregnant one, she's practically dying of starvation, or so she tells me, though you wouldn't think it to judge by her size.' He laughed. 'She'll be in labour by the time we get anyone to serve us in this place.'

'Then take it with pleasure,' I smiled, handing him my pie. 'Tell your wife the pie's on me.'

And the young man walked away, holding my pie aloft like a silver sports cup.

'Sorry, Walt, a small diversion.' It seemed I'd opted for the shut-down option. Walt was looking at me in a way that I thought might be disdain. Or hatred. I carried on speaking. To stop him speaking I suppose. Maybe if I could keep on speaking he'd forget about whatever it was he was starting to say and move on to something else, something safer. 'Look, it's a wrench for both of us, Katy going. For you in particular, I recognise that. I suppose it was a bit different when Tess first went . . .'

Walt exploded, spontaneously combusting before my eyes. 'Don't you understand anything, Julie? No, it wasn't different when Tess went. You think that because Tess had some other father that I don't love her like my own daughter. Well that's the biggest crap ever. I've always loved her like she's my own daughter. As far as I'm concerned she IS my own daughter.'

'Walt, I'm sorry. I do know that, about your feelings for Tess, it's just . . .'

'Did you hear what I said before? Were you even listening?'

My stomach clenched itself like a fist inside me.

'I am listening. You want to go away. On an extended holiday. Without me. To have a bit of time to yourself.'

'No, not an extended holiday. More than that. And I wouldn't call it a holiday. I'm thinking maybe a year.'

'A *year*!'

'Well, up to a year.'

'On your own?'

'Yes.'

'But what about your job?'

'I've resigned.'

'You've resigned!'

'Julie, you keep repeating everything I've said.'

'I'm trying to take it in. You've resigned.'

'Yes.'

'When?'

'Last week.'

'Last *week*? And you're only telling me now.'

'I thought it would be better to wait until Katy had gone. And anyway, you're always so busy.'

'You think I'm too busy to talk about a thing like this?'

'Well it's been about twenty years of thinking that I need to book an appointment every time I want to speak you.'

'You're not serious about that last remark, are you? Surely this isn't what it's all about.'

'I am serious about it, because it's the truth. But it's not all of what it's about, just a tiny bit of it.'

'I don't know how you dared to walk out on your job without

telling me. It's outrageous. I'm your wife. Your income is our income, just as my income is our income. It's what we need to live.'

'You see. None of it works between us any more. In any case, you always hated my job.'

'That's beside the point.'

'Is it?'

'Yes it bloody well is. And you hate my job, too.'

'I don't.'

'Yes, you do. Because I'm dedicated. Because I'm not cynical. Because I still believe in the NHS. Because however bad it gets I won't give up.'

'That's what I admire you for.'

'I don't want your admiration, I want your love. Sometimes I think you're jealous.'

'Sometimes I think you're cruel.'

'Twenty-three years, Walt.'

'I'm going regardless.'

'Yes, I've got that particular message. And to where, might I ask?'

'South America. Australia. India.'

'Got the whole thing planned then, have we?'

'Pretty much.'

'Well I'm glad you can afford it.'

'Is that all that you're concerned about? The money?'

'I shall ignore that remark. Are you by any chance thinking of coming back? I mean back to me?'

'Well, that depends . . .'

'On what?'

'A lot of things. Like if you and I can . . . Like where I decide I want to live. Lots of things.'

'And where might *you* want to live?'

'Maybe abroad.'

'But we've discussed this so many times. My work . . . My family . . . *Our* family . . . The kids.'

'The kids are grown up.'

'Katy? Grown up? You want to abandon Katy?'

'I'd never abandon her. We're part of the new Europe, remember. Travelling between countries is easy.'

'I'm not leaving England. And I'm not leaving Katy. Or Tess for that matter. Even though she's a married woman. And then there's the small business of my mother.'

'I know you're not.'

'It's easy for you. You've got two dead parents.'

'You're right, Julie. Two dead parents dying within six months of one another when I was twenty-one is a barrel of laughs.'

'So you'll go on a gap year, and then you'll live abroad?'

'I don't know . . .'

'So you want a divorce? And to sell the house?'

'I didn't say that.'

'You didn't say that but I assume it's what you meant.'

'I don't know.'

'Walt . . .'

'Yes.'

'Now I'm going to go.'

'Where?'

'To the toilet. I thought the food might make me throw up, but I'm going to throw up anyway, on which basis I might as well have kept the pie and eaten it.'

Walt managed the faintest of smiles. 'Stay, Julie. We have to talk about this.' He leaned forward, reaching out under the table, groping for my hands that were on my knees and clasping them between his. My hands were clammy with the sweat of fear. I pulled them sharply away, knocking them on the underside of the table and wincing with pain.

'Ouch, that was quite a bang,' said Walt, suddenly concerned. 'Are you OK?'

'Yes, I'm fine,' I replied, feeling the throbbing in my knuckles. As I interlaced my hands on the scratched wooden surface of the pub table I noticed a heart, etched into the wood. *Gav loves Laura. Forever.*

'When did you stop loving me, Walt?'

'I still love you. In some ways.'

'What ways?'

'Look, things haven't been good between us for ages.'

'Well, they're going to get a lot worse now.'

'That's not helpful, Julie.'

'It's not meant to be.'

'Well I'm going to eat my steak and chips, even if you're not.'

'You go ahead and I'll watch. I want to fix a picture of you chewing in my mind, one that I can conjure up at will when you're gone.'

Now Walt's knife and fork were poised above his steak. He put them down again, crossing them on the plate.

'This is hopeless. I can't eat with you staring at me like this.'

'When are you going?'

'Mid January?'

'Have you booked your flights?'

'Not yet, but I'm about to.'

'And what are you going to do when you get to wherever it is you're going?'

'I don't know. Well, I'm going to travel.'

'Am I expected to wait for you?'

'I don't expect anything. It's up to you.'

'Do you want me to?'

'I don't know.'

'There's an awful lot you don't know.'

'That's why I have to go. To see if I can find out what I want.'

'But why can't you do it here? We could see a counsellor. We wouldn't need to go further than our own postcode for that.'

'I'm going, Julie, and I'm not going to change my mind.'

'Is there someone else?'

'No.'

'There must be.'

'There isn't.'

'I believe you, I think. It's that bad you're leaving me for no one.'

'Julie, this is about me as much as it is about us. I'm hanging on by a thin thread.'

'Shall we get the bill?' I said in a monotone. 'And seeing as you no longer have a job, it might as well be me who pays.' That must have hurt. As it was meant to.

When we were back in the car he turned to me and said, 'Please try to understand. Please, *cara*.'

'Don't call me that, you bastard,' I screamed. 'Don't call me that ever again.' After more than twenty years of being called *cara* – 'beloved' always did sound so much better in Italian – that one small word of endearment felt like being stabbed with a knife. But for Walt, I suppose, it was reflexive, no different from calling my name, so automatic had 'cara' become to him over the years.

As we drove off in silence I closed my eyes and conjured up the time he first called me that, near the beginning, one night in Sicily some months after we first met. Then the very word sounded like an embrace.

I wondered how well Walt remembered Sicily. I'd left Tess with Gemma so we could go away, just the two of us, for a whole week. It was the first time I'd been away without her. I'd done nights at the hospital, but that was work. I missed her, but that day we hired the matching Vespas and drove to Mount Etna I didn't think of her at all until the evening.

It was on the way down from our hike, when we were almost at the bottom again, that I became aware that the undersides of both my feet were feeling particularly hot. I turned one foot over to examine it and discovered that my rubber-soled shoe was literally melting away. Although we could see the lava flowing freely down one part of Mount Etna in the distance we hadn't realised just how much heat the earth beneath us was generating. 'Oh my God!' I screeched and broke, laughing, into a run, Walt in hot pursuit. He caught up, grabbed hold of my hand, and we ran together the last few hundred yards, laughing all the way. That night, over a romantic candlelit dinner overlooking the bay, he called me *cara*, and I knew that we would be together and stay together.

After Sicily we went on to the Aeolian islands – Lipari, Vulcano, Panarea. We hired a small motor boat, and picnicked out in a deserted bay on bread and wine. Walt's tongue tasted of Taleggio, I licked his fingers clean of proscuitto and figs.

Then we took off what few clothes we were wearing and made love, right there on the boat. Goodness knows why we didn't fall overboard. Afterwards we swam naked in the sea. 'I love you, *cara*,' he told me, as we exchanged salty kisses in the water. Do you remember, Walt, do you remember, I wanted to ask as I looked across at Walt in the driving seat, stony faced in concentration. Well I was sure he'd remember, but perhaps he wouldn't want to be reminded.

We continued to drive home in silence. The warning signs had been there for ages. Of course they had. I had chosen to ignore them. But ignoring things, as we all know, doesn't make them go away.

Chapter Five

At 7.27 p.m. precisely the doorbell rings. It can only be Valentina. Gemma is never less than 15 minutes late, Aggie is always so late that you end up wondering if she's going to bother to turn up at all. She has been known not to, especially when she's in the first throes of passion with a new lover.

It's the only thing about Valentina that grates, this insistence on turning up early. Patients who arrive late and guests who turn up early have an equally negative effect on me. In my opinion the perfect guest is neither early nor even punctual but turns up at the same time as Gemma does, a good quarter hour after the time she was invited. An 'I'm sorry I'm late,' will always be greeted by me with a 'Thank God that you are, I was nowhere near ready.' From the day lastminute.com was launched on the web, it became Walt's new nickname for me. I'm *cara*, I'm lastminute.com and I'm also womb woman, in reference to my medical specialisation. I rather revelled in Walt calling me lastminute.com and even tolerated 'womb woman' until Walt started planning his new life, at which point every endearment began, to my ears, to sound like a personal slur.

Surely one of the main pleasures of down-time is *not* having to race against the clock. Whenever Walt and I went on holiday together I would remove my watch for the duration. 'The position of the sun tells me everything I need to know,' I told Walt, rather pretentiously, on that first-ever holiday together in Sicily. I think Walt was charmed by my quirks then, the hint of free-spiritedness so at odds with my disciplined approach to my profession. Being late, messy cupboards, those things comfort me in an odd sort of way, reassure me that I'm not the superwoman people always tell me I am. I loathe being called that. I don't get called superwoman because I'm a working mother, people have got over the novelty of mothers going out to work, but they still haven't quite got over the business of my being a woman, a mother and a hospital doctor all at once. GPs no longer carry much mystique, hospital doctors still do. It's the life and death thing, I suppose, the sense that once you're in a hospital setting you are putting your survival in someone else's hands. You can end up on a pedestal. Pedestals don't suit me though. And it's easy to fall off them. I don't have time to think about this now, but I think pedestals may have played a part in what went wrong between me and Walt.

I'm in the middle of trying to prise pre-sliced salami out of its plastic wrapping when the doorbell rings. My hands are greasy. So now I have to wash them before I can go to answer it. There's no soap by the sink so I rinse my hands under the tap and squirt Fairy Liquid on to them. I shout 'Coming!', even though I'm not, just as Valentina rings again, this time more insistently, with three sharp jabs at the bell. 'Coming!' I shout, wiping my hands on my jeans and sprinting down the corridor. This is why I don't like my guests turning up early.

I'm within an inch of irritation, but it's impossible to be irritated by Valentina. Out of the gloom of the porch and into the light of my hallway steps an open-armed energy force so great that its smile alone could power a super-tanker. Five foot two of fragrant femininity in fitted, fur-lined sheepskin, tan ankle boots and dark brown fishnets, clutching a bottle of champagne and sporting shoulder-length, chestnut hair so thick, so glossy that Aggie, Gemma and I have often suggested she shave it right off to cheer up her less fortunate sisters, namely us. I often wonder what temporary madness overcame Nature to bestow so much of its bounty on a single individual. No 51-year-old mother of two has the right to a 23-inch waist. And no one, mother or not, has the right to irises the colour of molten chocolate and eye whites that dazzle like fresh-fallen snow in the sunlight, even when their

owner has a humdinger of a hangover. Or has been crying. And
Valentina has more reason to cry than most, although I've only
seen her do so once. Gemma, Aggie and I reserve special envy
for Valentina's handspan ankles as opposed to English cankles. It
would be so easy to hate a woman with these advantages, unless
she happened to be as lovely inside as out. Unless she happened
to be Valentina.

'*Amore, amore,*' she trills, flinging her arms around me as I sink
my face into the forest of Chanel-scented hair that is the trademark
of my dear friend Valentina. 'This is so sad, but we must learn to
be happy again. I think the champagne will help.'

'Oh Valentina,' I reply. 'What is making me unhappy bears no
comparison to what you've been through. As much as I hate you
being early, I love having you here so we can talk before the others
arrive.'

'My enthusiasm is what brings me early. Always wanting to see
my friend sooner, not later. Although tonight there is something
else as well. Let me look at you, *amore.*'

Valentina stands back from me at arm's length and sighs, 'Not
so good, not so good.'

'And I thought you were here to lift my spirits, not to drown
them altogether.' I flick at Valentina's sleeve with a back-hander.
'I've even been to the hairdresser.'

'It's not the hair that is the problem, except for that most strange
tangled piece above your ear. It's the colour of your skin and the
dark circles under your eyes. How are you feeling?'

'Steam-rollered.'

'Shall I hug you again?'

'Oh, why not?' And I sink into her hair and her sheepskin once
more and for just a moment I feel safe. 'Come on, Valentina,' I say,
pulling away reluctantly, 'I need some help in the kitchen. Here,
give me your coat.'

Valentina married Rob the same year as I married Walt. Their
glamorous, no-expense-spared bash, with Valentina in a couture
meringue extravaganza that only she could get away with, with

Rob's Jewish family and Valentina's Catholic Italian family vying over which could be the noisiest, the most expansive, consume the most food, dance with most vigour, was in sharp contrast to our private, register office wedding with little Tess as ring-bearer, and not more than a dozen family and friends. It was the look of sheer delight on Tess's face, and her gorgeous cream silk dress adorned with pink silk roses around the hem, that I best remember from that day. I've found her a father, I thought, as Walt bent down to take the ring that Tess held in front of her on a small velvet cushion, and gently kissed the top of her head. Someone the two of us can love together. A man who loves my daughter as much as he loves me.

Rob and Valentina were our witnesses. Although it was Walt with whom I fell in love, his friend Rob was probably always the easier man to love. From the start Rob appeared to be at ease with himself and the world. Walt, I would say, is more of an acquired taste, having a darker, more cynical side to his nature. Walt questions everything, Rob lets things be. Walt's half-empty glass contrasts with Rob's half-full one. The fact that Walt came with Rob was a bit like a BOGOF. Not just one lovely new man in my life, but an extra one, thrown in for free.

I would never have expected to adore a man who starts jumping up and down like a hyper-active toddler if the words balance and sheet are uttered in the same sentence, but adore Rob I do. Rob is an accountant, though not one who suffers his job, or is constantly apologising for how boring it is. He genuinely enjoys his work. We used to tease him about his favourite tipple, which was vodka, and joke that unlike the message of the famous ad, accountancy only became his life *after* discovering Smirnoff.

Rob looks after performers in the music business, from *Pop Idol* winners to rock superstars. He does the unexpected. Like going to Glastonbury every year, on his own, with his own tent. And to Bayreuth, for the Wagner festival. He also plays guitar and sings to the old folks in the nursing home where his mother lived for five years before she died. His singalong is the social highlight of the week at Lavender Hall, though he keeps it quiet from his clients. He is exactly as he was when he first met Valentina. Short, bald, overweight and absolutely adorable.

Earlier in her working life, before she moved into fashion PR, Valentina had been working promoting a girl-band, one Rob did the books for. They met in the VIP area at a concert. She was so gorgeous she could have bagged a rock star. Sensibly she bagged Rob.

Valentina seems to know exactly how to keep Rob happy. She always looks wonderful, she's a great hostess, she never criticises him, either to his face or behind his back. But there's nothing airhead about Valentina. She set up her own PR business before she had the children, specialising in all things Italian, from food to fashion. Valentina is a gift to the PR world. Her glamour, her foreignness and her natural charm ensure that her male clients – gay and straight both – fall instantly for her. More surprisingly, her female clients also succumb to her girly warmth, because despite her obvious physical assets, there is nothing threatening about Valentina – she draws men and women into her orbit on a strictly no sex-discrimination basis. She manages to flirt with both sexes while coming on to neither.

Although Valentina first arrived in London from Perugia with her family when she was eleven she has lost barely a trace of her Italian accent. And still, sometimes, she gets words mixed up in a way that is far more pleasing to the ear than hearing it said correctly. To hear Valentina speak, Walt once remarked, is to feel your naked body, beneath a perfect, sun-drenched sky, being gently drizzled with extra virgin olive oil. 'And when I speak?' I'd asked, knowing that I'd get a straight answer.

'More like being hammered with hailstones,' he'd replied with a grin, and a warmth that was enough for me. I know my limitations, and I always trusted Walt to love me despite them. For so long he did.

★   ★   ★

It's two and a half years since Paolo's death. His suicide. Paolo was Valentina and Rob's beloved son, Carla's big brother. He killed himself in his student digs at university. His girlfriend came back from a seminar, and found him, hanging, in the bedroom they shared. Even she, who was living with him at the time, hadn't seen it coming. He was down, anxious, she knew that much. His exam results weren't good enough and he had re-sits coming up. The night before they'd partied, he'd got stoned, drank too much, but nothing out of the ordinary. He left a note with one word on it. 'Sorry.'

'You don't get over a thing like that. Not ever. But I have to live,' Valentina had said. 'For Carla, for Rob, and perhaps even for me. I just do the best I can with every day. I don't want pity. That's why I haven't let myself go. I don't want people to see my grief, or my guilt. It's mine, for me, not to share.' I've not seen Valentina cry once since Paolo's funeral. But there is a gesture she makes which she didn't make before. Sometimes, while speaking, she stops suddenly, crosses her hands on her chest, closes her eyes, and visibly breathes in and out once before resuming. It only lasts a second or two, but to me it seems as if Valentina is trying to contain her heart, for fear it will fall clean away from her body unless she clamps it in.

I am arranging salami on a plate in ever-decreasing circles. 'Grab a glass and help yourself to wine, there's a bottle just opened in the fridge. Or perhaps you'd rather drink the champagne. Trust you to bring Crystal, though I'm not sure exactly what it is we're celebrating.'

'Ah, my friend, that is your problem. You think champagne is only for celebrations. For me champagne is my daily bread.'

'In that case, forget the plonk and show me the bubbles.'

I have moved on from arranging salami to tossing the salad, with my bare hands, Jamie Oliver style. Well, I was doing it this way before Jamie Oliver had been born. Walt used to find it irresistibly erotic.

'I remember sex.'

'You *remember* sex? Was it so long ago that you have to remember it?' asks Valentina.

'I don't just mean going through the motions, I mean when it was urgent. When it took you by surprise. You see how I'm tossing this salad, no salad servers, no surgical gloves. Well it was enough to turn Walt wild. He got so turned on one time, seeing me do this, no more or less suggestively than I'm doing now, that he lifted my summer skirt, pulled down my pants, unzipped himself and screwed me from behind, right here in the kitchen.'

'Oh,' says Valentina, a little shocked. 'Oh.' And she flaps her hand in front of her face as if to cool herself down. 'Yes, I suppose so. You're right, there were times . . .'

'The children were out at the time, of course, or at least I assume they must have been. But now I'm not so sure. I wonder if there was a period when Walt and I were so hot for one another and sex seemed so necessary that we'd have taken the risk, even if the girls had been in the house and playing upstairs. It worries me a bit that I can't remember, but more curious is that my dwindling sex life has never given me much cause for concern. It's not the sex I've been missing lately, but the intimacy. The spontaneous hugs, the warm kisses. They lasted longer than the sex. Oh Valentina, I'm sorry, I didn't meant to embarrass you, it's just that these memories, these scenes from the past, keep flashing, half drawn, into my mind.'

'Julie, I do know what you mean. I really do. I'm not embarrassed, not at all, and I like that you are so direct. But it's interesting. We don't talk sex much, do we? Everything else, but not so much sex. Please don't think me selfish, but there's something I want to talk to you about, something connected to this conversation, before the others arrive. I know we will talk about you and Walt when Gemma and Aggie are here, but this is something I'm not ready for the others to hear.'

'Then talk, my friend. You're right, Gemma will be here any minute. We can drone on about me all night, it's my turn tonight, unless Aggie decides to take over. You know she and Charles . . .

never mind that, later will do for that as well. In fact I'm in no great hurry to talk about me and Walt, it's still so confused inside my head that whatever I say won't make a great deal of sense to me or anyone else.'

'Julie, I am so scared.' I look at my friend Valentina's expressive face. Her bottom lip is actually quivering. If my or Aggie's or Gemma's lip quivered you probably wouldn't notice, but when a bottom lip as full and pouting as Valentina's quivers, the effect is seismic.

'Scared? Of what?'

'Oh Julie, I don't know how to explain. It's as though he's slipping away from me.'

I think she means Paolo. That she can no longer quite conjure him up, see his face, imagine him as he once was. But I wait for Valentina to continue.

She has begun to pace back and forth along the opposite side of the kitchen island from where I am salad tossing. As she paces she runs her fingers through her hair, lifts her curls away from her neck, piles and twists a chestnut forest on top of her head, then lets it all go again. Valentina tilts back her head, shakes it from side to side. Her hair settles. Moments later the ritual begins once more. I watch in silence, mesmerised, head bobbing left and right, following her as though tracking the ball in a tennis match. Even in her anguish Valentina is so beautiful that it's almost impossible to see through to her suffering. Only the quiver of her lip gives something away.

Finally Valentina comes to a halt, and perches on a high bar stool, swivelling round to face me. Her usually mellifluous voice has a slight catch in it. 'For the first year, after Paolo, we were closer than ever. It wasn't like you're told by bereavement counsellors, how sometimes, when a child dies, their parents stop to communicate. With me and Rob it was the opposite that was true. We talked about Paolo all the time. Our lovemaking was the most intense. More even than in the beginning. Every night we held on so tight. We would wake up, in the same position, wrapped around one another, all our limbs mixed up, like we are one person. Like without the other the one could not survive. Now, he touches me for sex, only for sex, but it is like he is gone away. Unlike you I still have the sex, but like you no intimacy. I have no evidence, no reason to think, but maybe he has a mistress.'

'Oh Val, I thought you meant Paolo, not Rob. That it was Paolo who was slipping from your memory. But why would Rob have a mistress when you are more sexy, more beautiful, more lovely than all the mistresses in the universe?'

'Because that is not how the world works, Julie. Because I am just another human being and so is Rob and sometimes our needs and desires take us to another place.'

'You're right, that was stupid of me. But I don't think it's that Rob has a mistress, I can't believe that for a minute. I think it's part of grief. At some deep psychological level, or maybe one that's not so deep, he may feel guilty for finding comfort in you, and now he has to push you away. He may feel that it's not right for him to take joy in you when he has lost Paolo. It's just a phase. It will pass. I'm sure it will pass.'

'He also begin to criticise me. Before, never. Now, a lot. He say things like this sauce is not as good as you used to make. Or your skirt is too short. Or I don't want Gemma and Antony for dinner, he's so boring. Before, he never thought Antony boring. And he and Gemma, they always got on like house on fire. It's like he is looking for reasons to push me away. He can't find any big reasons, so he picks on small things. Stupid things.'

'You've handled it too well, the two of you. It's not natural. You are both such positive people. You have kept one another going with your zest for life, your love of Carla and one another, but maybe mourning hasn't been allowed its proper place.'

'Julie, I can keep going with Rob. Without him . . .'

'There's no case of without him. Dammit, the doorbell again.' I look at my watch. 'Gemma.'

'Promise me, Julie, you must not say one word. I don't want for this to be a four-way conversation piece.'

'Of course, not a word, but you have to promise to keep talking to me.'

'I will, *amore*, I will.'

'Would it help if I talked to Rob?'

'No, absolutely not. Well, maybe.'

'Think about it and let me know.'

A dismembered voice comes screeching through the letter box, down the corridor and into the kitchen. 'For God's sake, let us in, would you? I'm freezing my bollocks off out here.'

'What, Aggie here already?' Aggie here, at 7.45? The screech is familiar enough and Gemma would never use a word like bollocks.

I race back again down the corridor to find both Aggie and Gemma huddled on the porch, stamping their feet rhythmically on the tiles and batting at themselves, arms crossed, in an attempt to keep warm.

'Quick, quick, let us in before we die of pneumonia,' squeals Aggie, whose lips, I notice, are turning a worrying shade of blue, although it could be due to the porch light that's on the blink and creating strobe effects. Or her latest lipstick.

I snort. 'Well how do you expect to feel if you come out in below zero temperatures dressed like you're going to a barbecue on a blazing summer's day? I think I might leave you outside for another ten minutes, just to punish you.'

I put my arms out to the side as if to block the entrance. Aggie laughs and barges through, with Gemma close behind. Aggie is wearing a jade green, slinky halterneck top with jeans and open-toe stilettos. On top she's got some kind of cropped, furry jacket that barely covers her shoulders.

Gemma is kitted out in a brown version of my black puffa which we bought together in Zara, with a beanie hat on her head. Except for the large chattering teeth her little face is almost hidden from view.

Each of them is clutching a bottle of wine. 'That should be enough to get us started,' I declare. 'Come and get warmed up, the two of you. There's food, wine, heat and what I hope is a night of debauchery awaiting us. It's Sunday tomorrow and I'm looking forward to a hangover. There's not much else to look forward to,' I add ruefully.

'Bring it on,' says Aggie, almost tripping forward as she gets one of her heels stuck between the bristles of the doormat which is set into the wood floor of the corridor. 'Oh, sod this,' she says, kicking off the other shoe, and sending it skidding along the floor. She shakes her foot from the stuck shoe, yanks it out of the mat and bowls it along the corridor to collide with her first shoe. 'See what a good shot I am,' she laughs. 'And I'm even better when I've had a drink or two. Come on, girls, it's time to party.'

Chapter Six

There are those who loll and those who drape. Gemma, Aggie and I are lolling. Gemma is on the floor, legs outstretched and slightly apart under the glass coffee table, back propped up by the sofa. When she's not imbibing from it, which isn't very often, Gemma places her wine glass carefully on the rug, equidistant between her two knees.

Aggie and I are each tucked into a corner of the deep, cushiony cream-linen sofa, facing one another, feet overlapping, occasionally bottom shuffling and elbow manoeuvring to get more comfortable. When either one of us feels the need for a slice of salami or a crisp or an olive, before reaching over to the coffee table we have to swing our legs over Gemma's skull to avoid kicking her in the head. Valentina, meanwhile, is seated sideways in the tan leather armchair, turned towards us, crossed legs draped elegantly over one arm of the chair, her thin-heeled ankle boots creating interesting angles to the floor. Her own right arm rests lightly over the chair's back. I note that her fingernails, the russet of autumn leaves, tone perfectly with her chestnut hair.

Eyes may not be the windows to the soul, but they do reveal quite a bit. My own, I'm aware, are puffy and red veined. I can feel their tightness. Tears always leave me looking this way, unless I remember to splash my eyes over and over with cold water the minute the first tear has been shed. But eye-splashing isn't usually top of your mind when you need a good cry, and neither can you rely on being close to a sink. I've had one glass of champagne and two of white wine. I am drunk enough to have let down my guard, not drunk enough to be maudlin.

Gemma's eyes have gone glassy – she is holding a Grissini stick between two fingers, as though it's a cigarette, and she's sucking on it, pretending to inhale smoke. She has done this since childhood – with chocolate cigarettes, chopsticks, HB pencils, whatever is to hand – even though she has never actually smoked. Apart from that one-night stand of a few summers ago, it seems to me that inhaling bread-sticks is about as daring as Gemma gets, other than in her imagination. Her stories are a different ball game. Unlike her life, they're full of random violence and gratuitous sex. They're also very funny and aimed at a young, female audience which grows with each new book. Following *The Catwalk Killer*, *Lethal Lipstick* and *Photo Shoot*, her publisher reckons her next book will be her 'breakthrough'. This is book-publishing jargon for going from obscurity to the big-time. Gemma isn't sure the big-time will suit her, she'd really just rather write her books without getting too much attention. The mere idea of becoming a Richard and Judy book club choice horrifies her. Not because she's a literary snob, far from it, but because it would propel her into the limelight. Gemma takes another sip of wine.

Aggie's pupils have dilated alarmingly, to the point where they have taken over the iris completely. She has just finished smoking a large spliff. Her dealer had turned up at my door about twenty minutes after she arrived, waving a small, transparent plastic bag at her. I was not amused. 'What the hell do you think you're doing giving your dealer my address?' I'd screamed at Aggie.

'Well I could hardly have had it delivered by mini-cab, love,' Aggie had batted back, without apology. 'And given the fact that Charles isn't speaking to me, and doesn't know I do this stuff, I couldn't exactly have asked him to drop it round.' I ended up laughing. Aggie is simply incapable of a logical train of thought. It didn't occur to her that I, Julie, or rather I, Dr Julie Broadhurst, or indeed I, Miss Julie, consultant obstetrician and gynaecologist, Broadhurst, might prefer not to be implicated in my friend's dodgy drug dealings. That it wouldn't exactly be good for me professionally if it were to be found out.

Aggie is now so high that she has momentarily misplaced the knowledge of her husband Charles finding out about her affairs and being on the verge of throwing her out of her own house with a 24-hour deadline for departure starting this evening. At this particular moment she appears absolutely at peace with the planet and everyone on it.

Only Valentina's eyes remain crystal clear or, in this instance, Crystal clear. She is swigging back what remains in the bottle, from the bottle. I find myself thinking that if Aggie were to do this it would look cheap and somehow chavish, if I were to do it, it would look like a desperate, drunken cry for help but when Valentina throws back her head and drains the last drop it looks like a pose conjured up by Mario Testino for the fashion pages of *Vogue*. For all its surface appearance of carefree chic, of elegant insouciance, a pose is exactly what it is. Poor, poor Valentina.

A curious thing happens. Instead of the usual cacophony of chatter that erupts when the four of us gather together, there is a momentary pause. Conversation ceases and all is quiet. It occurs to me that this multiple pile-up of marital crises isn't a matter of coincidence. I may only have heard today that Valentina suspects her husband of having an affair, that Aggie's husband has found out about her serial infidelities and that Gemma is having serious thoughts about leaving Antony, but the shockwaves from Walt's announcement in October have been reverberating amongst us all for months. What has happened between Walt and me seems to have acted as a kind of catalyst for the rest, allowing Valentina's fears, Gemma's dissatisfaction and Aggie's perhaps subconscious desire to be found out, to bubble up to the surface. And what kind of effect, I wonder, might Walt's departure be having on Rob, Antony and Charles? What doubts of their own might have been stirred up by Walt's dramatic decision to take time out from his wife? Will they all shortly be demanding Gap Years? Asserting their right to their own mid-life, mid-wife crisis.

So far I'm the only one in the room who has been granted access to everyone else's current emotional imbroglios. My guess is it will be Aggie who'll be the first to blurt out her news, it always is. But even Aggie seems to need her moment of silent reflection.

For me, none of it has properly sunk in yet. Neither Walt's departure nor the possible demise of my friends' marriages feels real. As far as Walt's exit is concerned it's not as though he's emptied out his cupboards or even the bathroom cabinet. He's just packed a bag and gone off to catch a plane. It could be an assignment for the paper. Or a boys-only break with his mates. There's no real evidence of him having properly gone. And yet he has gone, and I know it, and I've been crying, so I'm definitely feeling his departure, just not the full brunt of it.

Since October, when Walt announced his exit strategy, I've been carrying on my life pretty much as though nothing has changed. Apart from the occasional confrontation I've been adopting the ostrich position. We've spent time with Katy as a family, had meals out with Tess and Pete, seen friends together as a couple, continued sleeping in the same bed. At least there's been no change in our sex life. We haven't had sex in over a year anyway. I don't want to think about that right now. I can't seem to locate my true feelings. Incomprehension is the strongest emotion I've so far conjured up. I'm not suffering from a broken heart so much as bafflement.

None of this is how it was meant to be. Not that I had anything mapped out as far as the future was concerned. I've been too occupied to think much about how life would pan out for me and Walt once both the girls had left home and started to lead independent lives. But if I'd chosen to think about it I suppose I would have expected our fifties to be a time of consolidation. Here I am just about getting used to the idea of becoming a grandmother. The contradiction between morphing into grannydom at the same time as waking up one morning re-minted as a fifty-something Bridget Jones doesn't bear thinking about. But there's one realisation that has taken me absolutely by surprise, and it's this. I don't want to live out the rest of my life in emotional or sexual purdah. If it's over between me and Walt then one day I would like to find a partner again, even while recognising that there may be no man out there for me to find.

All of this is too much to deal with all at once. These new circumstances need to be faced one step at a time. I'm going to need all my emotional reserves just to keep functioning. To go to work, do my job properly, come home. To not eat or drink too much. To be available to the girls and to support and be supported by my friends. Just how Walt and I are supposed to have any chance of sorting ourselves out when he's so far away, I have no idea. He hasn't even said that he'll write. I did ask him and he replied, 'Give it time, let's see how it goes.' As if the word 'let's' made it somehow inclusive, as if I wanted to 'see how it goes' too. What I wanted was for him to say he'd write, explain things, tell me why he'd done what he was doing, over and over again if necessary, in a dozen different ways, until I understood. But I let it drop, because whenever I failed to drop something we'd end up mauling one another.

On a day other than today, a day other than one on which my husband had left with a backpack and a one-way ticket, I would be feeling completely content in the company of my friends. As I have grown older my women friends, and I consider Gemma to be as much a friend as she is a sister, have grown ever more important to me. Even Aggie, whom I sometimes get the urge to slap, I couldn't contemplate life without. She may be at least ten times more infuriating than the rest of us, but she's no less loyal and loving. We need Aggie in the mix. We can bitch about her behind her back, and even to her face, but she gives the group a dynamism that it might otherwise lack. And she can make us laugh until we can barely catch our breath.

The conversation so far, until we fell spontaneously silent, has been on safe ground. We've discussed Valentina's incredible new boots, designed by her latest client, Giovanni da Pontedra. Aggie wants a pair at discount, I don't want a pair at any price on account of the fact that I get vertigo in anything higher than a kitten heel. Gemma's style tends towards Doc Martens teamed with black or stripy leggings, under layers of tops and tunics and long scarves. It's a look which doesn't go down too well with her barrister husband Antony who'd rather she shopped at Jaeger than in thrift shops and at market stalls. Antony saves himself embarrassment over the Doc Martens by saying things like, 'She's very creative, my wife.' Gemma would rather go naked than wear boots like Valentina's.

After the in-depth discussion about Valentina's boots, we moved on to the kids. Gemma, Valentina and I have two children each, or we did until Paolo took his own life. Aggie is childless, though not by choice. She goes down pretty well with all our kids because they see her more as a friend than a parental figure. She's forty-nine going on fourteen, as Walt is fond of saying. I've updated them all on Tess's ultrasound, Valentina has said she's worried about Carla losing too much weight. 'She's no wider than a chive,' she said, 'but I don't know if it's because of Paolo and is temporary or if she's becoming anorexic.' We talked of warning signs and the importance of vigilance at the same time as not over-pressurising her at such a vulnerable time. In other words we trotted out the usual clichés and silently prayed that Carla would get through it. Gemma, I noticed, has barely opened her mouth. She's always the quietest of our group, but it's as though she's not in the room at all tonight.

I've no idea how long the silence has lasted but as if on cue Aggie has started talking. I'm only half listening.

'Sexy Pilates instructor . . . Charles so predictable . . . just a bit of fun . . .'

'So how exactly did he find out?' asks Valentina.

'He found me on the mat with Raoul.'

This is beginning to get interesting after all. I sit up straighter and take another sip of wine.

'As in Raoul, the Pilates instructor, who does one-to-ones at your house?'

'I just said that, you haven't been listening.'

'But isn't that what Pilates instructors are supposed to do, get down on the mat with you and help you to stretch your muscles after you've done your hundreds and your stomach crunches and your leg lifts?'

'Yes, but they're not supposed to be down there with their head right between your thighs performing cunnilingus. At least not at the very moment when your husband walks in.'

A collective gasp goes around the room.

'My God, Aggie, you said on the phone this morning you'd never played so close to home before, but this is unreal. How could you be so stupid?'

'You're right, of course you are.' Aggie shifts uncomfortably in her corner of the sofa. 'But all that exercise gets my endorphins going. I mean you're a doctor, you know about endorphins. And Pilates teachers don't just bark orders at you like some personal trainers do, they get touchy-feely with you, encouraging you gently but firmly, and it's nice being touched gently but firmly when your endorphins are on full alert. And, well, one thing leads to another, and Charles is never home by four in the afternoon, but on this occasion he'd forgotten to mention that he'd arranged for the structural engineer to meet him at the house to discuss the possible underpinning because of the cracks and . . . and . . . well that's how I have so monumentally fucked up that . . .'

Valentina butts in. '*Mamma mia*, what were you thinking? So much humiliation. So much embarrassment. For poor Charles. And the engineer? Did the engineer see, too?' She is both horrified and agog, demanding more details. Gemma says nothing, and I wonder if she's making mental notes for her next novel. Me? I'm so discombobulated by events that I'm beyond even having an opinion.

'Yes, both. And I was so carried away, and my eyes were closed, I think I didn't notice at first. They could have been standing there for five minutes for all I know, but I think it was probably only seconds, and by the time . . .'

It must be because the whole of life feels so surreal on this particular day, or maybe it's the effect of too much alcohol but, like Valentina, I find myself interrupting Aggie, which mid-flow is no easy thing to do, and spluttering, 'Hang on, Aggie. This Raoul, how good is he? Do you think he could get *my* endorphins going? Help me find my core, that sort of thing.' I'm giggling now, but I'm not sure, from the look on Aggie's face, that I'm being very funny. 'I mean, what with Walt no longer being here, and the fact that I haven't had sex in God knows how long and Walt was never much one for oral sex which was a shame because . . .' And then I have to stop mid-sentence as well because Gemma has jumped up from the floor and turned towards me with a look of such fury that I half expect her to sink her considerable fangs into my flesh.

'Just shut up, will you! You're ridiculous. All of you. Ridiculous. Drunk. Immature. In short, pathetic. I don't want to hear any of this. Not about Valentina's boots. Or Raoul's magic tongue. Or your inebriated burbling, Julie. It's not funny. Not any of it. Not any of it, do you understand? I just want things to be like they were. Like they were before Paolo died. Before Walt went away. Before it all went wrong.'

And she is out of the room before she can hear me quietly say, 'That's what we'd all like, Gemma.'

I lift my leaden, wine-heavy limbs up from the sofa. By the time I make it to the corridor the front door has already slammed and Gemma has disappeared into the freezing January night.

I feel like crawling rather than walking back into the living room. Gemma's outburst has brought me back to my senses, but without clearing the fuzziness in my head. She has succeeded in making me feel slightly ashamed of myself.

'Sorry, Aggie, sorry for not taking you seriously. It's all been a bit much for me today.'

'Never mind that, what's got into Gemma is what I want to know,' says Aggie. 'She's usually so mild.'

'Whatever it is, it's pretty serious I'd say. Sorry, girls, but the party appears to be over.'

'Oh dear, I thought that for just this one night we were going to forget all our troubles. Are you going to be all right on your own?'

asks Valentina. 'I could stay if you wanted me to. Rob won't mind, he'd probably love it.'

'You're sweet, Val, but being without Walt is something I'm going to have to get used to. This could be the first night of the rest of my life. Aggie, we'll speak tomorrow.'

'You know I'd do anything for a friend,' says Aggie, winking at me like a saucy nymphette from an old Carry On film. 'I'd even lend you Raoul if I thought it would help. But Raoul is French toast as far as I'm concerned and in any case he's going back to Marseilles on Wednesday, for good, to open his own Pilates studio. From now on, no more affairs. The only thing that matters is getting Charles back.'

I close the front door behind Valentina and Aggie and lean back against it, so tired I want to slide down the door to the floor and curl up on the bristly doormat. I think about clearing up and realise I don't have to. There's no one to answer to but me. No one to see the mess but me. And it's Sunday tomorrow, and I have no plans to go anywhere or see anyone, although I'm going to have to find out what's up with Gemma. And speak to Aggie and Val as well. And the girls are bound to call to see how I'm getting on. My mum, too, probably, if Walt's departure hasn't slipped her mind. Life goes on. But the washing up can wait.

I go to bed, certain I'll fall instantly asleep, which I do. But at 4 a.m. I'm wide awake, my mouth parched. I grab hold of Walt's pillow and clutch it close, burying my nose into it, sniffing hopefully for his scent. Disappointingly it smells only of pillow.

Chapter Seven

I can't remember a time when I hadn't wanted to be a doctor. My father was a GP and he delighted in the fact that his younger daughter took such an interest in his work. Unlike Gemma, who was squeamish when it came to blood and gore and especially needles, but then went on to make it a special feature of her novels, I was fearless about bodily functions, and fascinated by the workings of the body. By the time I was six I was piecing together skeletons from kits and dangling the finished results from the ceiling of my bedroom. There were girls in my class who refused to sleep over because my grisly mobiles gave them nightmares, as did the posters of internal organs which I insisted on pinning to the bedroom walls on top of the pink flowery wallpaper.

One of my favourite games was memorising body parts, their exact location and the jobs they performed. At night, rather than reading stories, I'd mentally map out the body and go over which body bit did what. It was a bit like preparing for an exam. The difference was that it was fun, and it soothed me into sleep.

Friends who came to play were subjected to merciless body inspections which they were under threat of their lives not to report back to their parents. The boys who came for tea could never quite accept the fact that when it came to playing doctors and nurses it was always me who got to play the doctor. Male nurses were practically unheard of in those days, and the boys who found it too humiliating to be relegated to the role of nurse simply stopped coming after a while. I wasn't bothered. As far as I was concerned boys were a waste of space, except for the purpose of forensic examination.

The summer I turned six we had been on holiday to Cornwall. Our parents took us off to visit a church which was famous for its stunning stained-glass windows. But all I was interested in were the gravestones in the churchyard. I read the inscriptions of children who had died as young as two or three and one of a girl called Mary Elizabeth who was born in 1902 and died in 1908, the age I was at the time. Apparently I turned to my mother – years later she had to remind me of this as I'd quite forgotten – and said, with all the seriousness that only an innocent child can muster, 'I'm not going to let that happen when I grow up. I'm going to be a doctor for babies. And I'm going to save them all and make them better.' Goodness knows what path I might have taken if I'd been bad at science and failed my exams. There was never a time when I even considered being anything other than a doctor.

The GP surgery was located in our home with a special entrance at the side of the house. It would have been a simple enough job to create a second entrance from within the house itself so that Dad, and Mum – who was his receptionist – could get to work without going outside. But it was agreed that the internal door should be blocked off, and my parents would enter the surgery from the same door as the patients.

'Work and leisure shouldn't overlap,' Dad used to say. 'You should never bring your work home with you,' was one of Tom Broadhurst's most oft-repeated phrases, though it was one of the lessons I learned least well as Walt is constantly reminding me. 'I don't want to be tempted to pop back to surgery at the end of a busy day, which I might if it were as easy as opening a door from the hallway,' said Tom. This was more wishful thinking than reality on his part. A GP's work is never done, or at least it wasn't during the era in which I grew up when solo practices serving small communities were common and the local GP had little or no regular back-up for out of hours emergencies, unless he had a partner, which Tom didn't. He made do with a loose arrangement with a GP who had a similar practice a few streets away, and locum cover on the rare occasions he took a holiday. Tom liked it being just the two of them, him and Mum. Only later, by the time I was in my teens, did he employ a practice nurse on a part-time basis to administer jabs and dress wounds and deal with some of the simpler jobs that could be so time-consuming.

'But you wouldn't have to get wet and cold in the winter if there was a door from inside the house,' I implored when I was old enough to work these things out. 'It doesn't mean you'd have to use it all the time.'

What I actually wanted was a door *I* could go through whenever I fancied it, to check up on Mum and Dad and find out whether there was anything exciting going on at the surgery. Like an emergency. I loved emergencies. When the phone rang during supper – as it often did – it was always me who leaped up to answer it. The patient – and it invariably was a patient – would ask to speak to the doctor. And I'd reply in my poshest voice, 'The surgery is now closed. May I enquire as to whether it's a matter of urgency?' Of course it always was a matter of urgency, at least as far as the caller was concerned, otherwise they wouldn't have called in the first place. Sometimes patients even turned up at the front door, unannounced, at eight, nine or ten in the evening, demanding to be seen by the doctor, and Dad usually relented, leading them round to the side of the house and opening up the surgery.

Occasionally, if it was before my bedtime, he'd let me go with him. Then I'd sit in the reception cum waiting room and riffle through the index cards of all the patients. Or take the big copy of MIMS down from the shelf and randomly select a drug from the directory. Interactions, dosages, side-effects, I couldn't get enough. While Gemma was lost in *Little Women*, I was memorising medications. My ongoing battle to have an internal door to the surgery, however, remained a lost cause.

'I like my little walk, my little blast of fresh air,' Tom had responded. 'Does me good.'

'I'm not sure twenty yards quite constitutes even a little walk,' chipped in my mum, Annette, eyeing her husband's burgeoning paunch. Tom Broadhurst was fanatical about the exercise and diet regimes of his patients and his family, but took none of his own advice. Famously didactic, always explaining the benefits of a healthy lifestyle to anyone who was prepared to listen, he nevertheless ate too much, drank more than he should and exercised not at all.

'I didn't say it was exercise, did I, Julie?' he responded cheerfully, looking first towards his belly and then to me for support. 'It's more psychological, putting that bit of distance between my grim daily grind and the sheer joy of coming home to my adoring wife and children.' His jowls wobbled decisively in appreciation of his own good humour.

'I think you're getting your actives mixed up with your passives,' replied Annette, with a grin. 'Surely you mean *adorable* wife and children.' Gemma, who was seated on the sofa, looked up from the novel she was reading. Wordplay was much more to her taste than ulcers and fractured pelvises. Annette smiled at Gemma, then bent over and planted a kiss on the top of my head. This was not favouritism; there was no favouritism in the Broadhurst household. At that particular moment I just happened to be the daughter in closer proximity.

Looking back from the perspective of adulthood I've often thought how extraordinary my parents' relationship was. They never argued, despite working as well as living together, they always backed one another up over issues to do with us kids – much to my and Gemma's annoyance their solidarity was almost impenetrable – and they rarely got grumpy. They did tease one another a lot, and they bickered quite a bit as well, but it was always a good-natured thing. At the time we thought all parents were like them. As an adult, and more and more as the years passed by, I've caught myself comparing my own marriage to theirs and finding it wanting. Even when things between me and Walt were good, and they really were good, I sensed that Tom and Annette possessed something that Walt and I couldn't quite grasp.

I tried to quiz my mother about it. 'There's no mystery, Julie,' she'd said, 'I loved your father and he loved me and we looked after one another.'

'But Dad did have quite a big ego to haul around with him, in addition to all that body weight. Didn't you have to massage it all the time?'

'No, that's not how it worked. Maybe his ego could have got in the way of our relationship, but I didn't so much massage it – which suggests encouraging it – as indulge it, especially when it didn't do any of us any harm to indulge it. The important point is that he indulged me back – with love and affection and good humour and good sex.'

'Good sex? Did the good sex last?' I was always curious about other people's sex lives. Like my marriage, I wasn't always convinced that my sex life measured up, especially as the years went by. I'm smart enough to understand that everyone experiences sex in different ways, and that it isn't a competition, but I do find myself interrogating people whenever the opportunity arises. OK, I'm being honest here, my own sex life has been lacking lustre for a decade. I get this odd feeling that it ought to have bothered me more than it actually did.

Annette hesitated before answering my typically direct question. 'Well, you know that in his later years your father had a problem.'

'You mean his prostate . . .'

'Yes, he became impotent from the age of sixty-one, after it was operated on.'

'That must have mattered a lot . . .'

'Less to me I think than to him. I loved him enough to miss our sex life rather than mourn for it. He, though, felt unmanned, though he never said as much. Your father continued to insist on pleasuring me. We still had a physical relationship those last few years and he was completely unselfish in that way.'

How remarkable she is, I thought. Her openness and her unflinching honesty were just two of the things I admired her for.

What took me completely by surprise was her response to my father's death, and the revelations that came some time after he had gone. When Tom dropped dead of a massive heart attack at the age of 65 and the practice, which was still going strong, had to be shut down and Mum was out of a job, I thought she would fall apart. She didn't. Annette sold the big house, bought herself a flat, and invested the excess capital to provide herself with a decent pension in addition to the one she inherited from her husband. She signed up for the Open University and took a history degree and went on military history tours around Europe. On one of these tours, somewhere by the Somme, she met and fell in love with Paul, a retired headmaster.

'How do you do it, Mum?' I'd asked in amazement. It was only eighteen months after Tom's death that she blithely announced her intention to remarry.

'But Mum,' said Gemma, 'the ash has barely settled. It seems, somehow . . .' Gemma had been taking this whole romance thing far more badly than I had, and had already admitted quietly to me that the thought of Annette in the arms of some man other than her father, and so soon after his death, turned her stomach, as well as feeling like a betrayal of his memory.

'Somehow what?' Annette had interjected. '. . . Unseemly? Rushed? Hasty? Likely to get chins wagging in the neighbourhood? What do I care for such things?'

At the time of the announcement the three of us were sitting on a park bench with egg mayonnaise sandwiches, prepared by Mum, on our laps. It was a sunny spring day and ranged opposite us, in an indecently garish display, was a phalanx of rhododendron bushes. I found myself smiling.

'These rhododendrons remind me of you, Mum,' I said.

'You mean my face is all pink from the burst blood vessels too close to the surface of my skin?' Annette had laughed.

'No, not pink, you're not pink at all. Your complexion is wonderful, a whole lot better than mine, which doesn't seem fair. No, it's just that these rhododendrons don't appear to care at all for propriety or good taste or what their quieter neighbours in the next beds might think. They're having a grand old time flashing their booty and they don't give a damn who knows it. Congratulations, Mum, I'm really happy for you.'

Annette, who was sandwiched between me and Gemma, put one arm around each of us and squeezed us to her. It was lovely to have her girls to herself for a couple of hours. Now that we were both married, with kids of our own, such moments were rare – and all the more precious to her.

'Your father was a wonderful man. And it's because he was a wonderful man, and because our relationship was as it was, that I can love again. I'm sixty-two and I'm not dead yet, and I intend to go on living for quite some time. I believe that in the same way as it's easy to repeat the mistakes you make in relationships time and time again, you can repeat all the positive things as well.'

'But do you love him as much as you loved Dad? Surely it can't be the same?' Gemma was choked, she didn't want her father to be so readily replaceable. She knew she was behaving selfishly, but she couldn't help herself.

'Mature love isn't quite the same as young love, there's less intensity, at least there is for me, but I still crave the emotional and physical intimacy of a loving relationship. Paul is an intelligent, considerate and warm-hearted man. We have interests in common. I don't want to be alone. And don't forget the upside for you girls. The more reliant I am on Paul, the less of a burden I'll be to you two in my old age.'

'But you've never been a burden, Mum ...' Gemma was sniffling now. 'And I miss Dad so much.'

'And so do I, Gems. Which is another good reason for me not to be alone. I expect I'll go on missing him for ever, but it doesn't mean I can't enjoy the time I've got left.'

'Were there no times when you questioned your relationship with Dad?' I asked. 'Was it always as good as it appeared to be?'

'Once, yes ... It was when Gemma was five and you were barely two. I met him outside the school gate – a dad at the school gate was about as rare in those days as finding yourself living next door to a Russian immigrant. Now you wouldn't blink at either possibility. He wasn't a house-husband, of course, his wife had died of kidney failure leaving him with two young children.'

'And?'

'And I befriended him. Sometimes I used to sneak off with you, Julie, in the middle of the day between surgeries, and we'd meet him in the café or the park. You were a toddler and his two were both at full-time school, like Gemma. He declared himself, said he was falling for me. He seemed so vulnerable and I was swept away by the romantic notion that I could save him and his children.'

'What? And that we could all live happily ever after? You, him, his two, me and Gems? And what about Dad?'

'Exactly. But when you're right in the middle of something, when you're in the grip of infatuation, or whatever you want to call it, everything seems possible. At least for a moment or two.'

'Did you have an affair?'

'In a way, we did. But we didn't have sex, if that's what you mean. I put a stop to it. I had to. I loved your father and you girls too much to take the risk.'

'How long did it go on for?'

'About a year.'

'How did it end?'

'So many questions ...'

'Come on, Mum, this is interesting, how did it end?'

'I told him it was impossible. So he moved away to start over in another town. Away from memories of his wife, away from me.'

'Did he ever remarry?'

'I've no idea. It was the last I heard from him.'

'I wonder if you can ever really stop yourself from falling in love.' I didn't always agree with Annette, but I always wanted to know her opinion and to hear her point of view. Annette was so well grounded that somehow, just by listening to her talk, I felt more anchored, too.

'I think you can. There is a line, once crossed, that you can't step back from. That line may be drawn in different places for different people. The difficulty is spotting the line when it's in front of you. But I believe in free will. We do choose whether to fall in love or not, we do have some element of control. That was the only time I nearly went too far.'

Annette glanced from me to Gemma. I wondered if she was thinking how different the two of us are from one another. I wondered if our marriages caused Annette a certain amount of anxiety. I knew she hoped that Walt and I and Gemma and Antony would last the distance, but she often commented that commitment didn't seem to count for so much these days.

'And what about Dad?' I asked, warming to my theme. 'I bet he never strayed. You were everything to him.'

'For such a clever woman, Julie, you're really quite naïve. Think about it. Your father was a good-looking man with, as you've pointed out yourself, quite an ego. Doctors, a few years back, were still god-like figures. I could spot the she-devils a mile off. They'd come to the surgery looking like they'd come straight from the hairdresser, smartly dressed and in full make-up. And they were meant to be *ill*! It was so transparent it was laughable. They were damn brazen about it, too. The fact that I was the receptionist, on guard so to speak, didn't even figure in their thinking.'

'But surely he'd never . . .' Gemma was looking horrified. 'Surely not with a patient.'

'No, I don't think he ever did. But I know for sure he had a fling with Marina. And there may have been others.'

'Marina!' I screamed. 'Marina!' The name of the practice nurse was all I could manage to utter I was so stunned. Marina, who was treated like a member of the family, who befriended us all and stayed on for suppers after surgery cooked by Annette. And even once stayed in the spare room for three months, when her landlord decided to put up the rent and Marina couldn't afford it. Marina, who was young enough to be Tom's daughter.

So far, an hour of snatched time away from Walt and the kids had managed to produce three dramatic revelations from Annette, tumbling out one after another like Maltesers being poured from the packet into the palm of your hand.

'Enough, that's enough,' I wanted to cry. What more might she come up with? At the very moment that my mother had announced she was marrying again, everything I had believed to be true about my parents' marriage was being thrown into question.

'Marina!' exclaimed Gemma, echoing me. 'Marina!' Her face registered shock and bewilderment. Her eyes were wide and unblinking.

'Yes, Marina,' Annette said, the irritation showing plainly in her voice. 'I think we've all established that by now. What is it with you girls? Did I bring you up in some fairytale fantasy land in which the path of true love always runs smooth? In which everyone is faithful and no one is fallible. Why are you so shocked? You're modern women of the world. Did you think your father and I were different from other human beings? That we were immune to temptation? That's not at all the impression I wanted to give. Where did I go wrong?'

'But you seemed so happy,' wailed Gemma.

'What's the matter with you, girl? We *were* happy. He had an affair with Marina and it hurt. It really, really hurt. And I felt angry and jealous and betrayed. And then I calmed down. I realised it's this thing that men do. Women, too, sometimes, but in my experience not as often. He loved me, your father, more perhaps even than I loved him. But we loved each other enough. Enough to make it work. He'd never have left me and I'd never have left him. It was Marina who had to go, Marina who got hurt the most in the end, because she thought she could have your father, but she couldn't.'

That afternoon I had the strangest feeling. Perhaps for the first time I felt like a proper grown-up. The fact that I was thirty-six years old, a fully qualified doctor, newly appointed as a consultant, married and with two daughters from two different fathers, none of those things had made me feel quite so grown up as the conversation I had on the bench that spring day with my mother.

Talking about it afterwards on the bus when Annette had gone off to meet Paul for tea, Gemma said: 'I think I'd rather not have heard any of that. I feel a bit unhinged, like everything I've always believed has been a lie.'

'I know what you mean, Gems, but you're being terribly over-dramatic,' I replied, hoping I sounded at least sympathetic. 'I'm taken aback, too, but it was an important reality check, a reminder that no one's marriage, not even theirs, is perfect. And as for Mum and Paul, I think it couldn't be more wonderful.'

'I suppose so,' said Gemma, not sounding at all convinced. 'It's just so quick. I'm not over losing Dad yet.'

'Maybe not so quick when you're sixty-two.' I took Gemma's hand and gave it a little squeeze. 'You know the funny thing is all this stuff about Mum kind of helps me validate my own marriage. It means I can stop comparing us with them all the time. I would never have wanted to see Mum get hurt, definitely not that, but I don't feel I have so much to live up to any more, I can just get along with what I've got. I didn't even realise until today quite how the template of Mum and Dad's ideal marriage has been placing a burden on mine.'

'And are you happy with what you've got, Julie?'

'Happy enough,' I smiled. 'And you?'

'Ditto,' said Gemma, removing her hand from mine and using it to trace a smiley face in the dust on the inside of the bus window.

Suddenly I couldn't wait to get home. To Walt and the girls. I wanted to see Walt's face, his eyes, his smile. To check it for clues. Clues as to what, I wondered? His love, his loyalty? I want my marriage to last for ever, I thought. And then I moved on to planning other things, more pressing ones, like the girls' Sunday activities which had to be fitted in around school work; my schedule for next week; a teaching paper I was due to give to the new intake of medical students at the hospital.

Chapter Eight

'What the . . .?' Aggie is back on my front porch, this time with her luggage.

'I knew if I rang first you'd find an excuse so I went ahead and decided to . . .'

'Excuse me for interrupting, but you decided to pack your bags and come straight on over at the unforgivable time of seven forty-five on a Sunday morning and move in with me, safe in the knowledge that I wouldn't leave you to shack up on a park bench with the rest of the tramps. Sometimes you really do test the bounds of friendship, Aggie. We're supposed to be rational grown-ups. Not extras in *Desperate Housewives*.' I'm hung over and unamused. I love Aggie, as I keep having to remind myself, but having her move in is almost as bad as Walt waltzing out.

I need some time on my own, to try to come to terms with what's happened. I'm too weary – physically and emotionally – to cope with Aggie's verbal incontinence and 24–7 adrenaline rushes. But what am I to do? Refuse her entry? Tell her to go to a hotel? I'm supposed to be a friend. And this has never happened to her before, although it should have done.

'Well, darling, can you really imagine me camping out in the park with my Louis Vuitton trunk and my Balenciaga? I mean, there's no knowing who might like to help themselves to the contents. I was only reading in the *Standard* the other day that people won't even touch the stuff that's dumped in bins or skips any more unless there's a designer label attached . . .'

I'm desperate for Aggie to shut up. When the doorbell had summoned me, even though I'd hardly slept since 4 a.m., I'd stumbled out of bed, all bent over like an old woman, with a head as heavy and spongy as suet pudding and a mouth which had been vacuumed dry of saliva. Now, as I stand on the porch at the break of day, barefoot, dressed in a flimsy nightie, with an old woolly of Walt's flung hastily over it, my head is beginning to throb. But Aggie, mid-rant, is unstoppable.

'. . . Tramps are very into Balenciaga bags this season, don't you know. They're much more chic than they used to be. The tramps that is, not the bags. Problem is they prefer not to pay for stuff and there's something of a criminal element amongst the dossers. What is it with you, Julie? You're always leaving me out here in the bloody cold. Invite me in, would you?'

I'm determined not to laugh. 'You're impossible, Aggie. You only left my house a few hours ago. Judging by all this stuff you must have been packing ever since. What was the big rush? And why so much stuff? It looks like you're thinking of staying on a permanent basis.'

'The twenty-four-hour deadline from Charles was the big rush. The sooner I'm gone the sooner he'll realise how much he misses me. I have to move back in with him as soon as possible, it's really important that I do. As for all the stuff, well how am I supposed to know what I might need, what might crop up over the next few days? Look, I do know I'm impossible. That's what Charles says, too. But isn't it also why you love me? I mean, I may drive you nuts but I'm not boring, am I? Or likely to betray you in any way? And I know you want to laugh, and are trying not to. And you won't have to look after me, I promise . . .'

Aggie is wearing the same clothes as the previous night which, given the extensiveness of her wardrobe, is a genuine sign of trouble. She is also looking very much the worse for wear. Most of her Estée Lauder Thick-Lash Mascara has pooled halfway down her cheeks, soot-staining her sallow skin. Her big red salon-dyed, twice-weekly coiffed hair has shed its bounce and looks bereaved. My friend Aggie could easily be mistaken for a clapped-out middle-aged prostitute after a busy night on the streets of King's Cross.

'Don't worry, Ags,' I find myself saying, suddenly locating the compassion zone in my cerebral cortex. 'Of course I'll look after you. It's what friends are for. And you're right about Charles, he won't last five minutes without you.'

Between the two of us, Aggie in her stilettos, me practically naked, we drag the massive Vuitton trunk up the three steps and into the house.

'Leave it here in the hallway at the bottom of the stairs,' I command, 'and let's go and have a cup of coffee. The kitchen's a disaster area after last night. I decided to go straight to bed and to hell with the washing up. But now that you're here, and once you're settled, we can do it together and get it out of the way in no time.'

Fat chance, I think, Aggie doesn't have the housewife gene. Thanks to Charles's on-shore assets and off-shore investments, Aggie is blissfully unaware that not every household has a Filipina housekeeper. It wasn't at all the way she grew up, as the daughter of a Salford postman and a Morrison's cashier, but Aggie learned fast how to spend, after she met Charles, and Charles seemed happy to let her. I'd never quite understood what the deal was between them – why he put up with her infidelities and Viv Nicholson approach to money. It was something we had never discussed, but maybe, now that their marriage was in true crisis – he'd never gone as far as chucking her out before – it was time to try to understand the dynamic between the two of them a little better.

'Fancy some eggs?' I ask. Two poached eggs on toast with grilled tomatoes and bacon are my secret weapon in the fight against hangovers.

'Are you trying to make me throw up again? In addition to the three times I threw up when I got home last night?' Aggie looks horrified.

'Well, it works for me every time.'

'Oh, go on then.'

Pushing the previous night's debris to one side, I make just enough space at my kitchen island for the two of us to sit and eat.

I pile four dessertspoonfuls of fresh ground Colombian Reserve Arabica coffee into a cafetière, get a poaching pan from the cupboard and switch on the grill for the tomatoes and bacon. As I busy myself in the kitchen and feel myself slowly coming back to life, Aggie witters on and on about herself and Charles.

'I've tried to give up other men, I really have. But I'm too tempted. My therapist says it's understandable given the circumstances.'

'Therapists tend to be on your side, it's what you pay them for. So how exactly does your therapist explain it?'

'He says it's because I couldn't have babies of my own that I'm seeking assurance of my essential femininity through liaisons with as many men as possible. That I have to constantly prove to myself that I'm desirable in order to live with the pain of my empty womb.'

'Has he not suggested that perhaps this behaviour might be self-destructive?'

'Well, we have explored that idea a bit, but . . .'

'But what?'

'Look, I wasn't going to tell you, but he and I slightly overstepped the boundaries and I had to stop seeing him in the capacity of shrink.'

'Meaning?'

'Meaning, it all got a bit out of hand. Well I only slept with him once, well only once in the consulting room that is. And after that we did it a few times in his flat. And then he decided he couldn't see me any more, either personally or professionally, said it was all a big mistake and it was professional misconduct of the first order.'

The shell I have been attempting to crack on the edge of the pan splits dramatically in two and splatters raw yolk and gelatinous egg white all over the hob. 'Oh my God, Aggie, look what you've made me do. Look at this bloody mess. You are so stupid, so unbelievably fucking stupid. You said yesterday you'd never played so close to home before, that was bad enough, but this is unreal.'

'I'm sorry, Julie, I really am. It's all one big mess. So now I have no husband and no therapist and Raoul's going back to Marseilles. So I'm utterly alone and you're the only friend I can trust enough not to judge me.'

'But I am judging you, Aggie. I think you are ludicrous.'

Aggie's mobile rings and she rummages inside her fashionably huge designer bag to retrieve it.

'Hi there, sweetheart, not like you to be up so early. Great to hear from you though . . .'

'. . . No of course I haven't forgotten . . .'

'. . . Three this afternoon is perfect. Can't wait to see you . . .'

'. . . Whatever you feel like . . .'

'. . . Sure . . . absolutely . . . the movie is a great idea, and then afterwards we can decide . . .'

A beatific smile has crossed Aggie's face and she returns her mobile to her handbag with a contented sigh.

I feel such a rush of blood to the head I think I might blow up and splatter all over the kitchen just like the egg I have just dropped.

'What is it with you, Aggie? That wasn't Charles, was it? No, definitely not him. Was it Raoul? Or some other lover. You are simply the most immature person I have ever met. You really don't deserve Charles, you know.'

'It's not what you think, Julie.'

'Is that what you tell Charles? No really, darling, it's not what you think. Not at all. That man with his head between my thighs is just my Pilates coach trying to locate my core. No, Charles, of course not. I know it's three a.m. but I just popped out for some cigarettes and I got talking to the young sales assistant and before I knew it . . . Do you know something? I'd leave you if I were him.'

I poke aggressively at the bacon slices under the grill, then turn my attention to slicing bread for toasting with such a ferocious backwards/forwards motion of the knife I'm within millimetres of cutting off my own hand.

'Drop it please, Julie. I have to meet someone this afternoon and it's not a lover, I swear it.'

'Well it's not a business associate, is it, on a Sunday afternoon? Not even a bride who needs her make-up doing for her wedding. Who is it, Aggie? If it's not a lover surely you can tell me. Or are we just talking semantics here? Not yet a lover, but about to be a lover, once we've got the movie out the way. Someone you're planning to break in after the main feature.'

'Look, I will tell you. But I need time.'

'Honestly, Aggie, I'm so pissed off with you that I'm really not sure I can handle you and me being under the same roof. You are your own worst enemy. I mean what's even the matter with Charles? And on the subject of eggs, it's not as though it's his fault that you can't have children. He was desperate for kids, all along he wanted to be a dad. And then when you discovered you were having premature ovarian failure he supported you right through it. Said he loved you regardless. What better man could you have than that?'

'I wish it were that simple.'

'It could be that simple if you wanted to make it so.'

'Think what you like.' Aggie shrugs disconsolately. 'You're very self-righteous, you know.'

'Well I haven't done anything wrong.'

'Haven't you? Are you entirely blameless in the Walt department? Has his going off, escaping to halfway across the world, got absolutely nothing to do with your good self? I mean it can't be easy living with a cross between St Teresa and Nigella Lawson.'

'I don't know what you're talking about.'

'You're so fucking perfect, that's what I'm talking about. You're a doctor at the top of your profession, worshipped by your patients and staff. You're a perfect mother. You're a wonderful cook. And you're probably an absolute hooker in bed. I'd hate you if I was married to you.'

'Surely if I really was all those things and you were my husband you'd keep me under lock and key I'd be so precious.'

'Well that's exactly where you're wrong. If you're completely perfect, where does that leave Walt? Feeling like an absolute zero I wouldn't be at all surprised.'

I want to fight back, but I can't find the words. Maybe there are no words to counter what Aggie has just said. The smell of burning bacon reminds me of breakfast and I lunge at the grill to remove the blackened strips and overcooked tomatoes from under it, just as one slice of bacon is beginning to catch fire. I grab at the grill pan and with smoke rising over my face and saturating my hair I head for the bin with the charred remains.

'Ruined, of course.'

'What about the eggs?' asks Aggie.

'Shit, shit, shit. I forgot about the eggs as well. Unless hard-boiled poached eggs are to your liking, I'd better dump them, too.'

'No, Julie, I'll take them as they come. And at least the toast's not burnt.'

'By the way,' I say, 'I'm not sure I qualify on any of those counts you've just mentioned. As for being a hooker in bed, Walt hasn't been near me for so long I think I've sealed right up. I was thinking of coming to you for instruction in the dark bedroom arts.'

Aggie and I grin at one another. A major bust-up has been averted.

The eggs taste truly awful, like rubber pellets, but the coffee is good and the toast and fig jam are delicious, and we each have three fat slices before declaring ourselves sated.

'So how are *you*, Julie?' asks Aggie at last.

'To be honest I haven't got a clue,' I reply. 'I feel numb and slightly detached. I mean he's only been gone a day, so how am I to know?'

'I'm so sorry, Julie,' says Aggie. 'And sorry, too, to have been so me, me, me about everything.'

'I don't mind, honestly I don't. I'd actually rather hear you talk about you than talk about myself. I don't seem to know what I think or how I feel so there's very little I can say on the subject of Walt at the moment. I need to compute it quietly for a bit. You need to get it all out, I need to keep it in. That's the difference between us, I guess. And it's maybe why we're friends as well. Opposites attract and all that.'

'Julie, I didn't mean what I said before. He's an idiot for leaving you. It's only that you're so smart and attractive and capable and loyal that maybe sometimes you're hard to live up to. I can understand someone leaving me, I'm completely lunatic most of the time, but not you. You're a rock.'

'And maybe because I'm a rock he thinks I won't hurt when he kicks me. Maybe I've been too reasonable for too long. Oh hell, I really don't know, and as I said I think I need to mull it over for a while before I even attempt to talk about it in any way that makes sense.'

'Point taken, Julie. Thanks for putting me up. And now I wouldn't mind going and having a kip for a couple of hours. I need to look decent for later.'

I'm on the verge of launching a new diatribe against my friend. The mere thought of Aggie meeting up with a lover while feigning desperation to go home to Charles makes me crackle with fury.

'Spare bedroom's already made up,' I say instead. 'Towels in the airing cupboard, help yourself. I'm just going to clear this stuff up and I'll see you later.'

'We're going to have fun, aren't we?' says Aggie, fixing me with a smile which looks halfway between genuine and desperate.

'Yes, Aggie, I'm sure we will,' I say, turning my back on her and starting to clatter about the kitchen, sweeping up debris-encrusted platters and plates from the night before. Without even the most half-hearted attempt at offering help – a gesture I'd have appreciated even if I'd refused to accept it – Aggie leaves the kitchen. As Aggie huffs and puffs and swears loudly, thudding her way up the stairs with her heavy trunk, I glance through the window behind the kitchen sink. The sun has almost broken through the misty clouds and filled the garden with pale, wintry light. A cat sits contentedly on the lawn preening itself. I could do with some preening myself, I think, and make a mental note to book myself a facial and a massage for the following weekend.

At 2.15 p.m., while I'm attempting to read the Sunday papers, having tried – and failed – to go back to sleep, Aggie reappears looking refreshed. She is wearing tight blue jeans with low-heeled cowboy-style boots peeking out from underneath, a simple, tight cream polo sweater which emphasises her considerable breasts and an open double-breasted black woollen jacket with a knitted scarf. She's pulled her hair back into a shortish ponytail and her face looks as though it has benefited from exfoliation. She's definitely wearing make-up, but unlike the usual slap-fest she appears to have applied the lightest lick of tinted moisturiser, a quick flick of mascara and the merest dab of lipgloss.

'You look GREAT,' I say, and I mean it. 'I can't believe you've been hiding your natural assets under all that camouflage all these years. Look at you. You're forty-nine, for heaven's sake, and without the war paint you look a dozen years younger. I don't think I've ever seen you without your base coat, two layers of emulsion and top coat to boot. Does Mr Love-In-The-Afternoon like you *au naturel*?'

'Well, thanks for the compliment, Julie, but it really pisses me off that you don't believe me when I say I'm not meeting a man.'

'You mean you're meeting a woman? You've switched camps?'

'For God's sake, Julie, I'm not nearly as obsessed with sex as you seem to think I am. I'm really not that superficial.'

'But Ags, it's because you're so superficial that we all love you so much. You stop us being too po-faced and serious. No Aggie, no cabaret.'

'Well it's not funny. You're just mocking me and it's really not funny.'

'I wasn't trying to be funny. This started with me telling you how great you look.'

'And now I'm going to be late.'

'What movie are you going to see, by the way?'

'*Kung Fu Panda*.'

'*Kung Fu Panda*! You're not going to snog your way through *Kung Fu Panda,* are you? Shouldn't you be going to see something X-rated so you can canoodle without frightening the horses?'

'Fuck you, Julie. If I'm home late, don't wait up.'

'Our first marital spat, and we've only been married about . . . about five hours.'

Aggie turns on her stacked heels and stomps out of the living room. She gives me a two-fingered sign and I start laughing about a second ahead of her.

'Have fun, my impossible friend.'

'Love you really.'

'Love you back.'

As the front door slams, I pick up the newspaper and try to concentrate on it, but Walt keeps interrupting me – Walt invades my every thought.

The phone rings. It's Gemma. 'Sorry about last night.'

'What got into you? I know we weren't exactly behaving like mature adults, but it's unlike you to be so disapproving.'

'It's complicated.'

'It's to do with what you said about you and Antony, isn't it?'

'As I said, it's complicated.'

'So do you want to come over now? I'm only sitting here not reading the papers and chewing over the wreckage of my marriage.'

'No, not now. Andy's popping in soon. And we have to go to the vile Harold from Antony's chambers for dinner. His wife, I think you met Lavinia at our place once, is the world's worst snob. You know, the type who thinks she pees eau de cologne. I'd do anything to get out of it.'

I'm rather relieved Gemma won't be coming round today. I am too exhausted to talk, too worn out even to listen to someone else talk. 'Tuesday then?'

'No, I can't do this week at all. I'm going to New York, for the launch of the American edition of *Photo Shoot*.'

'It's amazing that they're paying for you to go there. They really are building you up for the big time.'

'Actually they're not paying, I am, and it's only one radio interview. The real reason I'm going is to see Sam. He's flying in from Whistler for the week and we're going to hang out for a few days together.' Sam is Gemma and Antony's elder boy. To Antony's eternal disappointment Sam dropped out of university to become a ski instructor in Canada.

'Of course. I'd forgotten.'

'That's all right, little sister. In the circumstances I forgive you.'

'But when are we going to talk?'

'When I get back. Tuesday week would be good.'

'Not sure I can wait that long.'

'Just look after yourself, OK.'

'Hug Sam for me, will you? Tell him it's time to come home.'

'Not a chance until the ski season's over. Are you all right, Julie?'

'Not really.'

'Me neither. Bye then.'

I pick up the newspaper again, but I don't know why I'm bothering. I pull the tartan woollen throw from the arm rest and wrap it tightly round me. Then I lie down on my side with my head on a cushion and curl up in the foetal position. I don't close my eyes. I stare sightlessly towards the floor and allow my thoughts to fill my head.

Chapter Nine

If Walt had simply said he needed some time, some time away from work, to have a break after so long slogging for that damn paper, I would have understood. If he'd said he needed to get away on his own for a few weeks, to conquer a mountain or drift around Europe on a motorbike, I would have said go for it. I'd even have chipped in for crampons or a Harley Davidson if I thought it would have helped. What I can't work out is what he expects to achieve by going off on a Gap Year. 'That's another of your problems, Julie,' Walt told me. 'You always want answers. You want answers before the questions have even been asked.'

This much I do know. Julie the workaholic wonderwoman can't have been a breeze to live with. Walt has put up with plenty all these years, although I'll leave it to him to catalogue my specific failings. But then I've put up with stuff, too. His dark moods. His self-doubt. His criticism of the way I relate to Katy. My sense of having to underplay my passion for my profession, to make up for his ambivalent, often negative attitude towards his. His insistence on tucking his vests into his underpants and his penchant for pink shirts. And the way he always overcooks spaghetti. It's the deal, isn't it? Putting up with stuff when you're in a long-term relationship. But at root Walt is a good man, good partner, good father, and I never once thought to let him go.

I did ask Walt how long the doubts about our marriage had been building up for. 'A long time,' was his clipped reply. I wonder if I'd have noticed Walt's mounting misgivings if I hadn't been so preoccupied by work and juggling my responsibilities at the hospital with Tess and Katy's needs. Or whether, if I'd been less preoccupied, Walt's doubts wouldn't have arisen in the first place. But I don't regret my preoccupations, they seem right to me. Shouldn't we adults be mostly able to take care of ourselves as we go about our everyday lives?

It's not that I was unaware of the shortcomings of our marriage. I've always been aware of them. But they didn't matter all that much to me. Maybe my not minding was at the root of the problem. I really did think Walt and I were all right.

I know now that I should have paid more attention to our sex life. Our non-existent sex life. How did I feel when our sex life petered out completely, more than a year ago? The truth is that any lustful feelings I felt for Walt had faded away long before our sex life halted. To get into the right groove when we did occasionally make love I had to conjure up some pretty extreme sexual fantasies. But even that I didn't think was a symptom of major malaise, more an inevitable result of our long-term partnership. I do know of a few long-term couples who have great sex lives, or so they tell me, but I also know there are a lot more celibate couples than there are those openly prepared to admit it. It's something I've talked about in passing to a relationship counsellor who's attached to the hospital. The celibate marriage, she tells me, is one of the last taboos.

I was more concerned that Walt was no longer interested in having sex with me, than with the absence of sex itself. Did it mean that he'd seek sex elsewhere? Well, probably. In fact why on earth wouldn't he? I was a fool not to speak to Walt about any of this, I realise now, now that it's too late. As with so much else in our relationship I let it drift. Thought it would pass, or could be dealt with later. But he didn't speak about it either, at least not until we reached the point where we could no longer discuss anything rationally.

Walt and I had our friendship, we were a family, our lives were intimately entwined. That had felt enough for me at this particular point in our lives.

Affairs were something I only ever thought about fleetingly. My instinct told me not to go there. I came to the conclusion long ago that I am rubbish at subterfuge, I'd never find the time, and no one, in any case, would want to have an affair with me. I'm not unattractive, it would be disingenuous to say I was, but I don't give out vibes of availability or even interest. I'm at ease with men, but I don't flirt with them. I shut up shop in that respect when I was training to be a doctor. To deal with the sexism and the harassment, I grew a shell of such thickness and cool indifference that I became a pretty worthless target. I realised early on that it would be a losing battle to fight the put-downs and sexual advances with anger and hostility, but if I could shrug them off I'd have won. And I did. Except when it came to Ed, my boss, who, as a pioneering doctor in the Active Birth movement, I hero-worshipped and fancied in equal measure and fell into bed with without a moment's hesitation. And look where that got me. Pregnant with Tess and a single mother at the age of twenty-seven, while Ed went off with his wife and son to work in the States and never made contact again.

Try though he did to persuade me to have an abortion, I was determined to go through with the birth. I fell out of love with Ed as easily as I'd fallen into bed with him, once I realised just how casually callous he could be. Not having an abortion was my best-ever decision. It gave me the gift of Tess. I'm grateful to Ed, for Tess, and for giving me the fire to carry on his work in campaigning for women to have greater choices about how they want to give birth. He was a great doctor, pretty useless in the human-being department. Could it be that I learned a little too much from Ed Auberbach, the guru of the birthing pool and the labour-ward squat?

My fidelity to Walt has nothing to do with taking the holier-than-thou approach. In fact my standpoint on affairs has less to do with moral conscience than with pragmatism. I had sex with Ed knowing he was a father and a married man. But since my own marriage, I've never needed to wrestle with infidelity. It hasn't been so much love or loyalty or belief in the sanctity of marriage that has kept me constant, but the idea of not wanting to rock the boat, not being willing to take a risk and endanger our relationship, having more important things to do. Except for when he told me he was leaving I've never asked Walt if he's slept with other women. I've never had reason to suspect him, but I can't know for sure. Does that imply complacency or indifference? To me it's a blessing not to be eaten up by sexual jealousy as women so often are. Best not to know. Best not to think about it.

It's not true, by the way, that thing Walt said about having to make an appointment just to talk to me. But if that's how it felt to him I suppose my denying it makes no difference. I gave him the impression of unavailability and that's what counted.

'It's lonely being at the bottom of the food chain,' he told me the night following his announcement of his Gap Year adventure.

It sounded so self-pitying, but I didn't say that. Instead I asked, 'And what or who, in your opinion, is at the top?' We were in bed together, though we might as well have been at opposite ends of the Clifton Suspension Bridge. If conversations could be measured in terms of temperature, ours had dropped to sub-zero.

'Your job of course.'

'Are you saying I'm a lousy mother as well as a lousy wife?'

'No, I'm not saying that. When you are around, you're a pretty good mother.'

'Meaning I'm not around enough?'

'You asked me what I think is at the top of your food chain, and I'm telling you. Your job, all those bonny little babies you bring into the world, followed by the girls, then your sister and your friends and your mum, and then, probably just ahead of me, the girl who waxes your legs.'

'So you *are* saying I'm a rubbish mother as well as a rubbish wife.'

'Why do you make it sound so extreme?'

'Because leaving me *is* extreme. Walt, I can't do this now, I really can't. I'm starting at eight tomorrow. Good night, Walt.'

'And there's our sex life, too.'

I was so tired. I tried to stifle a yawn and failed. 'What sex life?'

'Exactly.'

And that was as far as we got in talking about our sex life.

I've been thinking about silence as much as I have about sex. The worst thing about the past few months has been the silence. Worse even than those icy exchanges which punctured it. Silence sat so heavily between us that I felt I was being crushed by it. Insults hurled, accusations exchanged, verbal missiles launched, they were a welcome respite from the silence that followed Walt's announcement of his decision to take a marriage sabbatical. Neither of us could speak. At least not like the intelligent, rational, articulate adults we assumed ourselves to be. So we dealt with our reluctance to start verbal bush fires by saying very little. Words would rise like bile to my throat, then sink back down again. Sometimes I would even open my mouth to say something and nothing would come out. Not a single word.

Walt was just as bad, retreating as far into corners as it was possible to get without disappearing right into the cornice or the skirting board. Funny how so much space became too small to contain us both, each of us wanting to hide away from one another in our own home. Now the space seems absurd. So much of it all around me. Why, I wonder, did we continue to share the same bed? What on earth was that about? Our great, king-size bed, each of us on the verge of falling out from our own side, so desperate were we to keep as far away from one another as possible. Why didn't Walt move into the spare room? Why didn't I demand that he did? And not once in all those months did we touch. Not even a peck on the cheek or a hand reaching out in the dark. The electric currents of desire versus the electric currents of revulsion. The same currents, only a different interpretation.

As I lie here, waiting for the day to pass, I can almost laugh at the image of all those pillows piled up between us, the ones that in earlier times had sat decoratively on top of the bedspread by day, then at night were relegated to the armchair if Walt got there first, or flung on the floor if I did. But in the last few months they stayed right there on the bed, repositioned down the centre to become a physical barrier, an approximation of a barricade. Military sandbags is what they most reminded me of. What would have happened if one of us had decided to go 'over the top'? Would it have been a battle-to-the-death like when the soldiers emerged from the trenches in World War I? Or might we have laid down our arms and embraced, like that famous Christmas in 1914?

If they could do it, sworn enemies that they were, why couldn't we? Just for one night. It wouldn't have changed everything, but it might have broken the silence. Instead it was sandbags at dawn.

Some of Walt's behaviour these last few months I will never understand. Particularly the kindnesses. Like tea in bed in the morning, which Walt continued to bring day after day, knowing how much I needed that first cup of tea to crank me into action before I could even consider getting up. Like the way he still went down into the basement to polish my shoes and place them outside the bedroom door, mimicking hotels we'd stayed in when we were younger and a habit he'd had for years. And how he continued to replenish the white roses on the dining table as soon as they began to droop. Every week, without fail, a bunch of the white roses I loved.

Were these gestures simply force of habit or were they a way of leaving the door ajar, a signal that we might one day find a way back to one another through mutual kindness? Was I kind to you, Walt, these last few months? I think not.

However bad I feel about Walt going off and leaving me, the one thing that stings more even than his departure is the fact that he marched into the paper and resigned without so much as mentioning it to me first. This makes me feel more angry, more humiliated even than the prospect of divorce. I must be a truly dreadful wife for him to do such a thing without telling me.

I was shocked. I was more than shocked, I was wounded. Shocked that he'd done it and wounded that he thought it somehow had nothing to do with me, that it was his job and he could do with it what he wanted without reference to the woman he'd lived with for the past twenty-three years. Did it slip his mind that we were married, that we were a partnership, that we had mutual lives involving mutual decisions and joint financial responsibilities to consider? Would I hand in my notice as a doctor without discussing it first with Walt? It's unthinkable, unless my respect for him had worn away completely.

Afterwards Walt said the prime reason for not discussing it with me was that he'd absolutely made up his mind and I'd only try to talk him out of it, which would have led to a big brawl that wouldn't change anything, so what was the point. How could he be so certain how I'd have reacted? I'm not even sure how I'd have reacted myself. When did I become so predictable in his eyes? When did he decide that talking to me wasn't worth the effort and that my opinion didn't count? I suppose these things between couples are incremental. Petty at first, hardly noticeable, but slowly piling up, one on top of the other, until molehills really do end up as mountains. Mountains of resentment, disappointment. Loves labours, all lost.

What I would certainly have suggested, if he were really so unhappy, was that he ask for time off for good behaviour. That would have been the reasonable thing to do and surely the paper would have granted him that considering all the gongs he had won on their behalf over so many years. The *Record* was a smart outfit, probably the cleverest paper in the country in terms of understanding its audience and still building readership when new media was proliferating and stealing readers away from every other newspaper on a daily basis. They'd be alert to the fact that their award-winning, TV-friendly medical journalist couldn't easily be replaced. Walt on the breakfast couch at the

BBC, opining on why lettuce leaves contribute to obesity, or other spurious research, was a regular event. And they'd hate the idea of him going to a rival paper. But he didn't even give them the chance to reach a compromise. He told them he wasn't coming back and that was that and they could double his salary if they liked but it wouldn't change a thing. I didn't ask him if they actually offered to double his salary – that would have been interpreted as an example of my mercenary nature, something he's hinted at before – but I wouldn't be surprised if that's what they'd done.

Once I got over the initial shock I could see what was going on. Walt was testing out how it would feel to make life-changing decisions without reference to me. He was treating me as though I wasn't there, as though he was free of me.

He said I should be pleased for him . . . and for myself as well. That after bleating on for twenty years about how scare-mongering and sensational and downright dangerous his paper was, I should be hanging out the bunting in celebration that he'd finally had the guts to throw in the towel. And I had to concede his point. I *had* criticised the paper all these years – and I never fully recovered from the time my name was dragged into the mire along with Walt's over what Walt's rival paper dubbed The Waltergate Scandal. But I also knew Walt's own research and reporting to be exemplary, even if the sub-editors hoodwinked the readers with lying headlines and misleading stand-firsts. It was never what he did, well, apart from that one time, only the way they twisted it that enraged me.

And then things went completely crazy. One minute Walt was taking responsibility for his own life-changing decision, and the next everything seemed to be my fault. He laid into me like never before. He said that in criticising the paper all these years, I'd been scratching away at his self-worth as well. He must have been storing up his fury for years – and it hit me with the force of a truck. All this time, he told me, I'd towered over him like a Colossus, presiding over him as the heroic doctor, above reproach, while he was left to scrabble about in the mud beneath my feet, the sad and seedy reporter, dropping out of medicine, living in the shadow of my greatness. His language was so dramatic, so flowery, so unlike his concise sock-it-to-the-readers journalistic style. Maybe he needed to blow it up to gigantic proportions to give him the courage he needed to get it out. He even likened me to that giant statue of the communist dictator Enver Hoxha, the one we saw in Tirana when we went on that mini-break to Albania, just before communism collapsed all over Europe. Enver Hoxha? Julie Broadhurst! How thrilled we had been when the people razed that statue to rubble. We'd been there, only for a long weekend, but we had that smug sense that tourists get when they've been somewhere most other travellers haven't. Of being insiders, privy to a special, superior knowledge. 'Ah yes,' we could say complacently, 'we were there just before the fall.'

But Walt, I gasped, it's me, Julie, you're talking to. I love you and respect you and yes I do think your paper stinks, but this me you describe I don't recognise. I couldn't believe I was hearing him properly. Surely I'd never given him cause to see the balance of power in our relationship as he had just described it, to make him think I thought more of myself than I did of him. That I was somehow a superior being, a dictator even. The very idea of it made me feel nauseous. And there was something else. The ugliness that the Colossus conjured up, the brute force of Enver Hoxha, seemed to strike at the very core of my femininity. So that's how my patients feel, I thought, the ones who will never bear children. They feel stripped of their femininity in the way Walt stripped me of mine as he uttered those words. And almost at the same moment I thought, Walt's right, even now I am thinking about my work. The only way I could make sense of what was happening was to tell myself that Walt must be having some kind of breakdown. 'Is this something you've just thought of, this idea of me as dictator?' I demanded to know. 'Or have you always felt this way?'

Then he told me he'd been seeing someone.

'So, there is another woman,' I had said, without changing expression, certain that this was the cause of everything, and he replied, 'No, not that sort of someone, a therapist.' And then I really raged. 'She's been putting these ideas into your head, hasn't she? She's painted a picture of me as an overbearing harridan who has no respect for you, and you believe her. She's told you that I've infantalised you and the only way to move on is to leave both your job and me at the same time.'

'There,' Walt replied quietly. 'You don't even credit me with having opinions of my own. No wonder I feel I live in your wake.'

I felt so sad and stupid then. I didn't mean any of what I had said. It was sheer hysteria, the consequence of terror and utter frustration. But Walt doesn't easily forget. Once something is said, he stores it away. He doesn't buy the idea that things said in anger can be set aside, and that's one of the differences between us. I think angry words can be got over, he thinks once said they can't be wiped from the slate. But we all say things in the heat of the moment that we regret. And even if we mean them as they come out of our mouths we can unmean them later. That would be a topic worth talking over with his therapist. I think of the Truth and Reconciliation Commission, of the words of Desmond Tutu: 'There is no future without forgiveness.' If people can find a way to forgive the sins of apartheid, couldn't Walt find a way to forgive me?

After that it got even more confusing. He started on about 'living together apart'. Together apart? That set me off again. 'That's a great idea, Walt. Living Together Apart. It doesn't even make sense, which makes me think it must be the headline for one of those ridiculous stories your paper so revels in running. *Meet the Joneses, happily married and living on separate continents. Could it work for you, too?*'

Well no, it could not work for me.

'You're leaving me,' I said. 'Why don't you just come out with it?'

But he wouldn't. He wouldn't agree he was leaving me. He wanted things to be left open, was serious about the idea of a part-time marriage. He didn't see why it shouldn't work. I hated everything he said, and some of it seemed to me to be utterly nonsensical, but I also felt there was a kind of helpless honesty in what he was saying, that he actually wasn't sure he wanted to leave me, that even if we weren't together he didn't want to sever the cord completely. As for how I felt, I really didn't know. He was turning my life upside down for sure. There was fear, and there was panic. But did a life without him seem unthinkable? At that point I had no sense of how it might be to be alone, to not be with him. I couldn't access my feelings. The screen of my computer had frozen solid.

We've never lived in one another's pockets, we've always protected our independence. Sometimes, though, I think he must have mistaken my independence for a sign that I didn't really need him, but that's not at all how it was.

Oh Walt, remember when we first met? You had to take on not just me but Tess as well. We came as a pair, us two. One of the reasons I fell in love with you was because of how you were with Tess. And maybe one of the reasons you fell in love with me was because you fell in love with that sweet little creature who let you into her life with such wide-eyed innocence. We were quite some package, though not one that every man could handle.

You were wary with me at first, even perhaps a little intimidated by how well I seemed to cope with being a single mum in a profession where concessions to working mothers were non-existent. But I had Gemma, remember, and my mum, so I knew that Tess would never be neglected. It wasn't that hard, not like it was for some of the single mothers I came across in the hospital – with never enough money, living in some ghastly tower block, depressed and desperate. I never complained, or let on how exhausted I was, did I? I knew that compared to my patients I had nothing to complain about. And I suppose I felt that if I allowed even the tiniest chink in my armour to show, the whole, precarious edifice of my existence would collapse around me, and me with it. I didn't need you right away, but I wanted you. The need came later, when I saw how sweet life could be with a good man who loved me and loved Tess as if she were his own. Funny how, far from being a hindrance, Tess became the conduit through whom we found a way to reach out to one another.

That café where we met, the one just around the corner from the hospital where I was doing my senior registrar job, is no longer there. I've been retracing my steps, so to speak, in the months since Walt told me he was going away, and I wanted to remind myself what it was like. It's a grimy kebab shop now, but I managed to conjure it up as it was. I'd popped in with Tess, even though it was a Saturday and I wasn't on call, because I realised I'd made a mistake in one of my patient's notes and wanted to correct it before the wrong drug dose was given to her. Not that it would have done her any harm, it was a small mistake, but I was punctilious to the point of obsession back then. *Plus ça change?*

Walt had been up all night doing a reportage story, 'My Friday Night Hell in A&E' or some such shock-horror story, and he was knocking back black coffees because he had to go straight into the office to file his piece by the afternoon. The paper was on an all-out mission to expose the shortcomings in the NHS. After Tess had finished lobbing bits of lemon drizzle cake at him, Walt told me how he'd got into medical journalism after dropping out of medicine. He felt he could do more good on the outside, campaigning for better care, exposing drug companies who were dumping under-tested drugs on third world countries, speaking out against the ever-burgeoning numbers of NHS bureaucrats. An ethical man, I thought, quite a rarity. The cynicism set in later, when the devil that is tabloid Fleet Street stole his soul.

But it was that jagged scar zig-zagging down his nose that really did it for me. It was the sexiest scar I'd ever seen. In all my years of medical training I had never seen a scar that turned me on, until I unexpectedly found myself sitting opposite Walt's.

Have I lost you through carelessness? Are there things I can do to win you back? Is it too late? What an unnecessary mess we seem to have made of our marriage. Oh Walt, what will I do without you, without *us*?

Chapter Ten

A whole week has gone by since Walt's departure. I did two C-sections in my regular surgery session, one elected as the baby was breech, the second an emergency because the mother went into premature labour at 32 weeks and the baby was in distress. Both babies are doing well. I had to tell one expectant mother that her baby had died in the womb at 13 weeks, exactly the stage at which Tess is now. And I informed a 40-year-old woman who had given up all hope of having a baby, that the IVF had taken and she was having twins. She could, of course, still lose them in the next few weeks. There were too many at-term women for too few beds.

I am involved with a small study, part of a larger piece of research, to do with cord clamping in premature babies. We are trying to find out whether delaying the clamping reduces the chances of bleeding in the newborn's brain and also whether it cuts the need for transfusions. So far the results of delaying are looking positive. One of my senior colleagues has resigned, which can only add to the pressure on me. Thursday night I was doing my fortnightly on call and had to go in for another emergency C-section due to a protracted labour in a thirty-eight-year-old woman who was failing to dilate sufficiently. I'm not sure how many more years I can do of this sort of intense obstetric work.

Oh yes, and a new father who had gone out to celebrate the arrival of his newborn by getting paralytic, then popped back in to see his wife and child, when asked by me to keep his voice down on the ward threatened me by bringing out a switch blade and asking if I wanted to 'cop a feel of this'. He then grinned and said,

'Only jokin', love, didn't mean to upset you or anyfing.' I don't hold out much hope for his child.

No word from Walt. He didn't promise to write at all, but I'm hoping he will, once he's settled. *Settled!* What am I talking about? My husband is a Gap Year traveller, the whole point is to travel, not settle. At least I think so. It's all much too confusing. I've lost count of the number of times I've started emails to Walt this past week, and ended up deleting them. Why on earth would he want to hear from me when he's only just escaped my clutches? Katy had a text, though. Apparently the giant rucksack that had to go into the hold never arrived in Buenos Aires. I had to suppress a guffaw when I heard that.

'Mum, it's not exactly funny,' said Katy.

'No, darling, I know it's not funny, but it does feel rather like divine retribution.'

I was almost tempted to offer help in tracking it down. The only thing that prevented me was that if I did manage to sort it for Walt, it would end up being something else he could hold against me. You'd think incompetence rather than its opposite would be a problem, but in this case I suspect not.

Anyway it's Saturday again now and Tess is coming round in a minute. I couldn't resist spoiling her. I took the tube to Oxford Street this morning and went into Topshop and bought these great T-shirts and trendy smock-tops and jeans from the maternity range and a dress I think she'll look cute in. It's red, Tess's favourite colour. The bags are sitting on the sideboard waiting for her. She's working so hard she doesn't get a minute to herself and although she sounded like the usual cheery Tess when we spoke on the phone the other day she beefed a bit about feeling fat and frumpy and said that although Pete's being wonderful she's being a complete bitch back. I can't imagine her being beastly to Pete, and I'm sure she's exaggerating, but I thought new clothes might perk her up. I rather suspect she's upset that Walt isn't planning to be around for the birth. It's true he'd organised to go before he even knew Tess was pregnant and Tess hasn't said anything specific, but my guess is she's hurt.

'Look at me, I'm disgusting. Only thirteen weeks pregnant and I've already put on seven kilos. I swear I'm not even eating that much,' squawks Tess, reaching for her third biscuit in about as many minutes.

I'm about to say something, but Tess doesn't give me the chance.

'Don't start, Mum. Please, not now. I'm hungry, all right? Starving in fact. And that thing about not eating much is a complete lie. I'm eating like a whole stable-full of horses. But at least the tits are good.' Tess jumps up from the sofa, lifts, squeezes and thrusts her breasts in my direction in the manner of a Page 3 Girl. 'In fact they're magnificent, don't ya think! Before I was as flat as a Frisbee, now Pete says I look like Jordan, only better, because I don't have the surgery scars that she has. Pete reads *Heat* religiously, can you believe. My husband the research fellow in Physics at Cambridge University reads *Heat* and knows everything there is to know about Jordan's tits, including the name of her surgeon.'

'Well, he should make the most of yours while they're still standing. Once you've stopped breast-feeding he'll be dreaming of the glorious time when they were fully fledged Frisbees!'

Tess throws back her head with a full-throttle laugh. 'To be honest he's not much better off even now, despite my new improved boobs. They're so sore I won't let him near them. I even made this "Look But Don't Touch" notice which I hung round my neck before he came in the other night. There I was, naked but for my knickers and the sign, and in he walks with a pile of papers under his arm – too disorganised as always to carry anything as useful as a briefcase or even a plastic carrier. He took one look at me and dropped the lot. This enormous pile of his students' papers for marking, all mixed up and all over the floor. And there I was on all fours, scrabbling about with my big belly and huge boobs and this ridiculous sign hanging around my neck, like a beggar in the buff.'

I am bathed in Tess's sunlight. How did darling Tess turn out to be so wonderfully well balanced? She has never even met her real father, never wanted to, although I'd certainly not kept her heritage a secret. Walt was her dad as far as Tess was concerned and that was that. One little sperm did not, in Tess's book, a father make. But a lifetime of loving did.

Tess is flopped on the sofa now, legs out in front of her, and I've noted the puffiness of her ankles. Puffier than perhaps they should be so early on in her pregnancy. I'm going to have to watch her, I think, but for now I'll let things be. I don't want to say anything to cause her concern or dent her happiness.

'Your grandmother will be here in a minute,' I say. 'She's so excited about this baby it's all she ever asks me about. I suppose a first great-grandchild is quite something. As for your father's departure, she seems to have forgotten he ever existed. She hasn't mentioned him once since he left.'

'How's she doing?' asks Tess, suddenly serious.

'It's so hard to tell at this stage,' I sigh. 'To recognise the moment when the normal forgetfulness that is a consequence of ageing becomes something more significant. But Paul told me that the other day she put her cardigan on back to front and didn't realise what she'd done. She started fiddling for the buttons, but of course they weren't there, and Paul said he made a joke of it and helped sort her out. And then one evening they were eating steak for dinner and Annette said something along the lines of how it had been ages since they'd had a decent piece of red meat and then said, "My goodness, I've forgotten what it's called." If you've been eating steak all your life it's not something you suddenly forget the name of, not unless there's something organic going on. And they'd actually eaten steak the previous week as well according to Paul.'

'Poor Grandma. Thank God she's got Paul.'

'Thank God indeed,' I repeat, as the doorbell rings, 'though I've no idea how he'll manage if she rapidly deteriorates. Now see that huge carrier bag . . .' I get up from the armchair to go into the hallway, pointing with a smile at the Topshop bag on the sideboard. 'It's for you. Treats time. Not a baby shower, but a mother-to-be shower.'

'Oh Mum, you shouldn't . . .'

'Fashion show, please, Tess. Your grandmother will love it. And so will I.'

'Yeah, right. Queen of the fatwalk. Oooh, this is so exciting.'

I open the door to Annette. Even as I hope I'm imagining it the first thing I notice is that she's lost weight. When I put my arms around her, and feel how jaggedly her scapula protrude on either side of her back, I know it's no illusion. And then when I pull back to look at her face, I realise that something's wrong there, too. Annette's appearance has always been important to her. She prides herself on being groomed and well turned out. Even when Gemma and I were kids, Annette's weekly hairdresser appointment was sacrosanct.

I scan my mother's face, trying to work out what's wrong. It's her lips, they look funny. Her lipstick, normally applied so carefully and accurately, is all awry. One half of her top lip has been painted to make her upper lip look fuller than it is, to create a flattering shape, and the other half has been forgotten altogether. It's another sign I think anxiously, it's definitely another sign.

'How are you, Mum?' I ask brightly, trying not to let my voice reveal anxiety.

'Pretty good,' Annette replies, unbuttoning her coat and handing it to me. 'Now never mind about me, or indeed you, where's that granddaughter of mine? She's who I'm here to see.'

For the next twenty minutes Tess is in and out of the living room doing her 'fatwalk' show and loving every minute of it. With the exception of the dress, which Tess decides makes her look like a pregnant transvestite, with Annette and I laughing in agreement, she adores absolutely everything.

'Oh Mum, this is so what I needed,' she says, wriggling to adjust her cleavage to reveal her fabulous embonpoint in a glamorous black tunic top with a deep V front. 'I've felt really ugly trying to squeeze myself into clothes that no longer fit me. These are perfect, and there's room in them for me to grow.' She pauses. 'Hey, you, watch it, you're giving me that look again. I *will* be careful, I promise, but at this particular moment I could murder a cheese sandwich. Is there any chance that you might oblige, or do I have to haul this humungus body of mine into the kitchen and do it myself?'

'I'll do it in a sec, Tess. But it will have to be plain old English cheddar. You do know about unpasteurised cheese and the dangers of listeria, I hope.'

'Well, if it weren't for neurotic Pete I probably wouldn't. But since he's committed the entire *Healthy Pregnancy Manual* to memory, and is doing a grand job of playing pregnancy Chief of Police, I am absolutely up-to-date on every health scare imaginable. I get enough lectures at home, thank you very much, without Dr Doom Monger Broadhurst wading in.' Tess grins as she says this. If it were Katy saying the same thing, it would sting like a scorpion and I would worry that I'd been over-interfering or tactless in some way.

'Actually I've already prepared a salad for our lunch,' I tell Tess, 'but I'm happy to make you a cheese sandwich as well if you really feel you won't survive the day without one.'

Tess puts her hands together as if in prayer, and coyly tilts her head to one side. 'Thanks, Mum, you're the best person in the entire world.'

'I know I am, darling. I just wish your father knew it, too.' Damn, I hadn't meant to bring him up and interrupt the fun with a sour note.

'Oh Mum, I know it must be awful for you. But it's also awful for Dad in a way. It may seem as if he's just swanning around South America enjoying himself, but he's actually in complete turmoil, and this is his way of trying to work it out.'

'But if you have problems, you have to face them, not run away. You've said as much yourself.'

'Will you take him back if he wants to come back?'

'I don't know.'

'Do you miss him?'

'I don't know.'

'For an intelligent woman, you are being very stupid,' says Annette abruptly, looking up from examining her hands, which she has been turning over and over, as though seeing them for the first time. 'If you want him back he needs to know. Tell him, for heaven's sake. All this independence can go too far. I reckon it's one of the problems with marriage today. The man's an idiot, I'll grant you that, but you're behaving like a bit of an idiot, too. When your father had that affair with Marina, I made it absolutely clear that although I hated what he'd done, I wasn't going to let him go that easily. If you just give up on that ridiculous husband of yours, tell him he can do what he likes, that you can cope without him and he's a free agent, he's not going to feel he matters that much to you, is he? In which case, he might just as well not come back.'

Annette sinks back into the sofa, exhausted by her outburst.

'On the cheese-sandwich front,' I say, changing the subject, 'I think I'll make one for you as well, Mum, if that's all right, you could do with a bit of fattening up, and I don't think that salad will do the trick.' There's a certain logic in what my mother has just said, but I prefer to let Annette's words whirl around in my head for a while, rather than respond right away.

Over lunch I turn from my lusciously pregnant daughter to my increasingly frail mother and reflect on how, with these two, everything is in the right order. Tess, young, fit and healthy, and soon to become a mother. Annette, in her 80s, so lucky to have had not one, but two happy marriages, and now with old age beginning to catch up with her. As a doctor I've seen too much of death out of synch, lives snatched away, children dying before parents, adults dying too young, to feel that nature has cheated my family. And yet how hard it is, to accept with equanimity, the cruel dying of the light in someone you love. I need to spend more time with her, before it's too late.

The mood, despite the intrusive thoughts about our individual everyday dramas, is upbeat. Tess talks a bit about her thesis which will lead to the doctorate that's the final rung on the ladder to her becoming a clinical psychologist. She is researching into the incidence of obsessive compulsive disorders in adolescents of very low birth weight, and has been pleased that her research has found signification correlations to back up the former findings of other professionals. We discuss names they might call the baby. I favour Old Testament biblical, Annette likes traditional English names and Tess, as has become the fashion, fancies foreign, possibly Spanish in deference to Pete's heritage on his mother's side.

'Actually we're thinking Angel for a boy.'

'Angel!' Annette and I cry in unison. 'You can't call a boy Angel,' I say, not sure if my daughter is kidding or not. 'He'll be a laughing stock. Bullied all the way to the psychiatric unit.'

'Well, in Spanish they spell it Angel, but it's pronounced quite differently, with a ch in the middle for the g sound, from the back of the throat, like achtung in German.'

'It could be the Alzheimer's, but I'm completely lost,' says Annette, giggling. Tess and my heads shoot towards her, startled. 'I do know what's happening to me, you know, dears. But that doesn't mean I'm so far gone as to let any great-grandson of mine be called Angel.'

'It's all right, Gran,' grins Tess, 'I was only joking. Sebastien is possible though. Or Mercedes for a girl. We'll never be able to afford the car, but we can go around saying we have a Mercedes!'

So she knows. I've stopped listening to my babbling daughter. I should have given Annette more credit. My super-smart mother knows exactly what's happening to her. And then we move on to talk about Annette and Paul's plans for a cruise through the fjords of Norway, and for a while I think perhaps all is normal with my mother after all, she's so lucid about the trip and the places they'll be stopping off to visit. But five minutes later Annette is telling us the cruise plans all over again. Then in the way that conversation between people who know one another well flows seamlessly – and irrelevantly – from one topic to another, I find myself bringing up the subject of the second bathroom.

'So I've decided I can't live with those rusty, ancient taps and that stained bathtub and leaking shower hose a minute longer. At last I'm moving into the twenty-first century with my first nod at modern living, a trendy wet room instead of a traditional bath, no expense spared. I've even chosen the towels and the huge showerhead. A monsoon something or other. I'm so organised I've got two bathroom specialists coming next week to do estimates.'

'Oh, Dad would love a wet room. A shower of his own,' trills Tess, before realising what she has said. 'He . . .'

'Yes, but does he deserve one?' Annette butts in, as though she is discussing a disagreeable child. 'And if he's not going to come back anyway and you end up selling the house, it will have been a complete waste of money.' For a mean moment I think that maybe my mother's tact is going the way of her mind.

'Well, I'm doing it for me,' I say, defensively, realising as I say it that I'm not doing it for myself at all. It has always been Walt who's expressed a desire for a wet room, while I've preferred to sink into a bath with water up to my neck and bubbles. We'd been discussing it, in a perfectly amicable way, about a week before Walt announced his Gap Year plans. It's a two-bathroom household, I remember saying, and the kids have no voting rights because Tess is no longer here, and Katy's hardly ever here, and as long as we have one bath in the house, there's no reason why you shouldn't convert the second bathroom into the wet room of your wildest desires. Now, if I'm being honest with myself, this wet room *is* a way of keeping Walt in my life, doing something that he'd appreciate and therefore might want to come home to. A way of hoodwinking myself that he will come back. On a realistic financial level, without his salary coming in I shouldn't be even entertaining the idea of a wet room. And if he does come home, surely it will be to me, for me, not because of . . . I'm losing all capacity for rational thinking again and I'm wishing I hadn't mentioned the damn wet room at all. Nothing seems straightforward any more. Everything I do, everything I say, has implications – and repercussions.

'Coffee anyone?' I ask. Tess returns to the subject of the cruise and enquires of her grandmother how long she and Paul are going to be away for.

'I didn't mention anything about a cruise, dear. But you're quite right, Paul and I are going on a trip around the fjords in May. We are *so* looking forward to it.' And once more she proceeds to tell us all about it.

That night I dream I am caught in a hailstorm in the Pennines. I am wearing only a swimsuit. When I turn around to speak to my mother, who a moment ago was following me up the steep hill, Annette has disappeared from view. But how can that be, I ask myself in the dream, shivering uncontrollably as icy particles lash me from the sky and I recall my mother's funeral of the week before. I wake up, heart pounding, out of breath as though I've been running. It is 3 a.m. I turn towards Walt's pillow, as if to seek comfort in his sleeping presence beside me. But Walt is not there. Walt is no longer in my bed. Perhaps he has slept here for the last time and I will always be alone. Just me and my state-of-the-art wet room. It is 5 a.m. before I finally fall again into a fitful sleep.

Chapter Eleven

'Where have you been all my life?' I ask, not altogether jokingly, as Gemma bends down to kiss me on both cheeks. At 7.30 p.m. on Tuesday, as arranged before Gemma went to New York, I am already seated at a table in the corner by the window at Napoli's, my neighbourhood Italian. In an hour or so it will be so crowded and so noisy that Gemma and I will have to strain to hear one another speak, but for now we have the place almost to ourselves as well as a prime position to screen out at least some of the ambient chatter as it builds up later on.

We've been coming here for our sisterly get-togethers once a month for at least a dozen years. This place is something of an institution in the neighbourhood, an old-fashioned-style trattoria with white tablecloths, where not-too-raucous hen-nights and families consisting of grannies, parents and children happily share the same space and the sturdy Neapolitan dishes that are Napoli's hallmark.

'I'm convinced that Giovanni is a little in love with you,' says Gemma, ignoring my comment about her recent disappearing act, and waving at the chef/proprietor who is coming towards her to deliver his customary hug.

'Don't change the subject,' I say, already softening as I speak, glad to be seeing Gemma again. 'And he's not in love with me, just grateful that I told him to get checked out for diabetes after he'd described his symptoms to me, and it was in time for him to be able to control it by cutting back on the tiramisu rather than having to resort to anything more drastic.'

'Yeah, right,' says Gemma as Giovanni bounds up.

'Where you been?' he asks, smiling broadly. 'Your sister tell me you bad girl, too busy busy to make time for her. But she need you now that crazy husband of hers is run away. I offer to take his place, but she no interested.'

'You see,' says Gemma, laughing now, and looking at me. 'I was right. By the way, Giovanni, are you divorced?'

Giovanni furrows his brows. 'Me? Divorce? My wife would kill me. But maybe she let me have two wives. What you think and what you like to drink?'

'A bottle of Pinot Grigio please, Giovanni,' grins Gemma. 'You like the Pinot Grigio, don't you, Julie?' I nod and Giovanni disappears.

'So good to see you.' Gemma settles into her seat.

'And good to see you, too. But why do you look so young? I appear to have aged ten years since Walt left and you look like you've just shrugged off an entire decade. What's going on here? You should be feeling knackered. I'm the one who looks and feels jet lagged and I haven't been further than the hospital and back.'

'Nothing,' says Gemma abruptly. 'Nothing's going on. I don't know what you're talking about. The novel still isn't finished, and I'm up half of most nights writing.'

'I'm telling you, you've got this glow, and your eyes are all sparkly. And when you walked into the restaurant you were kind of bouncing on the balls of your feet . . .'

'For God's sake, Julie, your imagination is running wild, perhaps you're the one who should be writing novels, not me.'

'How was New York?'

'Well, it was great to see Sam. And we had a bit of a breakthrough. After three years – can you believe three years have gone by so quickly – he seems to have finally worked being a ski instructor and mountain guide out of his system. He told me he's going to come home at Easter and has already applied to complete his law degree. Of course if Antony hadn't been so typically tyrannical insisting Sam did law in the first place, none of this dropping-out drama would have happened.'

'But I thought that in a way you were pleased it did.'

'You know I was. I didn't even mind missing Sam desperately it was so important he got away from his father's clutches. It's the way it had to happen that I hated, Sam reaching almost breaking point, picking up every virus going, constant IBS. And me having to swear not to say anything about it to Antony. And then having to listen to Antony being so Antony-centred about it all. "I'm so disappointed in Sam." "I'm so hurt by Sam." It was always about what Antony wanted, what Antony felt about it, how it reflected on Antony, never about what was best for Sam.'

'Well it's interesting that Sam now seems to want to do law of his own accord.'

I note that every time Gemma mentions her son's name, her face is animated and glows with pleasure, but when she switches to criticising Antony it pinches and hardens.

'Yes, it is interesting, and of course I do recognise that Antony's enthusiasm for his work, his sense of the importance of it, was bound to rub off a bit on the boys. It's the way Antony always has to take the credit that I can't stand, and no doubt it's exactly what he'll do now. He'll turn the whole thing round to make out it was his idea that Sam went off in the first place, rewriting history as usual to ensure his place at the forefront of it. But Sam knows, and I know, that now it's something Sam genuinely wants to do. He's proved himself, he's shown he can support himself without a penny of his father's money, and now he's doing it on his own terms.'

I've never seen Gemma quite this angry with Antony before. She used to shrug off Antony's Antonyisms as we came to call them. As she delivered her diatribe against him her whole face was contorted, with an expression close to disgust.

'And the book?'

'Well I did the one radio interview and I moved my book to

front of store in the few places that stocked it, but apart from that, nada. I think I'm a little too ironic for American tastes.'

'So what's with you and Antony?'

'I hope Giovanni comes back with that bottle soon, I'm desperate. And starving, too.'

'You can't put this off indefinitely, you know. But all right, we'll order first, and then you're going to talk.'

'Am I?'

'I'm not having you making pronouncements like you're thinking of leaving Antony without any further explanation. I've been worrying about it for the past two weeks. We'll order, we'll drink, we'll do catch-up on all the usual stuff and then we'll get down to business.'

We've shared the tuna carpaccio for starters. I've downed a huge bowl of spaghetti with sage butter and prawns for my main course while Gemma has opted for a pizza piled high with roasted artichokes. Now we're prevaricating over which dessert to divvy up between the two of us – the almond tart or the legendary tiramisu. The tiramisu wins because it always does. The bottle of Pinot Grigio is almost empty. The catch-up is almost complete.

Mostly we've talked about Annette, comparing notes on any behavioural changes we've noticed while trying to avoid thinking too far ahead. Paul, we agree, seems to have it all under control. He has fixed an appointment for her to see a geriatric psychiatrist, and he updates us regularly. I am aware that neither Gemma nor I have yet faced up to the inevitable deterioration in the smart, sparky, lovable woman we have been lucky to have as our mother for so long. Neither of us is ready to absorb the possibility that she may become lost to us even as she continues to live.

We've covered everything, except the one thing that Gemma is desperate to avoid.

'That's it, spill . . .' I demand, slightly drunkenly.

Gemma drains the last drops from the bottle of Pinot Grigio into her glass and empties it down her throat immediately. 'Do you want another bottle?' she asks.

'No way. I've got a clinic at eight o'clock tomorrow. And you don't need any more either.'

'Believe me, I do.' She raises her hand to a passing waitress. 'One glass of white for me, please,' she tells her.

'Small or large?'

'Large,' says Gemma. She's flicking nervously at breadcrumbs on the table, then gathering them into a small pile. She picks up her half-empty glass of water and gulps it back in one go.

'Please, Gemma, what's going on? It can't be that bad. And in any case I think I already know. It's pretty obvious now I come to think of it – the glow, the bounce. You're having an affair, aren't you? You and the rest of the population. Almost everyone in fact except me.'

Gemma seems struck dumb, so I continue.

'Look I know I'm making a fuss about you and Antony, but I'm beginning to wonder if I make too much fuss in general about fidelity. I'm even beginning to wonder if I should have been faithful to Walt all these years. Well I was, and look at me now . . . I mean what's the harm, as long as you're not seriously thinking about breaking up your marriage. And it's not like you're having an affair with my husband or one of your friends' husbands, is it . . . Sorry, I'm talking over you. But I thought me saying something first might make it easier. Come on, Gems, it's me, Julie. Your sister. Your sister who loves you no matter what.'

'Oh Julie, you're right, of course you're right.' Gemma nods a thank you to the waitress who has just appeared with her large glass of wine, and immediately downs two mouthfuls. 'I AM having an affair. And it's with a lovely man. And I know I shouldn't, but I just can't help myself, and I feel reborn. I feel about seventeen years old. I walk around with this stupid grin on my face and I hardly care any more who sees my great big teeth. And instead of feeling dried up and sexually dead I'm producing enough natural lubrication for a KY Jelly factory. It's not even just the sex, although it's pretty mind-blowing stuff. I mean we actually talk to one another. Non-stop. We never run out of things to say and we laugh all the time, at silly, inconsequential things. He reads my books. And not because he feels he has to, but because my books are part of me, and he wants to know every part of me. He's amusing and clever and kind and he's mad about me, and I'm happier than I can ever remember being. Except when I'm being miserable about the mayhem I'm causing. And it's not surprising if I look young, because that's exactly how I feel and . . .'

'Stop right now!' I shout, with a ferocity that shocks Gemma into mid-sentence silence as I clamp my hands, one of top of the other, tight over my chest. My shoulders hunch and I curl in on myself over the table as if in pain. I am in pain, but I don't know where the pain is coming from.

'What is it, Julie, are you all right? You look like you're having a heart attack.'

My head shoots up again, but my hands, on top of one another, remain tight over my chest. 'No, I'm not all right. And you're not all right.' I know I sound hysterical, but I can't stop myself. 'You're infatuated, that's clear enough. But you need to keep it under control, be a little more circumspect. It's how it always is at the beginning of an affair. The crazy bit, the bit when all your thoughts are taken up by the object of your lust. But hang on and it will cool down, you'll see, it always does. You have to hang on to your marriage, you have to. Someone has to, or none of it makes any sense.'

Gemma sighs; she has this dreamy, dewy-eyed look about her. 'But I'm in love, Julie, properly in love, perhaps for the first time in my life. I was never in love with Antony. I married him because he seemed so solid and sensible compared to me, so certain of his ability to succeed. He just took me over and I went along with it.'

Now I'm clamping my hands to my ears. 'I don't want to hear it. I can't hear it. It's too much for me.' And without warning I'm sobbing, great wrenching sobs, for the loss of love, the loss of Walt.

Gemma realises instantly the mistake she has made. 'I'm so sorry, my sweet. I understand, I really do. But I was dying to tell you. And you nagged and nagged. And now that I have told you I so wish I hadn't.'

'What kind of sister are you anyway,' I splutter between sobs, 'abandoning me when I need you most? It's like you just don't care about me any more. Why did you have to do it now? Why couldn't you have waited?'

I wipe my eyes and nose with the napkin, registering in my peripheral vision that the two couples at the next table are staring at us, fascinated by the psychodrama taking place just within earshot.

'I'm sorry,' says Gemma again, so quietly that our audience leans in closer to better hear what is going on. 'I'm really very sorry. But you're sounding a bit like Antony. This affair of mine isn't about you, it's about me. I didn't plan it, I wasn't expecting or even wishing for it. But it happened. And I couldn't exactly have asked him to come back later, as in "Oh Rob, that's a lovely idea to have an affair with you, but it does rather hinge on Julie and Walt getting sorted first and whether or not they're going to get back together." '

'Don't listen to me, Gemma,' I say, now feeling foolish, selfish, unsisterly. 'And I'm sorry, too. It's not your fault that Walt has left me. And that words like love and sex and laughter fill me with despair. Or with envy, like a stab wound to the heart. No wonder you've been keeping your distance, I'm absolutely useless to you. The idea of keeping a lover on the back burner until your sister's got her act together is pretty hilarious. This guy . . . what did you say his name was . . . would think you completely nuts.' I start to laugh, in the uncontrollable bordering-on-hysteria way that catches those who only moments ago have been crying.

'I . . . I . . . didn't say what his name was,' stammers Gemma. 'And nor do I intend to.'

'Yes you did, you said his name was . . . Rob, that's it, Rob. Who is this Rob anyway and where did you meet him?'

I've put my hands on the table, palms flat to steady myself, and I'm trying to look squarely across at Gemma, but between the laughter and the tears I wonder if I am losing my mind. For a moment I feel I'm standing on the edge of a deep ravine, about to plunge into the void. I shake my head to dislodge the image. The waitress appears with a small mountain of tiramisu and two forks.

'Oh yummy, in the middle, please,' says Gemma in an anxious falsetto, 'and could you bring us another fork so we can share.'

'You already have two forks,' says the waitress.

'Oh yes, how silly of me. So we do. Tuck in, Julie, it looks delicious as always.'

Gemma sinks a fork into the creamy mass, raises it into the air, and just stares at it, playing for time.

'Where were we? Oh yes, I was asking where you met him, this Rob of yours.'

'Oh yes, where I met him, of course. Um, actually it was at one of my publisher's dos. Yes, one of them. He works as a commissioning editor.'

'So that's two lovely Robs then. The one that belongs to Valentina and the one that belongs to you. I wonder if there might be a third Rob out there, a Rob for me. Though to be honest if Valentina's lovely Rob ever came on the market I think I would be the first to want to snap him up.' I'm beginning to regain my focus.

Gemma lets out a little gasp. 'This tiramisu is a triumph,' she squawks, flushing bright red.

'Is that a hot flush you're having, Gemma? Please tell me it is. Finally my big sister is going through the menopause. And about time, too. I know I was always competitive, and wanted to do things first, but I hadn't banked on going through the change before you did.'

'Yes, yes . . . absolutely. I've been getting these flushes – maybe two or three times a day – for a couple of months. And sometimes I get night sweats too. But it's not so bad that I'm thinking of coming to you for advice. I'm managing OK. And I have no difficulties at all when it comes to sex.'

'I lost it for a minute there, Gemma, but I'm back with the programme now and there's no escape. Don't change the subject! Why are you so reluctant to tell me about this Rob? I want to know how serious it is.'

'It is serious, Julie. It's serious because as I've already told you, I'm in love. And he appears to be in love with me. He has a wife, too. But he doesn't love her any more. It's not that she's a bad woman, but stuff happened, none of it her fault and he wants to be with me.' Gemma pauses. 'I'm not sure how to tell you the rest.'

'Well you've got this far, so you might as well keep going.' I feel increasingly uneasy. Uneasy about how this affair of Gemma's makes me feel about myself, uneasy about the thought of Gemma and Antony's marriage going the way of mine and Walt's, and uneasy that the worst of it is yet to come.

'Will you promise to forgive me?'

'I don't know what you're on about. I can't imagine that you have a second lover, one you forgot to mention. Or that you've murdered Antony in his sleep and buried the body in the manner of one of your grisly plot lines.'

'I told you that Rob works in publishing. Actually that's a lie.'

'Why on earth would you lie to me about his job? Is he well known or something?'

'No, he's not.'

'But he does have a wife, I assume that's true.'

'Yes, but I didn't tell you her name.'

'Why would I need to know her name, I'm not exactly going to call her up and introduce myself unless . . . unless . . .' My shoulders involuntarily shudder. 'Unless Rob's wife is called Valentina.'

Gemma says nothing.

'No, Gemma, please. Please don't tell me that your Rob is Valentina's Rob, our Rob in fact, our very good friend Rob. Please tell me it isn't true.'

'I'm afraid it is true,' says Gemma. 'But, Julie, I'm begging you, try to look at it this way. His marriage is over in all but the paperwork. And if it hadn't been me, well it would have been someone else.'

'Anybody else would have been better than you.'

The foursome at the next table have given up all pretence at eating and are staring, goggle eyed, at the drama unfolding before them.

'I can't believe I'm hearing this. You're a complete fool. You are unthinking, selfish, disloyal and quite possibly unforgivable. You and Rob both! I mean, it's one thing having an affair, but to screw over your friend as well, I'm not sure there is any breach of trust greater than having an affair with the husband of one of your closest friends.'

Gemma bangs her wine glass hard on the table. 'Oh don't be so pompous, Dr sanctimonious Broadhurst. Valentina and I were never that close. She was always more your friend than mine. I tolerate her because she goes back such a long way and you always insist on inviting her to our get-togethers. You have this thing about her being an exquisite, exotic bird-of-paradise. You're in thrall to her.'

I start to get up, I have this sudden urge to walk over to Gemma's side of the table and punch my sister in her sweet little face, knock her off her chair and leave her wimpering.

'Sit down!' she screams. 'For God's sake, hear me out.' I sit down, shocked by the violence of my feelings.

'Look,' says Gemma. Her voice has a more pleading quality to it now. 'Maybe none of this would have happened if Paolo hadn't died, but maybe it would. Our friendship grew then, Rob said he could talk to me about Paolo, but he couldn't talk to Valentina about him, even though she spoke about him all the time. He said for the first year she would cling to him so tight every night that he felt she would steal the very last breath out of him. And after a year he couldn't stand it any more. He withdrew, and he knew it was cruel of him, but otherwise he would have suffocated. He began to rely on me more and more and gradually what I'd only ever regarded as friendship began to change and grow. And then came the sexual spark – well I suppose it must always have been there, but it was suppressed. And now it wasn't.'

I feel like a fire-breathing dragon. I wouldn't be surprised if there was smoke coming out of my ears. 'I don't give a fuck about you, big sister. Or about Rob. But I do care about Valentina and actually I care about Antony, too. You and Rob are despicable. You probably deserve each other.'

Gemma's gaze is steady now, it has a steely quality.

'This is why I've been keeping it from you, Julie. I suspected this would be how you'd react. But, Julie, we have to deal with this. Life can't always be as black and white as you'd like it to be. Look at you and Walt. It's not an either or situation. And no relationship in the twenty-first century is. I feel bad, but I also feel brilliant. I do have a conscience, but not that much of one given Rob and Valentina's situation.'

'Bill please,' I call, waving at Giovanni, now back up from the kitchen as the last orders have gone through. 'In fact I think I'll leave it to you to settle up if you don't mind,' I say, getting up from the table. 'I have this really nasty case of acid indigestion, brought on by a very sick spectacle.'

'Please, Julie . . .'

'Please what? Please tell you that it's OK to be responsible for breaking up my best friends' marriage. That it's OK to set up home with the husband of a woman whose son has so recently and tragically died. That it's fine to put your sister in the position of having to choose between loyalty to her sister and loyalty to her best friend.' I pick up my handbag from the floor and march off towards the coat stand.

'Goodnight, Gemma. Don't even think of calling me. I *will* call you . . . but not until I'm ready.'

'Are you going to say anything to Valentina?' asks Gemma as I turn and march towards the exit. I ignore her question.

Leaving the restaurant I am struck by the notion that this terrible thing that has happened is somehow worse than what has happened between me and Walt. And that if it really is worse in my eyes, what does that say about the flimsy nature of my own marriage, about the fragility of my own commitment? Does it tell me that I've already accepted the end of my life with Walt, that our marriage never did matter all that much?

Chapter Twelve

I haven't spoken to Gemma since last Tuesday week. Valentina is visiting clients in Italy so I've not yet had to face her in the light of what I now know about Gemma and Rob. I've three times started to dial Rob's number, then put the phone down. What the hell am I going to say to him that will make any difference? If the two of them have embarked on this thing they're going to work it out – or not – between them. The one person to whom I could talk about this is the one person who's no longer in my life. Walt. Walt. Walt. Walt. I silently repeat your name over and over, willing you back to me.

It's Sunday morning and I'm going up to see Katy at her university. Maybe, on the motorway, I'll have some time to think. I'm relieved no one has yet rumbled the ridiculous habit I've got into since Walt left. Sometimes, at moments when I feel utterly alone, and the house is like a huge, unfriendly cavern, I get into the car, press the lock button for the doors, turn on the engine and insert a CD into the audio player. Inside my car, a fifteen-year-old Saab, which I have always treated with maximum disrespect, littering it with parking stickers, chewing-gum wrappers and old newspapers, I feel cocooned, and quite safe. The car hasn't been washed since Walt went away, visits to the car wash being one of Walt's jobs, and I'm wondering how long I can hold out before it becomes an embarrassment to the neighbourhood. But I don't want a tidy, or even clean, car. If that's the way Walt would like it then he'll have to come home and see to it. Interestingly he went and got it washed the day before his departure. It seemed to me less a thoughtful gesture than an act of tidying loose ends. As though once he'd done his little jobs, once he'd done his bit, he'd be free to leave, without guilt or the sense of unfinished business. I did throw it in his face. 'You can't salve your conscience by getting my car washed, you know, or by remembering to renew the insurance on the household contents. If you think that cancelling me is going to be as easy as cancelling your subscription to the *BMJ*, you're wrong. You can't tidy me away and forget about me.'

Except that's exactly what Walt appears to have done.

My choice of CD when I lock myself away in my car like this is unfailingly upbeat, something I know the words to, and to which I would dance if I wasn't in the car. It could be Martha Reeves and the Vandellas with 'Dancing in the Streets', or James Brown singing 'I Feel Good' or Santana's 'Black Magic Woman', or one of a dozen other Julie all-time favourite hits. Checking that the windows are fully closed, I turn the CD up as loud as it will go and start to sing at the top of my voice. Within a few minutes, as my voice grows hoarse from uninhibited screeching, as I pound the steering wheel with my fists in time to the music, I can sense the mood-boosting endorphins coursing through my body and slowly I begin to unwind and relax. It's my little secret; my drug-free self-medication is how I think of it. I've sung my way out of a black moment at 11 p.m. at night and 3 a.m. in the morning, and once in the late afternoon after work when I couldn't face going inside the house and decided my off-street parking space offered enough cover to protect me from being seen and heard by passers-by.

If I were to tell my girlfriends or Gemma or Tess about this, they'd think I was starting to lose my grip. Except Aggie, who would probably join in if she got wind of it. I'm beginning to wonder if this tetchiness with Aggie has a touch of envy attached to it. The mysterious phone calls, the ongoing denial of anything illicit, leaves me convinced she's still carrying on with someone. And when I'm not mourning or railing against Walt I find myself wondering if my own sexuality has died or is simply in year-round hibernation. For the time being singing in the Saab will have to suffice as my secret vice.

This morning, however, there's no time for a singing session. I need to allow myself a good two hours to get to Katy by one o'clock.

Four months have gone by since Walt announced his Gap Year plans, since we drove up the motorway with a fractious, anxious Katy, and back down again in silence after the pub lunch that had sounded the death knell on our marriage. Despite Walt's ministrations about wanting to keep things open, I can only regard it as being over. A man who wanted to stay with his wife, even if he was going away for up to a year, would surely make the effort to stay in touch.

As I drive up the motorway to the Midlands in the direction of my daughter, on a wet February day, I find myself wishing Walt was once again in the driving seat, though for more practical reasons than those to do with the demise of my marriage. I haven't been at the wheel on a motorway for years, I have no idea how many, and I have been anxious about it, fretting over whether I'll miss the turn-off, concerned I don't have full control over the car at speed, that my reactions might not be quick enough if I were to suddenly skid. I have even mapped my route on the computer and printed out the detailed directions, just to be sure, though I remember the journey well enough from last time. What I now appreciate, perhaps for the first time, as I tentatively put my foot down and watch the speedometer climb to 70 mph, is that although Walt's own driving often makes me edgy, I trust him when it comes to motorways more than I trust myself. I trust him to get me to places alive. And I realise how much I like the idea of entrusting myself to my husband, and how much I miss being able to do so. *All this independence can go too far. Tell him you need him*, my mother had said to me. However trivial a thing motorway driving is in the scheme of a marriage, it is still an area for negotiation in which power, responsibility, compromise, dependence and interdependence are mapped out. Just as Walt could show his superiority on the motorway, I could show mine at entertaining in a way which appeared effortless, even though it involved a great deal of effort. And maybe these things matter more than most people realise. Perhaps that's what makes relationships work. Small things, done well, or even just done so the other doesn't have to, especially if they're acknowledged by their partner, are important building blocks in a relationship. Conversely, therefore, it must work the same way. The small things that too often are the catalyst for criticism – like my minor moans on motorways, and around town, too, when Walt, who so far has never had an accident, drives exactly as Walt wants to – build up pockets of resentment, incrementally, from year to year until finally, along with all the other peevish, petty complaints within a marriage, there is a river of discontent dividing husband and wife. A river that can't be crossed.

A horn is honking and hounding me from behind and with a start I realise that I have meandered from the slow into the middle lane, narrowly avoiding an accident as the driver just to my rear swerves his BMW into the fast lane. The driver, a man, is making a V sign and, to judge by the hyper-mobility of his mouth and the furled fury of his face as he draws parallel, simultaneously shouting obscenities. And now he's overtaking in the fast lane and coming back into the middle lane in front of me, deliberately braking in order to make me do the same. Shocked into full attention, I brake further and indicate to move back into the slow lane where I had intended to be all along. The other driver, he must be crazy with rage, nips over in front of me and brakes again. *He's trying to get me to stop*, I think, and I'm beginning to panic. *He's going to make me stop, then get out of the car and beat me with a car jack. He wants revenge and I'm powerless to prevent it.* My palms are sweating and it takes every effort of will to focus on my driving, to think about my next move, to check my wing and front mirrors before slowing even more and moving on to the hard shoulder. The only alternative to stopping is to try to out-drive him, which is what Walt would no doubt do but which I know I will never succeed in doing. The man in the BMW is clearly bonkers. If he stops and forces me out of the car I will have to try to talk him down before he lashes out at me.

As I slow to a halt on the hard shoulder I think at least I won't be killed while I'm actually driving, though I may yet be murdered now that I've stopped. And at the very moment that I become convinced I have only minutes to live the crazed BMW driver, also now on the hard shoulder, accelerates off and disappears into the distance.

I turn off the key in the ignition and lift the handbrake. I'm shaking all over. At noon on a wet Sunday in February, the wind-driven rain now lashing my car almost horizontally, stranded on the hard shoulder of the M1, just before junction 16, capable, clever me, Julie Broadhurst, learned doctor and woman of the world, leans my forehead against the steering wheel and weeps. I weep for my marriage and for my helplessness at the hands of a motorway bully, for my husband's calm assurance at the wheel and for every good moment of Walt's and my twenty-three years together that has been snatched away from me.

After some minutes, as the sobs begin to subside, I slump back against the head-rest and wait for self-composure to return, as I know it will. I deliberately slow my breathing and once I am sufficiently calm, I switch on the radio, hoping for solace on Classic FM or Radio 3. But one station is playing a Requiem Mass and the other Wagner, and I'm in no mood for either. Finally I settle for a discussion about prison reform on Radio 4.

Calmed by the reassuring tone of the BBC presenter, I delve into my handbag, mop up my smudged make-up with a wet wipe, and reapply lipstick and mascara. I can't let Katy see how upset I am. Katy's suffering enough, with her beloved dad gone away. And then, as though nothing untoward has happened, I switch the ignition back on, check all the mirrors, and manoeuvre my car back on to the motorway. I'll do what Walt does, I think, I'll just concentrate on my driving and obliterate all other thoughts from my brain. The discussion about prison reform rambles on.

The voices, soothing, solid and somehow reliable, are all I need. They represent continuity, the content of their discourse is of little interest right now.

All my focus is on the road ahead, and behind me, and to my left and my right. As I reach the outskirts of the campus, I call Katy on her mobile to guide me to her halls. *I've made it*, I think, with a sigh of relief. Anyone would think I'd been negotiating hairpin bends over Mont Blanc, not cruising up a quiet, four-lane motorway on a Sunday morning.

By the time I pull up outside my daughter's block Katy is coming out of the door clutching her arms around herself in an oversize sweater and tight jeans tucked into knee-length boots. My Katy the undergraduate I think with a flash of pride. I so hope it goes well today.

The rain has finally stopped and a feeble February sun peeks tentatively through the clouds as I get out of the car. 'Well, you seemed to have survived the motorway,' says Katy, hopping from foot to foot to keep the chill at bay. 'And you're all in one piece as far as I can see.'

'It was a breeze,' I reply, kissing Katy warmly, hoping the sweat of my fear hasn't turned acrid.

There appears to be something interesting going on behind my back, for Katy seems distracted, looking across in the direction of the halls opposite, and now waving animatedly. I turn slightly to follow my daughter's gaze and see outside the hall of residence a small group of male students and a car. Surely I'm mistaken. It's a dark blue BMW, but it could be one of hundreds, why on earth should it be *that* BMW. Then I see that there's an older man as well, and he's holding court, gesticulating dramatically as he leans up against the front door of the car, smoking a cigarette. He's telling a story, I'm sure of it, and I'm certain I know who the story is about.

The feeling of fear wells up inside me again. Any moment now he'll turn and recognise me, and if not me the car, and then what will happen? If he starts laying into me again in front of Katy it will ruin our day, or it's possible that he might even get violent. Maybe there's a way to whisk Katy inside before he spots me and by the time we go out for lunch he'll be gone. He must be one of the other dads, up to see his son for Sunday lunch; there can be no other explanation. If only Katy would stop waving.

I'm on the verge of saying, 'It's freezing out here, let's go in for a chat,' when the object of Katy's attention finally notices her and waves back with a broad grin on his face and a beckoning motion.

'Oh there's someone I want you to say hello to,' says Katy. 'He's my new friend, Chris.' I look at Katy and notice a slight flush to her cheeks. 'In fact he's a bit more than a friend, he's . . . Are you all right, Mum? You've gone a funny colour.'

'I'm fine, Katy, absolutely fine. This Chris. I don't suppose he happens to be over there talking to his dad by any chance.'

'How on earth . . .'

'Oh, just instinct, Katy. Do you want me to meet him right away? Or will you fill me in first and we'll do the introductions later?'

'Well, actually his dad thought we might all like to have a drink together, seeing as you were coming up and he was coming up at the same time.'

'A drink together!' It really couldn't get any worse. 'Yes, a lovely idea. What do you suggest? Shall we go over right now then and say hello?'

'You're really weird today, Mum. Are you absolutely sure you're OK, you sound a bit like a robot. I – am – a – Dalek . . . I – am – a – Dalek . . .'

'I'm just excited to meet Chris. And to be truthful I'm a bit strung out by driving up here on the motorway. Pathetic of me I know but I'm so used to your dad doing the driving. Now about this Chris. Is it serious? When did you meet?' And then in a whisper, 'Are you sleeping together? And if you are, is it good?'

'Muum . . .'

I only have to look at my daughter's face, so full of unaccustomed light on this grey day, to know that she is no longer a virgin, and that the sex is better than she could ever have imagined, and that for the very first time my little girl is in love.

'Come on then, Mum, let's get the introductions over with. Chris can be a bit quiet, but he's really clever and really funny once you get to know him. He says his dad is great.'

'I'm sure they're both great,' I reply, thinking that Chris's dad is surely a bullying bastard and that hopefully the apple that is Chris has fallen a very long way from the tree.

We walk the hundred yards to where the men are gathered by the BMW. Despite the cold I'm perspiring profusely again. As we approach, the other three students in the group start to walk away.

'See you later, guys,' says Chris, a tall, gangly boy with a goatee beard, wearing skinny red jeans and scuffed trainers and a black hoodie, the hood of which he pulls back before putting out his hand to shake mine.

'Pleased to meet you,' he says. 'Katy's told me tons about you and the amazing work you do.'

'Is that so?' I say smiling, grateful that Katy appreciates me when she's not around, even if she appreciates me less when she is. So far I haven't dared to look Chris's dad in the face.

'And this is my dad, Patrick.'

'So you're the girl who's been keeping my son out of trouble,' Patrick grins, bending down to kiss Katy on both cheeks, from which I see Katy recoiling just a little, taken aback by his casual, affectionate manner. 'He talked about nothing and no one else all over Christmas.'

And Katy didn't mention Chris even once, I think, bristling slightly at the idea of Chris having a more open relationship with that bully of a father of his than I do with my own daughter. It did help to explain why Katy spent even more time in her room than usual, making calls to Chris, no doubt, or going on to MSN to chat, which was an improvement on her disappearing in order to mull over how much she disliked herself. Not mentioning Chris would be typical Katy. She'd be far too scared to say anything until she was certain he really liked her back. Cautious, careful Katy. I check my negative thoughts. What matters is that now she is ready, eager even, to introduce him. Hurrah! Katy has a boyfriend and is beaming with happiness.

'And very pleased to meet you, too, Julie.' If Patrick has recognised me, there is nothing to suggest so by the expression on his face. Like his son, Patrick is a good six foot two. Unlike his son, even camouflaged by his Barbour jacket, I can see he has the build of a rugby player. His hands are huge, I note, as he shakes mine, in a grip which is firm rather than vice-like, as though he is aware of needing to keep his strength in check.

'What's it to be, Chris, Katy? Pub or union bar.'

'Well we can drink at the union, but not eat, and I'm starving,' says Chris.

'Then the pub it is, if that's all right with you two,' says Patrick looking from me to Katy for approval.

So not just a drink, but a meal. I can feel the anxiety pinching at my belly. Either he has failed to recognise me and he's a fool or he actually knows how to behave like a gentleman in order to save his son and his new girlfriend from any embarrassment.

And whatever happened to the quality time Katy and I were going to have together? Lunch with the boyfriend I knew nothing about, and the father who only forty minutes ago was intent on murdering me, and was now charm personified, had certainly not been on the agenda. Come on, you silly woman, I chide myself, you've had worse crises than this to deal with during thirty years practising medicine.

Over sandwiches and beer in a new-style pub with sofas and lounge chairs around a low coffee table, I'm lamenting the absence of traditional wooden benches lined up on either side of a solid oak refectory table. In those circumstances all four of us would have no choice but to sit in a four-square group, talking together. As it is, Katy and Chris have commandeered the small sofa. As the minutes go by they shift imperceptibly closer together until they seem to have meshed into a single being, quite oblivious of the presence of me and Patrick.

It had been bad enough piling into Patrick's BMW with the lovebirds seated in the back, me forced to suffer the indignity of being in the passenger seat next to a man who clearly despised me – and whom I despised in return.

To my surprise he drove extremely well, so that not even once did my right foot reach for the imaginary brake pedal. *He's just trying to prove a point I suppose*, I thought, *to show me up to be the worst driver imaginable.* But at least the conversation didn't falter, revolving mostly around how to find a decent pub and asking Katy and Chris's advice on places they had tried out together.

It's only now that we are settled in the pub of their choice, and have completed the business of ordering drinks and deciding on sandwich content, that I realise I cannot remember when I last felt this uncomfortable. Katy and Chris are talking, or rather canoodling, amongst themselves. Patrick and I are in armchairs facing into one another, and all I can think about as I scan this rather handsome, chivalrous man who actually stood up as I returned from a visit to the loo to calm myself, is that he is the monster who intimidated and terrified me on the motorway, and sent me sobbing into the steering wheel.

Glancing at the kids to make sure they are out of ear-shot, Patrick leans into me and says simply, 'I am so very, very sorry. My behaviour on the motorway today was unforgivable.'

I'm so taken by surprise at this apology that I clumsily thump the glass of lager I am holding on to the table, causing a large bubble of foam to break free from the top of the glass and float over towards Patrick, landing on his thigh.

'Oh gosh, look what I've done!' I instinctively reach over to brush away the froth from his corduroy-clad leg. Just as I realise, with horror, that I am touching this stranger's thigh, Patrick grabs my wrist, and raises my hand from his leg, forcing me to look up and into his face, which far from presenting as cruel appears to be utterly bereft.

'Wh ... what is it?' I stammer. 'I'm sorry about the froth. I mean I'm sorry about the other thing as well, I feel just awful, but my mind was on other things. It's no excuse, but I wasn't concentrating, I didn't know what I was doing, I . . .'

'How about you and I go for a little stroll and leave Romeo and Juliet to themselves for a bit?' says Patrick. 'There are some things we senior Montagues and Capulets need to say to one another, and this is not the place to say them.'

To my shock, he hasn't yet let go of my wrist.

'Well as long as it's not just an excuse to give me more verbal abuse,' I reply, trying to sound in better control of my emotions than I feel, noting that this Patrick is as determined to enforce his will as his bullying manner of earlier in the day would suggest, and glancing anxiously at Chris and Katy. Fortunately both seem to have completely forgotten that each has a parent in the pub with them.

'No more abuse, I promise,' says Patrick, and despite my misgivings, and without knowing much at all about this man, I know that he is telling the truth.

'Chris, Katy,' he says, 'Julie and I are going to take a little stroll. We've both been cooped up in our cars too long, and need to refresh ourselves before the long ride home.'

'Fine,' says Chris, uninterestedly, looking at Katy.

'See you in a bit,' says Katy, turning instantly back to Chris and nuzzling into him, as Patrick helps me into my puffa coat.

'Young love,' sighs Patrick as we leave the pub through the back door, and make our way across the garden to a gate which leads into the lane. 'Those two have got it bad.'

'Bad as in good,' I say. 'As far as I'm concerned it couldn't have happened at a better moment.'

'Funny you should say that,' replies Patrick, 'it's come at the perfect moment for my boy as well.'

'Do you want to expand?'

'Yes, I do, and it all ties in with what happened on the motorway today and my unforgivable behaviour. You see, it was only nine months ago that Mona, that's my wife Mona, died . . .'

'Oh, I'm so sorry, I had no idea . . . Katy hadn't told me anything about Chris being in her life until I arrived here today, so I know nothing of his background, or yours.'

'Keeping him all to herself, was she? Not that I blame her; most of the relationships the kids have don't seem to last more than about five minutes, so it's probably not worth sharing every sordid little encounter with the parents. Not that there's anything sordid about Chris and Katy together. They remind me of . . .' Patrick hesitates, leaving his sentence unfinished, and disappearing into his private thoughts.

'Chris is Katy's first boyfriend, so I suppose she wanted to be sure . . .' And now I stop myself as well. I shouldn't be revealing information that is personal to Katy to Katy's boyfriend's father whom I have only just met. I must learn to hold my tongue. '. . . But your wife, what happened?'

Patrick looks straight ahead as he speaks, and his words sound weary, as though they've been said too many times before. 'She died in a crash on the motorway . . .'

I gasp.

'. . . a bunch of drunken louts careering out of control. It wasn't an accident, I will never call it that, it was murder. The driver is awaiting trial on a manslaughter charge. I'd like to see the bastard hanged.'

'No wonder you . . .'

'I just lost it,' says Patrick, turning towards me now. 'I could see you weren't concentrating, and I had plenty of time to get out of your way, but I was exploding with rage. For those couple of minutes you were those drunk fuckers who killed Mona and I was determined to chase you down and hack you to pieces. By the time I'd come to my senses I realised that if I stopped to apologise I'd probably frighten you half to death in the process, so I just put my foot down and drove off. Mona was only forty-six. We were childhood sweethearts. I never stopped loving her for a minute.'

For a moment I am silent. I look up at the sky which has grown dark.

'I think it's going to rain again,' I say quietly.

'I think you're right,' says Patrick, looking up as well. 'We should turn back before we get drenched. So you see the reason I'm so happy that Chris has met your lovely daughter is that he has been shattered by his mother's sudden death. It happened in the run-up to his A Levels and I thought he'd flunk the lot. I even suggested he take a year off and finish them later, but he was determined to carry on. And then he refused to take the Gap Year he'd planned and got into the university through clearing. Didn't want to leave his sad old dad, I reckon. We're real mates, the two of us. He's my only son.'

'How we misjudge people,' I say. 'I thought you were a bullying brute, an absolute monster of a man, and you're right, I thought you were out to kill me. But look at us now . . .'

The rain has started to fall, and we pick up pace as we turn and walk back up the lane. Patrick turns up his collar against the elements, and I pull up my hood, grasping it under the chin to hold it tight to my head, suddenly aware of how unattractive this must make me look.

'You haven't told me your side of the story . . .' says Patrick, shouting now to be heard above the rain lashing the branches and the road.

'How long have you got?' I ask, smiling for the first time since we left the pub.

'The rest of my life, I suppose,' says Patrick, smiling back. 'But this is hopeless. Where do you live?'

'North London, close to the start of the M1.'

'Well I live in Hertfordshire, but I commute into town for my job. How about we meet up for a drink some time and you can let me tell you all my medical complaints by way of compensation for your appalling driving? Maybe your husband would like to come along as well . . .'

This is not the moment to explain. We're beginning to get soaked through and Patrick has linked his arm through mine and broken into a run, practically dragging me up the lane with the pub now in sight again.

'I'll write down my number before we go,' I suggest. What I think is, what an extremely pleasant man this Patrick has turned out to be, and I owe it to him to tell my side of the story. And what's the harm in meeting for a drink? Just the once. It wouldn't do to get cosy with the father of Katy's boyfriend, Katy would hate that, but a one-off drink wouldn't compromise anyone. At that moment I decide not to even bother mentioning it. There is certainly no reason to upset Katy by telling her what happened on the motorway this morning. And the possibility of a drink with Patrick really isn't important enough to discuss, especially as Patrick will probably forget to call, or more likely change his mind about the whole silly idea.

It's around six o'clock, far later than I had expected to leave, when I finally say goodbye to Katy at the entrance to her halls. After settling up at the pub – Patrick insisted on paying – he had driven us all back to the campus. Chris and Katy dominated the conversation by talking about their courses and how the race to find a house for next year, when they'd have to move out of halls, had already begun, and by discussing who they thought they might share with. There was no talk of them sharing a house together, and I was pleased at their maturity. They had obviously concluded themselves that they didn't know where their relationship was going, and that if they broke up when they were living together it would be extremely awkward to continue renting the same place.

After Patrick and Chris had gone off to Chris's room I went with Katy and the two of us sat on Katy's bed and chatted.

I didn't have to dig for information for a change, Katy talked about Chris non-stop. 'I've told him everything about me,' she said. 'Even the PCOS. He doesn't care about my thinning hair or anything, he thinks I'm beautiful.'

'Which you are,' I said, smiling.

'But you're my mother,' said Katy. 'You would say that. When Chris says it it's because he means it.'

'And I mean it, too. That boy has good taste.'

'His dad was nice, wasn't he?'

'Yes, an absolute charmer. Have you heard from your father?'

'He emails me a lot. Have you?'

'No. Is he OK?'

'Seems to be.' Katy didn't seem in the mood to expand, and I felt it unfair to press her.

'Do you miss him?'

'Well to be honest, no. I mean it's not as though he's going to be gone for ever, and he's pretty much in touch, and I'm so busy . . .'

'That's exactly what I was hoping you'd say. You're a grown-up girl. No longer just a daddy's girl, but some other guy's girl now.'

'You like him, Mum, don't you? Chris I mean.'

'Very much, sweetheart. He seems smart and sensitive, and he's clearly crazy for you. In fact I've had the loveliest day.'

'Me, too,' said Katy. 'I do hope you and Dad sort things out when he's back.'

'Well one way or another I suppose we will. Thanks for having me, Katy.'

'And thanks for coming, Mum.'

Katy's on her way, I think happily as I drive carefully home, back down the motorway, busy now with end-of-weekend traffic. Patrick keeps popping in and out of my mind – the sad look on his face when he spoke of his wife, his gentlemanly behaviour in the pub, the pleasure with which he spoke of his only son. Oh Walt, I find myself saying to myself, as I leave the motorway at Brent Cross, what are we doing with our lives? And what will become of you and me?

Chapter Thirteen

Aggie has been here a month. Walt has been gone a month. In Walt's absence I seem to have acquired a wife, albeit of the entirely undomesticated variety. Mostly I wish she'd go away, but I don't have the heart to throw her out. Charles has dug his heels in and is showing no sign of willingness to take her back. She could afford to rent a flat but she's terrified of being alone and I have so much empty space.

Most evenings Aggie's in, hitting the vodka bottle and ordering in the most expensive take-aways she can find. Whoever is her current lover clearly doesn't have much time for her. Or maybe it's a love-in-the-afternoon type of liaison. I won't ask for details and Aggie isn't offering them: she knows exactly how much I disapprove of her continuing to have sex with other men at the same time as claiming to be desperate about getting back with Charles. Her denials don't convince me. She talks, talks, talks, by turns amusing and aggravating. Sometimes I find myself longing for the horrible silence of the last few months with Walt, at others I'm grateful for the distraction.

At least I get the mornings to myself. Aggie's job as a make-up artist on a breakfast television show suits her (and now me) so perfectly it's almost as though it had been specially invented for her. She gets to meet everyone who is famous or nearly-famous or wannabe-famous, and picks up all the juiciest of gossip with which to entertain her women friends and itinerant lovers. Charles isn't the least interested in her gossip, but over the years of meals out and suppers at our place I've noticed how his habit of nodding while she prattles has become increasingly pronounced, to the point where it has almost become a tic. I'm convinced the nodding is a smokescreen for not listening.

Aggie says the only downsides to the job at the TV station are having to get up at 4.45 a.m. in order to be at the studio by 5.30 and being subjected to celebrity mouth odour – one whiff and she knows exactly which actress, Cabinet Minister, rock star or footballer has eaten what for dinner the night before. Many of them, she suspects, have dashed out of their homes or hotels, unaccustomed to such early rising, having quite forgotten to brush their teeth.

By 10 a.m. each morning Aggie is through and has the rest of the day free to shop, check in for her anti-ageing beauty treatments at various discreet Harley Street addresses, hit the treadmill at the gym and do a weights work-out. In addition there are her twice-weekly hair appointments, her regular mani/pedi and eyebrow threading, her once-a-week session with her cognitive behavioural therapist (recently discontinued following sexual indiscretion) and three sessions a week with her Pilates coach (also discontinued since being caught *in flagrante* by Charles). There are non-working friends to meet for lunch, and the mid-afternoon nap she needs after drinking slightly more than she should. Sometimes, depending on the day of the week, she has sex rather than a siesta, although she swears that particular activity is all in the past.

In her way Aggie is as busy as I am. I think I would find her life exhausting. Aggie certainly isn't working for the money, Charles is rolling in it. The job is easy and it's fun and as a chronic insomniac it suits Aggie not to have to spend the small hours staring at the ceiling and praying for sleep. Every day the same driver picks her up to take her to the studio, while she sits in the back and applies her own make-up, then picks her up afterwards and drops her back home or wherever she is due for her first appointment of the day. She treats herself as though she is one of the celebrity guests at the station rather than an employee.

If Aggie spent all her wages on taxis it wouldn't make a jot of difference to her lifestyle. Charles has been a canny investor and his property portfolio has netted him several million. How many millions exactly is of no interest to Aggie, she isn't one to count her cash or flaunt her fortune in front of others. She has as much as is required to do – and spend – exactly as she likes. And she's as generous with her friends as she is with herself, always lavishing her women friends as well as her lovers with gifts, treating them to nights out, and expecting nothing in return other than a willingness to be available whenever required and to listen to her incessant chatter.

For the work itself, Aggie has explained to me, she is mostly on automatic pilot. Ninety per cent of the time it's a case of camouflaging under-eye bags and blemishes with concealer in a shade to match the guest's skin tone, followed by a light pressing-down of powder to counteract the effects of the harsh studio lights which can make a face shine like newly polished silver.

I'm surprised by Aggie's assertion that the men in general are more vain than the women, especially male politicians. She has given me a crash course on politics and perspiration. Sweat apparently makes people appear untrustworthy. So politicians tend to be more demanding of Aggie in terms of moisture-absorbing camouflage than some of the hottest A-list stars who have flown in from LA for a premiere.

Aggie knows exactly which celebs wear hair extensions, which have tell-tale signs of self-harm or drug abuse up their arms. Her celebrity breath-ometer, by which she grades the famous according to the degree of offensiveness of the air emanating from their mouths, has had me several times crying with laughter over the past few weeks.

Last night Aggie was talking about her work and showed a side I hadn't seen before. She'd been banging on about some 'foul-tempered, stinky-breathed D-list car crash of a cow' who'd just been thrown off a reality show for popping amphetamines in full view of the cameras, and for whom she'd had to cover up several suspicious bruises, when she looked pointedly at me and said, 'Julie, I know my role is mainly that of comic relief as far as you're concerned, but it's not who I am. I do this job and I love it, but I don't just get to meet the rich and famous, I get to meet real people with real stories to tell. Brave people, worthwhile people, justifiably angry people, bereaved people, and people who are often all of these things at once. You don't watch this stuff, so you don't know. You can sneer because you read the *Guardian* but you don't see what I see.'

'Hey, Aggie,' I responded, bristling slightly at her remarks. 'You seem to be attacking me, but I'm not sure why. You think I don't see real life at the hospital? I don't work in the Portland, you know. Where everyone's too posh to push. I'm at the coal face of the NHS. Pregnant fifteen-year-olds. Single mothers on their fifth child by five different fathers. Girls six months pregnant and begging for abortions. Babies born with congenital heart disease or cerebral palsy. Mothers haemorrhaging. Still borns. Don't accuse me of living in a world removed from reality.'

'That's not what I meant, Julie, it's just that without doing anything specific, you always act slightly superior, like you're humouring me or making allowances. I'm not always as articulate as you, but just like you see real life on the wards, I see it in the studio. And I really talk to these people.'

'So why do you only ever talk to me about people whose names I recognise but don't give a toss about? How am I supposed to know if you don't tell me?'

'Because I feel it's up to me to make you all laugh. But I'm telling you now.' And she does. She tells me that in the last week there's been Anne, who's not yet forty, and whose sixteen-year-old kid was killed by a knife when he was on his way home from school. And Sue, who swam the Channel with one leg to raise funds for a cancer charity, and Gill who has just returned from Darfur where she was an aid worker and had seen so much horror that she was receiving medication for post-traumatic stress.

'Surprising as it may seem to you, these are the guests who make it worthwhile getting up in the middle of the night, who say please and thank you and make me feel appreciated. These are the guests who sit in the high make-up chair and tell me they never bother much with their faces or their hair, but by the time I've finished with them – five minutes is all it takes sometimes to perform a minor make-up miracle – they are wide eyed with surprise and gratitude.'

'So we both have healing powers. We're practically in the same profession.' I said this with what I hoped was humour, but it didn't work on Aggie.

'You're patronising me again.'

'I'm not . . .' I protested.

'Yes you are. But you wouldn't if you were an exhausted, overwrought mother who, with a few blasts of heat from the hairdryer, and a quick slick of my brushes, gets just enough of a confidence boost to get her through her four-minute on-the-sofa ordeal. I realise I always laugh at myself and this silly little job I do putting slap on celebrities' faces, but there's more to it, and I'm going to focus on that from now on.'

'Maybe you could make me over. I feel a bit like one of those overwrought women.'

'Like you'd let me anywhere near you.'

'I would, Aggie. In fact I'd be incredibly grateful.'

'Well I might,' said Aggie, beginning to relent. 'In fact it would be fun to have you at my mercy.'

I've never regarded Aggie as less than sharp witted and bright, and I'm aware her childhood was far from easy, but all the time I've known Aggie her life has seemed so hedonistic, so determinedly dedicated to the pursuit of pleasure. Aggie wanting to be taken seriously *is* new as far as I'm concerned. I decided not to cave in and apologise but resolved to try to see more shades to Aggie's character in the future. I could see that if we were going to remain close friends I might have to modify my approach.

'We could play tit-for-tat all night, Ags, swapping tales of our brushes with human tragedy and triumph. But actually, Aggie, right up until tonight, I've only ever heard you talking about the celebrity side of your work. And the fact is that I don't immediately equate make-up with good works.'

Before replying Aggie lit herself a cigarette and inhaled deeply. I don't smoke myself but I like the smell. It's probably one of the reasons Aggie invited herself to stay. I must be the only one of her friends who doesn't object to her smoking in their home. As smoke swirled around her face, making her features fuzzy and indistinct, Aggie said, 'I'm not comparing myself to you, Julie, I just want you to understand that there's a bit more to my work than you and Gemma and Valentina give me credit for. A bit more to me in fact.'

'Oh, Aggie, I know we all tease you, me especially, but you invite it. And of course I know you have depths, it's just that you're rather good at hiding them. I've never thought of your job before in the way you just described it because you've never explained it in those terms. What do I know about the workings of television? All I ever see is knickerless women with their legs open.'

Aggie snorted. 'Well I'm fed up with being labelled, of being cast as clown. I'm forty-nine years old and I feel it's time to take stock. In twenty years of marriage to Charles I've slept with at least a dozen other men. More, if you must know; it's just that after the first dozen I simply stopped counting. And I'm a bit ashamed of myself. Sometimes it was pure lust, sometimes boredom and finally, as I am only now beginning to see, desperation. My therapist was right. My empty womb left me feeling un-womaned. Now I need to accept what I can't change and move on.'

'You've come a long way in a short time, Aggie.'

'When I think of all that self-pitying, ranting at Charles I used to do, screaming, "Look what you've gone and landed yourself with. A dried-up, empty-wombed old hag. Why don't you just get rid of me, pay me to go away, you can afford it," I feel a complete fool. I know I can't play that particular hand and get away with it any more.'

'But he didn't want you to go away, did he?'

'No he didn't, but I wasn't listening. Over and over I'd ask the same thing, pushing him to the limits. But what about not having babies? What about never being a father? And he'd reply, "There was never any guarantee. I married you for you, not your womb." '

'Charles is a good man, and he loved you.'

'Why couldn't I just accept it? Why couldn't I believe he meant it? Every time he tried to reassure me it would make me fly into a rage. All that crap about being only twenty-nine and having to live my life with joy.'

'But you *have* lived your life with joy.'

'You're confusing joy with self-indulgence. Just like I did.'

There were tears in Aggie's eyes and a slight break in her voice. 'It felt like he wasn't giving me room to grieve. His serenity made me gasp for air. He was so, somehow, unmoved. Or at least that's how I saw it. And when he said, "This isn't about me, it's about how you feel about not being able to bear a child," I just blew. It wasn't his fault, of course not, but I needed to blame him.'

Aggie was learning a lot from this separation from Charles. I wondered if I could learn as much while being parted from Walt.

We met Aggie and Charles at a dinner party eighteen years ago. From the moment of meeting there was a spark between Aggie and me. Aggie had this way of telling stories against herself and with such wonderful self-mocking humour. Her words didn't come out of her mouth, they fell out, spilling over one another such was her rush to relay the latest episode in the soap opera of her life. And I think Aggie was bowled over by the fact that the 'brilliant' doctor as she insisted on referring to me ever after seemed to have taken to her so enthusiastically. She had this idea of herself as not being clever. When people she thought of as clever liked her, she felt elevated, smarter than her true self. And once she found out that

I had a special interest in fertility she convinced herself that fate had brought us together. She took my details.

On the following Monday, having decided she'd rather slum it and see me on the NHS than some private doctor in W1, with whom she could get an appointment the following day, she went to her local GP and got him to refer her. 'Miss Broadhurst is a new consultant and doesn't do privates,' he told her. 'You'll have to see her at the hospital and you'll have to wait.' Although Aggie baulked at the idea of a three-week time-lag, she couldn't persuade her GP to say it was an emergency and made the decision that I was worth hanging on for. That evening she rang and invited me and Walt to dinner, perhaps hoping to speed things up a bit.

'I don't do dinner at my house, not ever,' Aggie told me immediately after issuing the invitation.

'But didn't you just invite us?' I asked, already on the verge of giggling. 'I'm sure that's what you just did.' Despite enjoying the zaniness of my new acquaintance, I did have some small inkling that this effervescent woman might just turn out to be something of a liability.

'I did, but I meant out to dinner, to a restaurant. Yes, I know I've just had this incredible new Bulthaup kitchen installed, so incredible that Charles actually raised an eyebrow when I told him the cost – and as you will discover, when you get to know him, a raised eyebrow from Charles is the equivalent of an eruption of Vesuvius in anyone else – but I have no intention of using it. Unless, of course, I've got caterers coming in to do a party, and even then they usually do most of the cooking in their own kitchens. It's a showpiece, I admit it. If anyone wants to feature it in a magazine they're welcome. But as far as cooking in it is concerned, not me, not ever.'

'Well we'll come out for dinner, that would be lovely,' I told her, 'but I will take it that you are inviting us to join you, rather than taking us out, which is what you seem to be suggesting. We wouldn't dream of letting you pay.'

'Do you want to be my friend or not?'

'Well it's not really something I've given much thought to,' I replied, laughing again. 'But you are a most interesting and amusing person, that's for certain.'

'Then you need to know how it works. We invite you out for dinner and pay. Then you invite us back to your place and cook. If it makes you feel better, you can invite us twice for every once we take you to somewhere swanky with Michelin stars attached. Otherwise no friendship, no deal.'

'Then I suppose you have a deal.'

Over dinner Aggie had asked me if I might fit her in a little sooner than the time given by my secretary. I was adamant. 'No queue-jumping, Aggie, I'm afraid.' Aggie seemed to sense my frostiness at the suggestion and decided not to pursue it.

Eventually the day of the appointment came around.

'You'll never guess who I had in the studio this morning?' said Aggie as she tottered into my consulting room on four-inch heels, and before I had a chance to say hello.

Aggie's nerves were making her even more talkative than usual.

'George Clooney,' I replied, smiling.

'How did you know?'

'I didn't. He was just the first name that came into my head. Or maybe I've seen a picture of him in the paper recently and it triggered the idea that he was in town. Now let's get down to business, shall we? I'll take some basic details and medical history and then we can move on to your current concerns.'

'You don't want to know more about George Clooney? How extraordinary. There isn't a woman in the world who doesn't want to know more about George Clooney.'

'Well he's good looking and a good actor and I wouldn't mind him in my bed, but that's not going to happen, so what's to say? Now, have you had any serious illnesses or operations in the past?'

After a quick run-through of her details – there weren't many, Aggie was in perfectly good health – she told me about her irregular periods and how she sometimes woke up at night feeling hot and sweaty even when it was cold in the bedroom.

'I need to do some tests,' I said, without committing myself to a diagnosis. 'Just want to make sure that everything's functioning as it ought. We'll do the blood tests now, and you can come back in two weeks for the results.'

'Surely it doesn't take that long?' Aggie wailed.

'You know you could see someone privately if you have insurance. You wouldn't get better service, but it will certainly be quicker.'

'I'm prepared to wait' said Aggie. 'I just hope it's not bad news.' She was hoping that I would say something comforting.

But all I said was, 'That's what we both hope.'

But it was bad news. 'I'm afraid,' I told Aggie when she came back for the results, 'that you have premature ovarian failure.'

'What the hell is that?'

'In simple terms, Aggie, it means that you are going through a premature menopause. It's not so uncommon. Approximately one in every thousand women between the ages of fifteen to twenty-nine and one in every hundred women between the ages of thirty and thirty-nine are affected by premature ovarian failure.'

'But what does it mean? Will my vagina dry up like a grape left out in the sun? Will I wrinkle like a prune? Does it mean I can't have babies? Does it mean I'll be dead in five years?'

'The thing we know for certain is that you won't be able to conceive a child. If you are not producing the follicles that become the eggs which can then be fertilised, then you can't get pregnant.'

'Then my life is over.'

'There are hundreds of thousands of women who have long and fulfilling lives without children.'

'But a child is the only thing I've ever wanted.'

'Is that so?'

'Well it wasn't so. But now that I know I can't have one it is.'

Because I had only recently met Aggie, I was determined to retain my distance, to treat Aggie as a patient rather than a friend, to be compassionate but reserved, objective rather than emotional.

'I'm so sorry, Aggie, to have to give you these results,' I continued, resisting putting a hand out to comfort her, 'but there are alternatives, you know, we're getting better all the time at fertility treatments. But now is not the right time to discuss them. You should speak to Charles first, give yourselves time to digest this, and then come back and see me, both of you together preferably.'

'Thank you, doctor,' Aggie had said, quietly. She was too shocked for Aggie-style histrionics.

'I'm Julie to you, not doctor. We're friends now, remember, and you can call me any time, in or out of hospital hours. But when we talk medical matters I'll always maintain that bit of distance. It's better that way.'

Aggie didn't say anything, but I thought she was probably grateful for my dispassionate delivery which enabled her to hold herself in check for a few moments longer. It was only when she had left the room and closed the door behind her that she began to sob, her sobs reverberating off the walls of the waiting room, where other patients were waiting anxiously, hoping their news would be better than Aggie's.

Charles had wanted Aggie to consider egg donation but she was already way beyond reason. She didn't feel the baby would be truly hers. The idea of 'someone else's egg getting matey with one of Charles's sperm and then being dropped inside my tired old womb', as she put it, was an idea she couldn't handle. Even the fact that the baby would carry Charles's genes, and she would give birth, couldn't convince her. Aggie said she'd always hate the donor, the real mother, even though this woman would have given her something precious, and would almost certainly be a good person. Indeed these were the very things that would make her hate her even more.

Aggie had been in her mid-twenties, and Charles a decade older, when they first met. He was already raking it in as a property developer, building luxury apartments and villas on the Costa del Sol and in the Algarve. He had a nose for such things, selling up his UK portfolio just before the property crash in the home market, buying back in cheaply when prices were at rock bottom, and then benefiting from the rampant house price inflation of the later nineties and early noughties. Now he was predicting a new property collapse that everyone else was saying wouldn't happen, and was busy selling things off at sky-high prices and cashing in his profits.

From the age of twelve Aggie had been determined to get out of Salford, and she had been prepared to work hard to achieve her goals. After leaving school at sixteen, she had done what she called 'the treble shift'. By day she worked as a cashier at her nearest branch of Morrison's, in the same supermarket where her mum had risen through the ranks to supervisor. In the evenings she worked in a pub, and at weekends she did babysitting/leaflet delivering/customer surveys in the local shopping centre, anything so she could save enough money to come to London. She also had to hand half of her meagre wages over to her mum. What she didn't know was that her mum was keeping every penny Aggie gave her in a post office account so she could hand it back to her daughter as a lump sum when she hit the road for London. She had detected in Aggie a restless spirit that would never be satisfied in Salford, and wanted the best for her.

Aggie met Charles at a foreign property show at Earl's Court. She did a lot of trade fair work at the time, demonstrating, selling, standing around wrapped in advertising banners and attracting men to whatever stand she was attached to like iron filings to a magnet. She wasn't a great beauty, her nose had a wobbly bit at the end, and her large eyes slanted downwards, until a little light surgery fixed them. Her chin wasn't quite firm, but her breasts were large, her legs longs and her waist small, and she had a natural fizz and bounce that made her ideal for the work. What she had to spare was sex appeal.

Charles was one of those men from a wealthy English background who seem to sail through life, borne along by a gentle breeze. A minor public school, a degree from Durham; he wasn't quite smart enough for Oxbridge, but he could have followed his Lloyd's underwriter dad into the City. Instead he accepted a not inconsiderable nest-egg and turned money into more money by buying a dump of a flat in Fulham, doing it up and selling it on at a profit. He was neither playboy nor dullard, he was somewhere in between. He knew his comfort zone and stayed mostly within it – Chelsea pubs, Mayfair nightclubs, weekends in the country at the houses of friends. He was too comfortable with himself to commit to settling down, which is why girlfriends generally came and went once they realised this eligible young man had no wish to change the status quo. Until Aggie swept in like a whirlwind and made him feel that he had woken from a deep sleep that had lasted thirty years. He knew they were incompatible on paper, and perhaps in practice, too, and he knew he'd never let her go.

'I'm your bit of rough, aren't I, your Salford slapper?' she had joked with him.

'Actually, you're my blonde highlight,' he batted back, as she tossed her not quite natural locks.

'And you're my toffee-coloured toff,' she said in reference to his thick caramel-coloured hair.

Charles once confided in me how he would look at Aggie with her skirts that were too short, her heels too high, and tops too low, and think how easy it would be to have her made over, turn her into a sleek Sloane like the women most of his friends were married to. But he had no desire to do so. Aggie may have acted like an airhead, but she was smarter than she let on. She had grit, humour and good looks, and she punctured both his upper middle-class pretensions and his tendency to complacency.

Charles was smitten. Six months after meeting her he proposed. That first night I met her Aggie told me that when she saw the Tiffany blue box, before she had even looked inside it, she felt she was going to faint. I'm no gold-digger, she had thought, but I seem to have struck gold regardless.

'Yes please, Charles,' she giggled, opening the box and gasping with delight. They were in a restaurant, but she was no longer on her seat, she was on his lap with her tongue down his throat. The rest of the restaurant's customers were cheering in the background . . .

I do wish I'd been there to witness it.

Chapter Fourteen

Aggie's in again when I get home, sitting on the sofa in purple velour sweatpants and a matching tracksuit top, barefoot, channel surfing. Her toenails are the exact shade of purple of her outfit. My day has gone without incident: an ante-natal clinic in the morning followed by an afternoon of dreary inter-departmental meetings and admin.

'What's for dinner?' we both ask one another in unison.

'Well, I could do Japanese takeaway. Or Chinese if you prefer,' says Aggie. 'I didn't order because you didn't tell me what time you were coming home.'

'Oh, Aggie, I hope that's not a tinge of resentment in your voice.' This is getting more and more like a marriage by the day.

'No, darling,' Aggie sniggers, 'I'm not cross, but would it be too terrible to call me before you leave the office, I mean it wouldn't take much effort.'

I like Aggie when she's watching television, it curbs the verbal flow.

'I don't really fancy takeaway or cooking or even going out. How about if I defrost some leek and potato soup in the microwave, open a packet of salad, and bung this baguette I have here in my handbag in the oven.'

'Let's go for it,' says Aggie.

'By the way, I note your droppings are all over the hallway again.'

'What droppings?' asks Aggie, working two remote controls at once and staring straight ahead of her at the TV.

'The three pairs of shoes by the front door, the two coats over the base of the banister, the four handbags on the hall table.'

'Been counting, have we? Oh, come and relax and have a drink. Veg out for ten minutes in front of the telly and I'll make you a vodka and tonic.'

'No thanks, Aggie, I need soup.'

'I'm not your Filipina housekeeper, you know,' I'd told Aggie the other day after one trawl through the common parts had netted three earrings, a pair of boots, two pairs of Manolos, various scarves, gloves and hats, an assortment of make-up brushes and at least a dozen items of make-up.

'Funny you should mention that,' says Aggie, without looking away from the television, 'maybe I should ask Maria to move in with us. I mean she hardly has anything to do with me out of the house and she's bored out of her mind.'

'I don't want you in the house, Aggie,' I reply, 'and I certainly don't want your housekeeper as well. It's been six weeks now, I could do with knowing how much longer you are planning to stay.'

'Well, I thought Charles would have thawed long before now. He won't be able to hold out much longer, I'm sure of it.'

'Any evidence of a thaw?'

'Hang on, I'll switch off, there's nothing worth watching anyway. I'll come and talk to you in the kitchen while you do the soup.'

No reprieve then. Aggie continues to chatter as she follows me into the kitchen. I know I just have to go with the flow, accept that while Aggie is in the house my life will not be my own. 'Well, he no longer slams the phone down on me when I call and when I've popped in with the excuse of needing to collect stuff he's been polite.'

'Progress of sorts, I suppose. Look, Aggie, we do need to talk about this. I need some indication of when you might be moving out. I can't get my head around what's happened between me and Walt with you constantly about the place. I love you, you know I do, but solitude is what I need, not some menopausal version of a single girls' flat-share.'

'I suppose I could always move into a hotel. At least Charles hasn't frozen my credit cards.'

Sometimes I think Aggie has a PhD in the art of manipulation. 'You know I wouldn't let you move into a hotel. I was just hoping for a time frame, or maybe you could stay with one of your other friends for a bit. All those leisured ladies you lunch with, what about one of them?'

'To be honest, Julie, I think you're the only one who'll put up with me. And most of those women aren't true friends anyway. Since Charles chucked me out they all seem to have taken off for Barbados and switched off their BlackBerrys. It would appear that I have something of a reputation as a man-snatcher. A reputation that is entirely unfounded.'

Aggie is picking bits off the end of the baguette and popping them into her mouth. I snatch the loaf away from her. 'Hands off, Aggie, it's for the soup. And what's this about unfounded? Is that one of your little jokes?'

'That's the whole point, Julie. I've never wanted to run off with any of the men I've slept with. Their wives are welcome to them. And I've certainly never slept with one of the husbands of my so-called lunchtime acquaintances. I would never do that to someone who thought she was my friend, or even my acquaintance.'

No, but good little Gemma, the perfect wife and mother would, I think glumly.

'I think we're getting off the point, Ags,' I say, to bring myself back from thoughts of Gemma's appalling behaviour. 'We have to face facts. There's always the possibility that he won't take you back.'

'Julie, would you talk to him?'

'What about?'

'About us. About how much I love him. About how I'll never have another affair again. About how I'm finally coming to terms with my empty womb.'

'But surely *you* can do all of that.'

'But he won't listen, and he doesn't believe me.'

'And you think he's more likely to believe it if I tell him?'

'Coming from you it will sound so much better. My blondeness has always got in the way of him taking me seriously.'

'Even though I'm the blonde and these days you're a redhead.'

'Exactly.'

We snort simultaneously. Despite six weeks of her almost constantly irritating presence it remains quite impossible to be bad tempered for long in Aggie's company.

'I think it's your behaviour, not your blonde stroke redness that has got in the way of him taking you seriously. And he'll know you've primed me.'

'Please, Julie, please . . .'

'Look, I'll try, but I have to know you mean it. About the affairs that is. How is he ever expected to trust you again? And what about this mystery man you keep dashing off to see?'

'I'm still not ready to tell. And anyway he's a she.'

'So you've gone gay. Is that what this is all about?'

'No, you idiot, of course not. You're just going to have to trust me.'

'But how can anyone trust you on anything? It's so easy to use that word trust. I trusted Walt to stay with me for ever. And look what he did. I trust Gemma . . .' I stop myself just in time.

'What has Gemma gone and done?' asks Aggie, on instant tittle-tattle alert.

'Not *that* Gemma, one of the medical secretaries.' I immediately launch into a story about a fictitious medical secretary called Gemma who said that the urgent reports she was supposed to type had got lost when her computer crashed. And how I knew she'd come back drunk from her lunch hour and had almost certainly never even got around to doing them. As the words exit my mouth I realise that no one can be trusted to be truthful; the lies are as light on my tongue as candyfloss.

'Look, you *can* trust me. I've never lied to you. I've lied to Charles but not to you.'

I sigh. 'I think we need to talk this through properly first, Aggie. What makes you think you can suddenly give up on having affairs after all these years?'

'Well, I can lose seven pounds pretty quickly if I want to. And I gave up smoking, didn't I? For over a year anyway, until I started again. It's just a matter of willpower. Up until now I didn't want to exercise my willpower. I thought that what Charles didn't know couldn't cause him pain. Well, things have changed and so can I.'

While Aggie deals with the cutlery, I remove the bread from the oven, pour the soup into two bowls and carry them to the table. 'Are you happy with Charles?' I ask as we sit down.

'Yes I am, I always have been. It's like these men are a thing apart. I've never even come near to falling in love with one of them.' Aggie slurps appreciatively. She empties her bowl in seconds. 'Please, ma'am, may I have some more.'

'More!' I laugh, remembering the lines from *Oliver!* 'More! Never before did a girl ask for more!' I walk back to the stove to refill Aggie's bowl as she continues talking.

'In some ways I suppose I'm a bit like a bloke. I don't have to make love to every man I screw. Sex is sex. Making love is sex plus the feely stuff. The problem when I make love to Charles who, FYI, is just as good a lover as any of the men I've fucked since I married him, is that I am constantly reminded of the fact that we should be making babies, and that I can't.'

Aggie is telling me things that are quite outside the realm of my personal experience, but I'm beginning to understand what she's saying.

'You see,' she continues, 'these guys don't think of me as a woman with a useless womb; it's not my womb they want. We don't even discuss my womb. Except with my therapist of course. He knew everything there was to know about it, he seemed to know stuff about my womb that even I didn't know, but that was an exception. It probably doesn't make any sense to you, but it does to me.'

'Actually it makes a great deal of sense,' I say, aware once again that Aggie is far smarter than her ditzy persona suggests. And certainly more self-aware than I've ever given her credit for. 'The question is why should any of that change now?'

'Because I can't carry on hurting Charles. And because I have to grow up and accept the fact that I am never, ever going to have a baby of my own.'

'OK, I'll talk to him. But I'm not sure it will do any good.'

'You're a poppet, Julie, an absolute poppet. Mmm, this soup is delicious. Any chance of thirds?'

'Thirds, fourths and even fifths if you so require.' I smile at my impossible friend and know that I'm beat. Aggie will leave when Aggie is ready and until then I will simply put up with her.

'Any news from Walt?'

'*Nada*.'

'The bastard.'

'That's what I'm beginning to think.'

Aggie looks at her watch and lets out a small yelp. 'Oh no, look at the time, it's nine o'clock. I promised to make a call at eight-thirty and I'm half an hour late. Look, it won't take long, I'll nip upstairs and be down again soon.' She is already on her feet and dashing out of the kitchen.

'I'm turning in early, Ags. I've got ward rounds first thing and have some papers to run through before I go to bed. See you tomorrow. Are you in?'

'No, I'm busy in the evening, at least I think I am. That's what this call is about, to make arrangements. Thanks all the same.'

What on earth is Aggie up to? As I bend to put the plates and cutlery in the dishwasher something disturbs the tiny hairs at the back of my neck, and I instinctively put a hand there to check myself. I have the strongest sense of someone having passed behind me and planted a kiss on my most sensitive spot. He's back! I think for a fraction of a second before I have time to shake the absurd notion from my head. I turn round all the same to survey my Walt-less kitchen. No early night for me, I think, already beginning to compile in my mind my first carefully worded email to my errant husband. The phone rings.

★ ★ ★

'Hi, it's Patrick here.'

For a moment I can't remember who Patrick is, and I hesitate . . .

'Chris's dad Patrick. The mad monster man from the motorway.'

'Oh yes, of course, Patrick, the in-law.'

Patrick's hearty laugh reaches me down the line like a blast of welcome warm air when you've stepped in from the cold. 'Well, not quite in-law yet,' he guffaws, 'at least I hope not. And probably more like outlaw as far as you're concerned.'

'That's history,' I say, 'there's really no need to mention it ever again.'

'Well, I said I'd ring, and so I'm ringing. To invite you and your husband out for a drink, or maybe dinner.'

I had quite forgotten Patrick's casual invitation of a few weeks ago. I had thought about him though, on a couple of occasions, about the horror of losing someone you love in so shocking a way, about how he linked his arm through mine in the rain and I'd felt, for a brief moment, safe again. And then when I'd spoken to Katy a few days after my visit, Katy had said, 'You certainly scored quite a hit with Chris's dad. Charming, intelligent, amusing and attractive according to him.'

'It's the Irish gift of the gab,' I'd laughed, 'they're born flatterers,' but it had given me a boost nevertheless.

After that he'd pretty much slipped from my mind. My work at the hospital had kept me busy as usual. Aggie was taking over my life. And now there was the ghastly Gemma drama to deal with. I'd barely had a moment to think about Walt, let alone some bloke who'd cut me up on the motorway.

'Yes it would be lovely to see you, but it's a little complicated . . .' Whenever I have to explain the Walt situation I find the words stick to the roof of my mouth like cheap supermarket sandwiches.

'What isn't complicated at this stage in our lives? Complicated I'm used to.' Patrick seems almost to be laughing.

'Well, what I mean is it will be just me if you don't mind, and just me even if you do. You see Walt, Walt being my husband, isn't around. He's having a Gap Year.'

This time Patrick's laugh is unmistakeable. 'A Gap Year! Well, we could all do with one of those, you must be some wonderful sort of wife to indulge him so.'

'To be honest I didn't have a choice. So when did you want to meet?'

'I was wondering if you were free Friday evening. I have to be in central London for a meeting in the afternoon, so maybe after that.'

'I can make it for eight, I won't be through my list until six-thirty and would prefer to dash home for a quick shower and to change out of my scrubs.'

'Then we'll do dinner rather than a drink. Would you like to dine at the RAC, I'm a member. I'll have time to kill so I could have a sauna and a swim first.'

'That sounds lovely. I look forward to it.'

'And so do I.'

I put down the phone and realise I am smiling. I do believe I have a date, I think. And then, checking myself, it had better NOT be a date. This is Katy's boyfriend's dad we're talking about here. A date it most certainly isn't. It's merely Patrick's way of making up for what he did on the motorway, and in any case he was expecting Walt to come along as well. One sad, lonely man who could do with a bit of cheering up, I think. And who better to do it than a sad, lonely woman who hasn't quite lost her sense of humour or her bedside manner, strictly in the medical sense of course.

Hello Walt,

I miss you. I wanted to get that down and out of the way right at the outset. Whatever might follow should not detract from the single overriding fact that right now I miss you. Earlier this evening I was in the kitchen doing the washing up – my life has really taken an exciting turn since you went away – and I felt something rustle the hairs at the nape of my neck at the exact spot where you used to kiss me at unexpected moments. Remember how it used to turn me on, how it became our special code? Like when we were at a dreary party and you'd lightly kiss me there to signal not just love-making to come but our united front against the bores and dullards we were surrounded by. Well I felt your kiss this evening – most likely it was a tiny insect that flew by – but to me at that moment it was you. I was so sure that it was you that I actually turned around knowing that I would see you standing there, right behind me. Do you think of me at all, I wonder? Well of course you do, but how and in what context I have no idea.

Since you went away my smug little world of certainties has fallen apart. I probably shouldn't be sharing the sordid details of my best friends' lives, but I'm hoping that I might shed some light on the madness that seems to have overtaken us all. First and worst is the discovery that my big sister, she of the rock-solid marriage and best-mother-in-the-world award as well as the best-mother-substitute-in-the-world award as far as Tess and Katy are concerned – is having an affair. Not just any old affair, but an affair with Rob. And not just any old Rob, but that very same Rob who happens to be your great mate and married to my great mate Valentina. The real shit has yet to hit the fan. Valentina is worried that Rob is up to no good, but she has no real grounds. I've been going through hell since Gemma confessed to me. On the one hand I feel I have to tell Valentina, on the other I can't bring myself to do it. I'm not even speaking to Gemma at the moment. I'm feeling pretty sorry for myself in all this and fearful that I'm in danger of losing Gemma as a sister and Valentina as a friend, through no fault of my own. As I seem already to have lost you, that's three too many losses as far as I'm concerned.

Aggie, meanwhile, has been found out by Charles and chucked out of their seven-bedroom mansion. You'd have thought she could have simply moved to the east wing! Expect you've already guessed what's next, yes Ags and her Louis Vuitton trunks have moved in with me. It's getting to the point where I'm thinking of moving out myself and asking Tess if she minds if I stay with her and Pete for a while.

So there we have it. Love, marriage, fidelity, trust, companionship, loyalty, duty, all up the goddamn creek. I'm about as confused as it's possible for a supposedly sussed, mature woman in her fifties to be. Only the kids, so far, seem to be OK. Katy and the boy-saviour who is Chris are a serious item, and Pete and Tess are so bonded over the baby-to-be that I think he's developing moobs as we speak. He has certainly committed Miriam Stoppard to memory, a woman whose ideas I thought were as outdated as her false eyelashes, but who is apparently the guru du jour all over again. I'm rambling I know and you've probably dropped off by now . . .

Like it or not, reply or not, I'll be back again soon.

Me . . . xxx

Chapter Fifteen

'Can I help you, madam?' asks the uniformed retainer stationed just inside the door, beyond the columned façade of the Royal Automobile Club in Pall Mall. Even though the RAC has finally allowed women to become members in their own right, beyond the entrance it still feels very much a gentleman's club. I'm familiar with my surroundings, not as a member myself but as an occasional guest of various male consultant colleagues. When you've swum in the 26-metre pool and marvelled at the pillars and mosaics that surround it, eaten crustless sandwiches filled with cress in the Ladies' panelled drawing room, painted yolk yellow in deference to feminine taste, and congratulated yourself on remembering not to wear anything 'ripped, torn or dirty', or, should you be a man, made sure to tuck in your shirt, as laid down in the Club's rule book, you know you have left behind the twenty-first century. And that, I find myself thinking is surely the point. Once in a while to leave modernity to flash its brash booty just north in Oxford Street or to the east in Covent Garden is welcomingly reassuring. I wonder if Patrick O'Brien is a man of our times like Walt or a steeped-in-formaldehyde throwback.

'So it is you,' says a big smiling bear striding towards me. 'I wasn't sure at first. You'll have to excuse me, I'm still dripping from the pool.' A droplet of water from the front of Patrick's tawny hair slithers down his forehead and disappears into the crevice of his nose. 'And I haven't quite finished tying my tie as you can see, which could get me into trouble with the authorities, but I didn't want you to arrive without my being here to greet you. Shall we have a drink in the bar before dinner?'

I realise right away that Patrick is nervous. He's gabbling, talking too fast, trying to play the gentleman and somehow tripping over himself in his anxiety to do the right thing. Perhaps our road-rage encounter had a more lasting effect on him than it did on me, despite the fact that it was me who was the victim.

'Yes please, I'm more than ready for a drink. But hadn't I better put my coat in the cloakroom first? It's another of the rules, I believe.'

'Of course, I forgot, so this isn't your first time then. Here, let me take it for you.' I pass Patrick my coat and he makes rapidly for the sweeping staircase ahead. Then he turns and says, 'Oh I'm so sorry, I've left you standing. I don't know quite where to put you.'

I laugh out loud. 'I'm a big girl now, you know. I'll manage until you get back. Look, there's a magazine stand over there, I'll go and have a browse.'

'Right then. Back in a moment.' And Patrick bolts down the stairs as though there was a train waiting at the bottom, about to close its doors.

'Well this is very nice,' I say, resting back into the dark leather tub chair, surveying the warm wood-panelled walls of the bar and popping a pistachio nut into my mouth.

'Nice,' repeats Patrick. 'Is that the best the good doctor can come up with?'

I'm surprised by both the tease and challenge of his response to my bland remark. This Patrick, it would appear, is a man who would keep you on your toes. Or am I reading into this simple exchange more than I should? Maybe this is simply how it works when you meet a man for a drink when he's not a colleague or medical associate. It's so long since I've been in a one-to-one with an almost-stranger of the opposite sex that I have quite forgotten the art of social discourse. Despite the newness of it all, I feel rather comfortable.

'No, I can do better than nice. Two things come to mind, I suppose. The first, that I'm a bit of a sucker for old buildings and like the fact that this place reaches further back in time than the latest branch of Starbucks. It's the sense of continuity I suppose, the idea of it passing through the generations.'

'And the second thing?'

'That I'm a free woman, and there's something oddly nice about that, too.'

'By which you mean . . .'

'Gosh, Patrick, you do ask a lot of questions. Free means being with you in the bar at the RAC on a Friday evening. Free means not being expected to have dinner on the table. It means no washing and ironing piling up in the utility room. No homework to look over and no need to nag the kids to go to bed. It means no husband hogging the duvet or snoring so loudly that you have to kick him until he turns over and shuts up. It means the only person I have to think about is me.'

'And that makes you feel good?'

I'm laughing again. This Patrick isn't exactly funny, but he does somehow stimulate laughter. 'Actually no, it makes me feel truly terrible. I so miss the rhythm of family life, even the rhythm of dysfunctional family life. I miss the noise that sometimes made me want to stuff my ears with cotton wool or run out of the house, I miss teenage tantrums and doors slammed in my face, I even miss Walt's look of dissatisfaction. I miss boxer shorts and T-shirts, girls' knickers and bras, jeans and jumpers with a hand-wash-only label. I miss dirty dishes, would you believe.'

Patrick is smiling in an encouraging sort of way so I continue: 'Actually it's as though the pivot of my existence has been wrested away from me and I am doomed forever more to walk a tightrope without the comfort of a safety net below, though I know that sounds melodramatic. I'm reminded of this building again, with its sense of continuity; isn't that what families are supposed to be about? It's one of the reasons I'm so excited about this grandchild I'm going to have. I keep thinking it will make sense of things again, knowing that the family hasn't come to a complete halt, even as it's torn apart.'

I stop, quite shocked that I have blurted out so much so quickly.

'I'm sorry for the verbal incontinence, Patrick, but I'm not used to this kind of situation. It's as though I've forgotten how to behave.'

'You're doing just fine,' says Patrick. 'I hope you don't mind the barrage of questions, but I'm so curious about you. I want to know about your work. How it feels to be doing something that's important, something that actually counts.'

I sense that Patrick is doing more than going through the motions, and it makes me want to reply more thoughtfully than I otherwise might.

'You'd think I'd be answering this question all the time, wouldn't you. But your colleagues don't ask, your friends already know, so I rarely get to talk about this. Work remains my great joy. You never lose the excitement of a baby being born. And you never lose the edge of fear either, especially as I'm only likely to be present these days when there are dangers for the mother, the baby, or both. That fear is always there until the baby is actually breathing. The relief of the birth is almost orgasmic – all the tension build-up just goes.'

'Better than sex?' laughs Patrick.

'I can't remember that far back.' I am beginning to enjoy myself. 'The worst part of the job is the mistakes, the errors of omission. I'd be a better doctor perhaps if mistakes didn't leave me wracked with guilt, but they do. Fortunately I don't make too many, so I don't lose too much time beating myself up. Gosh, that must sound so arrogant . . .'

'Not at all.'

'I also work in the field of fertility. Despite the inexactitude of the science, despite the many disappointments, every time I help a couple with infertility problems to have a child, I know I have given the greatest gift they will ever receive.'

'It must be tricky not to get emotionally involved.'

'It's not that hard, it comes with time and experience. My husband, Walt, who was training to be a doctor, knew he'd never get the balance right and he quit, but it wasn't such an issue for me. The only pure sentiment I allow myself is this album in my desk drawer in my office. There's one photo each of Tess and Katy and the rest are of the babies I've helped happen for other people. The babies they might not otherwise have had. Those pictures make it all worthwhile, and every time I have to tell another couple that I can't help them, I look when they're gone at that album of babies and know I've chosen the right field. As for boredom, the dull ache of having done something over and over for decades, it's simply not a word in my vocabulary.'

I stop for breath. I've been talking at breakneck speed and I can feel my heart beating a little faster and my face becoming flushed. With the back of my hands I touch both cheeks to cool them. I have forgotten how animated I can get when I talk about my work. But there's an additional something too, something I can't quite define, although it certainly has to do with talking about the things I love in the presence of Patrick. A man who, unlike my husband, has not had his good opinion of me eroded by time, who has no ready-made responses to what I say, to whom everything is fresh and new and unsullied by the myriad miniature chafings that gnaw away at a marriage until one day you realise you no longer have a marriage at all.

Patrick is watching me as though he's trying to work something out. 'I suppose you're rather a God-like being to the couples you help achieve conception. It must feel fantastic to be on the receiving end of all that love and reverence on a daily basis.'

'If I really could play God I'd be handing out fertility pills like Smarties. And I'm certainly not much of a deity as far as the couples I fail to help are concerned. What drives me, and it's not a doctorly thing to admit to, is that I have this thing about the sanctity of babies. It's why, when I fell pregnant out of wedlock, I wouldn't even consider an abortion. Nor would I carry one out myself on a patient, though I'd fight to the death for her right to have one.'

I've said so much more than I intended, but I don't regret my remarks, not at this moment anyway. Patrick's manner invites openness.

'You'd make an excellent Catholic,' says Patrick with a grin.

'I don't do religion,' I reply, smiling back with equal warmth.

'Something occurs to me,' says Patrick. 'To be so loved and admired by your patients, to be put on a pedestal so to speak ... Is that something you need when you get home as well?'

No one has ever put the question quite this way to me before, but there does seem to be an element of truth in what Patrick says. How many times have I used the line, 'Well at least my patients appreciate me,' when Walt and I have got into an argument? *Sometimes I think you prefer your bloody patients to your family.* How many times has Walt used those words as a first line of attack?

I suddenly feel the need to deflect some of this attention. 'That is enough about me. I want to know about *you*. I want to know who the father of the young man who is courting my daughter is, what he gets up to when he's not scaring unsuspecting motorists with explosions of road rage?'

'I thought we weren't going to talk about that,' says Patrick, staring into his wine glass.

'We're not,' I reply, tilting my head slightly and appraising Patrick. It occurs to me that I might be flirting, though I can't be certain, so unfamiliar does this all feel. 'I've told you about my work. It's your turn.'

'For me, work is simply something to keep me busy. There's no passion in what I do these days, though there was in what I used to do, but for different reasons from you.'

'You're losing me ...'

'Well these days I'm a management consultant. Business has an inbuilt antipathy to people like me, we're about on a par with politicians and divorce lawyers when it comes to popularity. And nearly always we're a last resort, when a business is already going down the pan. Imagine how you'd feel if you'd been running a company for years and then some smart-alec who doesn't know the first thing about your industry came in and started telling you how to run things . . .'

'But surely that's the point, that's why they've called you in, to do exactly that.'

'In theory yes, but by the time they do call you in profits are already down so they resent spending what they don't have on your consultancy fees. Then they become defensive and start blaming everyone and everything except themselves. And of course they're terrified of change. But let's say you do get them back on their feet, do they thank you for your help? Like your adoring patients who send you pictures of their babies? Do they take you to Claridge's to celebrate the fact that they're back in the black thanks to the advice you've given them? Almost never. What they go around saying is that they came up with all the ideas for turning round the business themselves and that they'd never employ a pariah consultant again in their lives.' Patrick laughs, a little dolefully.

'But presumably you wouldn't keep getting work if everyone thought you were a waste of time?'

'Therein lies the mystery of it all. And the truth is I don't care much what they think or even if they take all the credit. I do my job and afterwards I disappear. Unlike your work, there's no emotional involvement at all, and that's how I like it.'

I'm tempted to ask Patrick if he treats other areas of his life with such emotional detachment, but I hold myself in check.

'Did you ever run a business yourself?'

'Well yes, at least I do have that, whereas the majority of young management consultants these days come straight from business school. I mentioned passion if you remember. The fact is that I was a condom manufacturer in Yorkshire. Our advertising slogan? *Because passion is never out of fashion.* You can imagine how well it went down with the deeply religious, Irish Catholic extended family back home.' Patrick throws back his head and laughs deeply, from his belly. For a second I think of my father, and how he too laughed with a lack of inhibition which would animate his entire body.

'I sold out for a fair whack a few years ago, having taken advantage of all my Irish contacts to grow the business when the condom ban was finally dropped. I'd been waiting for it to happen and I knew it would be the moment that I could cash in. In terms of money I never need work again, but I have to keep myself occupied, especially now that Mona . . .' Just as a moment earlier Patrick's face had been alive with pleasure, it now shuts down, becoming blank and almost featureless, as though it has been erased. What I note is that without his vitality he is barely attractive. Which in turns makes me realise just how very attractive I had found him up until a moment ago. Attractive? Not attractive? Why am I even considering these things?

'I'm not going to ask you uncomfortable questions,' I say, knowing without having to even think about it that I cannot be a source of comfort to him, only perhaps distraction. 'But maybe you could tell me something about your childhood, about what it was like growing up in Ireland.'

'It will be my pleasure,' says Patrick, 'but shall we move to the dining room first? I could eat a horse, or at the very least a suckling pig which I know for certain is on tonight's menu. I'll tell you what strikes me about us,' he says as he stands, smiling again, 'here we are, two mature grown-ups, successful in our careers, good enough parents, at least as attractive as most of our peers, and with our feet supposedly on the ground. But I look at you and I look at me and I think somehow that we are all at sea. Is that correct, Julie?'

I shrug, and say nothing.

As we walk towards the dining room Patrick, for no more than an instant, puts a hand to the small of my back. It has no specific meaning, I'm sure, it's what men so often do, a reflexive thing, protective perhaps, a small display of dominance, but so natural to the male sex that it doesn't bear interpretation. So why, at that moment, does something course through me, like a flow of energy travelling via invisible meridians? The language and indeed the practice of Chinese medicine has always rather appealed to me and it has long been my intention to find out more. I try to focus on this thought rather than the sensation in my body. Something is happening, but I choose not to articulate, even to myself, what it might be.

Patrick and I attack our dinner with equal relish, although Patrick's choices are considerably less healthy than mine. I order Green-Tea Smoked Duck followed by Pan-Seared John Dory while Patrick selects Lasagne of Loch Langoustines and the aforementioned Suckling Pig.

'You put me in mind of my father,' I tell Patrick. 'For the second time tonight in fact.'

'Looking for a father figure, are you?'

'I'm not looking for any sort of figure actually, father or otherwise.' I don't intend to be abrupt, but that's how it comes out. 'My dad was a doctor, too.'

'Aah, so it's in the genes. Did he live to a ripe old age despite his questionable eating habits?'

'I'm afraid he didn't. He was a wonderful man and we were furious with him for going too soon, purely as a result of his own self-neglect, but he did die happy I think. We used to ask ourselves how he could prefer the food and drink in his belly to his wife and children, his real flesh and blood. Which of course he didn't, he was the best of husbands and the best of fathers, but he was certainly a victim of his own excesses. I see we're back on me again, and it simply isn't good enough, you promised to tell me something about your childhood in Ireland.'

'Right then. We'll start with some edited highlights. Otherwise it will feel about as fun as reading the whole of *Ulysses* in one sitting, and we'll be here until Friday week. The name's Patrick O'Brien, as you know. I was born in 1952, the youngest of six siblings with three older brothers and two sisters. My parents ran a ramshackle hotel in County Clare on the west coast of

Ireland, within easy driving distance of the Cliffs of Moher. Those soaring cliffs haunt my dreams, and more recently my nightmares. But I digress. It really was a cross between Fawlty Towers and Bates Motel in *Psycho*. The *Psycho* bit relates to the guest who shot himself on the lawn and me being the one to find him. I was only five at the time. But there I go digressing again. I did warn you that once I get started I'm quite unstoppable.' Patrick pauses for a gulp of wine.

So something of a storyteller then. I feel like I've switched on Radio 4 for *Book at Bedtime*. I'm drawn to this big, warm, humorous man with the aching sadness barely below the surface.

'All was chaos and eccentricity, my parents pulled in the business because my father was renowned for giving free rounds once he'd had a few himself, and because my mother, despite the six children, was a professional flirt, though I'd swear she never went further than letting the men think they might just have a chance. Our own little cottage in the grounds had just three bedrooms, so we used the hotel as a home extension. So long as it wasn't full, which was the case most of the year apart from August, we'd spill out into whichever of the hotel rooms were available. So one night we might be sleeping three to a room on bunks in the cottage, the next I'd have a room of my own with en suite bathroom overlooking the vegetable garden and the croquet lawn. The only people who ever played croquet were us kids. It rained most of the time and after windswept walks along the crazy cliff face a gentle game of croquet wasn't quite the ticket for most of the guests who were looking forward to a log fire and a Guinness.'

'It sounds idyllic.'

'It was. I could fill volumes of books with the stories of my childhood, in fact I'm thinking of starting a memoir. Unlike all that miserable *Angela's Ashes* stuff, I'd like to present a picture of a different Ireland. The hotel was called simply O'Brien's, but my book, if I ever get to write it, will be called The Heartmend Hotel, with apologies to Elvis Presley. I still dream of that place, and I still have a dream of . . . well, we'll come to that later.'

Patrick picks up his glass of Bordeaux, and after taking another considerable gulp attempts to refill my glass with the Chablis he recommended to go with the fish. I cover the glass with my hand just in time to stop him and realise I am a little drunk. Looking up at the central chandelier in the ornate Gallery Restaurant I sense that the huge crystal drops, while shimmering, are more blurred around the edges than they should be. For a second I grab onto the rim of the table to steady myself.

'I want to hear more,' I say, 'but I need to go to the ladies first.'

'Shall I ask for the dessert menu?'

'No, just coffee please. An espresso. But don't let me stop you . . .'

'You just did, which is a good thing I assure you, especially after hearing about your dad. Decaff?'

'No, the real McCoy. I don't sleep well these days anyway, with or without the coffee.'

'So you're not just wonderwoman, you're a woman after my own heart as well . . .'

'What . . .'

'The coffee. I'm talking about the coffee,' says Patrick. 'Decaff is for wimps. Please hurry back, I'll miss you.'

'That's the sweetest thing anyone's ever said to me,' I say lightly, treating Patrick's remark as the little joke I'm almost sure it is.

It must be at least three glasses of wine that I've consumed and I'm feeling more than a bit wobbly. As I make my way across the dining room, my thoughts are racing. Why is this man making such an impression on me? Why do I want him to like me? No, not just to like me, but find me attractive. Why did I leave the table when I have no need of the toilet? Do I really believe that flicking a few droplets of water at my face will sober me up? The truth is that I have left the table so that I can go and check myself in the mirror, to repair what needs repairing, to see if I look good enough for . . . Good enough for what? What has got into me? What on earth do I have in mind?

I examine myself in the mirror above the sink. Then I reapply my lipstick and top it with clear gloss. I put my hand to the nape of my neck and lift my hair from the roots to give it body. In the full-length mirror at right-angles to the sink I examine myself from head to toe. Surely I wasn't showing this much cleavage when I started out, but my printed wrap dress seems to have parted at the front to reveal not just my bosom but a flash of lacy bra. I rummage pointlessly in my handbag for a safety pin and, failing to find one, pull at the fabric of my dress to bring it tighter over my chest. And then, in an act of complete contradiction, I hook my right thumb around the point of the bra that divides the two cups and with a shuffling movement from left to right adjust my breasts to ensure my cleavage is even more prominent than before.

I'm drunk, I'm horny, and I want to have sex with Patrick O'Brien, that's the truth of the matter. I must be out of my mind.

I walk back to the table, determined to give none of this away. I will not make a fool of myself by throwing myself at an almost complete stranger who has shown no sign of fancying me, let alone wanting to . . .

As I sit down opposite Patrick and wrap my hands around my water tumbler as tightly as a guy rope, endeavouringt to steady myself, he reaches across the table and attempts to unfold my fingers. 'You are a very attractive woman,' he says, 'I don't know how else to put this, but I want, right now, more than anything, to go to bed with you. You can walk out, you can slap me round the face, and you'd have every right to do so, but I'm telling you the truth and willing to accept the consequences. And you can believe me or not, but this is not something I am in the habit of suggesting to women I've only just met.'

'I want it, too, Patrick,' I say, with a calm that astonishes me. 'I think I wanted it from the second you came ambling towards me with water dribbling down your face. Such a sexy look.' We laugh simultaneously.

'My intention was to drive home to Hertfordshire, but they probably have a room available. Shall I go and check while you finish your coffee?'

'Yes, Patrick, you do that.'

★   ★   ★

Afterwards, as I lie in the crook of Patrick's broad arms, playing with the dark hairs on his broad chest, I note how different this big man's body is from the slim-torsoed, almost hairless figure of my husband, the husband who for over twenty years has been the only man I've had sex with.

'Patrick, I don't know how I did this, but I'm so glad I did,' I say, quietened now by the intensity of orgasm that followed our vigorous love-making.

And then all at once I realise what I have done. My colon twists and spasms violently. My breath is sucked out of me and I gasp at the pain.

'What is it, Julie, are you OK?' Patrick grasps me tighter towards him even as I try to pull myself away.

'We must be mad,' I say, 'we must be quite mad.'

'How mad can it be for two lonely people to make such pleasurable love to one another?' Patrick asks, not getting it. 'Surely you can't feel guilty? Surely you don't feel you have betrayed the husband who deserted you?'

'Oh my God, Patrick,' I say, as tears start to trickle down my cheeks. 'We're Chris and Katy's parents, we can't be doing this, they'd never forgive us. It has nothing to do with Walt, but everything to do with them.'

'I know,' he says quietly, while holding me firmly against him. 'I know, but I couldn't help myself either. You are the first woman I've had sex with since Mona died. Even that day when we went to the pub, even after my rage, I knew that this was where it would end up. Didn't you know it, too?'

'No, not at all, I didn't give it a moment's thought.' Or did I? 'But this has to be it, we have to promise ourselves, right this minute, that this is it. Finished. Over. You do know that, don't you?'

'I suppose I do,' says Patrick. 'But I'm not sure I can let you go.'

I wriggle away from Patrick, sit up, only half covered by the sheet, and raise my knees to lean on with my elbows, hands cupped around my face. I am completely sober.

I talk straight ahead of me, not even turning towards Patrick. 'You see, I love Katy, I love her so much, but it's an uneasy relationship. She has certain issues and certain difficulties. If this were to come to light it would ruin things for her and Chris, it would shatter her faith in me, sully what they have, throw everything into confusion. What's important is that their love remains something unique for the two of them. I feel sick just thinking about what this would do to Katy. And now I'm going to go. Thank you, Patrick, it was wonderful. More wonderful than I could possibly have imagined. But it has to be a one-off. Please don't even try to get in touch.'

'You won't stay just this one night?'

'Not even one, because if I do, I might not keep to my resolve.'

'They don't have to know, you know.'

'They'd find out. I'm not the betraying type. Maybe it's why I never even considered an affair all those years I was with Walt. I always felt that if, as a married woman, a mother, you had an affair, you'd be betraying your children as well.'

While Patrick lies silently on his back, hands behind his head, watching me in the slim shafts of light coming through the curtains from outside, I dress. When I am fully clothed Patrick says, 'See, you're doing it again. That's what did it for me. It was the way you twiddled your hair, outside Chris's hall of residence. That's when I knew that . . .'

I walk back towards the bed and lean over Patrick, putting my fingers to his lips to quiet him. 'Patrick, please. Thank you and good night.' I turn away and walk towards the door. Closing it behind me, I walk along the long corridor towards the central staircase with a growing sense that none of what happened actually happened, that it is entirely a figment of my imagination and that if I go home, shower, and get into my own bed, everything will be as it was before.

Chapter Sixteen

'I met up with Chris's dad for a drink,' I say casually to Katy when I call her at uni for a catch-up.

'You *what*?'

'I had a drink with Patrick, Chris's dad.'

'Like for *what*?'

'I don't know really. He was in town and we had talked vaguely, that day in the pub, about meeting for a chat sometime and then we did.'

I'm waiting for Katy to respond, but she doesn't.

'Katy? You there?'

Another silence and then, 'You're weird. You know something, you are really weird.'

'Well, it's not that weird. He was pleasant and charming and paid for all our drinks and food that day, so I thought I'd buy him a drink as a thank you.'

'So it was your idea.'

'Actually, come to think of it, it may have been his idea. Frankly I don't even remember whose idea it was and I'm sorry I even mentioned it. But it was a drink, and it was a one-off. We won't meet again before the wedding, I promise.'

'Whose wedding?'

'Yours and Chris's of course.'

'We're not getting married. I don't know what you're talking about.'

'Katy, I know that. It was a joke. But clearly not a very good one. So how's it going?'

'Oh, the usual. Boring lecturers, difficult essays, pot noodles for dinner every night, pot for dessert.'

'Katy, things are all right aren't they? With work? And between you and Chris?' I'm feeling the familiar anxiety, the sense of not-getting-it-quite-right that so often mars my conversations with my daughter. I'm genuinely concerned about whether Katy is managing her workload, but more concerned about Chris and Katy's relationship. I want so much for it to last, not necessarily for the long term, they're both still so young, but at least for long enough to give Katy the confidence to go forward and build new relationships in the future. More than once I've thought that if it ever has to end I hope Katy will be the one to end it. I know Katy has to learn how to handle being hurt, to deal with rejection, that it's an inevitable part of growing up, but I just hate even the thought of it. Walt was so right to criticise my over-protectiveness in respect to Katy, and point out it does Katy no good at all. And now, far from protecting her from hurt, I'm exposing her to it. At least I would be if she were to find out about me and Patrick.

'It was a joke, Mum. You made one, so I did, too.'

'Joke? What joke?' I ask distractedly. I've quite lost the thread of the conversation as my concerns about Katy have bubbled up into my consciousness.

'The pot noodles and the pot. What's up with you?'

'Oh I see,' I say, knowing I sound as awkward as I feel but hoping that guilt does not have enough material substance to be heard.

'Actually everything's fab. I'm really into my course and Chris is . . . Chris is Chris, and I'm happy.'

Katy is so smitten, or 'loved up' as the ghastly expression goes, that she appears to have forgotten about my drink with Patrick. I feel the muscles at the back of my neck relaxing. 'Oh, darling, I'm so pleased . . . Any news from Dad?'

'Yes, loads. Emails, texts, photos to my mobile. And he called me the other night. Says he misses us all, but he sounded good. Full of stories about the places he's been, the people he's met.'

'Misses us all? Or just some of us?'

It's another thing I wish I hadn't said.

'Haven't you heard from him then?'

'Not a word.'

'Sorry, Mum. I shouldn't have said about him sounding good and all that. He might just have been putting it on, for me. How are you otherwise?'

'Not so bad. Busy at work. Aggie is still here creating havoc and winding me up and tiring me out and making me laugh.'

We are on safer ground now, talking about other people.

'And Tess is looking glorious, and feeling great. Coming up for twenty-one weeks, more than halfway there. Which means your dad has been gone for over two months and you'll be back soon for the Easter holidays. The time is just racing by. Before I look around your father will be . . .' I stop myself. 'Can't wait to see you again, Katy.'

'Tess is coming up to see me this weekend with Pete. The four of us are going to a gig at the arts centre which should be fun. Do you think she and Chris will get on?'

'They will, Katy, I'm sure. Tess knows how to put people at their ease and Chris is delightful.' Like his dad I only just manage to avoid saying. 'Glad to hear all is well. We'll speak again soon, OK? I'll call after the weekend to see how it went.'

'Bye then, Mum. Oh, just one thing, if you're seeing Tess before she comes, could you give her my lilac T-shirt, it's on the fourth shelf on the left, about halfway down the pile.'

I smile to myself. Who other than order-obsessed Katy would know the exact location in her wardrobe of a lilac T-shirt she hasn't worn in perhaps a year? The fact that I have no plan to see Tess before the weekend I decide not to mention. Somehow I'll make sure to get the T-shirt to Tess before she goes off to see her sister.

'No problem, sweetheart, I'm bound to pop in on Tess before Friday. Bye.'

After hanging up on Katy I switch on my computer. Still no response from Walt. I know I should probably read into his lack of communication the silent message that he'd rather not hear from me. But I've been having all these thoughts. There's so much stuff

I want to say and although it doesn't relate to what happened between me and Patrick, it does seem to have come into sharper focus since that night. Shall I? Shan't I? My fingers answer for me, and I find myself typing.

Hello again Walt,

I assume you got my last email. Maybe this one will strike you as more worthy of a reply. I've been having a bit of a think about the meaning of love and of marriage, or at least the meaning of long-term commitment. I'm not saying I have any answers, just musings which may or not be coherent, and I want to share them with you.

At the very beginning, we fell in love differently, you and I. For you, at least the way you told it, it was a kind of wild passion. I filled your every waking moment, or so you said, and many of your sleeping ones as well. You wanted to possess me, mind, body and soul, to inhabit me, to seep into my every pore, and me into yours. And yet you knew right from the start that my passion was for my work and that while I could love with all my heart, my fire was for medicine. I've never told you this before, but the kind of passion you described, the passion of poets and dreamers, terrified me. It was the one thing that made me doubt we had a future. Because that kind of passion can never last. Once you've realised that the object of your desire is merely human – that she passes wind like every other creature, has breath that doesn't always smell of fields of lavender and flesh that with time heads south however hard she tries to ward off the ravages of time with healthy diet and exercise – how can the idealisation that comes with passion possibly keep its flame alive? A woman who loses her temper, leaves cupboard doors open and puts her knife in her mouth when she eats, how can she remain the object of a romantic man's worship? I was thinking this over the other day and it put me in mind of the story of the Pre-Raphaelite John Ruskin, who having grown up obsessed with the images of innocent young girls in paintings and Greek statuary, when faced with the prospect of womanhood in all its hairy reality was quite unable to consummate his marriage. I'm not saying that's how it was between us, but you did put me on some kind of pedestal, and I was bound to fall off.

Perhaps I'm too practical for passion in relationships. I cope, I get on with things, I see people as faulty and fallible, and mostly I try to accept their failings. Maybe it has something to do with my being a doctor. Just as our bodies don't always live up to our expectations, just as the wiring or the plumbing goes wrong in a physical sense, so emotionally, too, we are liable to disappoint ourselves and others. Maybe by loving you less, or with less ardour, I loved you better. From the moment we met I felt emotionally at peace. I thought here is a man I could stay with, someone with whom I could last the course. Tess's father had never been more than a casual affair. The fact that I got pregnant and refused to have an abortion didn't leave me wary of men. It was a stupid mistake, my fault as much as his, and I didn't expect him to live with the responsibility of my refusal to have an abortion. There, you see, being practical again.

Don't think I didn't desire you. I felt a frisson right away. How could I not with that jagged scar coursing down your nose, and the darks curls, and your natural sweetness with Tess? But you rarely interrupted my thoughts when I was working, I wasn't given to daydreaming even then. Whereas for months and months after we met, or so you told me, you lost your concentration altogether, found it almost impossible to meet your deadlines – although you always made it in the end. Maybe you never quite forgave me the imbalance. The sense that you loved me in a way that was more meaningful, somehow truer. I'd argue it though, even now. But back to the beginning. One minute you weren't in my life and the next you were all over it – lover, new best friend, almost-instant stepfather. It happened so easily and so naturally. Perhaps it worked for me because there seemed to be no doubts on either side, and because I had no time with work and Tess for doubts and the love games people play. There were none of those will he/won't he call moments, none of those does he/doesn't he love me agonies of insecurity. If I couldn't reciprocate the passion I could make it clear that I had no interest in anyone other than you. Does it sound strange when I say that if you lost yourself in me, it may be that I found myself in you? And it worked, didn't it? It worked for a very long time. In fact I've never had any interest in a man other than you. Even after all these years.

I've worn myself out writing this, and I haven't begun to talk about where it began to go wrong. What is it that you're looking for, Walt? Do you even know? The occasional meltdown aside, I'm managing really fine without you, but then we both knew that I would didn't we? Manage is what I do. But know this. I miss the nearness of you, the Waltness of you, the you of you. Write to me, please.

Mexxxx

Patrick texted me two days after our encounter at the RAC. Simply to thank me. *Thank you Julie. Patrick.* There was something gracious about that text, the simple acknowledgement and appreciation of what had passed between us. I'm aware, of course, that the words themselves are barely worth repetition, commonplace words, devoid of sentiment and with not a hint of flirtation or anything to suggest our relationship might continue. But somehow the words absolve me. Not of my guilt in relation to Katy, but of embarrassment about my eagerness. I cringe at the notion that Patrick might think of me as a woman who is sexually greedy, a woman who is so desperate for sex or reassurance that she would sleep with the first man she meets after her husband walks out on her, regardless of who that man was, and on almost the first occasion she meets him. And even though that's exactly what I did, I'm sure I wouldn't have slept with any man who came my way. This was something out of the ordinary, a chemical collision that seemed – at the time at least – both inevitable and impossible to resist.

The kindness conveyed by the thank you makes me feel both less exposed and less vulnerable than I've been feeling since I so willingly, and unexpectedly, allowed myself to be seduced. *Allowed myself to be seduced!* Who am I kidding? I was as much the seducer as the seducee.

I try to put Patrick out of my mind, reminding myself that it's a night to be filed away, and not brought out for constant re-examination. But two or three times a day I find myself opening that same text, *Thank you Julie, Patrick.* I replied, *And thank you, Julie.*

Now, days later, as I walk towards the hospital, there's a second text which says, *Please see me again. Patrick.* This time as I read the words a series of images flashes in front of my eyes, images that turn something inside me to liquid. And a memory of Patrick, whose topography is so new, so unfamiliar and yet in the picture library of my mind has the ability to excite me in an instant. I can't seem to stop myself, not just from recalling what happened, but from feeling it too, in a purely visceral way. I am walking down the street, an unremarkable middle-aged woman on her way to do a day's work, a woman who is probably invisible to every man who passes by, reliving the first time in twenty-five years that I have been touched by a man other than my husband, and wondering if I might explode with desire.

Even now, at 8.30 on a mid-week morning, as I conjure up the sensation of being totally engulfed by the sheer size of the burly stranger, the living tsunami that is Patrick O'Brien, I am aware of my shortening breath. This is madness! But now another image dances in front of my eyes: the look of anguish mingled with abandonment on Patrick's heavily contoured face as he came into me. And another picture: afterwards, Patrick weeping, silently, eyes closed, two tiny silent tears trickling between closed lids. Did he want me to notice or not? I didn't need to ask the why question. There had been something so melancholic, so plaintive in his howl of release that I instinctively knew what he must have felt. His *petit mort,* his wife's death, combining in a simultaneous outpouring of pleasure and pain. Curious to me is the sense that I don't mind that he should respond this way. That it was somehow appropriate that he should cry out and then cry quietly for his wife in the course of a sexual act with another woman. It would be understandable if I were to feel reduced to no more than a receptacle, but I don't. In fact I have the strongest sense that Patrick and I have exchanged gifts of equal value.

Seconds before the realisation of my betrayal of Katy had kicked in, as I lay in his arms, I said, 'That sound you made. The Lacrimosa from Mozart's Requiem has been swirling inside my head ever since.' And Patrick replied, 'How odd you should say that. It's what we played at her funeral.' It was the only time we made reference to his dead wife, to Mona.

But no sooner have I gone over these thoughts, as I read and re-read the second text than I begin to berate myself for my own naivety, for giving so much weight to something so ephemeral. When have women ever really understood what goes through men's minds? These are my ideas, my interpretations, a flimsily feminine take on the event, not his, and frankly it's preposterous to cast myself as a heroine coming to the rescue of a bereaved man. For him it was surely nothing more than a convenient fuck. One he barely even had to work for I was so blatantly up for it. *Wham Bam, Thank You, Ma'am.* It was an act of lust, performed with detached enthusiasm. Or perhaps, for a short while, lost in the physical intensity of the moment, he could convince himself that he was making love to his wife rather than fucking me.

I need to accept it as a one-night stand, an enjoyable aberration, and cast it aside. After all, I got exactly what I needed. A surprise bonus at the end of a pleasant evening; a gratifying sexual encounter to follow the sexual famine which had left me feeling that I might never be desired or desiring again. And now, why shouldn't Patrick be in the mood for more if it's available for the asking? I want him again, too, again and again if I'm honest with myself. So where does this need to give it meaning come from? Leave it be, Julie, I tell myself. It was an exception to the rule. The rule which states that however much I want Patrick I can't have him, because of Katy. And while Patrick is entitled to want more, he should also accept that more is not negotiable. A failure to care about the consequences for Chris and Katy would suggest a selfish, even duplicitous streak, mark him out as a man who can't be trusted. In which case all the more reason to forget about this Patrick, this man without the moral fibre or the sensitivity to sow his oats, to seek sexual gratification, anywhere but here.

A car screeches to a halt and sounds its horn. I have stepped out into the road in front of the hospital without looking first. I judder briefly from the shock and step back onto the kerb, scuffing the heel of my boot and almost stumbling as I wave an apologetic thank you at the driver, shaking my head, embarrassed to recognise her as a colleague from the hospital. It's how hospital gossip starts. 'Nearly ran Julie over on the way in today,' I can imagine her telling my fellow doctors in the department. 'She just walked straight out into the road without looking. Don't know what's got into her. Have you noticed how distracted she seems?' Since the scandal, the scandal that rocked the hospital almost as much as it rocked Walt and me, I have been so careful to keep myself at a distance. Not a soul knows about Walt going off. It's none of their business.

Only when I am working can I stop my thoughts from returning to Patrick. At all other times since that night at the RAC – in the car, in the bath, at the supermarket, last thing before I go to sleep – I play him over and over in my mind. How did it happen? How did I allow it to? And where did those overwhelming feelings come from? I've never regarded myself as a particularly sexual being. I had loved Walt, and there'd been a certain urgency in the early days. But over the years urgency had given way to a kind of libidinal lassitude. Sex remained a pleasurable if increasingly and, if I'm honest, gratifyingly intermittent activity until those last few months, when it ceased altogether. Once a week, or maybe once a fortnight, sometimes less, over the last few years, I didn't count or care how often. It happened when it happened. And then when we did make love, sometimes I would reach orgasm, more often I wouldn't. This wasn't something I minded either. But I did mind towards the end, in the period before sex ceased altogether, that sometimes Walt failed to reach orgasm as well. We would be making love and he would say quietly, 'I'm sorry, Julie, but I'm losing it,' and I'd feel that in some way I'd failed him, as though for a man orgasm was more important than for a woman to achieve. I never felt frustrated or disappointed when I missed out on orgasm for myself. Yet every time Walt lost his erection I felt that I was losing a bit of him. I wonder about it now: whether he had self-willed it, as a kind of early-warning mechanism, a subtle sign that soon he was going to withdraw from me in a far more dramatic way. *Please see me again. Patrick.* My head tells me one thing. My body tells an altogether different story. And yet sex begins in the head, too, doesn't it?

The one person who might be able to shed some light on what is happening to me is the one person to whom I'm not speaking. Following my dramatic departure from Napoli's neither Gemma nor I have attempted to contact one another. Valentina, meanwhile, returned from her working trip to Milan only to shoot straight back again a couple of days later, this time to Rome for a product launch. And now she and her daughter Carla are going to Sardinia for a holiday, just the two of them, for a week. I still have time to decide what I'm going to say to Valentina.

Outraged as I am, I'm desperate now to make some kind of amends with Gemma, or at least to listen to Gemma's side of the story in a more neutral way than I'd been capable of before my own lapse of . . . Lapse of what exactly? Composure? Self-restraint? Decorum? Decency? But the word I find myself silently repeating, over and over, is control. *I lost control.*

It reminds me of a game Gemma and I used to play as children. We'd start at the bottom stair in our house and jump to the hallway below. Each round we'd go one stair higher and jump until we dared go no further. I was always braver than Gemma. Knowing it wasn't safe, Gemma would bow out. Knowing that I'd pushed beyond sensible limits, I would goad myself to go just one step higher. Then, as fear and excitement merged in a pure rush of adrenaline, I'd bend my knees, close my eyes and launch myself off the stair tread into the unknown, relinquishing all control. On one occasion, as I closed my eyes ready for take-off, I lost my footing and tumbled down the stairs, breaking my arm in the process. And since that time I'd always had a certain fear of heights, a feeling of vertigo, especially at the top of steep stairs. It's exactly how I feel now when I think of Patrick. On the brink of losing control again, fearful and excited in equal measure.

Last night I left a conciliatory message on Gemma's mobile, but so far Gemma has not returned my call. Somehow I've got through my day without thinking about Patrick every five seconds. Now I'm home again, back to trying to process my rag-bag of mismatched thoughts, and drinking a strong black coffee with a stale, buttered bagel. Aggie staggers into the kitchen like a spent cyclone, dishevelled, bedraggled, exhausted. Only her forehead, pumped full of Botox, fails to furrow. The rest of her face is crumpled and creviced, like used paper scrunched-up for the wastepaper basket.

'Oh, Julie,' says Aggie, her cheeks streaked with mascara, 'it's happened. The worst that can happen has happened.'

'Is it Charles?'

'No, it's Maricel.'

'Who on earth is Maricel?'

'It's a long story. The story that explains my so-called mystery disappearances.'

'Well, I have nothing else to do this evening except check my emails yet again to see if Walt can be bothered to reply to the emails I sent him. You look in such a state, Aggie, I'll make it my turn to pour *you* a drink. And shall I pick up the phone and order Chinese?' Aggie's extravagant ways are creeping up on me.

'I couldn't eat a thing.'

'I'm not hungry either. Will egg fried rice, crispy duck with pancakes and lemon chicken do?'

'I guess so,' Aggie smiles weakly, 'and maybe a couple of spring rolls, just in case I get my appetite back.'

I open a bottle of wine and carry the glasses to the living room, Aggie shuffling along behind me. She slumps on to the sofa, and I sit down next to her, handing her a glass.

'Go for it, Aggie.'

'I don't know where to begin.'

'Just begin, and we'll see where it takes us. Start with telling me who Maricel is.'

'She's Ana's mother.'

'That doesn't really help, since I don't know Ana either.'

'I'm sorry, I can't seem to think straight I'm so upset. But OK, I'll start with Maricel.' Aggie explains to me that Maricel is the cleaner at the studio. How the two of them bonded from the beginning, from the moment Maricel started working there about four years ago. How cheerful Maricel always seemed, even at six in the morning. Singing, singing, singing, mostly Madonna and Mariah Carey. 'The words that came out were total jabberwocky, partly because of her English, partly because she's deaf in one ear as a result of measles when she was a kid. But she sang the lyrics with such emotion that you could almost believe she was making sense.'

'Where's this Maricel from?'

'The Philippines.'

'I see,' I say, pointlessly.

'She's such a hard worker. Have you noticed how these Filipina women, my Maria at home is just the same, are always amazingly turned out? And how they manage to make even the cheapest clothes look expensive and the way they take such pride in their job even when it's as menial as cleaning? She is quite amazing, she really is.'

Aggie continues with a synopsis of Maricel's life story. She describes to me how when she was no more than six years old she started taking the family's paltry vegetable produce to the city to sell by the roadside. How at twenty she left the Philippines to work on cruise ships, first as a cleaner, then later, following promotion, as a saleswoman in the duty-free shop. Eventually she arrived here and married a bloke she met at an Irish pub in Kilburn, although the man himself was an Englishman. 'And then they had Ana,' says Aggie, finally pausing for breath.

I have no idea where this is going but I'm intrigued. 'It sounds a familiar enough story,' I say. 'The Filipina women who clean the wards are equally hard working, in fact they're the only ones who keep the bugs at bay.'

'Maricel and I became such good friends. She even admitted to marrying for a passport rather than love, and the chance to stay here and send money home to her family. Bill was an OK bloke but too fond of the bottle and fell off a roof he was mending following a liquid lunch.'

'He died?'

'Instantly.'

'Gosh, how ghastly. When did this happen?'

'Maricel was six months pregnant with Ana at the time. She's done a brilliant job of bringing up Ana alone. Ana's this really smart kid, she was a bookworm from the beginning. A proper little English girl, which is exactly what Maricel hoped she'd be. Not because she's ashamed of her own background, but because she wants Ana to have the opportunities that were denied to her. At least she did before it all went wrong.'

'Sounds pretty admirable to me. So what's happened?'

'Well, you know I get all this free make-up. The cosmetic companies never stop sending me stuff. And I can't use half of it. So I got into the habit of offloading a lot of it onto Maricel. Maricel took it home to Ana who started experimenting and got a real taste for it. Then I started slipping magazines from the Green Room – they were going to get chucked out anyway – into Maricel's tote, and Ana apparently lapped them up.'

'Sounds pretty harmless so far.'

'It was fine when it all started and Ana was fourteen. At that time it was just about playing at being grown up. But then Maricel started whining to me about Ana – she'd never whined about anything before – about how Ana wanted to wear the make-up all the time, even to school, and how she had started to wear unsuitable clothes, clothes that according to Maricel made her look like a prostitute.'

'And it was all your fault?'

'Not exactly. But I did say when Ana was coming up sixteen last summer that Maricel would have to stop treating her like a baby. That clothes and make-up were her way of fitting in, and that fitting in is exactly what Maricel wanted her to do. And that she should be content that Ana preferred to read Jane Austen while the rest of them were lapping up Katie Price's latest, and that as long as everything else was to plan she shouldn't make a big deal about her clothes. And I remember looking at Maricel scrubbing away at a coffee-mug stain on my make-up counter as I spoke, and thinking she's trying to rub out my words. I've offended her in some way.'

'And had you?'

'It's as though she held me responsible for a whole chain of events which began with make-up and magazines, and then snowballed into Ana wanting to go out, OUT! As if out was the slippery slope to becoming a child of Satan. And then, just after her sixteenth birthday, all Maricel's fears proved founded. She caught Ana sitting cross legged on her bed, revising for her GCSEs and smoking dope.'

'I just don't see where you fit into any of this. What kind of relationship do you have with the girl?'

'Well, that's the crazy thing. At that point I'd never even met her. And then I came up with a plan that I thought might sort everything out.'

'And did it?'

'Well it might have done if . . .'

The front doorbell rings.

'Must be the bike delivery guy with the Chinese,' I say, jumping up and heading out of the room.

'I'm starving,' mutters Aggie.

'But I thought . . . Oh never mind,' I call, looking back over my shoulder as I disappear from sight, 'let's get the cartons open and you can continue your story.'

I note that the sum total of the remains of our Chinese takeaway are three grains of rice in the corner of one aluminium carton and a couple of bean sprouts that escaped the spring rolls. Not a bad effort for two women too miserable and stressed to eat.

While we've been eating Aggie has kept me in cliff-hanger mode, trying to prime me about what to say when I meet Charles for a drink tomorrow night. I told her it was up to me to decide how I play it with Charles, but she insists I tell him she is a totally reformed character and busy atoning for her sins.

'Can we get on with the story, Aggie, I still don't know what you came in so upset about.' And frankly, after three glasses of wine, Aggie doesn't appear to be anywhere near as upset as she was an hour ago.

'All right, where were we?'

'Ana taking drugs . . .'

'Oh yes. That day Maricel came storming into the studio, hysterical. "So now my daughter is a drug addict," she said. "I should take her back to the Philippines where she'll be safe. But if I do that I won't be able to pay my family's medical bills, and my father will die." She had convinced herself that perfect little Ana had so poisoned herself with drugs that she would fail all her exams and no sixth form college would take her. "No A Levels, No university. I think it would be kind if I kill myself," were the exact words she used.'

'A tad dramatic perhaps,' I say, 'but you can understand after all the effort she's put into Ana, and all the ambitions she has for her.'

'I *do* understand. But she has all these Victorian attitudes that are only going to drive Ana further away. And I suppose it shouldn't have been my problem, but I cared a lot for Maricel. Anyway, another of Maricel's major concerns were the summer holidays which were coming up. Since Maricel went all day from one cleaning job to another, she wasn't going to be able to keep an eye on Ana. She had this idea that Ana would run completely wild without the discipline of school and with her new drug habit. So that's when I came up with my plan. I said Ana could shadow me in the holidays. That she'd have to get up so early every day she wouldn't have the energy for staying up all night, and that if Maricel insisted she get a day-time holiday job as well, to help make ends meet, she'd be sorted. And that's what happened.'

'Sounds like a perfect plan to me.'

'In theory it was. Only I fell in love.'

'What's that got to do with it?'

'I fell in love with Ana. Beautiful, velvet-haired, doe-eyed Ana with skin the colour of maple syrup. We became incredibly close. She confided everything to me.'

'And the drugs problem?'

'There never was a drugs problem. She was just dabbling, like I do. But there was an over-controlling mother problem. And of course the closer Ana and I became the more jealous it made Maricel.'

'How come you never told me any of this?'

'For the first time in my life I had this special compartment in my life that I didn't want to broadcast. I wanted to keep Ana to myself. She gave me a quiet contentment that I'd never felt before. It wasn't a secret as such, because there was nothing to hide, but I did like the idea of it being a completely private pleasure.'

'I think you're trying to tell me you felt like you finally had the daughter you always longed for.'

Aggie smiles, and her face, which can look pinched and hard, softens, as though a veil of gauze has been draped over it. 'Having a daughter of my own is exactly how it feels, although Ana seems to regard me more as a sister than a mother figure. I tried to be careful, not to overstep the mark. Like when I started going out and buying all this stuff for her, all these clothes. Ana and I are the same size, so I could pretend they were cast-offs, when in fact I'd discovered that shopping for Ana was even more fun than shopping for myself.'

'Hmm, almost guaranteed to make Maricel feel inadequate, especially if she's the proud woman you've made her sound.'

'I told you, I said they were hand-me-downs.'

'Well Ana might have believed you, but I'm not sure Maricel would.'

'I seemed to be the only person Ana could really talk to. In the same way as Maricel had talked to me in the early days, Ana wanted to discuss everything about her relationship with Maricel. She really did want to make her mother proud of her, and she was aware of all the sacrifices Maricel had made, but at the same time she felt hemmed in by her. And then there was the business of boys and sex and clothes and make-up and movies and music, she just wanted to be a normal teenager. Ana could talk about all this stuff with me. Maricel, meanwhile, just worked her butt off and fretted about Ana going off the rails. Because Maricel did evening shifts as well I started to take Ana out – to the movies, or for a meal, just a pizza or hamburger, nothing flash, except that one time I took her to Nobu and Posh and Becks were sitting in the corner and Ana's eyes practically popped out. I suppose I became a bit of a fairy godmother.'

'And Maricel, I imagine, was torn between being grateful and resentful.'

'I think Maricel began to hate me. When Ana was helping me in the studio and Maricel would come in and start mopping around us I think Ana felt a little ashamed that her mum was the cleaner and would chatter away pretending Maricel wasn't there. And Maricel was reluctant to talk to me at all.'

'What a bloody mess. It's quite extraordinary how spontaneous acts of kindness can so backfire.'

'And now of course Maricel has cancer and only months to live and is going back to the Philippines to die and taking Ana with her.'

'She has *cancer*! Bloody hell, Aggie, this is awful.'

'Too right it's awful. It's awful what's happening to Maricel, and I know it's going to be ghastly for Ana, who'll be an orphan, but

Ana having to live in the Philippines, to give up all the chances I was going to give her . . .'

'Chances that *you* were going to give her? I can see how much you'll miss her, and how sad it is that she won't get to go to university, but where do you fit into her future plans?'

'Well I had this idea about sponsoring Ana's education, seeing her through university so she doesn't have to go into massive debt. I mean obviously Charles would have to rubber stamp it . . .'

'Had you spoken to him about it?'

'Well, I'd been planning to, but then he chucked me out, so there hasn't exactly been a right time. But the whole thing has become hopeless anyway.'

'Had you told Maricel about your big idea?'

'That's part of the problem. I did tell her and she accused me of trying to take over their lives, said she didn't take charity, and how she wishes she'd never met me.'

'Was this before or after the cancer diagnosis?'

'Before. Instead of at least thanking me, even if she didn't want to accept it, she threw everything back in my face, starting with the mobile phone I bought Ana as a present for doing so brilliantly in her GCSEs. I don't think I told you, she got two A stars, four As and two Bs, and place in college to do her A Levels.' Aggie smiles as proudly as if she really were Ana's mother. 'Maricel said it was some kind of friendship bribe. Actually I was doing it for Maricel as much as anything, so she could keep tabs once Ana started college, so Ana could call if she was going to be home late. It wasn't my fault that Ana got into this habit of texting me several times a day. Only of course Maricel found out and hit the roof. She literally threw Ana's phone across the room although she didn't say a word to me about it. I only know because Ana told me.'

'Oh, Aggie,' I sigh. 'The thing is I can see it from both sides. You, on the one hand, being warm and big hearted and generous and Maricel on the other feeling like she's being edged out, feeling she can't compete with your coolness and your cash, and that she's about to lose the one thing that she's managed to make a success of, her beloved Ana.'

'You think I haven't been over this a zillion times in my mind. But you know I have this problem with boundaries. Anyway we had this big confrontation in the studio one day. She was huffing and puffing around me while I was sorting out my kit before the first guest arrived and I just asked her what the hell was eating her up. Maricel fixed on her mop, wouldn't look at me, and then she said, "OK, madam, if that's what you want, I tell you." It had taken me a year to get Maricel out of the habit of calling me Madam and all of a sudden I was madam again. "You spoil her," she said. "You show her things she can't have with me. I know you buy all that stuff new and just pretend it's stuff you no longer want. You take her away from me. I have nothing left to offer her." She seemed so, somehow, defeated.'

'And what did you say?'

'That I only wanted to help. That I didn't want Ana for myself, only for us all to be friends, and that I cared as much for Maricel as I did for her daughter.'

'And how did she respond to that?'

'By telling me how tired she had become, how much her back hurt. I could tell by looking at her that she'd lost a ton of weight. It wasn't surprising that she was exhausted, but she'd been such a ball of fire to begin with, she had seemed to take the hard work in her stride. It was difficult to believe it was all down to worry about Ana. You need to take care of your health, I told her. Offered to pay for a check-up.'

'I bet that went down as well as the suggestion of sponsoring Ana did.'

'Well, to my surprise she agreed. And then she told me about the lump in her left breast, the one she'd ignored for an entire year. I fixed an appointment with the specialist, accompanied her to the scans. She's riddled with it.'

'And when did you hear about her wanting to go back to the Philippines?'

'She told me this morning.'

'And what does Ana say?'

'Not a lot. She has completely withdrawn from me, says her duty is to be with her mother and that she will happily go back to the Philippines with her and nurse her back to health.'

'And is there any chance of recovery?'

'None. She's going home to die, although Ana is in denial about it. And Ana will never come back, I know it.'

'I'm so sorry, Aggie, but it's natural for Maricel to want to be with her own family and for Ana to have some family to care for her when she's gone.'

'But what about me? I'd support her.'

'I know you would, but it's not the same as family. Maricel doesn't have a husband, she has probably been longing to return to the Philippines since the moment she left all those years ago. Now that she can no longer support them, they'll want to support her. Not in a financial way, perhaps, but emotionally and physically in her final days. They owe her a great deal. Poor, poor Aggie. You've put all your eggs in . . .' I stop myself mid-sentence.

'Go on, say it,' says Aggie, her anger flaring like a flambéed steak. 'You can say it, Julie. I've put all my eggs in one basket. But that's the trouble, isn't it? I don't have any eggs. And Ana was my one chance to put things right. Even if I couldn't have a daughter of my own, I could help someone else's. And by helping Ana – and of course Maricel as well – I'd finally done something worthwhile. I mean fixing hair extensions for spoilt divas and blotting moisture from the disgusting, grimy open pores of lying politicians isn't exactly useful, is it?'

'You've been wonderful to those two, you really have, and I'm sure they'll be forever grateful, but . . .'

'I don't know what I'll do without Ana, it's as bad as it felt when you first told me I'd never be able to have a baby. Worse in some ways, because then we were dealing with potential babies, not a living, breathing person who means more to me than anyone.'

'More to you than Charles? More than winning him back?'

'What happens between me and Charles seems the least important thing of all right now. But the funny thing is, the less I keep asking him when he's going to have me back the more he seems willing to talk to me.'

Aggie appears to have calmed down just a little, or at least enough to actually hear what I'm saying to her.

'Please, Julie, you have to tell me what to do about Maricel and Ana.'

'Apart from getting them an upgrade to ensure Maricel is more comfortable for the journey?'

'Hey, that's a great idea. I'll get Charles on to it, he always knows the right people to speak to. He has contacts everywhere and airlines are one of his specialities.' For the first time since Aggie stumbled in, there is a glint of light in her face.

'Ana isn't just one of my little flings, you know. All those guys I've shagged over the years, none of them meant anything to me. I can barely remember their names and don't even care to. With Ana it feels like so much more. I admit I've sometimes fantasised about being her mother, and hoped – as we wander down the street together arm-in-arm – that people might look at us and mistake us for mother and daughter, even though we look nothing alike. It's true she has become my project, and I admit that I've been thrilled and flattered by the fact that Ana has chosen to spend so much time with me. Tell me, Julie, I really want to know. This isn't just selfish old Aggie up to her usual tricks, is it?'

'Come here, my friend,' I say gently, opening my arms for Aggie and hugging her close.

As Aggie sinks into me and sobs, I stroke her hair and say, 'No, Ags, this doesn't remind me at all of your old tricks. I'm just astonished at the incredible muddles we all seem to have got ourselves into.'

'In a way,' sniffs Aggie, 'Ana has already left, she's stopped texting, and she won't see me because every spare minute she has she wants to look after Maricel. There's a bit of me that feels I stirred up stuff for both of them that maybe I should have left well alone.'

'The way it seems to me is that any clinging Ana might do to you right now would make her feel like she's being disloyal to her mother.'

'I guess you're right, Julie, you usually are.'

'Well you're wrong there, Ags. About as wrong as you could possibly get.'

'I need more wine.'

'Me, too.'

'And then you can tell me what's bothering you, Julie. I go on and on about me and you never talk about you.'

'That's because I'm fine. I'm a control freak, Aggie, remember. I have everything absolutely under control. Feelings, actions, everything. I'm beginning to wonder not why Walt left me, but why the hell he stayed as long as he did.' I think again of Patrick. Of that brief hour in the bedroom at the RAC when the fuse on my control mechanism blew and for a short period of time I allowed myself to surrender. Loss of control leads to trouble. Big trouble.

I walk to the fridge and take out a second bottle of unopened chilled wine.

By the time the bottle is empty Aggie and I are asleep on the sofa. It's 1 a.m. when I awake first, look at my friend and shake her gently. 'Bedtime, old girl,' I say. The two of us stumble upstairs together, before each retreating to our separate rooms. I dream of standing fully dressed in a room of naked men, all of whom are wearing masks. No one attempts to touch me. They are ghosts, and soon they begin to evaporate, turning into thin plumes of smoke that rise upwards before disappearing altogether.

Chapter Seventeen

At 4 a.m. I'm wide awake and at my computer.

Dear Walt,
You've not responded to my emails It doesn't feel great you know, being ignored. But then being abandoned isn't something I'd put at the top of my wish-list either.

God, I sound so bitter. Writing angry emails in the middle of the night when you are utterly exhausted and the alcohol levels in your blood are still sky-high is not the way to endear yourself to the recipient. Night-time emails should be slept on. Emails fired off in the dark of night will always be regretted in the light of day. I read that somewhere. On the other hand why should I be trying to endear myself to my husband? I'm not sure he deserves endearment. And angry and bitter is what I feel. At least it is when I'm not busy being fine and forgiving and trying to see things from Walt's point of view. I press the delete button and start again.

Dear Walt,
You might not welcome another email from me as you haven't even replied to my last two, but I'm finding this total lack of communication so hard to handle. It's been more than two months, and it's killing me not hearing a word from you direct, only heavily censored snippets via Tess and Katy.

Worse. Much worse. It's whiny and self-pitying. I'm not supposed to be the victim type, yet here I am playing the poor-little-me card. My finger hovers over the delete button. I press. The words disappear from my screen.

Dear Walt,
    I do think you're a bit of a bastard for not replying to my emails

This is better. A little barbed, but with a tinge of humour and certainly neither whingeing nor ranting. It occurs to me that instead of choosing my words so carefully I should allow myself to be myself, to be less careful, to not edit my responses. But what I feel is the entire gamut of emotions and an email is too precise a medium for expressing so imprecise a range of feelings. I suppose what I'm hoping for is to not blow my chance of ever getting a response. Walt is starting to have the effect on me of a phantom limb. Absent but somehow there. No longer attached, and yet so much of the time I can feel him as though he is physically present.

The thing that I've been running over and over in my mind is Waltergate. *Waltergate!* We promised never to talk about it again, and for four years we've not once mentioned it. But as elephants in the room go Waltergate has to be the biggest known to man. I need to ask Walt about it again, to understand whether Waltergate kick-started the rot for him, if Waltergate was the catalyst for all that came after.

Waltergate! That was the headline, albeit a small-ish one, on page 7 of the *Herald*, the mid-market tabloid rival to Walt's the *Record*.

How did we ever get into such a mess? I asked Walt not to get involved, to let it be, to allow the authorities to continue their investigation quietly, but once he had a nose for a story there was no stopping him. And the more the authorities dragged their feet the more determined he was to stir things up.

It started with that poor woman and her grievance – genuine as it turned out. If only she'd gone to some other paper. But she was a fan, a typical reader of the nation's favourite middle-England tabloid, the one with its finger on the female pulse. And Walt had the awards and the byline and that rather sexy headshot that accompanied his stories. It was hardly surprising that she went to him.

She'd certainly been doing her homework, pursuing her complaint against the hospital, against MY hospital, through the Health Trust and the GMC and the Health Commission. And all those other misdiagnosed women she tracked down. She was a real fighter. It was no wonder Walt admired her pluck and wanted to follow her story through. Eleven women given the all-clear only to discover that their screening results had been wrongly interpreted and that some of the equipment hadn't even been functioning properly and that the problems with it were being ignored. And Mrs A, who Walt decided to champion, discovering, several months after the screening that supposedly said she was in the clear, that she had aggressive cancer, and urgently needed a mastectomy, followed by chemo and radiotherapy.

So far, so understandable. But it didn't take account of the fact that Sally or rather Dr Sally Kettering, the consultant radiologist in charge of the screening unit, was my friend. Not just a colleague, but a special friend with whom I had trained in medical school, whom I liked and respected and who had always seemed to me to be a highly competent, dedicated doctor. And although Walt had never much liked Sally himself, saw her as someone who was more interested in hospital politics, sitting on committees and jockeying for power than she was in patient care, he always welcomed her in our home. He didn't much like her, but he did, I think, rather fancy her. In a way I think that was part of Walt's discomfort with her – he was both drawn to her and disapproving at the same time.

The investigation into Sally's work was common knowledge in the hospital, but I never breathed a word of it to Walt. Until he came home and announced that he was looking into the case. Right away I said don't go there, Walt, don't even think about it, but he wouldn't listen.

Even then he managed to turn the tables on me, though I'd

done nothing wrong. 'Why didn't you say anything?' he asked, in a tone which suggested he felt entitled to know.

'Medical confidentiality, of course,' I replied. 'The Hippocratic oath and all that.'

'You mean you don't trust me.'

'Of course I trust you,' I said, 'but you don't like Sally, and I don't want you to assume she is guilty as charged before anything is proven, and in any case I don't think she's done anything wrong.'

'She certainly looks guilty as charged from the evidence I've been gathering,' Walt insisted, and with more than a tinge of smug self-satisfaction.

I pleaded with him, begged almost. 'Please don't, Walter, please, please don't. For our sake if not for Sally's.'

Walt told me it was too late. That the big boss knew all about it and was gung-ho for a big scoop.

'And you accuse me of not trusting *you*,' I remember screaming. 'Well I'd be right not to, wouldn't I? I'm likely to be called as a character witness, and it's going to look great, isn't it, if I step up to defend her and you're covering the case and trying to crucify her. Do you think your rival papers might not notice? Do you not think the special relationship between the investigative reporter and his doctor wife might not get picked up?'

'Why would they care about us? We're not exactly celebrities.'

'I can't believe you're being so naïve,' I batted back furiously. 'Everyone's fair game these days and you should know it more than most. But because you've got your teeth into this you're blithely ignoring what could be catastrophic consequences. Or it's supreme naïvety. And I never thought of you as naïve.'

All Walt did was repeat what he'd already said. 'Sorry, Julie, it's too late now.'

The shit hit the fan as I was sure it would. Sally, when she discovered Walt was conducting a private investigation on behalf of the paper, accused me of being the informer, the one to tell him what had been going on. And then everyone at the hospital started taking sides, lining up with either me or Sally, the irony of it being that I had been a supporter of Sally all along. By this point the local paper had run an item about the investigation and just happened to mention that Julie Broadhurst, a consultant at the hospital, was not only a friend of Sally Kettering but married to Walter Wallace, the journalist investigating the case. And then it got picked up by the *Record*'s rival, the *Herald*, for their 'Not-so-idle gossip' column, and suddenly it felt as though I was the one being held up for possible misconduct, as though my ethics were under investigation. There was even a photo – God knows how they got hold of it – of the two of us walking on the Heath together. In a national paper, for heaven's sake, and the following day one of my patients bought it in to show me, as though I might actually be pleased to have become something of a celebrity. 'Nice to see you in the paper, doctor,' she said. 'Lovely photo of you and your hubby.'

It became ghastlier by the day. Eighteen months of ghastliness until, following the review of 3000 tests and the discovery of a slew of errors and a temporary closure of the unit, the GMC finally found Sally guilty of misconduct and deficient professional performance.

So I was wrong about Sally, and I accept that I allowed my loyalty to mask any suspicions I might have had about her, but Walt should never, ever, have pursued the case and compromised me as he did. The end did not justify the means as far as I was concerned, and although Walt remained convinced that the case outcome was influenced by the work he did, I'm not so sure. It may have taken longer, but the GMC would have found against Sally without his help. He was lauded for bringing a medical injustice to light, the paper bragged about it for a week when the judgment came through, and I was the one left under a cloud at the hospital. People stopped sharing confidences with me. No one doubted my medical competence, but they thought I was putting Walt first, and wasn't to be trusted with anyone's personal or professional secrets ever again.

So we were at a terrible impasse. Walt stuck to the belief that he was just doing his job, and that I should have supported him rather than sticking by Sally. I thought that he had made a fool of me in front of my colleagues and shown a complete lack of respect for me as a doctor.

And now Walt is gone, it's 4 in the morning and I'm writing emails into the ether to the man who maybe never forgave me for what surely it was up to me to forgive him.

Dear Walt,

I do think you're a bit of a bastard for not replying to my emails, but I'm willing to be big about it if you reply to me now.

I know we promised never to mention it again, I know we agreed that we would 'put it behind us' once and for all, but we never did wave goodbye to Waltergate, did we? Or at least you didn't. I will never accept that what you did was right, that yours was the moral high ground, but I think I forgave you. I think I accepted the awfulness of it, recognised the pressure you were under, and moved on. And I believed you when although you wouldn't exactly apologise you swore never to allow a situation which would compromise me in that way to arise again. I think I managed to incorporate the hurt, but for you, I sense, it was a watershed. A moment that would always divide our marriage into before and after, something that would hover for ever between us. It's when I fear it all started to go wrong.

For me, once the sore had healed, I genuinely felt it had been dealt with; the scarring would remain, but it would be minimal. But for you, I sense, the scar was a keloid, raised and pink and angry, a continual reminder of the original wound, more disfiguring in fact than the wound itself. And I don't understand why. Does it annoy you that I'm still overdoing it with the medical metaphors? How they used to make you groan, in the early days with affection, later with irritation. But they always did help me make sense of things.

But I do have this ability to let go. Without wishing to sound pompous I think I know how to forgive. I forgave you. But you didn't forgive me for refusing to acknowledge that you were justified in your actions. Nothing was ever the same after that.

*You stopped asking about my work, and I stopped asking about
yours. You even stopped the home delivery of the paper, with the
feeble excuse that you could read your pieces on the internet, that
it wasn't worth having it delivered since I loathed it anyway, and
that you would see the printed version once you got to the office.*

*On the surface things looked pretty much the same, but small
things in other areas were beginning to change. We stopped
holding hands when we went for a walk together, something we
had done for more than twenty years. We laughed less together.
I'd hear you, sometimes, laughing aloud with Tess or Katy, and
wonder why you no longer laughed with me. I've never said any
of this to you before. Maybe it would have been better if I had.*

*And although you professed to have been absolutely right to
pursue your story as you did, it was around this time that you
started to express increasing dissatisfaction with your work and
with life in general. Looking back I can see things weren't good
between us, but the thought of leaving you never crossed my mind.
It will pass, I told myself.*

*I'm wondering, even as I write these words, if you will read
them. I'm wondering, if you do, whether they will stir up the
old anger, and if I should not have set it down again. Whatever
happened to my famous clarity, my ability to cut through problems
to the core, my certainty? And what happened to your tender
loving? What happened to our so-special family unit? What
happened, Walt?*

Even as I click the mouse on 'send', an image of Patrick pops into
my head and a bolt of desire shoots through me. How can this be
possible? How is it possible to lament and long for your husband
at the same time as being overtaken by so urgent a sexual need for
someone else? A low buzzing alerts me to the mobile that's sitting
next to my computer. A text? At this hour? At 4.30 a.m.? I open it.
Not sleeping. Thinking of you. Hoping your dreams are sweet. Patrick.
Damn him. Damn him, damn him, damn him.

There is no chance of sleep coming to me now. I click on to Amazon, order a CD of Herbert von Karajan conducting the Berlin Philharmonic playing a Chopin violin concerto and a Nigella Lawson cookbook. I browse the best-sellers, read customer reviews. Next I go to the BBC website and check the five-day weather forecast. And after that to the *Telegraph* website to read the morning news. Back to the BBC and a replay of a jazz concert. It's 5.30 a.m. and tiredness is overcoming me once again. I could go back to sleep for an hour or so; now that I feel quite exhausted again I would probably nod off. I click back on to my inbox as a prelude to shutting down the computer. There is a reply to my email to Walt. No, it must be the email I sent him bouncing back. Why would he suddenly deign to reply after so long ignoring me? I feel myself bristling for a moment, thinking not about the fact that he might have written, but that it has taken him all this time to do so. I look again. It's not a delivery failed message, it's a Walt message. For a full five minutes I stare at the screen, not daring to open the email for fear of what it might contain. Supposing he insists I stop writing to him? Supposing he tells me he wants a divorce? Suppose . . . For God's sake, woman, open it. And then I do.

Dear Julie,

You don't give up, do you? Plaguing me that is. I'm kidding. In a way I'm pleased that you've been writing to me, it shows you care, and that's something I've doubted for a long time.

The reason I've not replied until now is that I simply haven't known what to write. I've had nothing to say that might shed light on you and me in a way that might be helpful, or move things along towards a resolution, one way or another. Even now I haven't really moved on, this is a courtesy call as much as anything else, but I'll do my best to tell you where I am.

What I've mostly felt is lost. Lost in lands where I am free to wander, but not free of me. Tess was certainly right on that score. But here on the farm in Australia, more than in South America, I

*am finally beginning to appreciate my solitude. I openly admit that
in Brazil and Argentina I succumbed to wine, women and song –
and some drugs that numbed the pain, at least for a while – but
none of it really helped me to see a way forward. It was an orgy
of hedonism, and I've never been much of a man for orgies. But
maybe the hedonism was a necessary transition, before I could start
to think. And so now, here, in the wide-open bush, in the silence, in
the vast wilderness, I am beginning to feel at peace.*

*I'm grateful to Guy and Petra for taking me in and giving me
work and accommodation. They say they've been waiting almost
twenty years to repay the hospitality we showed them when they
were touring Europe that time, and ended up staying with us
all those months. You probably can't imagine me, whose exercise
routine used to consist of tilting back a beer glass or hitting the
keys of my computer, rounding up sheep and learning the art of
shearing and chopping wood and putting out bush fires, but I'm
beginning to discover muscles I didn't know I even possessed. And
when I'm physically exhausted, which by the end of the day I am,
I sleep dreamlessly and long, or at least until Guy bangs on my
door at 5.30 a.m. so we can get started. Petra's a great cook, though
mutton seven days a week, even when it's dressed as lamb, can get
a bit tedious.*

*How long have I been gone? I've lost all sense of time. I think of
the girls a lot, especially of Tess and the baby. I so want to be there
for the birth, but at the same time I know she has great support in
you and Pete and that there's nothing I can do to be of any use.
It probably makes more sense for me to try and sort my head out
rather than rush back, still not knowing what the hell comes next.*

*Sometimes I think I could live this life for ever. That while
loneliness is a curse, solitude can be a blessing. I don't suppose that
thought will go down too well with you, Julie, but it's the truth of
how I feel.*

*It's so good to know that Katy is happy. That boy she's hooked
up with had better be good to her otherwise when I come home I'll
throttle him with some of the wire I've been using for making fences.*

I loved you for so long, Julie, but I always felt I was in your slipstream. It would have been better by far if our professions hadn't overlapped. If I'd been a teacher or a vet or anything other than a failed doctor turned hack journalist specialising in medical matters. I know it wasn't your hang-up, but it was mine. And you do have this way sometimes of taking the moral high ground. Julie at her most imperious can be quite intimidating.

And yet my respect for you is limitless. For the way you managed Tess as a single mother before I came along. For your absolute professionalism and dedication. For managing to juggle all those balls in the air. For being a still sexy woman and a loving mother. But the very things I so admired you for are the things that came between us. You grew in stature as I shrank. The more I expressed doubts the more sure footed and even didactic you became. I don't blame you but I lost my sense of being cherished and I lost the ability to cherish you. I don't know if it's recoverable. I don't even know if you have the patience for any of this. And I wouldn't blame you if you didn't. And neither do I know if I've had it with journalism or not.

So you see why I've not written sooner. You say you've lost your clarity. Well I'm way ahead: incoherent much of the time.

You're right about forgiveness. You are better at it than I am. So yet again I feel in the inferior position.

Take care of yourself, Julie. And the girls. I wish my crisis didn't cause you as much pain as it does me, but I fear it might.

I too miss what we used to have.

Walt

It's 6 a.m. My tears have plopped onto the keyboard. The i and the g are moist and shiny, like pebbles washed by the sea. Walt's email has left me none the wiser about *Waltergate,* but has suffused me with an all-encompassing sadness, a sadness I can feel in my toes, my fingertips, my skin, my hair, my whole being. Am I a fool for love or just a fool? Too late now for bed. I go to the bathroom, shower briskly and wash my hair as though, just like in the musical,

I'm trying to wash my man right out of it. Would Walt love me more, I wonder, if I were less able, more needy, more reliant? Well I'm not and I won't be. If he wants me back he will have to accept me as I am. I step out from the shower with a renewed sense that my strength will carry me through. And I have resolved to reply to Patrick, if only to stop him texting. I will agree to meet him. And when I do I will tell him face to face that this simply can't go on and that henceforth all communication between us must cease.

Chapter Eighteen

Charles is loping towards me with a grin. He's tall and lean and fair and expensive-looking. No matter how informal his clothes – tonight he is wearing dark blue jeans teamed with a pink and white striped shirt and a cord jacket – you can be sure that they have been chosen with great care, laundered to creaseless perfection and purchased in the classiest of Knightsbridge stores. He is the kind of Englishman for whom the word casual is always prefaced with the word smart. His loafers, unlike his eyes, gleam. Charles's eyes are that particular shade of barely blue, the colour of water, that renders them expressionless. To glean his mood from his face you have to focus on the lines that form around the eyes when he smiles rather than the eyes themselves. Even his nostrils speak louder than his eyes, flaring and narrowing with emotion while his long, bony nose has a panoply of expressive stances. When Charles leans down to kiss me he smells of sandalwood.

'Hello, Jules. Good to see you after so long.' He is the only person I know who calls me Jules.

'Well I've been rather occupied entertaining your wife,' I say. 'Good to see you, too.'

Charles and I are not what I'd call confidantes, and without Aggie I doubt we'd see much of one another, but I like him well enough and have a great deal of respect for his steadfastness in the face of Aggie's perpetual histrionics. This is the first time Charles and I have spent time together, other than in a foursome with Walt and Aggie. He is buying me supper at a gastro-pub close to the hospital.

'Will you have a glass of something to start?' he asks. 'Or shall I order a bottle of wine?'

'I'm going to stick to water tonight,' I reply. 'I've been drinking way too much of late and it's beginning to take its toll.'

'You look fine to me,' he says, but without conviction, and adds, 'a little tired perhaps.'

'Aggie can be quite exhausting. Quite apart from the rest of life.'

'Don't I know it,' Charles sighs, flicking once at his nose with the index finger of his left hand, a gesture he habitually makes when he wants to emphasise a point. 'Any word from the errant husband?'

'A word about sums it up. But he's definitely alive, that much I know for sure. What about you?'

'A postcard from Rio, written just before he left for Australia.'

'Much talk about the girls from Ipanema?' I ask as perkily as I can.

'No mention at all actually.' Charles averts his eyes from mine as he says this. 'So much for us smug-marrieds, Jules. Thought we'd last the distance, didn't you?'

'We might still,' I say. 'At least some of us might.'

'It would all have been so different if we'd had kids.'

'Maybe,' I reply. 'But look at me and Walt. Tess and Katy may have kept Walt at home until now, but it seems that with Katy at uni he feels free to do as he pleases. Even kids don't guarantee to glue you together.'

Charles raises his hand to attract the attention of the waitress. 'I probably shouldn't be saying this to you, Jules, but I feel sorry for Walt. I know he's the one who's gone off, but he seems so lost. You, on the other hand, seem so grounded. Even now.'

'That's because I put on a good show.'

'Please don't tell me it's all an act, I want to believe it's for real.'

'No, it's only partly an act. I won't go under because however much I want Walt in my life he's only part of it, and the other parts are precious too.'

'Without Aggie I feel the lights have been turned out.'

'Then take her back.'

'Let's order, shall we?' says Charles as the waitress appears at our table.

'What are you thinking of having?' I ask. I can't entirely relax with Charles, whom I know only in the context of Aggie.

'The calves liver and onions with mash.'

'I'll have the same,' I say, looking up at the waitress and then back at Charles. 'I'm too tired to make decisions tonight.'

We chat for a while about Charles's business and the state of the property market, but when the food arrives I turn the conversation back to him and Aggie.

'She wants to come home to you.'

'I know she does.'

'And are you willing to take her?'

'I can live with the humiliation, but I'm not sure I can live any longer with the lack of trust, the lack of honesty, the whole damn sham.'

'Any longer?'

'Don't think I didn't know what was going on. Aggie seems to think she was discreet, but discretion is not really one of Aggie's strong points. The evidence was everywhere.'

I'd always thought that Charles must have known, but until now it had been speculation. 'Then why did you put up with it for so long?'

'Because I couldn't bear to lose her. And because once I realised what she was up to I began to amuse myself with other women, too. It became our norm, I suppose. Me knowing she was screwing around; Aggie believing I didn't have a clue and me being so much better at deceiving her than she was at deceiving me.'

'You make it sound like a kind of sexual tit-for-tat, at least as far as you were concerned.' I'm beginning to wonder if I've lived a particularly sheltered life sexually speaking. Each new revelation shocks me as much as the last. I'm still in shock about me and Patrick.

'Well, it wasn't exactly what I'd call revenge. But I did take it as unspoken permission to indulge in lots of meaningless sex without feeling guilty all the time.'

'Is everyone unfaithful except me?'

'Perhaps.'

'So if you were playing around, too, why suddenly is it such a big deal?'

'Well, I guess she's told you the unsparing details . . .'

'Yes, I'm afraid she has . . .'

'Walking in on them like that made it so much more real. Made me realise how much of a chimera our marriage has been, and how sordid. I've no idea how many men Aggie's had sex with during our marriage, and nor do I want to know, but at least I'd not actually witnessed it for myself. What I couldn't see I had chosen not to imagine. Some men go mad with jealousy thinking about their wives with other men. I managed to cut myself off from it, to develop a kind of clinical detachment. But seeing her like that . . . it . . . it . . . well, it sickened me.'

I am not sure what to say so I just wait for Charles to continue. He takes a sip of wine and stares into the distance with his colourless eyes. 'There's not one single thing more I could have done for that woman. I dropped half my friends when they were too snobbish to take her on. I put up with her loudness and her brashness and I never criticised her for it. I offered to have a baby by any artificial means possible and told her I'd love her regardless of whether or not we had kids. I lavished her with affection and gave her carte blanche with the credit cards.'

'But you must have got something in return, Charles.'

'Well, that's exactly the point. I got Aggie. My funny, sexy, so much smarter than she seems, life-giving whirlwind of a faithless woman.'

I'm trying to make some kind of sense of this, but it's hard. 'I don't think I really get infidelity. I mean I know what drove Aggie, and that it wasn't about not loving you, but for myself infidelity was never an option.'

'Have you never once enjoyed meaningless sex? Even before your marriage?'

'For me even meaningless sex would have meaning.'

'Then you've clearly never experienced it.'

'I guess not.'

'I applaud you.'

We both laugh.

'I'm not sure there's much to applaud.'

'Meaningless sex is a great distraction. You can lose yourself for whole minutes at a time. Sometimes longer.' Charles raises an eyebrow, in a gesture of mock lewdness. 'You should try it some time.'

'Aggie would probably kill you if she knew.'

'That's my Aggie. She'd be murderous. But she thinks I don't have it in me to be unfaithful. And, Jules, just in case you were thinking of passing it on . . .'

'I wouldn't dream of it.' And I wouldn't, what would it achieve? I really do think that Charles and Aggie would be happier with one another than without.

'The odd thing is that with Aggie gone I've had all this time available to pursue other interests so to speak, and yet my great big two-metre bed has been lying fallow. I've lost all interest in women.'

'Including Aggie?'

'No, not including Aggie.'

'Changing the subject a little, how much do you know about the business with Maricel and Ana?'

'Not a great deal, other than that Aggie admires this Maricel greatly and has rather taken to her daughter. Oh yes, and the other day she rang and told me she wanted to secure an upgrade for them on a flight to the Philippines. I said no way, not without some kind of explanation, not that I gave her the chance to give me one.'

'Charles, I'm not sure how much longer I can have Aggie for. I need some solitude. There's so much I need to work out.'

'She can go to a hotel. I've not cut off her pipeline to the bank account.'

'Won't you give her one more chance? A trial reconciliation.'

'What's to say it won't start all over again with someone new? I want Aggie but I don't want this kind of marriage any more. A marriage that's become a shabby, grubby, sleazy farce.'

'There's only Aggie's word for it. But she says she's sworn off other men for good. I wouldn't say this if I didn't believe it myself, but I think Aggie will keep to her word.'

'Aggie needs to grow up and face facts.'

'Charles, she needs you right now, more than ever.'

'And why should that be?'

'I think it's best if she explains herself. It's partly to do with Maricel and Ana, but also a recognition that she can't carry on as she has all these years. She does love you, she always loved you, but this thing, this not having children . . .'

Charles partly rises from his seat, leans towards me across the table, grabs both my shoulders and shakes them roughly. 'Don't you understand?' he shouts. 'Don't you understand a bloody thing? I am so fucking angry I could . . .' He shakes my shoulders again. 'I could . . .'

'Charles, you're hurting me, stop it!' I try to bat him off and he releases his grip, dropping back into his chair and covering his face with hands.

My heart is thumping wildly and I rub at my shoulders to remove the sting where he gripped them. I look across at Charles, his face barely visible through his bony fingers. I find myself grabbing Charles's glass and taking a slug of wine from it. After a moment he lets his hands fall to his sides. 'Oh, Jules, you have no idea how miserable I am without her. It's pathetic, I know, but I went through her bathroom cabinet the other day and found an old bottle of perfume and then sprayed it on my pillow. Sorry if I hurt you just now.'

The beat of my heart has slowed. 'How sweet you are, Charles. No wonder Aggie can't bear the thought of losing you. You know,

I really do think she may finally be coming to terms with being childless.'

'I'm not sure that's possible for Aggie.'

'Do it, Charles, take her back, you can always change your mind again later if it doesn't work out.'

'I'm not even sure Aggie deserves me.'

'You may be right. But Aggie is one in a million as well.'

'I miss that woman so damn much. I don't know how it can be, but I still love her.'

'We can't intellectualise our emotions,' I say.

'That's wise, Jules, but I'm not sure knowing it helps.'

'Well, it certainly hasn't helped me, even though I know it to be true. Every feeling I've had since Walt left has to be explained away before I can accept it.'

'OK, Jules, I'll give it serious thought. But as I always say before agreeing to a deal, give me time to think it over. I'll get back before end of play Friday.'

'Thanks, Charles.'

'It's me who should be thanking you.'

'I so want things to work out for you and Aggie.'

'And me for you and Walt.'

'I wouldn't hold your breath on that one. Your wife's perfume on the pillow beside you . . . that's so romantic. The only thing Walt's likely to spray on his pillow is insect repellent. And sometimes I feel that poor little insect whose days are numbered is me.'

I'm in the middle of a busy general gynae clinic, seeing new patients for assessment and diagnosis following GP referral. Having just performed a colposcopy on a thirty-two-year-old patient whose routine cervical smear was abnormal, I should be calling in the next patient on my list, a teenager whose notes tell me she has had infrequent periods for more than two years. Instead I am just sitting and thinking, though not about the job in hand. This is not at all Julie-like behaviour. For the first time in my professional life I am not fully concentrating. The lapses began when I was seeing my first patient of the day, a middle-aged woman with pelvic pain, and taking down her medical history, all of which was standard procedure. Except that when I asked the clearly nervous woman whether she'd had any operations in the past and she launched into an unnecessarily detailed account of her appendectomy and her bunions, instead of encouraging her to move on I allowed my mind to wander. I looked at the date on my watch and noted it was only five days before I'd be seeing Patrick again, to tell him face-to-face that our one-night stand was definitively not going to be repeated. And then that now-familiar bolt of desire shot through me, a sensation strong and sudden like a stab of pain, but constituted only of pleasure. When it subsides I am left with a mild, yearning ache. 'Doctor . . .' I could hear an anxious voice in the background saying as I jolted back to the present.

Then just before, as I'd been preparing the microscope for the colposcopy procedure, I found myself worrying over the fact that protein has been found in Tess's urine, possibly suggesting the start of pre-eclampsia. It could be a minor kidney infection but I haven't been able to get hold of Tess since she texted me the news at eight this morning, so I haven't been able to ask if there are any other concerning signs, like raised blood pressure and swelling of hands and feet. I've texted and called but she must be busy working and unable to respond at the moment.

Now, instead of calling in the young girl sitting anxiously with her mother outside my door I find myself thinking about Socrates' maxim that 'the unexamined life isn't worth living' and wondering how I have managed to successfully navigate my own life for more than fifty years without dissecting, scrutinising and analysing at every twist and turn. Walt's departure and all the events of the past months have made me question everything. Once there had been a sense of 20:20 vision. Now it's as though I'm seeing my life through a sightline clouded by cataracts. I want proper answers, satisfactory explanations, to know what Walt thinks, feels, means, wants. Only by knowing, it seems to me, will I be able to absorb and assimilate and move on. It was easy for me to tell Charles that we can't intellectualise our emotions, but I can't give up on the notion in relation to me and Walt.

It had never seemed that complicated before. My *modus operandi* was to get on with things, making calm, rational decisions as I went. My path to becoming a successful consultant in obs and gynae might have appeared daunting to some, but not to me. Hard work plus the gift of intelligence, inherited from both my parents, paid rewards. Juggling my profession with my responsibilities as a mother and wife had never been easy, and it was certainly exhausting, but I had the energy and the grit and the grey matter and felt I was incredibly privileged to lead the life I lead.

Now I'm beginning to realise that all the elements of my existence fell very much within safe parameters, or at least within my prescribed comfort zone. Even having given birth to Tess as a single mother had felt relatively straightforward at the time, knowing I had my mum and Gemma to back me up. In those far-off days I took things in my stride, understood my goals and where I was heading. It had seemed a natural enough way to view the world. And then Walt came along. And once Walt was there, I had this sense that he'd always be there, like the tallboy I'd been given by my father, which had once contained his patients' files and which has stood in my hallway for the last twenty years. Walt, the fixtures and fittings of my life. Permanently there in the background, my bedrock. Great father and brilliant step-father, supportive husband, good friend. It was more than anyone could ask for. And maybe, I think now, it was only because of Walt that I was able to hold it all together. I took him for granted because he was a given. His presence was never in doubt. But had I underestimated his value to me personally?

In the time of Walt I knew exactly where I was. Post-Walt, or PW as I'm starting to call it, I have this sense of having been placed blindfold in a field in the middle of the countryside, spun around a few times, and instructed to find my way home without either a map or a compass.

What I need is a break. In fact I need what Walt is having. A Gap

Year of my own. What gives him the right . . .? I feel so tired that if I were to place my head on the desk in front of me I would fall asleep in the middle of my busy clinic schedule, while the queue of patients, lined up on chairs outside my office door, snaked beyond the waiting room down the long hospital corridor.

Before I can rouse myself sufficiently to see another patient I need more coffee. My caffeine intake has been rocketing skywards ever since Walt left, and I'm up to at least seven cups a day. I know it's contributing to my general agitation, and my increasingly wakeful nights, but I still find myself returning compulsively to the coffee machine at diminishing intervals throughout the day. A coffee machine which dispenses coffee so offensive to my palate that I wince every time I drink it. Coffee and wine are turning into my staple diet.

I go to fetch a coffee, stare into its blackness as it cools for a minute or two, then knock it back in one go. Mother and daughter look up at me expectantly as I pass on my way back to the consulting room.

'I won't be a moment,' I say.

Inside my room I dial Gemma. She picks up immediately. 'Gemma, it's me. I need to see you, urgently.'

'Oh,' says Gemma coldly. 'I only answered because I thought it was . . .' I resist saying Rob for her. She switches tack. 'You're not talking to me if I remember rightly . . .'

'Look I'm sorry, Gemma, truly I am. I may have been overly harsh and overly judgmental. I didn't take the time to think it through. But you shocked me, you really did, and the thought of poor Valentina . . . I'm in a state of permanent shock these days. There's so much I want to say to you but I'm right in the middle of a clinic and . . .'

'You! Calling me *in the middle of a clinic*! Gosh, Julie, I had no idea things were that bad.' Gemma's voice has taken on a new tone, changing in an instant from cold indifference to concern.

'It's not that things are so bad. I'm managing, I really am. But there are these moments when I feel I'm on the verge of toppling over a cliff, and that you're the only person who might be able to stop me.'

'Oh, Julie, I'm sorry, too. It's just . . . Look, tonight I'm seeing . . . No, no it's OK, how about tonight?'

'I'm free tonight, and most every other night, but if you're seeing . . .'

'It's not important. I want to see you, of course I do. And other stuff has happened, stuff that's so overwhelming . . .'

'The boys? Are they OK?'

'They're fine, it's other stuff . . .'

'Then tonight, the sooner the better. It had better be Napoli's. Otherwise I've got Aggie and you've Antony.'

'Napoli's, eight o'clock.'

What more could have happened? I wonder if Antony has found out. I disconnect from Gemma and look again at my watch. I've allowed 15 minutes to pass between patients for purely personal reasons. It's inexcusable.

'Many apologies for the delay, do come in,' I say, stifling a yawn and with a forced jauntiness to my voice as I usher in the mother and daughter duo.

'Now, I see from the GP's letter . . .'

'Yeah,' says the mother, cutting across me, 'but that was weeks and weeks ago. Things have changed a bit since then, haven't they, Shawna? Accounts for the no periods, that's for sure.'

'I'm up the duff,' says Shawna with a tone of defiance in her voice. 'I did a test, didn't I? And I want an abo.'

'How old are you, Shawna? Ah yes, you're just fifteen. And how pregnant do you think you might be?'

'I 'aven't had no period for about six months, but then I was 'ardly getting 'em before anyway. But I only did the test a couple of weeks ago. I knew I was getting fat as a cow but I didn't think anyfing of it. It ain't too late is it, doctor? I mean it ain't too late to have an abo, is it?'

I keep my tone absolutely neutral. 'Well the first thing I need to do, Shawna, is confirm the pregnancy and examine you.' The girl is clearly several months gone, and I already sense that she won't be persuaded out of an abortion. I'm not going to mention that I don't carry out abortions myself, and it's not my way to lecture teenagers on the ethics of abortion. After checking her over, I'll send her for an emergency ultrasound and as long as she's not past the cut-off date will hand her over to a colleague. My colleague can do the pep talk about sexual health and sexual responsibility and contraception. Doing abortions this far into pregnancy always carries extra risk, but again one of my colleagues can deal with that.

I glance at my watch. Another hour of clinic, an hour's break and then this afternoon my weekly gynae theatre list. By tea-time I'll be elbow-deep in fibroids and hysterectomies.

Chapter Nineteen

Last time I saw Gemma she sashayed into Napoli's looking ten years younger than her true age. Tonight, as she walks towards the table, her gait is that of a woman far older than fifty-six. She looks as though she has folded in on herself, as though she would like nothing more than to be able to roll herself up into a small ball and hide herself from the world like a hedgehog. How is it possible to age so dramatically so quickly? Something awful must have happened, but surely Gemma would have picked up the phone to tell me, despite our falling out.

'Gemma, you look grim.'

'I am grim.' Gemma plonks herself down in the chair opposite me without bothering with our customary hug or to remove her jacket. She clearly hasn't thought to comb her hair which instead of being a slick, dark bob is sticking out in little clumps. I don't need to ask if she'd like a glass of wine, I just pour.

'Is it you and Rob?'

'Not exactly.'

'So you've told Antony then? I bet the shit's really hit the fan now. In fact I'm surprised Antony hasn't been in touch demanding I cure you of sudden onset psychosis.'

I realise I haven't let go of my anger with Gemma. Hence my little stab at ironic humour which is quite lost on her. My loyalties are so split between my friend and my sister. Once Valentina got back from her various trips to Milan and Rome and Sardinia I had no excuse for not seeing her. We met, we talked, she voiced her continuing concerns about Rob and I stayed schtum. Lying by omission is as bad in my book as lying to a person's face. Keeping up the façade has been agonising.

Gemma shakes her head, picks up the white paper napkin from her side plate and starts to separate the filmy layers.

She's not offering up anything, so my only option is to continue to try to prise information out of her. 'Come on, Gemma, you've got to fill me in, does this mean Rob's already told or is about to tell Valentina? I think I have a right to know.' My mind is darting all over the place. It could be why Valentina hasn't yet got back to me since I left her a phone message the other day. I so hope not. The thought of Valentina handling this on her own or perhaps feeling I have somehow condoned the affair between Gemma and Rob, or at least knew about it all along, makes me feel quite queasy. But what should I have done? What could I have done? Gemma is still silent.

'I was on the verge of telling Valentina myself, you know, but because it involved you I just couldn't bring myself to. Not yet anyway. Instead I churn it over and over in my head, getting nowhere. For God's sake, Gemma, stop playing with that paper napkin. It's driving me nuts.'

Gemma shakes her head again, but lets go of the napkin. As if in slow motion she looks up and starts to speak. 'Well it's a good thing you didn't tell Valentina. Antony doesn't know about Rob. Rob hasn't told Valentina. Nothing has been said.' I can't help it. I breathe a small sigh of relief. It feels like a stay of execution. Valentina still not knowing feels like maybe Valentina need never know.

Gemma's delivery is clipped, dispassionate. Her tone resembles a recorded announcement, like the one on the tube: *The doors are now closing. Please mind the gap between the doors and the platform.* This holding in of her emotions is a temporary tactic, and she won't be able to keep it going. I'm fearful of the emotional outburst that is sure to follow, the flow of feeling, like a ruptured femoral artery, which will be hard to stem.

'*Nothing?* You mean nothing has been said by anyone to anyone? So what is it? Are you getting cold feet? Do I have to guess or are you going to tell me?'

'It's Antony. I think he's done it to spite me, I really do. I think the conniving bastard has done it to spite me.'

'Done what?'

'Got MS.'

'Got *MS*! What are you talking about? Antony has *MS*? But you never said a word. How can this be? When did you find out? What are the symptoms? Are you sure? Oh God, Gemma, this is horrific. Just when I thought things couldn't get any worse.'

Gemma's voice continues to be a dull monotone. 'The MRI scan says it's definite. Apparently MRI picks up ninety per cent of suspected cases.'

'You're going to have to play this from the beginning, Gemma. I can't believe you didn't consult the family doctor, i.e. me, about this. You must have had some inkling for quite a while.'

'But I didn't. You know how elsewhere I've been, with the book, with Rob.' As Gemma says the name Rob her voice sinks to barely a whisper. 'With Rob,' she repeats, bowing her head again. She talks into her lap. 'I'm trapped, Julie. I can't leave Antony now.'

I reach over and place a finger under Gemma's chin. 'Look at me, Gemma, please. I can't talk to you with your head on your lap.' Reluctantly, with my help, she lifts her head again. Her little face appears smaller than I've ever seen it.

Slowly, hesitantly, Gemma pours out her pain. Her voice is weak, hoarse, and she has to keep clearing her throat so she can continue. Leaving Antony now she tells me would be like watching a man fall over in the street and rather than helping him up on his feet again kicking his head in instead. In fact falling over in the street is exactly what did happen to Antony. Only when he arrived home with stitches in his elbow and a cut hand he nonchalantly told Gemma he'd tripped over a paving stone while answering his mobile, not even considering that there might be more to it than that.

'Well it's easily done,' I say, 'people fall over all the time. What about other symptoms?'

Gemma describes to me the blurred vision in one eye, which

he kept quiet about. Apparently he thought it might be the start of a cataract, but after a few weeks it cleared up again so he didn't bother to do anything about it. The only thing he did mention was a bit of tingling, a bit of pins and needles which was recurring.

I ask Gemma how long has this been going on.

'Six months, nine months, maybe more. You know Antony, it's one of his better traits, being too busy with more lofty matters to worry over his health.'

I remember how it used to infuriate Gemma that he'd dismiss any ailments the boys got when they were little, and how she'd end up having to worry for both of them, but I also remember her telling me that she was rather grateful not to have a hypochondriac husband.

'Anyway the eye symptoms came back and he decided to mention it to the GP and then all the other stuff came out and then a while later he had the scan.'

'And when did he tell you?'

'Last Tuesday evening. The same evening I was planning to tell him about Rob and Rob was planning to tell Valentina.'

I involuntarily shiver. 'Simultaneous revelations. Synchronised bombshells. The mind boggles. So you managed to stop Rob telling her.'

'The minute Antony told me I ran straight to the bathroom and texted Rob to not say anything. Goodness knows what Antony must have been thinking . . . There he was saying, "Darling, I've got a bit of bad news," and no sooner had he told me what the bad news was than I was scooting out of the room like a rabbit on LSD. So there we have it. Antony has an incurable illness. I'm in prison. Life. Over.'

This is too much to take in. 'Surgery is a doddle compared to all this,' I say unhelpfully. 'Uterine haemorrhage at four o'clock this afternoon just a walk in the park.'

'You doctor, me nurse by the looks of it.'

I grope for something positive. Straw-clutching more like it. I start with the stuff I do understand, even though it's not my speciality. I tell Gemma not to focus on the worst-case scenario. That the disease might not progress rapidly, that he won't necessarily be very debilitated and may remain quite well for many years to come. I also point out that many people who get MS cope very well indeed. How much the drugs have improved. And the fact that the relapses can be very far apart.

'You're missing the point, little sister,' says Gemma. This comment doesn't surprise me, I was deliberately missing the point, playing for time before having to express an opinion or give advice on matters which are quite beyond me. 'The truth, Julie,' Gemma continues, 'is that I'm thinking about poor me rather than poor him. I know that getting MS is not his fault, and that it's an awful thing to have, but I'm furious with him anyway for putting me in this position. I mean why couldn't he have got MS, if he was going to have to get it, next month, or next year, when I'd have been gone? Why does it have to be right now, just as I'm about to leave him? I don't want to be his wife any more, Julie. I don't want to be Antony's wife.'

'Oh, Gemma, I feel utterly at a loss as to what to say that might help you. But maybe if you're absolutely sure that your marriage is dead it would be better to go now rather than ruin your whole life.' I'm not sure I believe this, something at the back of my mind is clinging to the forlorn hope that two marriages can be saved here, but at the same time I don't want Gemma to be miserable for the rest of her days. Miserable, bitter and full of regrets. Poor Gemma. The blue-grey circles under her eyes seem to take up most of the available space on her cheeks.

'I'm damned if I do, damned if I don't, aren't I? Can you imagine what Sam and Andy would say if I left now? They'd say I'd cruelly abandoned their father just when he needed me most and they'd probably never speak to me again. They wouldn't forgive me, I know they wouldn't.' I sense that Gemma could bear the loss of Sam and Andy's love even less than she could bear losing Rob.

'If I'd left before, I really think they'd have understood. In fact there have been times when each of them, individually, has asked me how Antony and I ever managed to get together in the first place. But this is different. This changes everything.'

'You've always put the boys first, Gemma,' I say, and realise that this is something I am quite sincere about. 'All those years while they were growing up and you put your writing on the back burner to look after them, and look after my two as well whenever I needed you to. Perhaps it's time to think of your own needs now.' I'm trying to explore all the angles, see every possible point of view, before committing myself to any one of them.

'Get real, Julie. How could I live with myself? He's not been a bad husband. I mean not really bad, as in mentally cruel or physically violent. Selfish, yes. Bombastic, yes. A bit of a tyrant, yes. But not evil, and a generous provider, and maybe not that much different from a lot of successful, ambitious men whose fathers never thought them good enough. The trouble is I just don't want to be in his company, don't want to listen to his droning on about things that don't interest me, don't want to share a bed or even the breakfast table with him. It's not like you and Walt who have so much in common.' Do we, I wonder. 'We inhabit different planets, always have. And now that the kids are grown up there's no point in us remaining together as far as I'm concerned, no point at all . . . except for this.'

I look at Gemma and want for us to be little children again, me piecing together skeletons on the floor, Gemma sitting cross legged on my bed, scribbling madly in her notebook, the one with Jumbo the Elephant on the cover. Everything seemed so simple and so certain back then. If I start casting moral judgments, like I did when Gemma first told me about her and Rob, I will risk losing Gemma altogether. I can't afford that. I love my sister too much.

'I can't make your decision for you, Gemma, and nor can I play down your dilemma, but I owe it to you to express myself honestly. I'm going to say this once, and then I'm never going to say it again: a bit of me wants to crack open a bottle of champagne to celebrate the fact that Valentina and Rob have the chance of staying together if you don't leave Antony. On the other hand you're my big sister and I so don't want you to be unhappy. And if you and Rob really are meant to be together for the next twenty-five years or for however long you live, then you're as entitled as the next person. And Antony, well I care about him, and think this MS business absolutely awful, but if I have to have a pecking order of people I care about he's not at the top of it. Oh Gemma, I've become a born-again romantic. I just want happy ever after for everyone. All this marital mayhem is not supposed to be happening at this point of our lives.'

'I can't bear to think you hate me for falling in love with Rob.'

'If I were to hate you for anything, it would be for hurting Valentina. But I know you're not a predatory man-snatcher or deliberate, callous marriage wrecker, I know that you wouldn't have done this lightly. I don't blame you for not wanting to be with Antony, I just wish you'd found someone less close to home to fall in love with.'

'You've certainly changed your tune since last time.'

'Well I've had time to think. And stuff has happened, stuff that has changed my perspective a bit.'

'What kind of stuff? I'd be rather grateful not to talk about me for a second or two.'

I can see Giovanni coming towards us.

'Good evening, beautiful ladies,' he says. 'Tonight I see no disturb sign at your table. Give me order and I leave you alone.'

I smile up at him gratefully. 'Yes, we have much to process tonight, Giovanni. Shall we share a pizza, Gemma?'

Gemma shrugs. 'Whatever you like.'

'OK, Giovanni. A pizza margharita to share and a mixed salad.' He is gone.

'That man sees everything,' I say. 'No wonder this place is so successful.'

'So tell me about the stuff,' says Gemma.

'Well you're not the only one with a dilemma and you're not the only one with a sex life.'

'You mean you've . . .'

There's nothing to smile about, but when I think about Patrick I can't help myself. I smile.

'Who'd have thought,' says Gemma, smiling, too. 'Who? When? Where? How? I want details. All of them.'

'A man. A couple of weeks ago. At the RAC Club. As for how, I'm not sure I can answer that question. And in any case it was a one-off.'

'Well that's all very informative I don't think.' Gemma's grinning now. At least I've managed to distract her. 'Why the one-off? Married, is he? Or a doc at the hospital and you don't want to start a scandal?'

'Neither actually,' I reply enigmatically.

'So what's stopping you? Surely you can't feel guilty about Walt.'

'He's off limits, that's all.'

'Are you going to tell me or not?'

'Of course I am, it's just that I feel I've been so foolish, and I don't like you to think me the fool.'

'I'd rather we were both fools than be a fool on my own.'

'Well you know Katy has this boyfriend Chris . . .'

Gemma interrupted. 'Didn't I tell you? No, of course not, we weren't speaking, but Katy actually rang me from university last week and told me all about him. It's lurve, isn't it? The real deal.'

'So it seems. The thing is Chris has a dad . . .'

'Well there's a surprise.'

'I mean a dad who . . .'

'No!'

'I'm afraid yes.'

'Holy shit!'

'Indeed. So you can see I have a dilemma, too.'

'Don't go there, little sister.'

'But I already have.'

'I mean don't go there again. Mother screwing daughter's boyfriend's dad not good. Especially when the daughter concerned is Katy.'

'I know that. He keeps texting, though, clearly not as bothered about his son's sensitivities as I am about my daughter's. I'm seeing him one more time, to put the lid on it once and for all.'

Gemma raises an eyebrow quizzically. 'Is that so?'

'Don't look at me like that. Nothing will happen, I swear.'

'So why the up close and personal then? Haven't you heard of the Dear John text? Or the Dear John posting on Facebook? They're all the rage these days. Or you could take the old-fashioned route and write him a letter.'

'I . . . I . . .?'

'I'm "on fire" perhaps. I'm "hungry for more" perhaps? Can't say I'm quite convinced that you have the resolve you feel you ought.'

'Actually I'm hoping that I'll see him and think him crass and boorish and unattractive, which was my first impression when he nearly murdered me on the motorway, which is another long story I won't go into now. I'm hoping that when I went to bed with him I was simply too drunk to notice the negatives.'

'And how likely is that?'

'Not likely at all. I should cancel, shouldn't I?' I am astonished to find myself sounding like a sixteen-year-old, although thinking back I have the feeling I was a lot more grounded and sensible then than I am today. Could it be that I was actually more mature as a teenager than I am as a fifty-three-year-old? 'I don't really need to ask, Gemma, I *know* I should cancel.'

Gemma clamps her hands at the back of her scalp, and elbows to the fore, squeezes her arms against the side of her head. She rocks back and forth as if in prayer. When she's stopped rocking she crosses her hands on the table in front of her and says, 'I'm hardly in the position to tell anyone what to do. But it's not love is it, not after one meeting. So if it's simply sex you've discovered you need there are plenty more blokes out there who'll be willing to take Patrick's place. The danger is in getting to know and like him more and I wouldn't have thought you'd want to give yourself that opportunity. Not in the circumstances. Rob and I allowed ourselves to creep up on one another, and by the time we realised what was going on it was too late. But this, you can nip in the bud.'

'You're right, Gemma, of course you are. I'll cancel him.'

And I would have done, honestly I would, but that was before the weather changed and the temperatures shot up and the forecast was for a prolonged heat wave. Katy rang to say she needed more stuff, Patrick was going up the following weekend to see Chris, and it would be great, she said, if I could just meet up with Patrick for a quick drink and give him what she needed.

'But Katy,' I protested, 'you're coming back for the Easter holidays straight after that.'

'Please, Mum, it's not that big a deal, is it? And I thought you liked Patrick. I mean your social life isn't that packed is it, it's not as though you don't have the time.'

'No, Katy, it's not, but you didn't sound too pleased the other time I had a quick drink with Patrick.'

'Please, Mum.' And so I agreed.

Chapter Twenty

Time works in mysterious ways. In the dead of night, when you cannot sleep, so slowly does time move you feel you could pluck the seconds out, one by one, and hold them in the palm of your hand before they slip away. I'm not sleeping much lately.

In theatre, time can mean the difference between life and death, every second counts. Take a crash section, the highest grade of emergency in which there's an immediate threat to the mother or the foetus. Thirty minutes, say the guidelines. You have thirty minutes to get from decision to delivery.

With no time even to sign the papers, it's common practice to verbally consent the mother as she's being whisked off to theatre, giving her the essential information but without having time to explain properly. Everyone swings into action, but none of the medical procedures can be disregarded. A full blood count is taken, and a 'group and save' done so blood can be put on standby in case a transfusion is required. We all get into our scrubs and the team members at the sharp end must scrub up so they are totally sterile. A Foley catheter is inserted. The anaesthetist gets one shot only at the spinal block. If it doesn't take full effect fast it's straight on to a general anaesthetic and the dad, if he's in the room, is asked to leave. If the dad kicks up that's precious seconds which are ticking by and he needs to be told in no uncertain terms what delay might mean.

There are plenty of other examples where time is critical. I was recently called in to facilitate a delivery in which the baby's head was out but the shoulders were stuck. Shoulder dystocia to give it its proper name. Usually it's plain sailing after the head is out as the head is the biggest part of the baby, but with mothers who are diabetic, as was the case in this instance, there is often the added complication that the baby carries a lot of fat around the neck and shoulder, with a larger ratio of shoulder to head circumference than in babies of non-diabetic mothers. The baby's anterior shoulder was lodged behind the mother's pubic bone. The registrar had tried a number of the techniques, but the baby wasn't budging. We have protocols for such situations.

In the case of shoulder dystocia we use the mnemonic HELPERR, and go through each stage in careful, planned succession. H signifies to call for Help. If a midwife is in charge at this point she bleeps for the obstetricians and the paediatricians. E is Evaluate for Episiotomy. You need to make a cut so you can get a hand in to do the necessary manoeuvres. L is for legs, getting them into the McRoberts position, which means one helper on each side of the patient, each holding up a leg and bringing them as close as possible to the woman's abdomen. This reduces the curvature of the spine, and makes the tailbone tip back to create a crucial extra centimetre in the pelvis. For the mother, each stage is progressively traumatic. If still no joy the next protocol is P, which stands for pressure. Suprapubic pressure may work at this stage to dislodge the shoulder, but on this occasion the registrar had tried all of this, and nothing was doing the trick. That's when I got bleeped in. The baby was beginning to turn dark blue and the mother, who had declined analgesia, except for gas and air, was in horrific pain. Her husband was panicking and shouting. 'Get off my wife,' he was screaming at the team. To him it must have looked like they'd descended like locusts and he was ready to haul them off her. I calculated we had about three minutes before that baby was in serious trouble, and the mother soon after. 'Your wife and baby might die if we don't get the baby out soon,' I hissed in the ear of the desperate dad, hoping his wife wouldn't hear and shocking him into silence. In a situation like this you don't have time to think, you just follow the drill, the drill which the team has rehearsed on mannequins in training and again on refresher drills. You do what you have to.

E is for Enter, placing your fingers into the vagina to try to dislodge the shoulder with internal rotation. And then it's on to the first R. E and R were my job. R was trying to remove the posterior arm by performing something called the 'cat lick' manoeuvre, sweeping the baby's arm over its face like a cat licking its face, only in reverse. That's when I heard it go. That's when I heard the pop that told me I'd broken the baby's humerus. We all heard it, it was that loud. The baby was delivered, safely, without resorting to the final R which involves rolling the patient onto all fours.

Afterwards you feel drained, elated, conscious that you've saved lives, conscious that you could have lost them. Sometimes the images stay with me for days. A deeply distressed mother in horrible pain, a distraught dad and a baby with a fracture, albeit one that will hopefully heal without complications. Lay people think you're immune from emotional involvement. It doesn't work like this. You care, you have to. But if you treated everyone as though they were your sister or your daughter you wouldn't be able to look after them objectively. That's why you don't operate on your relatives. Too much emotional involvement can get in the way. But you have to care, you can't be indifferent. The passage of time or experience doesn't change this.

It's not over when the baby's out. Then comes the writing of the notes. This can't be rushed, for two reasons. The first is that precise recording can be useful reference for how to deal with such incidents in future. Second, obstetrics is the most litigious branch of medicine, and it's becoming increasingly litigious all the time. Sometimes there is come-back years after a baby is born if developmental problems manifest themselves later, and can be traced back to the birth. That's why every manoeuvre is recorded and timed during the actual procedures so it can all go in the notes. In case one day it ends up in court. By the time we'd done the debrief on the shoulder dystocia case, written it all up, agreed between the team that the notes were accurate and complete, explained to the parents exactly what had taken place and why, completed the audit and clinical incidence form, almost two more hours had gone by. It was two in the morning. Shattered? The whole team were.

Sometimes I think Walt sees me as an automaton, working as if programmed to do so by some internal computer, but not actually feeling anything. It's my own fault in a way. I don't let on to him, the girls or any of my friends how, when things go wrong, the guilt lingers, even when I know I've done everything I could. I regard this lack of detachment as a fundamental flaw, so I keep it hidden, from my colleagues and juniors of course, but also from those I love. What we, in medicine, call reflective practice, is our way of learning from experience. When reflective practice morphs into beating yourself up for not always being perfect, you know you're heading for trouble.

If you do have the luxury of time in surgery, as in an elected Caesarean, you should use it. With the mother awake, but not in pain, the atmosphere can be relaxed and informal, joyful even. A natural childbirth may be the ideal, but a C-section can also be a positive experience for the mother. There might be music on in the background, and there's time to explain everything that's going on. Hurrying, when you don't have to, is bad practice. I remember, as a junior doctor, being bullied by a consultant to 'get a move on' as I stitched up a patient after an appendectomy. The consultant had a dinner appointment, and I'm not proud to admit I wanted to impress him. The result: a nasty scar on a fifteen-year-old girl that would never fully fade. I like to give my patients time if I can; I see it as my duty of care.

Time. Five months have passed since Walt left and he is ebbing away from me. I no longer turn over in my bed and expect to see him there, no longer obsessively check my emails. It seems like both yesterday and forever ago that he was here. Just as Aggie moved out, the builders moved in. Quite what I'm doing spending several thousand quid on a wet room I neither need nor particularly want makes no sense to anyone I know, me in particular. But I have spent four entire Saturdays choosing tiles and taps and sinks and towel rails and sometimes I picture Walt standing under the shower, singing at the top of his voice, and slathering himself in soap, and I feel better. As the dust rises so does the sense that I am deluded.

My mother, caught more tightly in Alzheimer's determined grip, has lost all sense of time. She gets up in the middle of the night and wants to know why it's dark outside. During the day she closes the curtains and goes to bed because she thinks it's night. Last time I saw her she said, 'A long time ago, didn't you used to be my daughter?'

'I still am,' I said, choking back the tears. 'And I always will be, and I love you very much.' What else was there to say? Annette is taking Aricept, one of the few drugs thought to be effective, and she has suffered no discernible side effects other than mild nausea at the beginning. There's no way of really knowing whether her symptoms would be progressing faster without it, but neither do we want to take the risk of her stopping taking it at this stage. Fleetingly I wonder if my own father would have been as patient and dedicated as Paul who cares for her round the clock without complaint.

Tess is 34 weeks pregnant, the pre-eclampsia confirmed some weeks back. She may require a Caesarean section. I count the days, knowing that each one she can hold on will allow the baby to grow stronger. The baby needs more time.

Aggie has moved back in with Charles. She says they've discussed nothing beyond her promise of future fidelity. Charles is being so damned English about it. He told Aggie that it was in the past, he didn't want to rake it up. I think of Pandora's box and hope, for both their sakes, the lid remains tightly closed. We had a meal, the three of us. Aggie talked incessantly about Ana and Maricel, now back in the Philippines. I have this sense that she's waiting for Maricel to die so she can claim Ana for herself. Biding her time so to speak. I haven't said this, of course, because to accuse her of such a thing, whether I am right or wrong, would be the death of our friendship. Aggie has persuaded Charles to sponsor

Ana's further education and living expenses. But she hasn't yet mentioned that she wants Ana to move in with them. That Ana may not wish to come back, or go on to further education in this country, is a no-go area.

In bed with Patrick, time is suspended, it simply no longer exists. In a way I no longer exist when I am with Patrick. I am a person outside of myself. Perhaps this is why I have continued this affair, despite my promises to myself to the contrary. In bed with Patrick I enter a territory that is quite apart from my life, a kind of dream world that doesn't impinge on my reality as a doctor, a mother, a friend, a sister, a daughter, an abandoned wife. We meet in hotel bedrooms, not restaurants, bars, cinemas or theatres. We don't walk in the park together or go for country rides. I won't allow Patrick inside my home, for fear of traces; I don't go to his home, it's too far out of town for mid-week trysts. Too far out is fact, but it's also an excuse. I am curious about how and where Patrick lives, but at the same time I don't want to recognise anything that is his, the flowers in his garden, the paintings on his walls, the colour of his front door, in case I inadvertently say something to Katy, in case I expose my treachery. So I don't go to Patrick's home and he is not permitted in mine.

Here, in bed, is what I want. I want only this space with Patrick. A parallel universe of unfamiliar beds in unfamiliar rooms, pillows, sheets, towels, skin on skin, a time to be without thought, only sensation. Am I becoming addicted to the very thing to which I had become so indifferent? Sometimes, the morning after Patrick, the smell of him, of us, is still lodged just inside my nostrils. I breathe in and I am back in that space that I've never before so intensely inhabited. I am tempted not to wash at all after sex with Patrick. I love the damp, loamy scent of our love-making and how it lingers. Sweat and saliva, sweet and sour, fluids sticky and silky and elastic. It astonishes me, this sense of sexual self-discovery. This side of me that has taken more than fifty years to reveal itself. And yet I feel it can only ever be a thing apart. I'd trade it in a moment to regain the status quo, to wind the clock back to a time when Walt and I were secure in our love for one another. But would I wind back to Walt as he was when the left? No, I would not.

A routine of sorts has been established between Patrick and me. We meet on average twice a week, but never the night before I have an operating list. I am fanatical about getting a decent night's sleep before I operate, although recently it has been more a case of lying in bed and resting, eyes wide open, than actually sleeping.

Patrick fits in with me, because his work as a management consultant is intermittent and doesn't rely on regular hours. When Katy and Chris were back for the Easter holidays we didn't meet at all. I demanded we didn't even send one another texts so fearful was I of Katy finding out about us. Katy was home for a whole month and I only saw Patrick twice, in the week that Katy and Chris went down to Cornwall. But since the end of April a pattern has been re-established. Now another term has sped by, and any day now Katy will be home at the end of her first academic year. She and Chris are showing no signs of wear and tear. They're planning a month-long trip to Thailand. Maybe then, with them halfway across the world, I'll go out for supper with Patrick. Maybe then it will feel safe.

Patrick is beginning to become frustrated with the clandestine nature of our affair.

'It's good in bed with you,' he told me the other night, 'very good indeed, but I want to find out if it's good out of bed with you as well. I'm beginning to think you only want me for my six-pack, which is both flattering and somehow not.'

'Well it's a nice body,' I replied, 'not bad at all considering its great age, though I've yet to find the six-pack lurking beneath the layers of flesh. Does it worry you, being my sex object?'

'No one's ever called me that before,' he grinned. 'But I rather expected, at this stage of my life, to be spending my evenings playing bridge, not holed up in some hotel room with a sexy lady doctor who can't get enough.'

'And what's to stop you?'

'Nothing, I suppose, but we'd need a foursome for a game, and I can't see you agreeing to that.'

'A foursome? Try me,' I laughed, running my fingernails down his breast bone and through the dark hairs, flecked with grey. 'I think a foursome could be fun.'

'I'd like to have a proper relationship with you, Julie, not one confined to the four walls of a hotel room, with meals delivered on trays. And you creeping out in the middle of the night when you've had your evil way with me.' Patrick smiled, but I could tell that it was a forced attempt at casualness.

I drew my hand back from Patrick's chest, felt my body shifting away a centimetre or two, an automatic response to Patrick's request for a different level of intimacy, a level I am unable to supply.

'Hey, my girl,' he said, 'I hate it when that cloud passes over your face.'

'It's impossible, Patrick,' I replied.

I am surprised at how coolly I can lock this affair with Patrick into a box so separate from the rest of my life, how the cycle of desire, its brief fulfilment in the act of sex and rapid rekindling, playing on an unbroken loop, over and over, has become, for me, a complete world in itself. I better understand now Aggie's affairs. A sexual relationship can serve many purposes; hers provided temporary respite from the burden of her infertility, a burden she felt every time she made love to her husband, never when being fucked by a man who meant little to her. I don't put Patrick in that category, he does mean something to me – more perhaps than I am prepared to face up to. But for me, for now, sex with Patrick is exquisite escapism, something I can excuse myself for, vis à vis Katy, so long as I don't overstep the emotional mark. I realise I'm playing with fire, but my resolve to keep away from Patrick has proved a feeble thing. *Frailty, thy name is woman.*

We do talk, Patrick and I, for hours at a time in anonymous rooms, but we've not once met without having sex. I have this idea, spurious as it must seem, that the night we don't have sex is the night it will end between us, because to curl up cosily in Patrick's arms, just to hold one another, would be a definite danger sign. A signal that we were becoming emotionally entangled, something I dare not even contemplate. Only Gemma knows about me and Patrick. Having ignored her advice and having gone to see Patrick again with the clothes Katy wanted taken to university, I knew the minute I set eyes on him that we would have sex again.

Gemma and I are back at Napoli's, in our usual corner.

'I was all ready to lie about it to you, Gemma, but when it came to it I couldn't. I couldn't keep this thing with Patrick going without telling you.'

'Well, I hope you realise just how dangerous a game this is,' she replies. 'You are jeopardising your relationship with Katy and possibly even screwing up Chris and Katy's relationship at the same time.'

'Sometimes I wonder why it should be so taboo,' I say, realising I sound petulant, realising how supremely selfishly I'm behaving. 'I know that it *is* taboo, but I haven't quite got the measure of why.'

'Well, it seems pretty obvious to me. And the only reason for it not being obvious to you is that you don't want to face facts. Look, there might not be consanguinity, but there's a definite whiff of incest about it. And think how awful it would be if Katy and Chris broke up, and she was left bereft and broken hearted while you and Patrick continued to have an affair. Or if she knew about the affair and then the two of you fell out, how would that affect her and Chris? And how could Katy introduce Chris to Walt, and perhaps Walt to Patrick, knowing that Chris's dad and you were screwing one another? The more I think about it, Julie, the more I can see the myriad possibilities for resentment, misunderstanding and a deep sense of betrayal.'

'The thing is, the betrayal has already happened. And I'm going to have to live with it until such time as I have the strength to end it with Patrick.'

'So how do you really feel about Patrick?'

'As a person you mean?'

'As opposed to a fish or a root vegetable or a DVD? Of course as a person.'

'I think he's funny and sexy and probably kind. He's smart and successful, both of which are attractive characteristics. He's also still very much in mourning. There's something that worries me. He just doesn't seem to share my guilt about having an affair with his son's girlfriend's mum.'

'Don't take this badly, little sister, but at least he's following through. Surely the guilt thing is a bit of a cop-out.'

'You mean I'm a hypocrite.'

'Not exactly, but I can't see the point of the angst. Either stop the affair and put an end to the guilt, or carry on the affair and ditch the guilt.'

'It's easier said than done, Gemma. And talk about guilt, *you're* wracked with it.'

'But that's because Antony has become ill. I didn't feel guilty before, not about him, not about Valentina. But now I'd feel appalling if I left.'

'And what about Rob? You've committed yourself to him. How do you feel about backing out? He'll be heartbroken, won't he?'

Gemma stifles a sob. 'Right now I don't believe that any of this is happening. Not having Rob will make life impossible. Not staying with Antony is impossible, too.'

'I suppose you could carry on your affair with Rob indefinitely and stay with Antony.'

'That's not helpful, Julie. We want to be together, not adulterers.'

'Then you're fucked.'

'You and me both.' Gemma's eyes are glistening with tears. 'I think it's time we changed the subject, don't you?'

'How's the book going?'

'I typed my favourite words in all the world this morning.'

'Which are . . .?'

'THE and END.'

'Gemma, that's brilliant. We should be celebrating, not sitting here like two miserable, menopausal old biddies. Giovanni!' I call. Giovanni is at our table in less than two seconds. 'Two glasses of champagne. My clever clogs literary genius of a sister has just finished writing her new bestseller.'

'Then you should be very happy,' says Giovanni, bending down to kiss Gemma on both cheeks.

'Indeed I should,' she replies.

Until the champagne arrives Gemma and I say very little. We sit, clasping each other's hands across the table, deep inside our own thoughts.

'I'm so lucky to have you,' I say to Gemma as Giovanni places the flutes in front of us.

'And I'm lucky to have you. I have so much to be thankful for,' says Gemma.

'Me, too.'

'What shall we drink to?' asks Gemma.

'Your book, of course. To your first Number One bestseller. To "The Nail in the Coffin".'

We clink our glasses and sip.

'And now,' says Gemma, 'we must make another toast.'

'To whom?'

'To us. To the sisterhood of secrets and lies.'

We clink again and sip.

'And now,' I say, 'let us drink to our children.'

'To the offspring who make it all worthwhile.'

More clinking, more sipping.

'To the men without whom our children wouldn't be possible?' I pose this more as a question than a statement.

'Do we have to?' asks Gemma, giggling now.

'I'm afraid we do.'

'And what about our lovers? Do we toast them as well?'

'Probably best not to,' I snigger. 'Probably best to leave them out.'

'Except we can't leave them out,' says Gemma.

'I suppose not. Oh, all right, to husbands and lovers.' Further clinking and sipping.

'There's enough in my glass for one more toast,' says Gemma. 'What shall it be?'

'To love,' I say, but this time I can't manage to clink my glass. And neither can Gemma. We both have tears pouring down our faces.

When the pizza arrives neither of us has the appetite to eat it. Gemma prods at her side with a fork, putting down her fork and then picking it up again moments later to prod at it again. I peel the crusts and nibble at them disconsolately.

'I'm whacked,' I say.

'Me, too,' says Gemma. 'I'll ask for the bill.'

When Giovanni looks at what's left, he says, 'The pizza no good? You no eat, you no pay.'

'The pizza's fine,' I insist, 'but neither of us is hungry.'

'Then you no pay,' he repeats.

I look at the last dregs of champagne, for the final toast we never managed.

'To Giovanni,' I say.

Gemma smiles. 'To Giovanni.'

Our mood is broken.

'It's OK, Giovanni,' I say. 'I've suddenly got my appetite back.'

'Me, too,' echoes Gemma. Giovanni walks away, looking pleased with himself.

'Time,' I say. 'Time will sort it out, one way or another. How is Antony by the way?'

'Well, he seems to be in remission. In fact he seems almost well, which makes me wonder if now might be a good time to . . .'

I sense a commotion, coming from the direction of the entrance. Raised voices, brought into sharp relief by the effect they have of quieting the chatter of the other diners. I turn around to look at what's going on. A woman's voice, screaming in Italian. '*Dove la puttana? Dove la puttana?*' I know what this means. It means 'Where's the prostitute?' Giovanni shouting back, something about *tranquille*, about keeping calm.

Gemma is looking, too, but I need my glasses for this distance and I pick up my bag and begin to rummage, fascinated at the prospect of a major row and wondering how the generally genial Giovanni will handle it. I hear a small whimper. It's coming from Gemma.

'What is it, Gemma? What's going on?'

Gemma whimpers again. 'Over there, near the door, by the reception desk . . .'

'You mean where the screaming's coming from . . . the ranting Italian woman who I can hear but not see?'

'Yes, her . . .'

'What is she on about? Something about a whore . . .'

'Yes,' says Gemma quietly. 'Something about a whore.'

'A case of mistaken restaurant.'

'No, I don't think so.'

'You mean we have a whore in our midst.'

'Not exactly. No, not exactly.' A strangulated squawk emanates from Gemma's mouth.

And then it dawns on me. 'No,' I say, 'it can't be . . .'

'It can and it is . . .'

'Oh no, this is the worst . . .'

'And it's about to get worse still . . .'

Valentina thunders towards us, eyes wide and flashing, hair swinging. Gemma is trembling. I'm paralysed. '*Puttana!*' cries Valentina as she reaches our table, grabs Gemma's water glass and flings its contents in her face. 'And you. You, too. *Puttana!*' My water glass is empty, but Valentina turns to the next table where there is a small espresso cooling in a cup. To the sound of gasps from the couple sitting there she picks up the cup and flicks the contents at my face, scalding me. I shriek as the hot coffee burns my skin. 'Stop it, Valentina, stop it.'

'I hate you. I hate you both,' she screams. 'First they steal my child, now my husband. You have ruined my life. You were meant to be friends, both of you. You, Julie, were my special friend, and now this, gloating over . . .'

I try to wipe away the coffee from my face.

'No, Valentina, please, it's not like that, not like that at all.'

Valentina seizes the white tablecloth, and in one huge dramatic sweep pulls it and everything on it from the table. Glass shatters, china fragments, food flies, as Valentina turns on her heels and runs out of the restaurant. Diners jump up from their chairs in fright and fascination as Gemma and I stand facing one another, stunned, silent, unable to do anything at all.

'Is OK, is OK everybody,' says Giovanni, making his way towards us through the thronging, gawping diners. 'These two of my best customers. Crazy lady. You know she Italian. All Italians crazy. Like me.'

One of the other customers shouts out, 'For a moment, Giovanni, we thought she was your jealous wife.'

'Or jealous mistress,' shouts another regular.

'I wouldn't put it past him,' shouts a third. 'Quite a stunner she was.' And they're beginning to laugh, perhaps a little nervously. The drama has given them something new to talk about, it has made their night.

As Giovanni and his staff clear up, Gemma and I are ignored again. My face is hot but the coffee had already cooled and I'm not properly burnt.

'Go, go,' says Giovanni as we make our way towards the coat stand.

'I'll come in and sort out the damages,' I say.

'Sure, no worries, go home.'

'The unravelling has begun,' says Gemma as we step out into the night.

'It's like one of your books,' I say.

'Well, no one's been murdered.'

'No, not yet.'

We hug one another and turn in separate directions. As I walk along the street in the direction of home, I pull out my mobile from my bag and text Valentina.

'I was still working out what to do. I would have spoken, I just needed more time.'

Time moves in mysterious ways, I think again. And I head home, to my empty house.

Where are you when I need you, Walt? Don't you know you should be here? Why don't you? Why don't you know it?

Chapter Twenty-One

As I approach my front driveway, beyond the forecourt where my car is parked I can see an outline of something in the porch. The light is not on so at first all I can make out is a dark mass. Then, as I accustom my sight to the gloom, I startle at what appears to be a figure, sitting sideways on to the street, knees bent, head hanging forwards, arms hugging shins. My instinct is to reach for my mobile to dial 999 and make ready to run. But there's something familiar about the outline. For a split second I think, *Walt! He's home. He must have forgotten his key.* It's late and I'm tired and my mind is playing tricks on me, as it often does where Walt is concerned.

Realistically it could be a tramp, taking shelter from the rain that started to bucket down a few minutes ago. I'm already drenched through without my umbrella, quite forgotten following the furore caused by Valentina, probably picked up gratefully by another diner. I try to blink the rain from my eyes, to get a better view. I'm hoping the person in the doorway hasn't spotted me. My eyes dart anxiously up and down the street, looking to see if there's anyone else around in the event I need to call for help.

The question is what action do I take. I'd certainly better not go any closer to the person in the doorway, and it definitely is a person, a person who might be not just a sad old tramp but a drunk and violent one, or maybe not a tramp but a junkie or a housebreaker waiting for a chance, waiting for a vulnerable woman to turn up alone at her front door. A vulnerable woman *alone. Alone.* My heart is beginning to race. I take a step or two back in the direction from which I've come.

I stop again, bedraggled, wet, exhausted, *alone.* A wave of almost pleasurable self-pity washes over me, an alluringly masochistic moment of thinking, *I could simply succumb to my fate, I could allow this stranger to attack me, perhaps even murder me, and my life will be over, and everything will be simple once more.* There is a strange sweetness in this notion, like the siren's call, and I find myself wanting to stay with the moment, edging tentatively forward again in the direction of the figure in the doorway. Almost simultaneously my survival instinct kicks in and a jolt of fear, like a small punch from inside my belly, brings me back to the possibility of danger.

The person in the porch slowly raises his – or is it her? – head, and turns towards me.

. 'Julie, is that you? Quick, come in from the rain.'

I recognise Rob's voice right away.

The drama of the situation has dissipated. I am saved, but being saved means nothing has been resolved, nothing is as it should be. 'Thank God it's only you,' I mutter, unconvinced, as I approach the doorway.

Rob hauls himself up with difficulty, as though uncertain he can carry his own heft.

'You're soaked, poor thing,' he says. 'Look at you.'

'You've no right to be here, Rob,' I say, exploding into anger. 'You frightened me half to death, what the hell do you think you're up to? If you so much as dare to ask if you can stay I might have to come at you with one of my most lethal surgical instruments. I've only just got rid of Aggie, remember, and if you think you can come between me and Valentina you are so wrong. She already hates me, and if anyone's side needs taking it's going to be hers not yours.'

'But, Julie . . .'

'But nothing. You'd better come inside and we'll talk. About bloody time, too.' I know I'm contradicting myself but I'm angry at Rob for being here, and even more angry at Rob for not being here sooner. Much sooner. I don't appreciate ranting in other people, and even less in myself, but I can't seem to stop. 'It's not like you haven't known for ages that I know all about you and Gemma. You didn't have to wait for Valentina to find out. But not once in all this time did you think to call me. Even putting you and Gemma aside for a moment, even putting Valentina aside for a second, didn't it occur to you that I could do with a friendly male ear with Walt gone? We're supposed to be mates, aren't we? Not withstanding that you've been screwing my sister, you bastard.'

It's as though all my anger, not just at Rob, but at Walt, at Gemma, and at my own inability to make everyone see the light and stay dutifully married, has finally coalesced in an outpouring of outrage.

'What was I to do, Julie? How could I talk to you? The situation was impossible.'

I turn the key and usher Rob in.

'It's preposterous, Rob. We're preposterous. All of us.'

'No, Julie, we're just human.'

'Human, maybe. But certainly not evolved.'

'Do you mind if I remove my coat? I think it might be a good idea if you removed yours, too. Either that's a puddle beneath your feet or you've just peed yourself.'

'Don't even think about trying to make me laugh, Rob. I'm angry, very, very angry. And I want you to remember that.'

'I'd like to tell you you look beautiful when you're angry. But right now you look dreadful. Maybe a quick spin in the tumble dryer would sort you out.'

'Just shut up would you, Rob. Your lame jokes aren't working.' But they are. 'I'm going straight upstairs to have a hot shower. By the time I've dried off and come down to the kitchen I want the water boiled, the tea made, and you ready to start talking. Me, I'm talked out. I have nothing left to say.'

'Somehow I doubt that, Julie. And I need your input, you're the sanest, most grounded of us all.'

Rob has taken off his jacket and hung it at the bottom of the banister. I notice he has put on weight. At little more than 5ft 6in he can't afford to carry such a paunch. Or that new chin. It occurs to me that Rob's attractions, unlike Patrick's, are most certainly not of the obvious physical variety, and yet Gemma says the sex is the best ever. And sexual chemistry, as I have so lately discovered, cannot always be accounted for. Rob, when he's not destroying marriages, is the most lovable man I know. Who wouldn't want a Rob, despite the blubber, in their lives?

'I thought you might have lost a bit of the excess adipose with all that's been going on,' I say, deliberately cruelly. What I really want is a big Rob bear hug.

'Comfort eating,' he says glumly. 'But your sister doesn't seem to . . .'

'I'll be ten minutes,' I say, cutting him off mid-sentence, not wanting to hear how Gemma loves her roly-poly man just as he is. If it's going to be Gemma this, Gemma that, Gemma, Gemma, Gemma, I may not be able to avoid another emotional explosion. 'And in the meantime, Rob, the biscuit tin is barred to you.'

'Sure, Top Doc,' says Rob, and I allow myself the faintest smile. Top Doc has been Rob's nickname for me from the time we first met.

'You're meant to have stayed out of my life, Rob.'

'Well, now I've come to ask for your help.'

'Bad move that, I'm in no position to help anyone. But I'll listen.'

I drag my legs up the stairs, one tread at a time, not sure I'll make it to the top without them buckling beneath me. On the landing I drop my coat, and I walk through my bedroom to the en suite bathroom, shedding wet clothes on the floor, on the bed, as I go, not caring about the mess that no one but me is here to see. Once inside the shower cabinet I turn the hot water up as high as it will go and the jets on full blast, then I stand there, arms at my side, unmoving, not washing, not smoothing back the hair from my face, allowing the steam to gather and mist up the cubicle windows. I've no idea for how long I stand like this, letting the water wash over me, leaving it to wash away the grubbiness that has attached to all of us, the taint of betrayal, lies and disloyalty. It's only when I hear a faint knock at my bedroom

door and a muffled 'Are you all right?', that I realise I must have
been here for far longer than ten minutes, for so long that the
hot water has run out and I am starting to shiver. I emerge from
the shower, trembling with the cold. I grab my large towel from
the radiator and wrap it around my chest, tucking in the ends
so it stays up, but I'm still quivering. I grab a smaller towel and
wrap it round my head turban style. But I can't get warm. I look
at the towel hanging on the hook on the inside of the door and
grab that, too, draping it around my shoulders and hugging it
close. It's Walt's towel, or would be if he were still here. I know
Walt doesn't need a towel when he's halfway across the world,
but there are some habits I can't let go of. Washing my towel
with Walt's and replacing it with a fresh one every time I do the
laundry is another of my pathetic little ways of keeping him in my
life. I may no longer look for him in my bed or expect his name
to pop up on my email, but I can't let go altogether. Not until I
know what it is he wants to do with his life. I open the bathroom
cabinet. There's the bottle of Acqua di Gio, Walt's signature
scent, citrus with a touch of melon. I pick it up, examine it and
spray it behind my ears. 'You smell so good, I love your scent,'
Patrick told me. I didn't tell him I smelled of Walt.

'Why, Rob, tell me why.'

'It's because of Paolo, it would never have happened if it hadn't
been for Paolo. I don't want to die, too, and if I stay with Valentina
I will spend the rest of my life fighting for breath. Gemma is . . .
well Gemma's wonderful.'

'You've known about Gemma being wonderful for twenty
years, it's nothing new. But Valentina, she's grieving, Rob. It's a
phase. Why didn't you give her a chance to heal, just enough so
that she can carry on and lead a meaningful life and find her way
back to you? Why have you been so quick to jump ship? It doesn't
make sense to me. You loved each other, didn't you? Before Paolo,
I mean. There weren't any problems to speak of as far as I know.
Or had I been missing something?'

Despite the fullness of his face, the rotundness that can give the illusion of jollity, Rob looks like a man in pain. The pronounced pouches under his eyes have a purple-bluish tinge. His eyes are piggy, as though the strain of keeping them open is hard labour, as though a metal band has lodged itself behind them. His cheeks are waxy, the usual high colour drained from them. I think of a decaying apple, turning to mould.

'You can't know what it's like, Julie, having the life-force sucked out of you. She has become a vampire, an emotional vampire. I don't blame her, I know it's a living hell for her, but you don't see what I see. You see Valentina breaking out the champagne, the show-must-go-on girl, full make-up, cloud of scent, hair so thick and glossy you could drown in it. Which is exactly what I've been doing. Drowning in it. Sometimes I think she's holding my head under water so I drown. So I drown alongside her.'

I lean back on the kitchen chair, rocking it on its back legs, appraising the easy-going, ain't-life-great guy I once knew.

'I'm not getting it, Rob. Isn't this what marriage is supposed to be about? Seeing one another through the bad times. Stuff happens. When you work in a hospital you see tragedies every day. I'm not downgrading Paolo's suicide, the opposite in fact. It's bigger than anything I can think of, to lose a child in this way. But it's what we're supposed to do, be there for one another.'

There are tears trickling down Rob's cheeks. It's old fashioned of me I know but I still hate to see men cry. We women cry easily, without shame; it takes a lot for most men to weep in front of you.

'My son, Julie, he's dead. Think if it were Katy or Tess, think what that would do to you. Paolo, my beloved boy, is dead. I should have been able to keep him alive. I should have been able to save him. I failed. I hate myself for not having been able to save him. And if I couldn't save him, then Valentina should have been able to. We've both failed. And sometimes I hate her for it, too. But however much pain I'm in all she does is take, take, take. With Gemma I feel free again, free to be me, to be heavy when I have to be but to be light as well. With Gemma I know I can survive, and be happy again.'

I know I should tell Rob that he and Valentina were good parents, that it's not always possible to 'save' someone however much love and warmth and generosity you lavish on them. I saw how they were with Paolo, and they were never less than they should have been. Paolo's demons were not of their making and nor could they undo them. But I can't bring myself to give Rob reassurances, not now, not while I am still angry with him. I glance at my watch. It's already 11 p.m. It shouldn't matter but already I am conscious of my operating list in the morning. Even now I am thinking about tomorrow's early start.

'Is that what it's about? Being happy. The relentless pursuit of happiness. Who said we have the right to be happy? When was happiness ever part of the deal? For better or for worse, for richer or for poorer, in sickness and in health. But for happier? I get the feeling that happiness is a luxury of our times, a construct of the late twentieth century. It's all about me, me, me and nothing about us.'

'So, Julie, the woman with nothing more to say. It doesn't sound like nothing to me. But it's not a philosophical argument. This is about how I feel, how Gemma feels . . .'

'And Valentina? What about how Valentina feels?'

Rob slaps his hands against his eyes despairingly.

'It's over, Julie, and there's nothing you can say to stop it being over. And it may well be over with me and Gemma soon as well, if she continues to insist on staying to nurse Antony, which will probably be one good result as far as you're concerned.'

'Rob, that's not fair. I acknowledge your right to happiness, because that's the way of the world today. I was just questioning where that notion comes from, and wondering whether if we focused less on being happy, and were more accepting of the way relationships are, with all their difficulties, all their ups and downs, if we were less vigorously pursuing perfection, perhaps happiness would somehow sneak up on us, and we'd be more content.'

'Are we talking about you and Walt?'

'Aah, Walt. I did wonder if you'd ever get around to asking.'

'I'm sorry, Julie, I'm sorry for my selfishness, but my woes are more than I can handle right now. I'm a lousy friend, aren't I?'

'Yes, you are actually. An extremely lousy friend. And you have a lot of ground to make up. But I guess if we're here to talk about you that's what we should do.'

'Gemma won't leave Antony, I'm pretty much convinced of it.'

'So she says, although with Antony in remission . . . Christ, I've just thought of something. Now that Valentina knows it can't be long before Antony finds out, too.'

'More shit, more fans.'

'What a mess, what a goddamn mess. Has Valentina thrown you out?'

'No, she says I can stay in the spare room until I find myself somewhere to rent.'

'That's generous.'

'That's Valentina.'

'She came flying into Napoli's accusing me of being a prostitute. She seems to think I've played a deliberate part in all of this.'

'I've tried to explain . . .'

'Well, perhaps you'll try again. She's not returning my calls.'

'Oh Julie.'

'Oh Rob. What will you do if Gemma stays with Antony?'

'Shoot myself.'

'I don't think you'll do that.'

'You're right, I won't. Gemma has shown me that I can be happy, and despite your objection to the word, happy helps. Even if she won't leave Antony and the result is that I live the rest of my life in misery at least she has shown me that there is life after Paolo.'

'So she's shown you how to be happy so you can survive in misery. One day perhaps it will make sense, but not now. How am I going to get Valentina to talk to me?'

'She'll come round. She has to see that this has nothing to do with you.'

'Hasn't it got something to do with me? I have this idea that Walt's decision to go off disturbed a hornet's nest in our nuptial neck of the woods.'

'Well, if it's any consolation I told Walt he was nuts to go off without a plan, and nuts to go off and leave you.'

'Because, like Gemma, I'm a wonderful human being?'

'Exactly. You two sisters are something else . . . So different and yet so . . .'

'Wonderful?'

'Exactly.'

'Rob, do you think us two might have a hug? It wouldn't be misinterpreted, would it?'

'Unless someone has installed CCTV in your kitchen, I think it's highly unlikely that we'll be spotted.'

'I'll meet you halfway,' I smile. Rob and I get up simultaneously. Even barefoot I'm taller than him, and when he puts his arms around me I have to bend my head a little to nestle into him. His heat enters into me like a blast of Mediterranean sunshine in August. He strokes my still damp hair.

We hug and hug and then we hug some more. 'Time for bed,' I say, pulling back and leading Rob by the hand into the hallway. 'Don't panic, Rob, I didn't mean with you.'

Rob looks embarrassed. Embarrassed that it even crossed his mind that I might think of such a thing. He removes his coat from the bottom of the banister.

'Onwards and upwards,' he says as I open the front door for him to leave.

'Or backwards and downwards,' I smile feebly.

A woman alone, I repeat to myself as I make my way upstairs again. Something stirs inside me, a tiny welling up of resolve, a barely perceptible sense that passive acceptance of my situation is no longer appropriate. There may be nothing I can do about the marital wreckages all around me, but isn't there something, anything, I can do about my own? Is it time, I wonder, to try to win Walt back?

I fall asleep and dream of Patrick. I dream of having sex with him in my hallway when a key sounds in the lock. Is it Katy? Tess? Walt? I wake up with a jolt before I can find out. When I fall back to sleep again I dream of nothing. Oblivion, I decide, when the alarm rings at 6.45, is my preferred or, perhaps, dream destination.

Chapter Twenty-Two

After a week of stalking Valentina with phone messages left at her home, on her mobile, with her PA at her office, as well as repeated texts and emails, she has finally got in touch. The text buzzes through to me just as I'm entering the doors of the hospital on my way to the monthly specialty meeting, which will be attended by representatives from the whole department, including Finance and HR as well as consultants, pharmacists and senior midwives. People don't realise just how much of a doctor's time is taken up with admin. Consultants meetings, protocols meetings, incident review meetings, clinical governance. As if I didn't have enough to do, what with being on call one night in five, and one weekend in five as well, which means I regularly end up working twelve days at a stretch, I'm also obstetric rep on ICU, the critical care delivery group.

Another thing the public doesn't get to hear about is that once you are a consultant you can begin to apply for what are known as Clinical Excellence Awards. There's something addictive, well there is for me, about working your way up through the grades, and I've been climbing this particular ladder for many years now. Gemma, when we were kids, used to accuse me of being a boring, beastly swot. Always winning a prize for this, a prize for that, especially in science. Truth is, I still am a bit of a beastly swot, the nerd who never grew out of it. 'The early nerd catches the worm,' I used to say to Gemma. Or maybe it's a case of needing constantly to prove to myself that I'm good enough, and all the awards I've won give me just sufficient reassurance to last until I get the next award. There are twelve levels in all, the highest being

Platinum. I'm at Level 11, which is Gold. Only one more to go to be right at the top of the consultants' tree, but lately I've been thinking I might not bother. Lately I've been wondering if it's time to call a halt to my workaholic ways and start to loosen up my lifestyle a little.

In recent times, leading up to when he scarpered, I've felt that Walt would rather not see me at all, that the more I was out of the house the better, but that could have had something to do with the fact that I was never there earlier on when he needed – or at least wanted – me. He may have gone way beyond the bounds of exaggeration in saying that he had to make an appointment to speak to me, but I'm beginning to wonder if he suffered from benign neglect. If, as a wife, I wasn't wife enough. I could spend more time with Walt, getting to know him again, less time doing research and sitting on committees. If he could hear what I'm thinking, the planning I'm doing in my head, Walt would probably laugh. He's left me, hasn't he? He hasn't even hinted that he'd like to come back. But then neither has he said he won't.

Walt, at his most cynical, on the trendy blog that he launched a couple of years back, has described these awards I work towards as a way of giving back-door pay rises to consultants. It's another of his old-school-tie conspiracy theories. I sometimes think he does it just to spite me, or at least to play devil's advocate, without really meaning what he says. He puffs up with pleasure when angry medics post messages of outrage on his website. It's a mark of Walt's cleverness that he could argue most cases either way; no wonder they've loved him all these years on the tabloid whose editor thinks you can never be too outraged for the readers of his paper.

We had quite a shouting match about Walt's rant against the consultants' merit system. Each level of the Clinical Excellence Awards is worth an additional salary, and the rewards at the highest levels are substantial, but since the whole system is completely transparent I don't see where back door comes into it. Also, as I have so often pointed out to Walt, I could be working in private practice and earning several times what I'm earning now. Instead I've chosen to stick with the NHS while most of my colleagues are raking it in with private work. Some, e.g. Walt, might call what I do clinging to the wreckage, but nothing will shake my fundamental belief in free medical care, however faulty the system is at present. And it's not as though you get these awards for sitting on your backside; you have to prove you're contributing above and beyond your normal duties.

Walt and I have always clashed on issues to do with medicine. I used to find it quite a turn on, the way we'd verbally josh and joust. He did, too. We regarded it as a form of foreplay, a mutual teasing of minds that got the sexual juices flowing, too. We were never going to be one of those dull couples who lose their individual personalities and find themselves choosing the same things off a restaurant menu without even having consulted one another first. Whether it was standing our ground or sometimes being persuaded to the other's point of view, we both got a buzz out of it. It was an important part of the dynamic between us, this ability to debate and disagree and accept our differences. But in relationships that go wrong, there has to be a turning point, a point at which respecting one another's differences becomes dismissal of their point of view, when debate turns to argument, when acceptable disagreement becomes unacceptable conflict. I can't place that point with any accuracy in my relationship with Walt.

Valentina! At last. I text back as I enter the lift. She's told me she's coming over this evening, at eight o'clock. Without bothering to enquire first whether I'm free. I am going to be absolutely honest with Valentina about how I feel in relation to Rob and her and Gemma. And then it's going to have to be up to Valentina whether she can continue our friendship while I continue to support my sister. But I have to put that aside now, try to keep tonight from interfering with my concentration. All day I'm going to be in and out of meetings, which frankly I find more enervating than clinics or surgery. With surgery you get the adrenaline to see you through; with clinics you are often presented with new and challenging cases; but with meetings what you need most is stamina, the stamina to keep going, stay alert, not nod off. Since tired is my permanent physical state at the moment, staying awake will be an achievement in itself.

As the lift doors open to the fifth floor I remove my coat, hook my finger through the loop inside the collar and fling it over my shoulder. I walk down the long corridor, listening to the familiar clickety clack of my heels against the lino floor. 'We always know when you're coming,' one of the junior registrars said to me the other day. 'That particular sound, it's like an early-warning system that Miss Broadhurst is on her way.'

'I only wear heels to keep the junior doctors on their toes,' I replied with a smile. Tough but fair minded and flexible is how I hope to be seen. Who knows, perhaps they think I'm the bitch from hell.

Today I am dressed in a just-to-the-knee straight black skirt, with a Chanel-style boxy jacket, black trimmed with white, underneath which I am wearing a sleeveless, cowl-necked cream silk blouse. My shoes are slim-heeled courts with pointy toes and my black tights are sheer. The diamond stud earrings, which Walt bought for me as an anniversary present more than a decade ago, are a permanent fixture. Anything dangly around my neck or hanging from my ears would be both unhygienic and an obstacle if I had to bend down over a patient. I like to play up my femininity at work. Since I became a consultant I've not had to bother myself about sexism, about dressing to deflect ribald remarks. If there's a certain aura of steeliness about me, something that keeps my male colleagues at bay, commands respect rather than flattery, reserve rather than flirtatiousness, then I'm quite OK with that. I dress to please myself, in a way that I hope nods at both elegance and authority, without shouting their presence.

Last year I was much amused when one of the fashion magazines, *Harper's Bazaar* I think it might have been, rang and asked me to do a fashion shoot for a story they were doing in their 'working woman' section on professionals with 'stand-out style'.

They'd heard, goodness knows where, that I had a bit of a thing for Chanel suits. I laughed, and told them I had a bit of thing for suits in the style of Chanel, and that I thought Chanel was a great liberator of women by putting them into trousers and simple, pared-down clothes, but that my so-called Chanel suits came from places like L K Bennett and Wallis. I could hear the researcher at the other end of the phone clearing her throat with embarrassment. I decided to put her out of her misery. 'I'm delighted to be asked,' I said, 'most flattered in fact, but I'm way too busy I'm afraid.'

'Oh thank you, thank you so much,' said the girl gratefully, as I saved her the indignity of having to reverse her offer on the grounds that only the real deal would do in a magazine as elevated as hers.

In a poky office at the end of the corridor, with a table barely big enough for six to sit around, I count eight people already in place. 'Morning, everyone,' I say, squeezing into the last available chair, looking at my watch to make sure I'm not late. It's two minutes past nine and I'm the last to arrive.

'Cool suit,' says Alison, my favourite of all the midwives.

'We have a lot to get through this morning,' says the voice of our Chair at the other end of the table rather snippily. 'Shall we begin?'

The air in this cramped, windowless room is already beginning to smell a little stale. There is a distinct whiff of last night's curry coming from my left, morning coffee breath from my right and stale nicotine from the direction of Toby from HR. If the girl from *Harper's Bazaar* could see me now she'd understand just what a lucky escape she had. 'I'd like to get the finance issues out of the way first,' says our Chair. I stifle a yawn. As if on cue, my bleep buzzes. 'Sorry, emergency.' I try not to grin, but I can't help myself. I'm outta here. 'I guess one of the guys, one of the other consultants, failed to turn up this morning,' I say. I get up with renewed vigour. I don't walk, I practically sprint down the corridor. As I approach the labour ward, Emily, one of the junior registrars, is coming to meet me, clutching a clipboard.

'Thirty-five weeks. Sky-high blood pressure. Decelerations in foetal heartbeat. I need you to review her right away.'

I'm about to say, 'Sky high is not the appropriate medical terminology . . .' but the registrar is still talking.

'Miss Broadhurst, I don't want to alarm you, but the patient is called Tess and she is apparently your daughter.'

I stop dead in my tracks. I almost stop breathing. 'What do you mean, "apparently"?' I scream as though it's all Emily's fault. 'Of course she's my daughter. Give me the notes, give them to me right this second.' I grab them from the registrar's hand. 'Good God, it's Tess, it really is her.' All the signs are of rapidly deteriorating pre-eclampsia. Presenting with vision problems, flashing lights and upper adominal pain. Severely raised BP, deranged blood tests. It's fulminating pre-eclampsia for sure. 'There's nothing in the notes about fitting, is there, she hasn't fitted, has she?'

'No, Miss Broadhurst, she hasn't.'

'Have you fixed the magnesium sulphate drip?'

'So far, not. I wanted you to . . .'

'Then fucking do it, and do it NOW. It should prevent fitting. Where is she?'

Emily looks shocked. She's never heard me swear before.

'She's in Room Six.'

'And we have to get the blood pressure under control. First we stabilise her, then straight off to theatre.'

'Yes, Miss Broadhurst.'

'There must be someone else who can do this job. It can't be me. Get Raj, he's on today, isn't he? Get someone to get Raj, now, this instant.'

'Sorry, Miss Broadhurst, but Raj, I mean Mr Singh, is dealing with a post-partum haemorrhage and Miss Blackstone called in sick. You're the only consultant available.'

'Then you're right, it will have to be me. You'll do the LSCS and I'll supervise. And, Emily, you're going to have to forget it's my daughter on the table and my grandchild who is about to be delivered, and treat it like any other emergency C-section.' Emily is ghostly pale.

'Where's Pete? Her husband . . .'

'Her husband brought her in . . . She woke up with these flashing lights, and the pain, which they thought might be labour, but didn't feel right for labour. He panicked and drove her straight here to A&E, said it wasn't where she was going to have the baby, but it was the nearest hospital to where they lived.'

'Then he did the right thing.'

I arrive in the labour room to find Tess lying on the bed, close to tears, doctors and nurses swarming around her, organising drips and catheters and bloods.

'It's going to be all right, my darling,' I say, walking towards her. 'Everything will be all right, I promise.'

'Mum, are you sure?'

'I am absolutely sure, sweetheart. Just as soon as you're stable we'll do the C-section.'

'Does it have to be a Caesarean?'

'It does.'

'I so wanted a natural birth. Pete was going to support me through it.'

'I know, darling, but we have to do what's safest for you and safest for the baby.'

Pete is beside Tess, ashen faced.

'Did I do the right thing, bringing her here? To this hospital rather than . . .'

'You had no choice, Pete, of course you did the right thing.'

'Mum, are you going to do the actual operation?'

'No, pet, that's Emily's job. You wouldn't want me fumbling around down there and Emily's quite the expert, aren't you, Emily?'

'Yes,' says Emily quietly, 'you'll be fine with me. And your mum will be watching me every step of the way.'

'Now,' I say, turning away from Emily and back to Tess and

Pete, 'I'm going to explain to you exactly what we're going to do. The intravenous drugs will control your blood pressure and prevent fitting. The catheter will monitor urine output, and there'll be another drip for restricted fluids. We'll do some bloods, we'll continue to monitor the baby and the senior anaesthetist will be here any minute to review you for surgery. Whether we decide to do a general or local anaesthetic will depend on the results of your blood. Either way, there is absolutely no need to panic. You are in the right place, and you came in at the right time. Now there's something I have to quickly see to. I'll be back in a couple of minutes.' I go and kiss Tess on her forehead once, twice, three times. She's clammy and weepy.

'I promise, darling, everything will be OK.'

I leave the labour room and head for the toilets. Locking myself in the cubicle, I throw up into the toilet bowl. Everything is under control, except me. This is my daughter we're talking about here, and my grandchild, and I'm mildly in shock. After pulling the chain and leaving the cubicle, I wash my hands, splash my face with cold water, remove my jacket and wash my underarms as best I can. There are sweat stains on my silk top. I dry myself off with paper towels, reapply my lipstick, pop a mint into my mouth and take three slow, deep breaths.

Tess Broadhurst gives birth to Lara Alice Broadhurst Roberts, weighing 2.65 kilos, at 12.30 p.m. on 26 June, following a Lower Segment Caesarean Section conducted under general anaesthetic. Mother and baby are doing fine. The baby is well enough to stay with Tess under close observation. Tess will continue to be monitored for 24 to 48 hours on the labour ward. The flashing lights are beginning to resolve. The upper adominal pain has gone. None of the things that could have gone wrong – fitting, difficulty in getting Tess's blood pressure under control, bleeding during the Caesarean because Tess's platelet and clotting blood tests were abnormal, the baby being delivered in poor condition – materialised. Never has the rule that you don't operate on your relatives seemed so apt. I felt like a person of two halves throughout – treading a tightrope between cool professionalism and gut-wrenching anxiety. Under my instruction and guidance, in an atmosphere of subdued tension, Emily performed her duties with heroic restraint. Afterwards I hugged and hugged her, I couldn't help myself.

'I just did my job,' she said quietly. 'And I couldn't have done it without you.' Later, I saw her talking to a colleague and punching the air with her fist. Showing off a little perhaps, exaggerating the drama of it all. Well, why not. Emily has the makings of a very good doctor indeed.

Pete is overawed with gratitude. 'Thank God for you, Julie,' he keeps saying, over and over. Tess is too tired to express anything very much, other than to ask, 'Is Lara OK? Are you sure she's OK?'

I just make it to my 2 p.m. meeting. Afterwards, I hang around, pretending to Pete and Tess that I'm still on duty, whereas in fact I'm supposed to finish at 5. I have quite forgotten that Valentina is coming round. I'm aware that all I've eaten today is the banana, yoghurt and granola I had before leaving for work this morning. And even that didn't stay down for much more than an hour. I should eat something, but I'm not hungry. I'm just getting ready to leave the hospital at 8.20 when my phone rings. It's Valentina, waiting on my doorstep.

'Where are you? Why are you not home? Are you standing me up? This is too much, Julie, too much.'

I am almost too weary to explain. 'Tess,' I say, and then, 'Tess.'

Valentina's voice switches immediately to one of concern. 'Is everything all right? Tell me, tell me.'

'Everything is fine. Now. But it nearly wasn't.'

'Has she had the baby?'

'She has, yes, she's had the baby. An adorable little mite called Lara. And I, Valentina, am a grandmother.'

'Then we must have champagne. Are you coming back?'

'I'll be at least half an hour. I'm sorry.'

'Sorry, what for? You're a grandmother, aren't you? And

everyone is fine. I'll go and wait at the café round the corner from you and be back in half an hour.'

'Are you very, very angry with me?'

'I don't know, Julie, I just don't know any more. I'm trying to focus more on hating your sister than on hating you, but it's not easy. We'll talk when you get here if you're not too exhausted.'

'I won't be too exhausted,' I say. 'I'm just relieved everything is fine with Tess and the baby. I'll see you soon, Valentina.'

I go back to Tess's room. Pete hasn't moved from her side. The baby is fast asleep, in his arms, wrapped in a blanket.

'See you in the morning, darling,' I say to Tess. 'If at any point in the night you need me the nurses are under strict instructions to give me a call.'

Tess smiles weakly at me. 'Pete has rung Katy, but what about Dad? Will you let him know? Do you mind letting him know?'

Ah yes, Walt. Just as I had forgotten about Valentina I had completely forgotten about Walt. All of this has happened without Walt. And at this precise moment I can't remember exactly what it is I need Walt for, and yet something tugs at me, and I want so much to hear his voice. Later. When Valentina's gone, I'll try to call him then. I don't even know what country the man is in.

Although the last thing in the world I need right now is to listen to Valentina and her woes, in a way I'm grateful that she's coming round. I want the distraction. I don't want to replay, over and over, what might have happened, how wrong it could all have gone. And exhausted as I am there's not the remotest possibility that I could go home and go straight to bed and to sleep. Whether or not I'll survive the battering I'm expecting from Valentina remains to be seen.

When I arrive at my home just before nine, Valentina is standing in my porch. Except for the evidence of a bottle of champagne, which she must have picked up from the off-licence next to the café, she might have been standing there since we'd spoken.

'Congratulations, *amore*,' she says, wrapping herself around me.

'Oh Valentina, it was so very nearly so very awful.'

'But it wasn't and all is well.'

I'm starting to tremble. I try to put the key into the lock but my hand is shaking so much I can't get the key to fit.

'Here,' says Valentina, 'let me do that for you.'

We enter the hallway and whatever tiny reserves of strength I've been hanging on to to get me home evaporate. I make it as far as the staircase, and sink on to the steps. My whole body is quivering.

'You don't need champagne,' says Valentina, 'you need brandy. Don't move a muscle.'

I couldn't, even if I wanted to.

When Valentina returns, she is clutching two brandy balloons, one in each hand, filled generously.

'Move along your bottom, please,' she says, and sits down beside me. 'Now drink.'

I swig back a large gulp, and the brandy hits the back of my throat with a burning sensation. With my hands cupped around the big glass balloon I stare into the liquid as though seeking answers in a crystal ball.

'How about some more?' says Valentina.

I take another swig and already it's beginning to work, the trembling is beginning to subside. I feel light headed, which is not surprising.

'So, Valentina . . .'

'So, Julie . . .'

'You abandoned, me abandoned.'

'I've made a decision.'

'And what decision is that? Apart from the decision that all men are bastards.'

'And that there are some women who do not know of boundaries, who cannot make a difference of right from wrong, who have no respect for friendship, for whom morality means not anything.'

Valentina has gone straight for the jugular; if not mine, Gemma's.

'Valentina, I hate what Gemma's done, I really do, but I've tried to imagine cutting Gemma from my life and it's impossible. I know sisters fall out, stop talking to one another, and this is a bigger reason for falling out than all the petty financial wrangling over wills and sibling rivalry that sisters generally come to blows over, but I simply can't do it. Gemma should never, ever have allowed this thing with Rob to happen. But I still can't turn my back on her.'

'I know you can't and I wouldn't ask you to. That's one of the reasons why I've made the decision I've made.'

'Which is . . .'

'To go and live in New York. To get away from everyone who has to try to split their loyalties. I've lost Paolo, I've lost Rob, I've lost you, I've lost Gemma. There's no one here for me to stay for. And Carla, thank God for my daughter, Carla says she'll come with me. She wants to join the business.'

It flashes through my addled head that Rob will be heartbroken if Carla moves to New York, but I can hardly say that to Valentina, not after what he's done to her.

'Many of my clients have been asking me for ages to have a New York office, to start promoting them in the US so they can have consistency of PR strategy in Europe and the States. It's the perfect opportunity.'

'You're remarkable, Valentina, you really are.'

'No, I'm a survivalist. This I've told you many times before. To tell the truth I think Rob's way out is the behaviour of a coward. He is a white flag man. He lose himself in another woman but this is not the right way to come to terms with the loss of Paolo. It doesn't respect his death, it just avoids facing up to it. My way is different. I will survive alone. I will remember Paolo every day, all day. Rob chooses to forget. He thinks Gemma can help him forget. I don't want to forget, not ever.'

'You do know, don't you, that Gemma has said she's going to stay with Antony.'

'Maybe she will, maybe she won't. But if Gemma turns him down and Rob tries to come crawling back to me . . .'

'You loved each other well enough, didn't you?'

'We did, but Paolo's death changed everything. Love doesn't conquer all; circumstances can kill it. I thought that maybe if I stayed very close to Rob, held him to me all the time, things would be easier, but they weren't. I thought I could save Rob and Rob could save me, but another soul you cannot save, only your own.'

'Are you quite sure you wouldn't take Rob back if things didn't work out with him and Gemma, if Gemma decides to stay with Antony long-term? I mean, it's an affair that could work itself through.'

'I'm not going to wait to find out. And I'm not going to take Rob back just because he is not able to start a new life with Gemma. I'm going to New York, Julie.'

'God, I'll miss you.'

'You can come and visit.'

'Oh, you can be sure of that. It will be like *Sex and The City*, thirty years on. It will be Hot Flushes and the City and Grey Pubic Hair and the City and Dowager's Hump and the City.'

'That is so disgusting, Julie. What has got into you?'

'The brandy's got into me. Today has got into me. Matters of life and death have got into me. And the absence of Walt. That's got into me as well.'

'Do you hear from him?'

'No. But he's about to hear from me. If I can track him down.'

'How do you feel about him not being here with all this going on?'

'I've asked myself if he'd have been here if it had been Katy who was going to have a baby.'

'Meaning?'

'Sometimes I wonder if the fact that Tess isn't biologically his makes a difference. Whether he is that bit more detached, knowing that none of his genetic inheritance is going into Tess's baby. Or maybe he's just given up interest in his entire family, Katy included.'

'That doesn't sound like Walt. Family, it means everything to him. From what I've observed he has always been wonderful with

Tess, always treated Tess and Katy equally. If I didn't know I would never think for one moment that Walt wasn't Tess's natural father.'

'I'm tired and emotional, Valentina, and I find it quite extraordinary that all this drama has been going on and Walt is waltzing round the world knowing absolutely bugger all about it. Can you imagine if the positions were reversed? If it had been me who had gone off and left my husband, my kids, when one of my children was about to give birth.'

'Put that way it does sound very bad, I agree.'

'Everyone seems to accept Walt going off and doing his own thing. Oh yes, they nod sympathetically, having a bit of a mid-life crisis, is he? Got himself a Harley, did he? Having a Gap Year? Sounds good to me.'

'Would you take Walt back?'

'The question is would Walt take me back?'

'I'm asking would you take him back?'

'Do you think I should?'

'You're not answering my question.'

'That's because I don't have an answer. When are you going to New York? Who will run the London office?'

'Jon, my senior director, is coming in as a partner. We've been talking about this for months. He's really good, and he is able to run things here no problem. I will commute myself every three weeks, and will be in constant touch. I trust him.'

'I've forgotten about trust.'

'What do you mean?'

'Well, look at us all. I trusted Walt. You trusted Rob. Antony trusted Gemma. The only person who never trusted was Charles. He never trusted Aggie. And yet those two are back together. Maybe trust is overrated.'

'Maybe life is overrated.'

'Is that how you feel?'

'No.'

'Me neither.'

Valentina and I stay sitting on the third step of my staircase, hugger-mugger for comfort, sometimes talking, sometimes silent, for a very long time.

'Do you want to stay the night?' I ask. 'You've had a lot of brandy.'

'Yes, please,' Valentina replies.

'The spare room's already made up,' I say.

'Actually I would like very much for you to hold me,' says Valentina.

I hug her closer to me.

'Not now. All night. But you have to lend me pyjamas, I always wear pyjamas, otherwise I can't sleep.'

And so we do a most curious thing. Valentina and I climb into my bed together, me in my nightie, Valentina in a pair of Walt's three-sizes-too-big, blue-and-white-striped pyjamas.

'You don't remind me of him at all,' I laugh, as Valentina snuggles into me. Then I quietly hold her in my arms, stroking her luscious hair, until she falls asleep. I lie awake a while longer, thinking about Tess and the baby, and Paolo. And then I too fall asleep. I never did get around to telling Walt about the birth.

Chapter Twenty-Three

'Why are you so forgiving?'

'Am I?'

'You never say a bad word about your husband.'

'He's not a bad person.'

'So him going off like that, leaving you to contend with the business of earning a living, paying the bills, an expectant daughter and a mother with Alzheimer's is the right way to behave?'

'I didn't say that.'

'It's a selfish, adolescent way to behave.'

'I know.'

'What does he expect to achieve?'

'You'd have to ask him that.'

'You amaze me, Julie.'

'But not in a good way.'

'You are clever, sexy, funny, competent. I'm crazy for you. But I don't understand you.'

'Oh Patrick, this is hopeless.'

'What's hopeless?'

'You and I. We're a hopeless proposition.'

'Don't you like talking about you and Walt?'

'I can't really see the point.'

We are sitting opposite one another in a Japanese restaurant in Charlotte Street. Today has been a delight, both for its normality and for the sense of sexual gratification delayed, the knowledge that unlike in those countless hotel rooms where sex is all that matters, we have been able to behave like an ordinary couple, doing ordinary things, but with the added pleasure of the spark between us, self-igniting unexpectedly at random moments throughout the day. Until just a moment ago Patrick and I were laughing and joking, feeding one another from chopsticks, popping morsels of sushi and sashimi into each other's mouth and knocking back too much sake, oblivious of the other diners. I was allowing myself to think of later, when I would invite Patrick back to my house, my bed. Now the bubble has been punctured. Walt has come between us.

This day we've spent together. One entire, glorious day. Our first. With Katy and Chris safely ensconced in Thailand I agreed to break the golden rule of seeing Patrick outside of the four walls of a hotel room.

He came into London from his home in Hertfordshire this morning, Saturday, to collect me at ten. We drove back out of London to Wendover Woods, a lovely spot high in the Chilterns, and set off on a ten-mile hike, through thick woods and open fields, on to a pub for lunch, where the sun was so hot that we had to seek out some shade. I realised, with a shock, that I'd only once seen Patrick in the daytime before, our first meeting all those months ago. That day it rained and rained. Patrick in the sunlight looked different. Paler, older, apart from his size somehow less distinct, more blurred around the edges. But I didn't mind. In a way it emphasised his vulnerability, and for a moment I wondered about his wife and felt a rush of tenderness. Lunch over we headed back through woodlands again. We stood in a hide, hoping to catch a rare glimpse of the firecrest, a tiny bird with orange head that flits through the evergreens. To our amazement one suddenly appeared, flying across our sightline and then disappearing.

'It's a sign,' Patrick whispered in my ear, before kissing it gently.

My heart sank a little, and I said nothing. Too deep, I said to myself, we're getting in too deep. But then I allowed myself to kiss Patrick back, knowing we were alone in the woods, and he walked me backwards as we kissed, pressed me up against a tree, kissed me harder, and I was lost again.

Mostly we walked companionably, chatting, Patrick regaling me with stories of his chaotic, bohemian childhood, of family life with his wife, of the contrast between having one child and growing up with so many siblings. I told him tales of the hospital which, for reasons I cannot fathom, seem to fascinate him.

'It's like listening to *ER* as read by a Radio 4 announcer,' he joked.

I talked about the girls, the new baby, my ailing mum. We skated lightly over topics in the news, books we've read. Sometimes I'd look across at Patrick and quite suddenly I could see us naked, limbs entwined, totally without inhibition, hostages to desire, and I would smile. Who would ever think such passion could exist between two such ordinary middle-aged people?

Patrick refills the tiny cups with sake.

'I want to be integrated in your life, Julie, not a sealed-off segment. I want openness and honesty. I want to know where I stand. I need you to tell me what you really feel for Walt and whether you want him back. And when we can tell the kids about us. I'm falling in love with you, Julie, can't you see it?'

'Oh Patrick, please not that. Be in like with me, in lust with me, but not that. It's a mirage. You're still mourning the loss of Mona. You think you're in love with me, but you're not.'

'For heaven's sake, Julie.' Patrick sounds angry now. I'm taken back to that moment on the motorway. I can see the rage building inside him and feel the fear welling up inside me. 'You can't tell me what I think. What I feel. You may be able to control your emotions but you can't control mine. Don't even try to. If I say I'm in love with you, and you can't bear to hear it, then . . .'

'Patrick, please, you're shouting . . .'

'I don't care, Julie, I really don't care. I don't want to be your gigolo, and I don't want to be your fuck-buddy. I want a relationship, an open, loving, caring, giving relationship. As for Mona, she's dead, and I'd do anything to bring her back, but I can't. Loving you doesn't mean I loved her less. It's because I loved her so much that I can love again. I'm good at love, it's what

I do best. Apart from make money, that is. I'm good at that, too. I'm a catch, in fact, a real catch . . . And you should count yourself lucky, woman. A VERY LUCKY WOMAN INDEED,' he booms, close to a roar.

The Japanese couple at the next table haven't turned to look at us. Perhaps they don't understand English. The two young men to our left are speaking Spanish and holding hands and looking into one another's eyes across the table. No one it seems is interested in what's going on between Patrick and me.

So this is how it will end, I think. And the fool that I am will be alone. No Walt. No Patrick. But at least I'll have Katy, at least I won't lose Katy.

'We can't tell the kids, Patrick. We can't. It would destroy Katy.'

'Do you know what I think, Julie?' Patrick's face is turning red. It makes him look florid, ruddy, less attractive. This is good. Maybe I can turn myself off from this huggable, lovable hulk of a man. 'I think Katy is one big excuse. She's the impenetrable shield you hold between us, but rather than *protecting* her you're using her to keep me at bay. She's the ace in your pack. Whenever things start to get real between us, you play the Katy card. It's not fair on me and strange though it seems it's not fair on her either.'

'That's cheap, Patrick, twisting things to make it look as though I'm exploiting my daughter.'

'I only want to get through to you, Julie.'

'No, you want more than that. You want me to declare my love, tell you that Walt and I are definitively through and reassure you that Chris and Katy will find it really sweet that their parents are bonking one another behind their backs.'

'I'm going to drive you home, Julie, and then I'm going to drive myself back to Hertfordshire. Sort yourself out first, then decide what you want to do about me. I can't live with you in the dark, and you can't live with me in the light. But I will wait. What I won't do is carry on like we have been doing.'

Outside my front door Patrick holds my face up to kiss me goodnight. I kiss him back greedily, hear my own small gasp as he puts one broad, strong hand to the small of my back and presses me into him. I pull back. 'Stay with me, Patrick, just tonight, just so we can see how it feels to be lovers in the light, albeit with the lights out.'

Patrick laughs. And so we go to bed together in the bed that belongs to me and Walt, and which has never seen another man until tonight. When I come, easily, powerfully, as I always do with Patrick, I find myself crying. I assume Patrick does notice, but he makes the wise decision to ask no questions. Why can't it be like this with Walt, I ask myself? Why wasn't it ever like this with Walt? And why, if this is so good, do I still want Walt so badly?

Walt is in India now. The day after Lara was born I tried to contact him, but he was nowhere to be found. Every day for a week I sent another text or email, just to be sure that if his communications had broken down he'd hear from me as soon as they were up and running again.

Lara was eight days old by the time Walt called.

He told me he'd been trekking in the Himalayas, in northern India, starting off from Dharamsala, which is home to the Dalai Lama in the Kangra Valley, then hiking over the Dhauladhar Range to Lamu in the Ravi River. Walt described it as the traditional migratory and grazing route of the Gaddis, the semi-nomadic Hindu shepherds of the region.

'Has the Dalai Lama sorted you out then? Or are you going to give up journalism and become a shepherd?' I couldn't resist asking once I'd updated him on Tess and the baby.

'Very funny, Julie, I shall ignore those remarks.'

'Everyone keeps asking me when you're coming back, expecting me to know your itinerary. I tell them I haven't a clue, but still they ask.'

'It's none of their business, is it?'

'Well they are your friends. And mine.'

'Is this your way of asking me yourself?'

'Would that be so unreasonable?'

I could have kicked myself. I so wanted to stay sounding neutral but the sarcasm crept into my voice before I could do anything about it.

'Soon,' he said, without committing himself.

'Are you having fun?'

'Some of the time. I've certainly seen some amazing things. But it's painful, too, Julie, not knowing who you are or what you want. It's even painful knowing that I'm causing you pain. But things are starting to make sense. I'm beginning to see a way forward.'

'Well that's something, I suppose,' I replied. 'A way forward. For you, for me, for us, I wonder. I miss you, you know.'

The line crackled, then it went dead.

And now it's August, Sunday morning, seven o'clock, seven months and one day from when Walt left, and I am in bed, my bed, with my lover and thinking about my husband.

Patrick stirs beside me, rolls onto his side and pulls me closer, so we are in a spoon position. He lifts my short nightdress and presses his naked torso into me. I can feel him hardening and I am ready, right away, to receive him.

'I'm going to fuck you one more time, darling woman,' he whispers. 'And then I'm going away and leaving you alone until you have made your decision.'

I like the way Patrick uses language to seduce me. It turns me on when he graphically describes what he wants to do to me before or while he does it. I wonder if Walt and I could . . .

I give myself over to the moment. So many questions, so many unknowns. But for now only this.

Chapter Twenty-Four

Now I have two men to miss, which some would say is better than none, although I'm not so sure. I miss both the familiarity of Walt and the unfamiliarity of Patrick. I long for each of them, but differently. For Patrick, the ache is that of sexual desire, as well as the strange mingling of danger and security I feel when I am with him. There is the excitement of the illicit, of course, the frisson that goes along with the fear of being found out, and even the dark, angry side that flares in Patrick unexpectedly has a kind of allure; but there's also the wonderful feeling of protection that Patrick's sheer physical bulk affords me whenever we are together. I have this image of myself, curling up inside the breast pocket of his jacket, listening to the steady beat of his heart.

The ache I have for Walt has more to do with my sense of what's right, what ought to be, the respect I feel our shared history deserves. The sense that we can't possibly be throwing this away, and for what? But it's also for Walt himself. The man who was always there, clever, sharp-tongued Walt, my intellectual sparring partner, the man who would keep me on my toes when my thinking got lazy, who was also the man who loved Tess and Katy without reservation. If he was judgmental with me, with them he never was. Where I was worried or impatient he was calm and ready to let things take their course. Always, at the back of my mind, when dealing with a gritty problem – to do with work, the children – what would Walt say, how would Walt handle it? I'll ask Walt, Walt's perspective is what I need. And now I see all the things at which Walt was so competent, which I hadn't noticed until he was gone. The filing, the paying of bills, the organising of repairs. These things, too, are important in a relationship, the filling in of each other's gaps. I think of Walt's scar, the one that runs the length of his nose, and touch my own nose, running my finger down it, remembering exactly the jagged course of the cut that never fully healed. I know him by heart. In my heart. Could it work with a man like Patrick? Could it work again with Walt? Walt is neither callow nor callous. He's not the type to just run off. It may appear selfish, indeed what he has done is undeniably selfish, but such an action in a man like Walt has to be for a reason. I should have better heard him out.

From that mid-August morning until now, early October, Patrick has kept out of my life. He asked me not to call or text and I have respected that. When Katy returned from Thailand, I was relieved not to have to sneak about, deleting texts, only calling Patrick when she was out of the house. Chris stayed over, often, and for a week she stayed at his place, with him and Patrick.

'What do you think of Chris's dad now that you know him better?' I asked. Casually, I hoped.

'I think he's great. So warm and welcoming and such a storyteller. It's funny, I thought you two got on, but . . .'

'But what?'

'I'm not sure I should be telling you really, I mean I don't want to upset you or anything.'

'Come on, Katy, you've started so you might as well finish.'

'Well, Chris had this idea. His dad has been pretty down in the dumps lately. Chris thought he was getting better for a bit, suddenly he seemed more like his old self, joking and laughing all the time according to Chris, but recently he's been all gloomy again. Chris thinks he might be depressed. So on the basis that you and he liked one another, or at least we thought you did, and what with Dad still being away, he thought that we might all spend the weekend together at their place. I mean it has six acres, it's a proper country estate, as posh as one of those country house hotels you see in the ads and with these amazing grounds to get lost in. So he suggested it to his Dad and . . .' Katy hesitated.

'And?'

'Well Patrick went ballistic, really lost his temper. It was quite scary actually. He said it was a completely stupid idea, except he didn't use the word stupid, he just shouted, "Over my dead body" and stormed out of the room. It was really weird.'

'Well that's the effect I seem to have on people these days, Katy. I can empty rooms in an instant. If it weren't a matter of life and death I could probably empty theatre, too.'

Katy snorted. I had succeeded in making it sound as though Patrick's approval or disapproval of me meant absolutely nothing. 'And in any case it would have all been a bit uncomfortable. I mean I hardly know the man. For what reason could he possibly want me hanging around him for an entire weekend?'

'Yeah, I guess you're right, but Chris was only trying to be kind, and I know you'd fall in love with the place.'

'He's a kind and lovely young man, your Chris, and you are lucky to have found him.'

'I know that, Mum.' And Katy gave me a spontaneous hug, the sweetest of solace.

Grandchildren. All the clichés are true. You think no child will capture your heart in the way your own children did – and still do – and then this little creature, progeny of your daughter, comes along, and you are head over heels in delight. You wheel the baby out in its pram, and you beam with pride at everyone who passes, not because you think, even for a second, even on a very good day, that you could be mistaken for the child's mother, but because this is simply the most gorgeous, adorable, perfect baby in all the world, and you want the world to know it. You quite forget that small babies who aren't related to you, with whom there's no familial bond, are rather boring, one-dimensional little creatures and that playing pass-the-photograph should be reserved for your closest friends, and then only on an occasional basis. Forwarding dozens of baby jpgs to everyone in your email address book the moment they arrive on your computer courtesy of your daughter or son-in-law is not good etiquette, at least not unless you want to lose all your friends. I'm an obstetrician, for heavens sake, I'm awash with newborns, and even if I still regard every birth as little short of a miracle no one would have suspected just how gaga I'd go when Lara came into my life. And there's this other thing as well, which I hadn't given any thought to before. The absolute pleasure of seeing your own child become a parent. Behind that pleasure is perhaps a sense that you and your daughter can now forge a new bond, one that accounts for how it feels to be a parent, something your child cannot possibly know until she has one of her own. Walt is missing out on so much by not being here.

Lara is such a tonic for my mother, too. Annette whispers sweet nothings over Lara's cot for hours at a time. And her sweet nothings are becoming wilder as time passes and her Alzheimer's gets worse. She's also taken to singing songs that she never had any inclination for in all the years I was growing up. 'Daisy, Daisy', 'We'll Meet Again' and 'Lily Marlene'. Curiously, she is word and tune perfect when she sings these songs. The baby appears to love her warbling, gurgling and smiling happily in return.

Tess and Pete are just as I expected. Totally devoted. Pete one hundred per cent competent to take over without instruction whenever required, even admitting to me that he'd be quite happy for Tess to stop breastfeeding as he's jealous that he can't feed the baby himself until she moves on to a bottle. I look at Tess and Pete, exhausted, somewhat anxious, but emotionally complete in their love for one another and as a new family unit. I wonder what will become of them, whether twenty years down the line they'll still be together, or just another divorce statistic. Were Walt and I ever like Pete and Tess? Yes we were, and it's partly why each time I leave their company I allow the tears I've been holding back to fall. They remind me of us, I am happy for them, and at the same time it compounds my pain.

Apparently Pete and Walt have become best email buddies. By now half the population of India must know about Walt's grandchild.

'Tess tells me you and Walt are in regular contact,' I said to Pete the other day.

'Yeah, we are actually,' said Pete, raising Lara by the ankles with one hand as he expertly slid a nappy under her bottom. She was lying face up on the changing mat, kicking back and forth as Pete held her in his confident grip.

'I was just wondering if he'd found himself yet.'

'I know I should ask, but all he wants to discuss is Lara.'

'Then he's probably on some kind of guilt trip.' I sniggered at my own poor joke, but no one else did.

'Mum,' said Tess, as she gathered up discarded Babygros, dummies and muslins from the floor. 'Will you have him back?'

'Do you think I should?'

'It's not up to me.'

'No, but you can tell me what you think.'

'I think you've been extraordinarily patient. Not sure I would be. I also think that Dad has been suffering more than he lets on.'

'He has a funny way of showing it.'

'But surely that's the point. He doesn't let it show. He's being a man about it, by walking out into the wilderness.'

'Do you think it's manly?'

'I think it's not untypical male behaviour.'

'How many men your father's age do you know who have decided to go off with a backpack on a Gap Year?'

'None, besides Dad. They just leave their wives instead, go off with a younger woman.'

'What do you think is better?'

'Neither. But at least this way it gives you the chance of a reconciliation.'

'Mind if I hold the baby for a bit?'

'Of course,' said Pete, handing the newly changed, clean-nappied Lara over to me.

'I love you soooo much,' I whispered into Lara's sweet little ear. She rewarded me with a burp.

★   ★   ★

Today, Sunday, is an anniversary of sorts. It's a year since Walt and I drove Katy to university for the start of her first term at college. She was jangling with anxiety. Today, as we load the car, she is full of happy expectancy for the year ahead. I'm helping her to move into the house that she'll share in a village a few miles from the campus. She could have chosen a much livelier spot in the nearby town but she wanted somewhere quiet, to be surrounded by woods and fields, and she and two other like-minded second years found the most charming of thatched cottages. She intends to cycle the four miles to the campus, and although I hate the idea of her going down dark, unlit lanes in winter, I've buttoned my lip. She's a big girl now. Chris has a car and a place in the town and they've worked it out that they can have the best of both worlds with this arrangement. Katy has come such a long way in so short a time. I love to see my girls taking the reins of their own lives, even as I watch my own life unravel.

It's also a year to the day that Walt told me he was leaving. I replay that conversation in the pub over and over in my mind as I drive Katy up the motorway. Last year she was plugged into her iPod, silent, morose. This year she still has the iPod in her ears, but now she's singing and jiggling in her seat and tapping out the rhythm of the music with her feet. Chris certainly came along at the right moment. For a girl who was as reliant on her dad as Katy was, and who had never had a proper boyfriend, Chris was manna from heaven turning up at the time of Walt's departure.

So my girls are doing fine. It's we adults who don't seem to know how to behave.

Chapter Twenty-Five

Katy's cottage may be clean by some standards, but not by mine. I am keen on hygiene, indoctrinated perhaps by my medical training. I leave Katy to vacuum and dust her room, and organise her possessions in her own orderly fashion, while I spend two hours scrubbing everything in the kitchen from the grime-ingrained tiles on the splashback to the burnt debris of hundreds of roasts in the rickety oven, to the fridge that has a distinct whiff of old fish about it. Katy's two housemates – a petite Malay girl studying anthropology, and a geeky-looking lad with thick spectacles and the beginning of a beer belly, like Katy reading geography – are sitting on the sofa with their feet up on the coffee table and watching television while eating a pizza. Apparently they arrived earlier in the week. They certainly look settled in. Like most youngsters I assume they are immune to dirt. And motherless. Well, probably not that, but they clearly have sensible mothers who are not prepared, like me, to do their housework for them.

At four o'clock I declare my work done. 'Time for tea and Hobnobs,' I say, putting my head round the door of the living room where Katy's housemates are still watching TV. I've said the magic word. Hobnobs. 'Coming,' says Suki, 'I love Hobnobs.'

'Yeah, me, too,' declares Ethan the geographer. It's not obvious at first sight why Katy has chosen these two to be her housemates, they look a little lethargic to me, but I have to assume she knows what she's doing.

As the four of us gather round the small kitchen table and I determine to get Suki and Ethan to open up to me a little, there is a ring at the doorbell.

Katy jumps up. 'Must be Chris,' she smiles excitedly. 'I'll go.'

She opens the door. I hear Chris say, 'Hi, babes, you all right?' then another male voice. Older, gruffer. Irish. Surely not . . . Why the hell didn't Katy say something? Why didn't she tell me that Chris was going to turn up with Patrick? But then again, why should she have done? She knows nothing about what has passed between the two of us.

I feel a wave of panic. Since we started our affair, I've not been in a room with Katy and Patrick at the same time. Will it show? Is my duplicity written on my face, in my eyes, my smile? My face has turned quite red. I touch my cheek with the back of my hand and feel the heat. I've been getting these hot flushes lately, especially when I'm under stress.

Katy enters the kitchen, pulling Chris in behind her. Patrick follows, his bulk taking up most of the doorway. He has to bend his head so as not to knock it against the doorframe. Patrick is not a man designed for cottages. From the start I thought that Patrick's personality could fill a room; in this tiny house he seems to have swollen to the point where he is taking up all the physical space as well. I get up to greet Chris, and Patrick, and feel quite dizzy.

'Hi, Chris. Patrick. Sorry to seem rude, but I think I need to get some fresh air. I'm feeling a bit out of kilter. I'm not used to all this housework, forgotten just how physical an activity it is . . .'

I'm burbling, but I can't stop myself.

'This house isn't big enough for all of us,' says Patrick, staring at me quite directly. 'And it's certainly not big enough for me. Come on, Julie, I'll go with you.'

'But . . .'

'No buts. I could do with the walk myself. Been cramped inside that car for far too long.'

Outside the cottage, a wave of brisk breeze cools my cheeks and we head off together. The moment we've left the little pathway to the house Patrick tries to put his arm around me.

'No, not here,' I snap, wriggling away from his touch, looking back over my shoulder.

'No one is looking, Julie. And the kitchen, where they're all sitting, is at the back. I'm being careful.'

'The kids might not be looking, but you can't vouch for the neighbours.'

'Julie, you're being completely paranoid, it's ridiculous. I've missed you,' he says, 'for two whole months I've missed you and I don't care who knows it, and that includes the kids.'

'Well I do care,' I reply sharply. 'In fact I care more about that than I do about . . .'

'About me?'

'For heaven's sake, Patrick. Now is not the time. I haven't seen you for two months, as you say. Can't we talk about the weather or something neutral, just to get us going?'

'Frankly,' says Patrick, 'I can't see the point in talking about the weather.'

And so for the next few minutes, until we leave the village well behind us, we walk in silence.

Patrick reaches out and grabs my arm, holding me back from walking.

'You're hurting me,' I say, trying to release myself from Patrick's iron grip around my upper arm.

'Come here,' he says, pulling me roughly towards him. I try again to pull back, but I'm no match for Patrick.

'Kiss me,' he commands.

'I won't,' I say, as his lips descend on mine. For no more than a second or two I keep my lips firmly closed, resisting him. Then, like a woman who has been on a strict diet for far too long, I allow myself to feast, greedily, knowing even now that when it's over I will be full of remorse.

When finally he draws back, my lips feel swollen, bruised almost, and I say, 'Look what you've done to me. Katy might notice I can't go back just yet.'

'If you let me stay with you tonight,' says Patrick, 'I'll leave you be for now.'

'But you're the one who refused to see me. And you were right. And we agreed.'

'I've been thoroughly miserable, Julie. Chris says I'm a nightmare to live with. Why can't we just take our pleasure where we find it? I mean what else is there? We're not getting any younger, either of us. I just don't see the point of denying ourselves. And over time, the Chris and Katy thing, I'm sure we'll come up with a way to work it out.'

I almost mention Walt, but what purpose would it serve? Walt isn't here. And because I am weak, and lonely, and because Patrick's touch has reminded me so urgently of what I've been missing, I agree.

'Do you rue the day you met me?' Patrick asks.

'You're hard to rue.'

'Well that's something, I suppose.'

'Indeed it is.'

Suddenly tonight feels much too far away.

So Patrick tails me home, keeping a respectable distance. As I drive up my street I notice a car straddling my driveway, preventing me from entering.

'Bastard,' I say aloud, wondering what thoughtless person would do such a thing, especially on a Sunday when there's plenty of available parking in the street. I draw closer and see a back door of the car swinging open. It must be a drop-off, not so selfish after all then. I'm so quick to judge these days. It's already dark and the street lamp outside our house has blown. I've been meaning to call the council for weeks to get them to come and fix it.

I can't see who has exited the car but the outline looks ... it looks ... I'm always doing this, always seeing Walt where he isn't and this time I'm not going to be fooled. I stop the car some distance back, determined to wait patiently rather than honk my horn. I notice in my wing mirror that Patrick has already parked a little way behind me, and now he's getting out of the car and walking towards me.

I press a button and the window to the passenger side rolls down.

'Why've you stopped?' he asks.

'There's someone ahead blocking my driveway, but he appears to be unloading, so I won't be a minute I'm sure.'

'OK, I'll go check it out.'

The figure in the car in front of me has walked round to the boot. Now he's opening it and lifting something heavy out, a suitcase perhaps. A small light has come on in the boot. I can see a head framed in the light, it . . . no, of course it's not Walt, the shape of this man's head suggests baldness or a short crop, Walt's curls . . .

Now Patrick and he appear to be talking. The man who has unloaded slams shut the boot. Patrick is turning to walk back to me, but before he does he shakes the other man's hand. What on earth is going on? As Patrick approaches my car, the other vehicle speeds off leaving a man on the pavement.

Patrick leans over and puts his head to my open window.

'OK, Julie, you can get into your driveway now. I'm off.'

'But Patrick . . .'

'That man who just got out of the car . . .'

'The one you just shook hands with. Bit matey, I thought, for a complete stranger who just happened to be unloading his luggage outside my house.'

'Not so matey when you consider the circumstances.'

'What circumstances?'

'That the man unloading the boot is returning unexpectedly from a rather long journey.'

I feel sick. 'You mean . . .'

'Yes, Julie, I do mean. I introduced myself as the father of his daughter's boyfriend. So you'll understand if I don't stay the night . . .'

'But . . .'

'No buts, sweetheart. Get in touch when you decide . . .'

'But he can't just turn up like this. Not without warning. Not after so long . . .'

'Well that's exactly what he's done.'

'Then he is a bastard, he really is.'

'I was hoping you'd say that. Bye for now, my sweet woman.'

I am shaking like a dodgy washing machine on full spin. I intend to put the car into drive but I ram it into reverse instead and with my foot on the accelerator start zooming backwards, slamming my foot on the brake only just in time to avoid crashing into a parked car. I breathe. I breathe again and I shift the gear stick into drive, and then edge forward slowly, before turning left into my driveway. In the light of the porch I see a slim, shaven-headed man with a suitcase and a backpack.

'You've lost weight,' I say as I approach. 'And your hair. Where has that gone?'

'Aren't you going to say hello?'

'Hello, Walt.'

'How about a hug?'

I can't do it. I can't touch him.

'I was thinking a hotel rather than a hug.'

'Meaning?'

'Meaning I think you should check into a hotel.'

'But this is my home.'

'Was your home.'

'But we need to talk, Julie, there is so much I want to say.'

'First a hotel, then later, perhaps when I've got used to the idea, we can talk.'

'Are you serious about this?'

'Deadly.'

'What about the spare room?'

'Not far enough.'

'If you say so.'

'I do.'

Still standing on the porch, determined not to let Walt into the house, I ring a reasonably priced hotel I know near Bayswater. One I'm quite familiar with actually. Patrick and I have become quite regular visitors, but always under his name. The ironies are piling up. I drop Walt off outside.

'I'm sorry to have surprised you the way I did, but I thought you would have got my email . . .'

'Well I didn't.' Why don't I quite trust Walt's statement? 'Have you spoken to the girls?'

'No, I thought I might surprise them. I can't wait to meet Lara.'

'Yes, I'm sure she feels the same way about you.' I don't want to appear sarcastic, but I am so wound up, so tense, so fearful of allowing tears or fury or any extreme expression of my vulnerability to show, that sarcasm seems the safest reponse. 'Goodnight, Walt. I would say welcome back but I can't quite get the words out.'

'When can we talk?'

'I'm working late tomorrow.'

'Plus ça change then . . .'

'Actually a lot has changed, Walter, since you've been gone, it has had to.'

'So how about Tuesday?'

'No, I'm seeing Aggie.'

'Wednesday?'

'No, I'm seeing Gemma.' I am determined not to change my arrangements to accommodate Walt. He can't just turn up and expect me to drop everything. 'I'll see you Friday. I need a few days to get used to the idea of your being here. Come for supper if you like.'

'I'd like. It will give me a chance to catch up with the girls. Julie . . .'

'No, Walt . . . whatever it is you were about to say, don't say it now. Don't say anything at all. Please.'

'Good night then.'

'Good night.'

I look at the sign ahead of me which says No U-turns and

decide to do one anyway. What's a fine or a police reprimand or a few points on your licence compared to your husband arriving on your doorstep unexpectedly after a nine-month absence? I execute a U-turn, almost willing the sirens to sound behind me. It's as though I want something to happen, something that will break through the numbness that seems to have overtaken me. The street is quite empty, however. And silent. When I get home I strip off my clothes, pull on a baggy old T-shirt from the cupboard and without washing, removing my make-up or even brushing my teeth, I get into bed. For a very long time I lie flat on my back under the duvet, arms tight against my sides, rigid, like a corpse, staring at the ceiling and wondering if the last nine months have been one long dream – or would nightmare be a better word for it?

Chapter Twenty-Six

Her feet may be encased in skyscraper-heeled, snakeskin gladiator shoes, and her body in a Herve Leger bandage dress (I only know this because when I ask, 'What's that extraordinary tourniquet you're wearing?' she replies, 'Herve Leger', of whom I'd never heard), but Aggie is in an unusually sober mood. 'So he's back,' she says, sitting on the sofa and tugging at the hem of her skirt to preserve what remains of her modesty.

'Yes.'

'But is he back back? Or just here, if you know what I mean.'

'I know what you mean, but I don't have an answer for you. I don't know if he wants me, and I don't know if I'll have him even if he does.'

'Splitting up feels like having a boob job without the benefit of an anaesthetic. Excruciating.'

'I'm supposed to be the expert on the medical analogies, Aggie, not you. But you're right about the pain. You know, I really did think you and Charles had got it sorted.'

'So did I. But it turns out that Charles has been behaving even worse than me. Can't blame him for that, I suppose.'

I say nothing about Charles's confession that night in the pub. Aggie wouldn't appreciate my holding out on her. But he seemed quite desperate to have Aggie back. Men are hard to figure.

'And now,' says Aggie, more resigned than angry, 'he's reverted to type. Found himself a genuine Sloane, the real McCoy. As bland and beige and boring as porridge, naturally blonde and up to her ears in mulch, green wellies and fox hunting. Everything I'm not and everything he said he didn't want. Plus, the thing I hate her for most: all of thirty-two and four months pregnant.'

I'm trying to make sense of this. Trying to figure out how Charles could be both so desperate to have Aggie back and so quick to dump her when she returned. And that thing he said about his bed lying fallow since Aggie went away?

'An accident, he told me. Not on her part, you can be sure of that. Can you believe he had the nerve to say he wouldn't let her have an abortion. That it would have been unbearable after all those years of me trying to conceive. That it would seem like a crime. Like it was supposed to make me feel better or something. Like I was supposed to thank him for it. Well, you know what? The minute he said that I thought, that's it, it's over. I'll manage . . .'

'I can't believe you're taking it so well, Aggie. That you've rented a flat and are being so cool.'

'I've changed, Julie. I seem to have developed this thing called perspective. But I haven't been taking it well, it's been awful coming to terms with the idea of no more Charles in my life. Charles a father of someone else's child. And then this morning I got this long email from Ana and the future looks bright again.'

'Goodness, I've not thought about Ana and Maricel for ages, I'm just so preoccupied at the moment.'

'Of course you are. Poor Maricel, she died a fortnight ago.'

'She died! And Ana didn't tell you right away?'

'She's such a mature and intelligent girl, she didn't want to rush it, didn't want me wading in offering to wave my magic wand with the pound signs printed all over it. She wanted to think about what she wanted to do. Whether or not to make a life in the Philippines with her extended family, even though she feels British in so many ways.'

Life doesn't resemble a soap opera. Life *is* a soap opera.

'I'm sorry about Maricel, I really am, even though I never met her. But poor, poor Ana. An orphan. So has she now decided what to do next?'

'She's going to come back to London. And live with me. Once I've sorted out a permanent place for myself. She'll stay with me while she studies, and after that ... well, after that, who knows where any of us will be.'

'Oh Aggie, that's wonderful news.'

The hint of a smile that shows on Aggie's face is in contrast with the soft sadness of her eyes. It's not Aggie in brash, triumphant, let's-pop-the-champagne-corks mode, but a quieter, more thoughtful Aggie who is revealing herself. Aggie all grown up after all these years.

'It is wonderful news. It's also going to be the most responsibility I've ever had. To care for her, Julie, like a mother, to make sure she doesn't go off the rails, to give her security. And love. I do hope I'm up to the task.'

'Like a mother yes, but not as her mother. It's important to remember that. I have no doubt you're up to the task, Aggie, but Maricel will always be her mother, and a pretty wonderful one given her own difficult circumstances. Don't try to replace her.'

'Yes, like a mother, but not as a mother, I'll have to remember. The way I see it is that I'm expecting to learn as much from Ana as she will from me. At least as far as anything useful and true is concerned.'

'Don't put yourself down, Aggie.'

'Charles and I were never really right together, were we? I realise that now, probably always did, but neither of us was willing to face up to the fact that we were just too different. I don't know how we hoodwinked ourselves for so long. He and his Fulham floozy are made in heaven, or rather Sloane Square. I can already picture the children, the grandchildren, even the great-grandchildren. Bland, boring and naturally blonde for generations to come.'

'He loved you for years, Aggie, I know he did. He seemed quite broken without you. But I guess men are rather good at moving on when they have someone to move on to. And maybe his acceptance of no kids was another self-deception. As well as the infidelity. Not many would stand for that.'

'Do you think I'm ridiculous, the way I look?' Aggie asks, tugging at her rising hemline again. 'Is it time for black slacks and long sleeves and sensible shoes? Will I be an embarrassment to Ana dressed like this? Is it time to be less, oh I don't know, less Kim Cattrall and more Grace Kelly?'

I look my friend up and down appraisingly, trying to keep a straight face.

'Aggie, you are a one-off. You are funny, sexy, over-the-top, noisy, outrageous, irrepressible and sometimes irresponsible. You are the most tremendous life force. If you stopped dyeing your hair and started buying your clothes from the classic range at M&S the world would become a more miserable place. As for Ana, she's coming to live with you not because she has to, but because she wants to. Because of who and how you are. Something fundamental has changed about you, and I think that will be good for you in the long run. Your surfaces? They're fine. More than fine, they're fabulous.'

'You're a true friend, Julie. I wonder what next for you and Walt.'

'Well, the wet room's finished. I kept telling myself it was for me but of course it wasn't, it was a way of kidding myself Walt had just gone away on holiday. Six grand I've spent on that crazy project.'

'Cheaper than a divorce lawyer,' says Aggie. 'If it works . . .'

'Shall we watch a movie?' I ask, not wanting to dwell on Walt.

'Yes, let's. How about *Some Like It Hot*?'

It's always *Some Like It Hot* when we need a little light entertainment.

'Would you like a drink?'

'A cuppa would be nice.'

A cuppa? Aggie, a cuppa?

And so we sit on the sofa, drinking tea and watching telly, tears of laughter rolling down our faces as Jack Lemmon and Tony Curtis blag their way, dressed as women, into an all-girl band. At the end, when Lemmon reveals himself as a man to his fiancée

Osgood, we turn to one another. 'Well, nobody's perfect,' we say in unison with the actor on the screen. It shouldn't be that funny, not after so many viewings, but it is, tonight somehow more than ever. Not just funny, but pertinent as well. And far better than any advice I might have to offer.

I am remembering that evening at Napoli's when Gemma bounded in looking ten years younger, unable to disguise the glow of a woman in love. She's lost that sheen now, not because she feels differently about Rob, but because it has been tempered by all that's followed. Gemma is sitting in the same position on the sofa as Aggie was last night. It's getting to be a pattern, my friends and family popping in to update me on the unravelling of their marriages.

Valentina has gone to New York, taking Carla with her. But she did not go quietly. She called Antony at his chambers and asked if she might pay him a visit. Before Gemma had gathered up the pluck to tell him herself, Valentina marched in and announced that her husband and Gemma were having an affair.

When Antony stormed in later that evening and demanded that Gemma, 'GO! Go now,' Gemma told Antony she was willing to give up Rob and be a dutiful wife.

'I don't want you as my nurse,' Antony had told her, sounding as coolly certain and in control as though he were in court doing his summing up for the judge. 'I can pay someone to look after me and a lot better than you are capable of. I'm not even that ill. Yet. And if and when I become so I don't want you mooning around after me, the tragic victim of your pathetic, doomed love affair, always blaming me, loathing me as you so clearly do.'

'Whatever you say,' she'd replied. 'But I don't loathe you.'

'I'll tell you one thing, I'm not moving out of the marital home, and I'll fight you in court – and win – if you demand that I do. I'm an invalid now, remember, as well as being a lawyer.'

'I know what I'm entitled to,' Gemma had replied quietly. 'But I won't ask you for anything over and above that, Antony. I can keep myself by my writing.' And so Gemma packed her bags and moved, with Rob, into a small rented flat. They've been there for a month now.

'How's it going?' I ask.

'Between me and Rob it's wonderful,' says Gemma, 'at least it is when we can forget about all the hurt we've caused everyone else. Sometimes, though, we sit across the table from one another, in silence, lost in the memories of our marriages, and then I can't help wondering if it's really worth it. I do know I want to be with Rob, and I'm secure in the knowledge that he wants to be with me, and that we truly love one another, but you can't shrug off what's gone before.'

'It's so simple when you're young, isn't it?' I reply. 'But not now. Every gain seems to incorporate a loss. Not only can't we erase the past, it seems never to leave us for an instant. How are the boys taking it?'

'Sam sort of gets it. He's spent most of his life trying to escape his father's clutches so he's hardly immune to his faults. But naturally his loyalties are split. Andy is disgusted with me. I mean, he and his dad alone in the house isn't a great scenario. I said it would be a good time for him to move out, get a flat share. He's twenty-four, and he's earning. They pay a pittance on these graduate trainee schemes but I'd be prepared to top him up, and I'm sure Antony would too. But he says that if I'm leaving he's going to have to stay put and look after his dad. It's not true, but that's the way he chooses to see it. It's the worst thing of all, Andy turning against me.'

'Give him time.'

'I have no choice. He said he doesn't want me to contact him at all and I have to respect that. It's horrible, but there's nothing I can do.'

'So where are we on the happiness scale now?'

'If I could take everything but Rob out of the equation, right at the very top. But taking account of the fall-out I'm not sure where I stand, or if I stand at all. When are you seeing Walt?'

'Friday.'

'What was all that about? Turning up and expecting to move straight back in and sort things from there.'

'Well, he said he wrote.'

'And I'm sure he did, but the cheek of it.'

'I can't talk about Walt, Gemma. I just need to see him, see if I recognise him. It's late, hadn't you be getting home to An— I mean Rob?'

'I suppose I had. He'll be waiting up. We're still at that stage in our relationship when things like going to bed at the same time matter.'

'Do I detect a hint of cynicism?'

'I hope I can do this.'

'Do what?'

'Start over with someone new and make it work.'

'After wrecking two families you'd better be able to.'

'Thanks for reminding me, little sister.'

'You're welcome, Gemma. Now go home to Rob and be loving.'

'Being loving to Rob is easy. Loving myself is rather more of a problem.'

'You'll get used to the idea.'

'Perhaps. Now don't you forget to tell that idiot of a husband of yours that I missed him. That I still do. Good night, Julie. And good luck.'

'Good night, Gemma. And thank you.'

'Thank you for what?'

'For being born of course.'

'Gemma wants you to know that she missed you.'

'I appreciate that. How's her writing?'

'Her new book is finished. Going through the editing process as we speak. She's taking some time off to sort things out before starting on the next one.'

'I was planning on seeing all the guys this weekend. Rob, Charles, Antony.'

'Not all at once I hope.' Walt and I snigger at the same time.

'No, thought I'd see them one by one, get the men's perspective, before I start on the women. Though not Valentina of course, I'll have to go to New York for that. But Gemma and Aggie, providing I'm not *persona non grata*.'

'If we worked on the *persona non grata* principle none of us would ever see one another again. It's becoming like one of those Feydeau farces, or an Alan Ayckbourn romp, but a lot less funny.'

We both snigger again.

'Simultaneous sniggering,' smiles Walt. 'Well it's a start.'

There's an edge of unreality about this, but it's fun all the same. This pretending to be normal, this suspension of disbelief, won't last. I give it a few more minutes max before it explodes into something nasty.

Nine months my husband has been gone, and we're skating over issues as comfortably as if we only parted for work this morning and reconvened over supper.

I wanted supper to be a good one. To show him what he's been missing? Or to show myself that I can survive without him?

'This is all new stuff,' Walt says appreciatively, 'absolutely delicious. I've not tasted anything like this from you before.'

'Mmm,' I reply casually, determined not to let on how carefully I've planned this meal. 'It's my mid-life, Middle Eastern phase. I have this whole new culinary lexicon, all these amazing ingredients I've discovered. Like sumac, made from the crushed berries of a Mediterranean tree. Za'atar, which is a blend of dried thyme, toasted sesame and salt. And I'm into lashings of yoghurt. Pomegranates with everything. I'm practically a new woman, Walt,' I say, passing him more of the chicken pieces cooked with honey, nuts, spices and rose water.

'You never cease to amaze me, Julie.'

'That may be one of the problems,' I say. 'Amazement, like admiration, is no substitute for love.' And then, before he has the chance to answer I ask, 'Did it do the trick? Did you find what you were looking for?'

'That depends on you.'

'I wasn't looking for anything.'

'But you've been thinking, I bet.'

'Between my job, and the kids, and my car-crash friends, and my ailing mum, yes I've been thinking . . .'

'While I've been chasing dreams, being a selfish bastard and all that . . .'

'And all that . . .'

'You know, sometimes self-preservation, survival, call it what you will, demands drastic measures.'

'I didn't know survival was such an issue for middle-class blokes with well-paid jobs living in well-appointed houses close to the centre of London.'

'That's not worthy of you, Julie.'

'I know. But while you're busy thinking me admirable and amazing and not very lovable you should know that I'm not always worthy either.'

'I think the time has come for us to talk, Julie.'

'I thought that's what we were doing.'

'To tell you the truth, the whole truth.'

'Sometimes the truth is dangerous. I've been pretty economical with it lately.'

'Well I'm prepared to take the risk.'

'Go for it.'

Walt puckers his eyebrows, and does something funny with one shoulder, raising it to his cheek and pressing his cheek hard into it.

'That's new,' I say, 'that thing with your shoulder.'

'Not only did I get bitten by ticks on my travels I developed some tics of my own,' says Walt, willing me to laugh.

'How were your travels, by the way?'

'Extraordinary.'

'I'm not sure if I really want to know about them. It's going to be hard to listen to you talking through your holiday snaps.'

'Look, I understand. One day, maybe, but I'll wait for you to ask.'

'What made you think you could come home like that?'

'I did email.'

'I know, you've already told me that but I never received it. You left me. Why did you feel you could come back? I still don't understand.'

'Because I didn't see it as leaving you. I went away, for a period; that's different.'

'You didn't write, except for one lousy email, you didn't tell me what you were doing, you didn't seem to care at all about how I was getting on.'

'I can explain.'

'You look so different,' I say. The gunmetal curls gone, Walt's hair so close cropped to his tanned head he has the appearance of a soldier on leave from a tour in the desert. He's wearing loose khakis, a black T-shirt and flip-flops, even though it's early autumn. He has a thin, woven leather strap around his wrist. And he's so lean, perhaps three or four kilos less than before. Although his body looks toned, youthful, his thinned-down face makes him look older, and the scar that courses along his nose more prominent. I want to touch the golden hairs of his forearms, but I resist.

'I had an affair,' he says.

'Well we can all lay claim to one of those,' I reply sharply. 'I haven't exactly been a saint since you've been gone.'

'I spotted that right away,' says Walt, with an edge to his voice. Jealous? Surely not.

'What do you mean, spotted it?'

'It was the look of fury on the face of that Irish bloke, the father of Katy's boyfriend. I forget his name.'

'Fury?' I say, attempting to sound astonished. 'What on earth do you mean?'

'When he realised who I was on Sunday night I honestly thought he was going to thump me. I mean what else was he doing here if not coming to spend the night with you?'

'I don't want to talk about this, Walt.'

A sly smile turns up the corners of Walt's mouth.

'So what does Katy think about it? Who got in there first? You or Katy? Or was it a joint decision to keep it in the family? He's a big guy, isn't he? I'd hate to cross him, he could crush me to death. Could crush you to death if he wasn't careful.'

I feel my face flushing. I'm not sure Walt has the right to be ironic or cynical or even teasing with me after so long an absence. 'Walt, I'm warning you, this is no joke. I'm not admitting to anything. And the thing I'm not admitting to is not for Katy to know about. OK?'

'OK, my Julie,' says Walt, reaching across and touching my cheek.

'*My* Julie?' I say, pulling away. 'Don't do this. You're confusing me more than ever. You wanted to tell me about an affair you had while you were away. I don't really have to know, you know.'

'I'm talking about the affair I had before I went away.'

Something tugs at my intestines.

'It went on for five years.'

'I see.' These are the only words which will come out. For five years. Walt has been living with me while having an affair with another woman for five years, and the funny thing is I'm thinking, well who could blame him?

I picture Walt in the confessional, determined to blurt out his sins before he loses the courage to speak of them. 'It started around the time of the hospital scandal. Francine's an assistant editor on the newspaper, she was gung-ho for the story, we'd have drinks to talk it over, she convinced me to see it through. One thing led to another.'

I say nothing. How many lies do you have to tell to carry on an affair for five years without your wife having even an inkling?

I wonder if Walt's been practising his confession, and whether this might explain why it's coming out so fluently, without the usual hesitations that accompany awkward revelations. 'I fell in sex and in love,' he continues. 'We'd practically lost it sexually, you and I. We hardly saw one another, we were both so busy working, you in particular. We sniped at one another over the girls. I always felt like the lesser mortal. It wasn't great, Julie, not on any level.

Francine kept telling me what a great journalist I was, what a great lover I was, and I started to believe her.'

I feel a rush of blood to my head. Anger at last. 'So why didn't you leave me for Francine? She sounds perfect. Is she married? Does she have kids? Is she twelve years old?'

'She was single and she was willing, but I couldn't.'

'And why couldn't you, if she was so fabulous and I was so awful?'

'That's just it, Julie, no one could ever live up to you. Not in my mind anyway. What I wanted was you back again, only I didn't know how. And Francine seemed to recognise that she couldn't be a substitute for you, but she hung on in, hoping.'

'Is it over with her?' Five years!

'I resigned to get away from her, to make the break. But also because I couldn't bear to be part of that cynical, tabloid culture a moment longer. One that she thrived in and I increasingly loathed. I went away to get away from her. And from you. I needed to think about what I wanted to do with my life and what I wanted to do about us. I was on the verge of a breakdown. I didn't tell you about the panic attacks, the sense that I was losing my mind.'

Already my anger is dissipating. No matter how hard I try, how justified I feel, I can't seem to hold onto it. Walt is here, the husband I feared I might never see again is here in front of me. And his pain is as palpable as mine. But as for where this conversation is leading I have no idea.

'You should have explained to me, Walt, what you were going through. Couldn't we have talked about any of this before? Properly I mean. Before you made the decision to go. We never really talked, did we?'

'I tried. You tried. But sometimes we just don't have the language.'

There's a sad truth in Walt's words. You build a relationship on your ability to communicate and then, when things go wrong, it's as though you've forgotten how to use your mother tongue, other than as a weapon. 'That's true enough,' I say. 'But after you told me you were going I did suggest counselling instead of abandonment.'

Walt slowly shakes his head. 'I wasn't ready for it. I needed to understand for myself that it wasn't your commitment to your work that was the problem, but my dissatisfaction with mine that made me see it that way.'

'I need to know something, Walt. Did you think about me at all? The effect that your going away might have on me? The possibility that I might not want you back, regardless of what you decided you might want, and I still don't know what that is.'

'It was a chance I had to take. I did know I was hurting you, of course I did, and it may be weakness on my part, or selfishness, or even cowardice, but it was the only way I knew to save myself. How could I save our marriage if I didn't know how to save myself?'

'And Francine?'

'I told her it was finished, but she flew to Australia to see me. We spent ten days together. I wavered, but then I told her it wasn't going to happen, that I already had a family and that I could never agree to give her children.'

'But why? If you love her. You're not too old to start another family. Thousands do.'

'She's not a patch on my wife.'

Five years. For five years he betrayed me, five years in which the deceptions and excuses must have become so commonplace he probably barely noticed them. But I still don't blame him. I'm not even vengeful or jealous. I'm just sad that we so easily bypassed one another. What's the matter with me? Is it perverse of me to understand? Does it mean I don't care enough? No, I feel plenty, but in a quiet, deep inside sort of way. I hurt in my head and my heart. The ache of loss and longing is lodged in my bones and cartilage, in my ligaments and tendons, in the blood coursing through my body, in my skin, my hair, my fingernails. I shut my eyes tight, holding in a whole world of feelings, a universe girdled with tears. Something huge is happening, but I'm not sure what it is.

'I've been hurting all over, Walt. I've missed you so much.'

'I know.'

'I don't know what to say or do.'

'Can I come closer?'

'Maybe.'

Walt takes me by the hand and we leave the dining table and head for the sofa. We sit where last night I sat with Gemma, the night before that with Aggie, and discussed the unravelling of their marriages. As Walt holds me tight I bow my head, I cannot hold my face up to his, but I allow him to kiss my hair. I say, 'I fear it may be even harder to re-ravel than unravel.'

'Re-ravel? Is that a word I should know?' asks Walt.

'I'd like you to go now, back to your hotel,' I say.

'How about a date tomorrow night?'

'On call,' I say.

'But of course . . .'

'That's what you get when you get me.'

'Sunday night?'

'I'll be wrecked, but yes . . .'

'We've not talked about our grandchild.'

'We will.'

'Or the girls.'

'There's time.'

'Or the fact that I've got living abroad out of my system.'

'As I said, no holiday snaps.'

'Or my brilliant new career.'

'You can tell me on Sunday.'

'Or the future,' says Walt, quietly.

'I think we should see how our first couple of dates go first.'

As I get into bed, alone, I feel I am acting in a play, the ending of which I haven't yet been told, the lines of which I've not yet learned. I think about Walt and this affair of his, the one that lasted five long years and I think of my mother, and of how steadfast she was in the face of my father's affair with his practice nurse, Marina.

I remember what she said to me about how in a way she felt sorry for Marina, because in the end it was Marina who lost out, and my mum who got to keep Tom, my father. It wasn't the same thing, of course, Marina was a fling, not a five-year relationship. On the other hand it's a five-year relationship that appears to be over, that Walt has made a decision about, one that took him halfway round the world before he could make up his mind, but one that has returned him home. In a way this Francine person barely exists for me. I've not seen her, met her or even heard her name until now. Rather than seeing her as a living, breathing person perhaps I can turn this Francine into a metaphor for what can happen to a marriage when you don't tend it sufficiently. Even as I think this a part of me knows that feelings can't be so neatly filed away, but at the same time it does make a certain sense that if this Francine didn't exist for me then, there is no reason for her to haunt me now. Am I ready to receive Walt back? Was I ready all along? My last thought before I fall asleep is . . . a date with my husband on Sunday night, now there's a thing . . .

Chapter Twenty-Seven

On the Sunday of our first date Walt has a surprise for me.

'I haven't been entirely idle these last nine months,' he told me. 'I've been writing.'

'You mean you've been freelancing for the paper?' I interrupted. 'I've not been keeping up with it since you went away.'

'No, not the paper. That's over. For good. What happened after the first few months was that I found myself as free to wander mentally as I'd been doing physically. I was spending all this time alone and gradually this idea began to form, a plan which would use all my skills as a writer and medical expert, in addition to my new experiences as a traveller. By the time I reached India I had worked out an outline for a series of medical thrillers . . .' Walt paused for effect. He smiled at me, with a look that made me think of a young boy about to own up to his mum about something he shouldn't have done, but at the same time confident he could twist her round his little finger. '. . . Yes, medical thrillers based on this feisty female doctor who works for a *Medecins Sans Frontiers* type organisation, and whose job takes her to some of the exotic locations I'd been visiting.'

Walt's excitement was infectious. 'Is she modelled on anyone we know?' I asked, tilting my head, in a simulacrum of coquettishness. I'm not sure it's possible to play the coquette with a man you've known as long as I've known Walt.

'Well she's pretty smart and sexy and can be a complete pain in the ass, but I think you'll like her.'

My body felt suddenly warm from within, but for a change it wasn't the beginnings of a hot flush, it was more like a remembered sense of something nourishing, sustaining, secure. 'This *is* exciting, Walt. This could be the start of something to really get your teeth into, something you really do care about.'

'Well I've managed to do loads of research, I have a dozen notebooks full of stuff I wrote down on my travels, and I've got story-lines for the first three in the series already mapped out. I got in touch with Gemma who put me on to her agent who recommended this guy for me to approach. He read my stuff and offered to take me on.'

'Wow, Walt, that's great. But Gemma? You were in touch with Gemma while you were away?'

'Only on matters to do with writing, we didn't discuss you and me. Or her and Rob. But she did tell me about Antony's MS.'

'She's a dark horse. She didn't mention a thing.'

'Well we're all dark horses one way or another. Anyway, three publishers are really interested. I'm waiting to hear who we're going to go with.'

I looked at Walt and despite the loss of his distinctive curls I could see the young Walt I first knew, the free-spirited Walt who loved life and had once loved me. 'I'm so pleased for you, Walt. No more office politics, no more tabloid piranha pool. So you'll be working from home, I take it?'

'That's the idea,' Walt replied. 'Although the way things stand I'm not exactly sure where home is. I'm not presuming . . .'

'Quite right, Walt. I wouldn't presume anything if I were you. But I do have a surprise for you, too.'

'Which is?'

'Your very own wet room. The wet room of your . . .'

'Wet dreams . . .?' My clever, quick-witted, life-loving Walt.

When I think now about relationships I am interested less in why they go wrong, and more in what makes them go right. Walt moved back in a couple of weeks after our Sunday night date. At some point I did reach out and touch those sun-bronzed hairs on his arms that I'd wanted to touch before, and what I felt was a tiny frisson. Sex with Patrick, it occurred to me, had perhaps paved the way for sex with Walt again. And I was right. When we did go to bed, it worked. It was good, really good. Not as exciting as with Patrick, not with that illicit edge, but loving, familiar, intense.

What a difference a year makes. It's Christmas Day. This time last year the traditional gathering around my table had consisted of me and Walt, Katy, Mum and Paul, Tess and Pete. If someone had told me of all the dramas that were about to unfold I wouldn't have believed them. Of course I already knew that Walt was about to disappear from my life, and that was drama enough. The atmosphere was mostly light, but little moments of tension kept puncturing the festive spirit.

'Where are you off to exactly?' Paul had asked Walt, as casually as if Walt were planning a weekend mini-break.

Walt's response had been clipped. 'Well I'm starting in Argentina, but I'm not making many plans as such. Anyone for more roast potatoes?'

'He's heading for the open road,' I had said, a little sarcastically. 'My husband, he's a travelling man. Doesn't like too much baggage, and certainly not this particular baggage. Here, Mum, let me pass you some more dark meat, I know you only eat the white to be polite.'

Later, my mum had asked, 'When's the baby due, Tess?'

'Not until right at the end of July. Will you be back by then, Dad? For the birth.'

Walt looked shifty. 'Can't say at this stage, sweetheart. Not that I'd be much use. More your mum's line than mine.'

Damn him, I thought. Damn him, and damn him again. I butted in. 'Walt, you do know that I won't actually be delivering my daughter's baby. You do know it's not what we doctors do, getting down and dirty with our relatives.' Little did I know.

'Yes thank you, Julie, I do know that.'

Poor Tess, she looked so uncomfortable.

'I'm sorry, darling, I just can't say right now.'

'It's all right, Dad. I just thought you might . . .'.

Paul had been knocking back the port like it was . . . well, like Christmas, I suppose.

'Bon voyage, old chap,' he tittered, raising his glass at Walt. 'Annette and I are going to visit Auschwitz in the spring.'

'That'll be a barrel of laughs,' said Pete.

But generally speaking it went quite well. After lunch we had played charades, as we always do. Then we'd got out the old family photos and I became a bit weepy, a combination of too much wine and all those snaps of when we all looked so happy together as a family.

As I said, what a difference a year makes.

If I'd had to take a bet last Christmas on which of the couples in our immediate circle would still be together, I'd have said the lot, with the possible exception of me and Walt. How wrong I was.

There are plenty of things I've learned this year. Although my experience as a doctor has taught me always to expect the unexpected, I'd never really applied it to life before. I'd not fully understood about the fragility of love, the seismic social changes that have so altered people's views about marriage and long-term relationships. Naïve, perhaps, but I really did think that if you had survived the hurdles of courtship, muddled your way through parenthood and seen your kids to adulthood, succeeded in making ends meet, accepted that the hurly burly of the chaise longue would give way to the peace of the double bed, then you would make it to old age as Darby and Joan, squabbling but content, accepting.

Here's how my gathering looks this year.

Well, there's me and Walt for starters, seated at either end of the long table. In between there's Pete and Tess. Lara, mercifully, has decided to sleep through lunch, giving her parents a bit of a breather in which to enjoy the meal. There's Katy and Chris. And next to Chris there's Patrick. Yes, Patrick at my table. We agreed to this for Chris and Katy's sake, so Chris could come and be with us and so that he and Patrick could avoid a miserable just-the-two-of-them Christmas dinner. I know this is hard for Patrick, but he's a good man, and he's putting his son ahead of his feelings. Walt hasn't asked me anything else about Patrick and I've never actually admitted to our affair. I look at Patrick, he looks at me, and for a moment our eyes are locked. In a special private part of me, his imprint will remain, always. Sexually I gave him everything, more than I had ever given Walt, but I couldn't give him the thing he wanted most. My heart.

Annette, my lovely mum, is getting worse. She got lost on her way back from the bathroom. Paul trails her almost everywhere. He's a saint.

Rob and Gemma are here. I can tell from the angle at which their arms are held that they are holding hands under the table. I sense that their need to cling to one another is a way of reassuring themselves that they have made the right choice. Their families are fractured. Gemma's boys are with Antony. Andy's still not talking to her.

Valentina and Carla have decided to stay in New York for Christmas. I'm going to visit her in the New Year.

Aggie and Ana are here, too. What Charles is up to Aggie has no idea, they only speak through lawyers now. Aggie assumes he's with the girlfriend's parents at their county pile in the Cotswolds.

I've put Aggie next to Patrick. They're both drinking like fish and laughing uproariously. I see Patrick glancing sideways at Aggie's cleavage. Well, you couldn't miss it really. Her plunge-necked red dress leaves little to the imagination. I wonder if the two of them . . . I feel a small stab of jealousy. Yes, I did put them together for exactly that reason, but the thought of Patrick in bed with . . . I have no right to think this way. I can hear Patrick telling Aggie about O'Briens, how he is planning on going back to Ireland to restore the hotel. That's news to me.

Ana is quiet, reserved, polite, grateful, still in shock most likely. She answers every question put to her with great care, but she doesn't ask questions of her own and she doesn't volunteer information. To make her feel welcome is the most we can do.

And that's about the sum of it.

Walt and I are determined to repair things. We have started to see a counsellor, once a week. It's painful, exposing all the hurts of the past, the misunderstanding and the things that sometimes we each understood too well. But we seem to have learned from our mistakes. If we don't make it, at least we'll have tried our damnedest.

While everyone else is talking and laughing I am reflecting on the fact that there's no road map for relationships any more. That sex, however powerful, is no substitute for love. I didn't fall in love with Patrick, but desire almost kidded me into believing I had. I know now that it can be easier to be cruel to your partner than to be kind. That proximity to what you've got can obscure the view, and sometimes you need to step way, way back. That it can be better to lie than tell the truth. Thank God Katy never found out about me and Patrick. That if you don't pay attention to your partner they will pay attention to someone else. But paying attention won't necessarily do the trick. I've learned that staying together is harder work than splitting up. That itches, when they're scratched, can get worse. Or they can mysteriously go away.

The phone rings. Yes, the on-duty registrar knows it's Christmas, yes he knows I'm not on call, but they're short of staff and there's a rash of emergencies and I'm desperately needed and there's been a car crash with a seven-month-pregnant woman and . . .

'I have to go,' I announce.

I walk calmly over to Walt and kiss him on top of his head.

'I'm sorry,' I say.

'Not to worry,' he grins, 'we're used to you skiving off just as it's time to do the washing up.'

'Happy Christmas, Julie, Happy Christmas, Mum,' cry the assembled crowd, as little Lara wakes suddenly with a wail.

I assemble my things. Just as I am about to leave, Walt comes walking down the corridor, clutching Lara in his arms.

'Say goodbye to grandma,' he says, holding her towards me so I can smell her delicious baby smell and kiss her head. 'Thanks for having me back, Julie. I wasn't at all sure you would,' says Walt.

'Isn't she adorable?' I say.

'Like her grandma.'

'Oh Walt, that's so sweet I may have to throw up.'

'Bye then, old girl.'

'Bye, old man. Happy Christmas.'

'Come back soon, will you, there's no way I'm going to do all that washing up on my own.'

'So do you love me, Walt? Do you?'

'I suppose I must.'

'That's good, because all of us need someone to love.'

I so missed the banter. That's one thing back for sure.

I drive through the deserted Christmas-day streets in the direction of the hospital. Thinking about Walt's absence it occurs to me for the first time that he was gone for almost exactly nine months. How very apt. After a nine-month gestation period, a difficult nine months with certain worrying indicators, the marriage of Walt and Julie was born again, weighing in at a healthy twenty-three years. Close monitoring advised. To date, husband and wife are doing well.